Cry of the Hawk

BOOKS BY TERRY C. JOHNSTON

Carry the Wind
Borderlords
One-Eyed Dream

SON OF THE PLAINS SERIES
Long Winter Gone
Seize the Sky
Whisper of the Wolf

THE PLAINSMEN SERIES
Sioux Dawn
Red Cloud's Revenge
The Stalkers
Black Sun
Devil's Backbone
Shadow Riders
Dying Thunder

Cry of the Hawk

Terry C. Johnston

cop. 2

Bantam Books
New York / Toronto / London / Sydney / Auckland

for Bruce and Sandra,
and all they've meant to me

CRY OF THE HAWK
A Bantam Book / September 1992

All rights reserved.
Copyright © 1992 by Terry C. Johnston.
Book design by Ellen Cipriano
Map on page viii designed by GDS/Jeffrey L. Ward
No part of this book may be reproduced or transmitted
in any form or by any means, electronic or mechanical,
including photocopying, recording, or by any information
storage and retrieval system, without permission in
writing from the publisher.
For information address: Bantam Books.

Library of Congress Cataloging-in-Publication Data

Johnston, Terry C., 1947–
    Cry of the hawk : a novel / by Terry C. Johnston.
        p.   cm.
    ISBN 0-553-08936-6
    1. United States—History—Civil War, 1861–1865—Fiction.
I. Title.
PS3560.O392C78   1992
813′.54—dc20   92-46
                                                          CIP

Published simultaneously in the United States and Canada

PRINTED IN THE UNITED STATES OF AMERICA

BVG   0   9   8   7   6   5   4   3   2   1

CAST OF CHARACTERS

Hook Family

Jonah Hook
Gritta (Moser) Hook
Hattie Hook
Jeremiah Hook
Ezekiel Hook

Hook's Mentor

Shadrach Sweete   Toote Sweete / Shell Woman
Pipe Woman—daughter
High-Backed Bull—son

Danite Freebooters

Colonel Jubilee Usher
Major Lemuel "Boothog" Wiser
Captain Eloy Hastings
Riley Fordham
Laughing Jack
Healy Stamps
Sam Palmer

Major Military Characters

General William Tecumseh Sherman—Commander, Military Division of the Missouri
Lieutenant-General Philip H. Sheridan—Commander, Military Dept. of the Platte
Lieutenant Caspar Collins
General Patrick E. Connor—Commander, Military Dept. of the Plains
Captain Henry Leefeldt—Co. K (Camp Marshall)
Captain A. Smith Lybe
Sergeant Amos Custard—11th Kansas Cavalry
First Sergeant William R. Moody—Co. I
Major Martin Anderson—Platte Bridge Station, post commander
Captain Henry Bretney—11th Ohio Cavalry
Lieutenant George Walker—Platte Station Adjutant
Corporal James Shrader—11th Kansas Cavalry
Captain Henry E. Palmer—Powder River Exped. Quartermaster
Colonel Henry E. Maynadier—Commander, Fort Laramie
Dr. Henry R. Porter—surgeon, 7th U. S. Cavalry, Ft. Hays

Captain Frederick W. Benteen—7th U. S. Cavalry
Major Wycliffe Cooper—7th U. S. Cavalry
Captain George W. Yates—7th U. S. Cavalry
Lieutenant Myles W. Moylan—7th U. S. Cavalry
Lieutenant Colonel George Armstrong Custer—7th U. S. Cavalry
Lieutenant Thomas Ward Custer—7th U. S. Cavalry
Major Joel H. Elliott—7th U. S. Cavalry
Captain Louis M. Hamilton—7th U. S. Cavalry
Lieutenant Lyman S. Kidder—2nd U. S. Cavalry
Lieutenant Edward Godfrey—7th U. S. Cavalry

Pawnee Battalion

Major Frank North
Captain Luther North
Lieutenant / Captain James Murie
(Co. B)

Lieutenant Issac Davis (Co. B)
Half Rope
Sgt. Bear Runs Him

Major Indian Characters

Crazy Horse—Oglalla
Spotted Tail—Brule
Roman Nose—Cheyenne war chief
George Bent—half-breed Cheyenne
son of fur trader Bent
Blind Wolf—Cheyenne chief (father to
High-Back Wolf)
Spotted Wolf—Cheyenne
Porcupine—Cheyenne

Whistler—Brule
Grass Singing—Pawnee
Black Kettle—Cheyenne
Pawnee Killer—Brule
Young Man Afraid—Oglalla
He Dog—Oglalla
High-Back Wolf—Cheyenne
Turkey Leg—Cheyenne chief

Major Scouts

Jim Bridger
Captain E. W. Nash—Omaha and Winnebago scouts (Powder River)
California Joe (Moses) Milner—Hancock Expedition
Jack Corbin—Hancock Expedition
James Butler Hickok—Hancock Expedition
Will Comstock—Platte River Expedition

Major Civilian Characters

Nathan (Nate) Deidecker—newsman, Omaha *Bee*
Artus Moser
Samuel Hosking
Eldon Boatwright
Major Edward W. Wynkoop—government agent to the Cheyenne
Colonel Jesse W. Leavenworth—government agent to the Sioux
Sidney Gould—mercantile sutler, Fort Larned

It is not easy to visualize the enormous spread of frontier where these 6,000 [galvanized Yankees] marched and fought and endured the tedium of garrison duties. From Fort Kearney to Julesburg. From Julesburg to Laramie and along the Sweetwater through South Pass to Utah. From Julesburg up the South Platte to Denver, by Cache la Poudre to the Laramie Plains and Fort Bridger. . . . They made themselves a part of all the raw and racy names on that wild land of buffalo and Indians—Cottonwood Springs and Three Crossings, Lodgepole and Alkali Station, Medicine Creek and Sleeping Water, Fort Zarah and White Earth River, St. Mary's, Fort Wicked, Laughing Wood, Soldier Creek, Rabbit Ear Mound, Dead Man's Ranche, and Lightning's Nest.

—Dee Brown
The Galvanized Yankees

Led by desperate men . . . the guerillas, most of them only boys, fought a total war. West of the Mississippi they plunged a fairly stable . . . society into intense partisan conflict that was felt by every man, woman and child. This was not a war of great armies and captains, this was bloody local insurrection, a war between friends and neighbors—a civil war in the precise definition of that term. Here organized bands of men killed each other and the civil population hundreds of miles behind the recognized battlefronts. Here there was ambush, arson, execution and murder; warfare without rules, law or quarter.

—Richard S. Brownlee
Gray Ghosts of the Confederacy

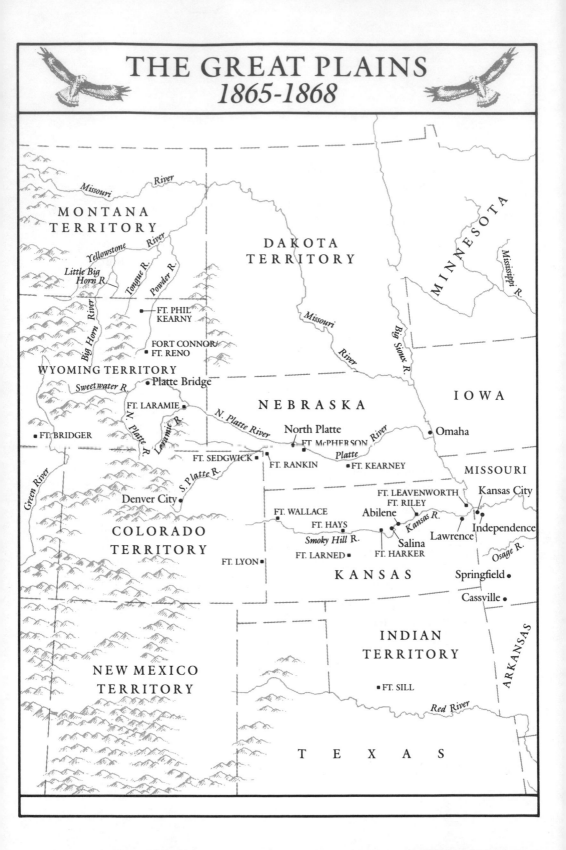

THE GREAT PLAINS
1865-1868

MONTANA TERRITORY

DAKOTA TERRITORY

MINNESOTA

Missouri *River*

Yellowstone *River*

Little Big Horn R.

Tongue R.

Powder R.

Big Horn River

FT. PHIL KEARNY

FORT CONNOR
FT. RENO

WYOMING TERRITORY

Sweetwater R.

Platte Bridge

FT. LARAMIE

N. Platte R.

Laramie R.

FT. BRIDGER

Green River

Missouri River

Mississippi R.

Big Sioux R.

N E B R A S K A

IOWA

N. Platte River

North Platte

FT. McPHERSON

Platte River

Platte

Omaha

FT. SEDGWICK

FT. RANKIN

FT. KEARNEY

MISSOURI

S. Platte R.

Denver City

COLORADO TERRITORY

FT. LYON

FT. WALLACE

FT. HAYS

Smoky Hill R.

FT. LARNED

FT. LEAVENWORTH
FT. RILEY

Abilene

Kansas R.

Salina

FT. HARKER

Kansas City

Independence

Lawrence

Osage R.

K A N S A S

Springfield

Cassville

NEW MEXICO TERRITORY

INDIAN TERRITORY

FT. SILL

ARKANSAS

Red River

T E X A S

Prologue

"THERE AIN'T TIME for you to make it back to town before dark," the old frontiersman said. "I best make you comfortable here."

Nate Deidecker marveled at the old man's vitality. Something on the order of seventy-one years old now, and still the former plains scout stood as straight as a fresh-split fence rail. Only the careful, considered pace he gave to all things betrayed his true age.

"I appreciate that, Mr. Hook."

"Told you—you're to call me Jonah." The old man smiled, a few of his teeth missing. Not unexpected. "We're friends, Nate."

Nathan appreciated that, having made a friend like Jonah Hook so quickly. Yet there was something that bothered the newspaperman who had traveled to Wyoming from Omaha, on a hunch and a limited budget begrudged him from a tightfisted managing editor at the *Omaha Bee*. In 1908 there weren't many newsmen actively following up the old warriors who still had stories to tell.

Having heard whisper of an unknown former scout living somewhere at the base of the Big Horn Mountains, Deidecker had finally convinced his editor and publisher to open their wallets and spring for a round-trip rail ticket, along with expenses for hiring the horse and carriage he had driven down from Sheridan.

Stepping off the railroad platform, he had been met by the aging newsman who had founded and owned the Sheridan *Press*.

1

"How'd you end up picking me, Mr. Kemper?" Deidecker asked as the two sat down for coffee once a carriage and horse had been secured outside the bustling Sheridan café. The summer sunlight was startlingly bright on the high plains. Even here in the café, Deidecker found himself squinting.

"You been writing stories, haven't you?"

Nate swallowed the hot coffee, its scorch something akin to the hot August weather that had accompanied him all the way west across Nebraska. "What stories?"

The old newsman chuckled. "Your stories about the old plainsmen. I don't mean those goddamned bragging, strutting peacocks we've seen time and again." He quickly leaned across the table, head close, grasping Deidecker's wrist between his old hands. "We're talking a different sort of man here, you understand."

Nate Deidecker looked down at the waxy hands gripping him, the ink forever tattooed in dark crescents at the base of the man's fingernails. "I understand, Mr. Kemper. Just as you said when you wrote me—not like Buffalo Bill over at Cody, or Pawnee Bill down in Oklahoma. You said Will Kemper would steer me to the real thing."

Kemper leaned back and seemed to suck on a tooth a moment before speaking. "This man's the real thing. Those others you've been writing about either been honest-to-goodness grandstanders or they simply aren't the caliber of the man I want you to meet."

"What's his name?"

"Jonah Hook."

"Why haven't I ever heard of him?"

Kemper smiled, running a single finger around the rim of his white china cup. "As long as I've been writing stories out here, it seems the ones who got the best stories to tell are always the ones who keep most to themselves."

Deidecker ruminated on that, sipping the hot coffee he really didn't relish on this hot summer afternoon. Something else to drink was on his mind, like a beer in that shadowy, beckoning place across the street. Unconsciously he wiped a hand across his lips before he replied.

"One thing's bothered me ever since that first letter you wrote me."

"You write good stuff, young man," Kemper said. "That's why I came to you first. I've been reading everything you've written about the old scouts you've found on your own. You can be proud your copy's been picked up by the *Tribune* and the *Herald*."

"I am—but I want to know why you want me to talk with this particular fella. Why don't you?"

"Don't get me wrong—I've talked with the man many a time," Kemper said, without the least bit of defensiveness.

"Surely you could write this story yourself. Why don't you?"

Kemper once more leaned in close to the young reporter. "Because you write as well as I did when I was your goddamned age, Deidecker." Slowly he creaked back in the chair. "I don't write that well now. Don't do anything that well now."

Deidecker pushed his cup and saucer aside, glad to be through with it. Itching to get on with the long ride south out of Sheridan. "He knows I'm coming?"

"Like I said, when you told me you'd be here—I went down there to tell Jonah."

"No problems?"

Kemper shook his head. "No problems. Just take it slow. Don't rush things."

Deidecker had patted his coat pocket, knowing he would be shedding the wool suit coat as soon as he stepped outside to the carriage. From inside the pocket came the reassuring sound of the folded map Will Kemper had drawn him of the route to the cabin where the Omaha newsman would find this reclusive Jonah Hook.

"I best be going."

Kemper looked out the window. "Yes. It's a long ride."

Deidecker held his hand down to the Sheridan newsman, who did not rise from his chair, as if he were comfortable right as he was and was not about to be disturbed from his perch by the formalities of another man's leave-taking. Kemper took Nate's hand. They shook, then the older man held Deidecker's for a moment longer, looking directly into his eyes.

"Find out about the woman—his wife," Kemper whispered. "No man's ever found out about her."

Nate remembered how at that very moment the cold splash of something had run down the length of his spinal cord. "Is she—was she killed somehow?"

Kemper removed his hand from Deidecker's sweating palms. "Not exactly. No. You'll see her . . . meet her."

"She's there? With the old man."

"He loves her deeply. And she's all he has now. Except the stories."

"The stories."

"Best you go now."

"Yes, Mr. Kemper. I'll come round when I get back to town."

Kemper was gazing back out the window at the bright splash of liquid sunshine spraying the hot, dusty street.

"Like I said, Mr. Deidecker. Take your time asking—and you will be richly rewarded."

Funny how things had turned out on that long ride south from Sheridan, Wyoming, crossing the Tongue River and heading toward the country where Colonel Henry B. Carrington had decided to raise the pine stockade for his Fort Phil Kearny in the middle of Red Cloud's hunting ground some forty-two years gone. Not that long, Nate had thought at first. Many a man that old or older.

But as the horse hit its comfortable stride and the wheels of the jitney clattered and rumbled along the jarring ruts of the old wagon road that led him south toward the foothills of the Big Horn Mountains, Nathan Deidecker himself slowed down.

His heart found a new pace. What's more, his own youthful and impetuous hurry to get on with things was seeping out of him with every drop of sweat pulled from him by this high, arid land. What was normally the aggravation of summer's heat now became something to be savored as richly as the smell of green-backed and white sage, stunted cedar and juniper.

He turned again now to look at the woman in her old rocking chair, remembering Kemper's cryptic admonition.

"Find out about the woman."

Deidecker watched as the thin old man descended the five creaking steps from the porch into the grassy, dusty yard in front of the old cabin nestled here in the foothills, beneath the shadow of Cloud Peak.

Jonah Hook went about pulling firewood from the cords of it he had stacked against the north and west sides of the cabin. A few pieces he selected for kindling and split them agilely. One final thin sliver of kindling the old man furred into curls that he laid atop a generous pile of ashes filling an old fire pit. Dragging a wooden lucifer across one of the flat stones ringing the fire pit, Hook started his supper fire as the sun sank closer and closer to Cloud Peak.

Swallowing hard, just as he had when preparing to commit one of the deadly sins of a schoolboy in class with the teacher's back turned, Deidecker glanced again at the old woman. For the first time all afternoon, finding himself amazed that she continued to rock in that dark, cherry-wood, ladder-back rocker with its old arms rubbed down to the color of yellow pine.

She hadn't spoken to him all afternoon. Looking at him only once with those cloudy blue eyes of hers when the old man first brought the newsman up onto the porch when Deidecker arrived. Here out of the sun at that moment, she had seemed to study something in his eyes only, and only for a moment—not really looking at the newspaperman, rather looking through him, somewhere—then went back to staring up at the green hills gone summer brown and gold, beyond them the blue and purple and lavender of the high places tucked beneath the clouds of this high land.

Never a word. Not a sound from her except for the incessant creaking of the rocker's bows on the plank porch.

"I built this place for us, you know."

Deidecker started at the old man's voice. He found Hook standing in the yard, halfway between the porch and his fire. Hands stuffed in the pockets of his canvas britches.

Nate felt nervous again. "I—ah—"

"She don't talk much, Mr. Deidecker." Hook came up the steps. "I'm the only one."

"She talks to you?"

He settled on the top step, next to the reporter. "And you're the first I've talked to in a long while, son."

"You've decided?"

"You can stay till you got all your questions answered. Gritta don't mind."

He looked at the woman, then caught himself and turned back to Hook. "You—you asked her?"

Hook tossed a stick toward the fire. "Don't have to. Sometimes—a man and woman been together for a long time, they can just tell. It's all right with Gritta if I talk to you. Just like, well—just like it's all right with me if Gritta don't talk to no one else no more."

"How long you been married?"

The old man smiled, his bony face creasing all the more. Deidecker was amazed that many hard miles could show on a man's face when he smiled or frowned. A face that nonetheless did not look to have seventy-one years of war and trails and tragedy indelibly scarred into it.

Hook gazed up at the peaks. To Deidecker, the old man might very well be looking at that same place the woman was staring. Far away. But somewhat nearer just by the mention of it aloud.

"Eighteen and fifty-four." Hook tossed another twig at the nearby fire. "We'll put meat on as soon as we get some good coals."

"I can wait."

Hook patted the newsman's knee. "I wasn't always as patient as you when I was younger. Didn't get this way overnight neither."

"I want to know everything." And he couldn't help it, but found himself flicking his eyes at the woman slowly rocking, rocking, forever rocking as if she were truly a part of the chair.

"I know you do, Nate. And if you're patient—that's just what you'll find out."

"You and . . . and Gritta were married in 1854?"

"I was seventeen. She just turned fifteen. Had eyes on her for some time, I had too. We were living in a valley between the Rappahannock and Shenandoah rivers."

"Virginia?"

"You know it?"

"Only from schooling. The great war and all."

Hook looked down at the palms of both his old hands. "Yes. The great war."

"So I figure you fought for the Army of Virginia? Robert E. Lee, eh?"

"No. We left Virginia two years after we was married. Gritta and me decided we wanted to spread our wings. Find our own place in this big country. Hattie had come to us by that time."

"Hattie?"

He sighed, rubbing his big hands across the shiny thighs of his threadbare canvas britches. "Daughter. Our firstborn. Come to us in the spring of fifty-five. Next year we was gone from that valley below Big Cobbler Mountain. Where Gritta's folks had farmed for generations."

"Gritta . . . is German?"

"Her folks was about as German as folks could get, that many generations out of the old country."

"And you?" Deidecker asked.

"German too. There was some little Irish blood a ways back, my mother told me of a time. On her side. Scotch too, as I remember. But my father was firstborn to folks who came over from the north of Germany. Named Hecht."

"Hecht? How—"

"Somehow got changed on some paper. Wrote down as Hook, so Hook it was from then on." The old scout got up without explanation and stepped to the far edge of the porch. The old dog dozing alongside Gritta's rocker raised its head and watched its master pee off the porch into the yard.

Self-conscious, Deidecker looked away to watch the sun settle on Cloud

Peak, impaled with a rosy summer light that gave a rich, rose luster of alpenglow to these foothills. Leaves in the nearby trees rustled with the cool breeze that seemed to immediately sweep down out of those high places, down from those never-summer ice fields as soon as the sun began settling for the coming of twilight.

Hook came back to the steps and strode down off the porch, across the wide, dusty yard toward the smokehouse, a last, unshakable remnant of his southern heritage. The old dog raised its snout, then slowly rose with a shake of its rear quarters, a languorous stretch, and loped off the porch as well.

"Only damned thing that ranger will get up for." Hook strode away, finding the dog at his leg. "If it ain't a bitch in heat nearby . . . it's meat."

Hook disappeared into the darkness of the shed. A moment later a big bone came sailing out of that dark rectangle where in another moment Hook himself reappeared, two large steaks draped over his bare forearm.

"Best meat gets aged. Don't ever let anyone else tell you different."

"What is that, Jonah? Buffalo?"

He laughed a little. "Wish it were. No, buffalo good as gone now. We seen to that, Nate."

"Elk?"

"You ever had yourself elk?"

"No."

"Then you're in for a treat, son."

"This whole . . . this meeting you. It's a totally different world out here. Something I've never experienced before."

Hook trimmed the steaks and laid them in a huge cast-iron skillet. "Certainly is something different out here. I had no idea how different it was when first I come out."

"You didn't tell me where you went when you left Virginia."

"Missouri. To homestead with an uncle."

"You came on here to Wyoming from Missouri?"

Hook set the skillet atop the coals, where the steaks began to hiss as the cooking fire's heat seeped across their bloody surfaces.

"We'll talk more after dinner and Gritta's fed."

Nate cursed himself silently for pushing. "I'm sorry, Jonah."

"No offense taken. Just . . . out here, you slow down a bit so that you can read the sign. A man in a hurry is going to miss most of what there is to read. The way a bird is calling out. The lay of a clump of bunchgrass. Maybe even the way the ants are acting on their hill. You slow down—you'll get all your questions answered.

"Time was, I wasn't one for it. This being slowed down. But—I learned from the best teachers there was back then how to slow down and read the sign. I learned from the best these plains ever could make out of white men."

"The men who taught you to be a scout?"

"The best ever set a moccasin down out here."

Book I

The
Captivity

1

February, 1865

H E HAD GROWN to hate the sound of that door sliding open against its three rusty hinges. But he suffered it this one last time.

Jonah Hook stepped from the tiny cell into the narrow hall running the length of the entire building, one of the hundreds of cells here at the Rock Island Federal Prison for Confederate prisoners of war. He was fourth in line coming out of the cell, two more behind him. The rest staying behind in the bull pen hooted and spat on those few who had decided they'd had enough of rotting away in this stinking place.

Eighteen hundred had signed an oath of allegiance to the Union they had of a time fought so hard to tear themselves away from in those long, bloody years of insurrection and rebellion and ragged defense of what mattered most to a man who had himself a small plot of land down in southern Missouri.

All those years of wondering on Gritta and their young ones.

"All right, boys! Let's march out into that sunlight, you Johnnies!"

The bellowing voice erupted volcanically from somewhere behind him, echoing off the rafters of the dirty prison building, built on the order of a warehouse, now smelling of piss and decay and souls rotting away month after month until the time spilled together into years of captivity.

Jonah Hook had vowed allegiance to the Union. He would put on a Yankee's blue uniform as long as he did not have to fight his former brethren dressed in butternut gray. He would go west with the others to hold back the Indians. He would keep the freight roads open and the telegraph wires strung across that expanse of open wilderness yawning out there in his imagination.

Hell, Jonah would do anything just about to get out of that stinking cell where one more man had died before the winter sun came up to make the whole damned building steamy again.

He wasn't going to wait until it was him they dragged out by the ankles while everybody turned away. Jonah Hook was going west dressed in Yankee blue.

In the North for the past few months, President Lincoln had been engaged in a fierce campaign against his former chief of the army, George B. McClellan. Lincoln won a second term. But as the terrible human cost of the war mounted, the President's Union found it harder to recruit soldiers for the effort. Draft laws and conscription edicts did nothing but incite the Northerners into riots.

Then there was Gettysburg, and the thousands of bodies piled up all in those three long days. Along with so many other less glorious battles with little-known and easily forgotten names, where thousands more lay waiting for a shallow grave, perhaps no grave at all, lying there for the animals and the seasons to reclaim their nameless mortal remains.

There were damned few substitutes left among those Yankee states by 1864—substitutes who would be paid a handsome bounty to serve in the stead of a man drafted to go fight the rebellious Confederates. So the Union continually drew manpower from its frontier army until it hurt, like an old-fashioned leech bleeding to cure a hopeless patient.

With little else to do, the army figured these Confederates they would galvanize into Yankee soldiers could hold back the red tide on the frontier until Grant and Sherman and Sheridan finished their nasty little business in crushing what was left of resistance in the South.

Make 'em all good Yankees by opening the doors for those who would go west—what with the promise of more and better food, dry clothes and some fresh, clean air.

So the eighteen hundred marched into the sunshine of this winter day. Still this place stunk of death, no matter the cold. If not of rotting flesh, then heavy with the stench of decaying souls.

"Gimme a double column, Johnnies!" hollered the throaty voice. "Double column . . . and march!"

The blue-bellies marched them between the low warehouses, past one row of high fence, then a second, and at last beyond a line of trees Jonah could make out the huffing of smoke and the familiar cry of iron on iron as the huge engines scraped to a stop near a much-battered rail-station platform. He had not seen this place in years. Since a train much like this one had brought him here.

But now this homely rail of a man all strap and sinew was headed west. Starved down to hide and bones by the years of hanging on, he was ready to be going anywhere. Jonah was scared nonetheless.

The promise of rations enough to fill his belly sounded the best. No matter that he had to fight Injuns out there. He had volunteered last September, then waited all these months into the maw of winter until the Yankee officers got their galvanized conscripts organized into two new regiments of Injun fighters to help General Pope out on the frontier.

Jonah damned well had lived on the frontier, leaving his birthplace of Virginia for the promise of rich land in southern Missouri, homesteading beside his uncle's place. He arrived to find it a land embroiled in fiery turmoil between free-staters and slavers. The Hooks had never owned a slave, but—by God—a white man had a right to his property, and no so-called government was going to take it away except at the point of a gun.

As soon as Fort Sumter fell, the Union rushed their forces into Missouri to hold the line against the slavers. The state had a bad reputation for being a lawless land of bloody insurrection. A few zealots had been tramping back and forth across the southern forests and fields of Missouri, gaining converts and what money they could when they passed the hat. And when Sterling Price showed up down in Cassville, Jonah Hook told Gritta he had to go.

At first they were nothing more than freebooters themselves, living off the land and the gracious help of other free-state sympathizers. Price kept his growing legions moving: destroying bridges, removing rail ties, setting fires beneath the iron rails until they could be bent shapeless, firing into passing trains until most rail traffic slowed and eventually halted.

But then Brigadier General Samuel R. Curtis, a West Point man from Iowa, marched with his army into Missouri to destroy the State Guard. The Union soldiers met Price's ragtag volunteers near Springfield, down near Jonah's new home where Gritta and the children stayed on to work the fields. And Curtis drove Price farther south, beating his rear flank like a man would flog a tired, bony mule.

A beating so bad that there were only twelve thousand of them left who stayed on with Price by the time they got to Pea Ridge in northern Arkansas in March of 1862.

It was there that Price rejoined McCulloch and turned to fight. But

General Earl Van Dorn and Curtis made quick work of the Southern farm boys on that bloody ridge strewn with bodies and torn by grapeshot and canister.

Price escaped with a portion of his command: those who would still fight, those who had not headed home shoeless and demoralized.

Jonah followed Price east into Mississippi for the great Corinth campaign. Saddened already: the best the Confederates could muster had not been good enough to push back the Yankees from the western borders.

After his capture in Mississippi, Jonah had been marched and wagoned and railed mile after mile northward to a squalid prison that was swelled with new prisoners every week. Rock Island.

For the longest time, Jonah had feared it would be the last place he would sleep in his life. Come one morning and never waking up again.

Word was from one of the officers on the platform as the eighteen hundred were herded onto railcars that they were heading south and west.

"I know that place," Hook had whispered when someone mentioned their destination.

"You been to Fort Leavenworth, friend?" asked the fellow behind him on the platform.

"No, but, it's close to home . . . closer to home than I been in years now."

"Don't go fooling yourself, friend," whispered the disembodied voice behind him. "You ain't gonna be nowhere near home—what they got planned for us."

"What's that?" asked someone farther back.

"Ain't you heard?" responded still another voice off in another column. "We're being sent out yonder to fight all them Injuns the Yankees cain't whip."

Never before could he remember such a glorious chance to clear the white man's Holy Road of emigrants in their wagons. So few soldiers left out here now that the white man was making war on himself back east.

Crazy Horse pulled the buffalo robe tighter beneath his chin. The sun shone brightly on the patches of old snow, it and the breeze cold enough to make his eyes smart.

For the past three winters while the warrior bands roaming to the south had hacked at the Holy Road, and the Santee Sioux to the east had waged war against the whites in Minnesota, this young Oglalla warrior had stayed north among the villages of his people, living off the buffalo grown fat on the tall grass. He had discovered that the solution to the white man moving onto the plains was to stay away from the white man altogether. Everything north of Fort Laramie was tranquil. The white man did not venture north into the land of the Lakota.

Yet in the time of drying grass last summer, even Crazy Horse had grown restive and yearned for the excitement talked about on everyone's lips—ponies and plunder and coup to be found far to the south in the white man's settlements just south of Fort Laramie.

Crazy Horse wanted to stay clear of the fort and its soldiers, not because he was afraid, but for more personal reasons. Fourteen winters gone, soldiers from Fort Laramie had come out to argue with a small band of Lakota over a skinny cow some warriors had appropriated for their families from one of the wagon trains passing through. There was shooting and much killing—more than enough blood for a young boy to remember.

But now in his twenty-fourth winter, Crazy Horse had formed a bond with a young soldier named Caspar Collins, who was stationed at Fort Laramie, where his father, Colonel William O. Collins, served as post commander.

Through the past winter the two young men had become friends. Oglalla teaching soldier to shoot the bow, taking him on hunts among the coulees and hills, instructing Collins on the rudiments of the Lakota tongue.

So when Crazy Horse had come south to raid with the southern bands, he gave Fort Laramie wide berth. Making war on the white man was one thing. Fighting a friend was something altogether different.

And now the bands of Shahiyena and Lakota were migrating north again, slowly. Herding before them their new horses and the hundreds of cattle stolen in their raids along the great Holy Road, not to mention the many travois groaning beneath all the plunder taken from the wagons and ranches and stage stops. Never before had the Sioux or the Shahiyena been so rich.

But for Crazy Horse—it was still too little salve on the wounds of the massacre at Sand Creek.

Three moons ago, white soldiers had attacked at dawn and killed not only the fighting men staying behind to cover the retreat of their families—but the white men had cut down women and children that cold November day, still fresh and painful as any open wound after all this time.

Black Kettle's survivors sent out pipe bearers to other bands of Shahiyena, Lakota, and Arapaho, calling for a wholesale war on the white man.

The warrior bands had argued and disagreed as to strategy, but when the vote came down, all the villages but one marched north from that council held near the Bunch of Timber on the Smoky Hill River. Only Black Kettle and the remnants of his band headed south. They would not carry the war pipe against the white man.

In that first week of the Moon of Seven Cold Nights, what the white man called January, the warrior bands had arrived on the hills overlooking the settlement of Julesburg. At least ten-times-ten-times-ten fighting men had prepared for this major attack on the white man. A small number of women had accompanied the horsemen north from Cherry Creek to cook meals and wrangle the herd of extra war ponies. Their march had been orderly, for this had not been a simple raid by a handful of warriors. Flankers and scouts had been thrown out along the path of their march, with camp police to assure that no hot-blooded young warrior eager for an early coup would ruin the surprise the war chiefs had planned for the white men along the South Platte River.

The Brule Lakota of Spotted Tail and Pawnee Killer led the way, carrying the war pipe. They knew this land better than the Southern Cheyenne or the Oglalla from the north. They brought the warrior army to the sand hills where Julesburg lay, nearby Fort Rankin.

Julesburg was a small settlement compared to Denver City farther south on the river. It served as a stage stop and crossing place of the river for the Holladay coach lines going on west to Salt Lake City. The stage ranch itself was constructed of cedar logs hauled in from Cottonwood Canyon a hundred miles away. A cluster of low-roofed buildings: telegraph office, stables and corrals for fresh teams, in addition to a large store and an adobe warehouse filled with Ben Holladay's Overland Stage property and commodities. Only a mile to the west stood the strong stockade of Fort Rankin, established in August of 1864 and garrisoned by one company of the Seventh Iowa Cavalry.

At dawn the following winter morning, Crazy Horse and six other decoys joined the Shahiyena Crooked Lance Society chief named Big Crow in riding out of the sand hills into plain sight of the settlement and soldiers. They hurried their ponies down to attack a small body of soldiers who withdrew, escaping back into the stockade. Minutes later a large body of horse soldiers and citizens burst from the fort gates in pursuit of the decoys.

Big Crow and Crazy Horse retreated into the sand hills, drawing the eager soldiers behind them.

Yet some impatient young warriors spoiled the trap and burst past the camp police too early, alerting the soldiers before they had ridden into the noose.

The soldier chief called to his sixty men, turning them about in a clumsy group, and tore off at a gallop. Crazy Horse wheeled about with the white men and was soon riding among the stragglers, hitting the frightened ones with his bow before he shot them from their horses.

Some of the white men reined up and dropped from their mounts to fight on foot. When the main body of warriors came up, most of the soldiers were quickly overrun. The rest cut their way back to the stockade, where the gate was hurriedly shut behind them, abandoning the bodies of fourteen soldiers and four civilians for the warriors to mutilate.

The rest of the thousand warriors then turned their attention to the settlement of Julesburg and the stage station. By the time the women came up with the extra ponies, the warriors were hauling plunder out of the warehouse: bolts of colorful cloth, sacks of shelled corn, flour, sugar, along with canned oysters, catsup, and an entire display case filled with gold and silver watches dragged out the door using a buffalo-hair lariat tied to a pony. Some of the warriors located a sturdy box they hacked open with their axes, finding inside bundles of green paper, which they promptly sliced apart and hurled into the cold breeze of that winter morning.

It was not until late that afternoon that the ponies were loaded with everything they could carry and the cattle herd across the river was herded south for their return to the great encampment at Cherry Creek.

Less than ten days later, the warrior force was back to pillage Julesburg again. Other parties ranged up and down the South Platte, searching for more road-ranches to plunder. Crazy Horse joined some of Pawnee Killer's band, who carefully spread sand across the frozen river west of the plundered settlement of Julesburg and crossed to the north bank. They attacked Harlow's Ranch and killed everyone there but a lone white woman and her child, who were taken prisoner. The place left a bad taste in the Horse's mouth for he would never forget how the warriors found some small kegs of the white man's whiskey and got drunk. So drunk that a Cheyenne waving his pistol around accidentally shot an Arapaho warrior in the head, killing him to the raucous laughter of many others.

Crazy Horse had escaped that place, moving upstream a mile before he halted among some willow and cottonwood and made himself a lonely camp for the night.

For five more days the warriors ranged up and down the river, cutting off the supply routes and dragging down telegraph poles, using their ponies to pull the white man's talking wire far across the prairie. More stations were burned, their employees killed. Cattle were driven off by the young men.

By the time their week of raiding was complete, the villages were brimming with plunder. Nervous ponies were hitched to many wagons groaning under sacks of flour and cornmeal, rice and coffee. There were barrels of the white man's pig meat and crates filled with sugar-coated citron fruits along with small tins of dark, sweet molasses. Shoes, clothing, boots, belts, and hats, besides the bolts of bright cloth the women argued over.

And on the last day of raiding, a party of Shahiyena and a few Oglalla led by Crazy Horse had chanced across a party of nine men who had been members of Chivington's Colorado volunteers and were on their way east when they were ambushed. Searching the valises belonging to the dead men, the warriors discovered two scalps. To one of the scalps still clung the peculiar shell that identified it as Little Wolf's hair. The other scalp was identified by its light color as having been White Leaf's.

Both were warriors killed at Sand Creek.

Yet what stirred the maddening hate within Crazy Horse even more were those other bits of hair and flesh the soldiers carried as souvenirs of the massacre at Little Dried River—easily recognizable as the genitals hacked from the bodies of Shahiyena women.

After their second raid on Julesburg, the entire armada moved north, unhurried in crossing the South Platte, Lodgepole Creek, then the North Platte. Heading for the Niobrara, and away from the bluecoat soldiers at Fort Laramie.

2

I T HADN'T ALWAYS been this cold. Nor had it always taken so long for the morning sun to drive the chill from his marrow.

But for a man with fifty-four winters behind him, come morning Shadrach Sweete moved a touch bit slower, shedding himself of the thick buffalo-hide sleeping robes, than he had when first he came to the mountains with General William H. Ashley back in 1825.

A big bull-sized kid whose immense size belied his youth back then, Shad Sweete had parlayed that muscle into a spot among Ashley's One Hundred. Across the next few years that quickly wore the green off his novice hide, Sweete trapped elbow to elbow in the mountain streams with the likes of Jim Bridger, Davey Jackson, mulattos Jim Beckwith and Edward Rose, Billy Sublette, Joe Meek, and all the rest who went on to have their names given to rivers, creeks, passes, and mountain peaks.

Yet among them in those early years Shad Sweete had stood out, and stood out did he still. Six and one-half feet tall and nudging something shy of three hundred pounds, he was the sort who more readily blocked out the sun than moved with nothing more than the whisper of wind beneath his huge moccasins. Times were when he had been faced with riding a short-backed Indian pony, his buckskin-clad toes almost dragging the ground when he did.

Shad glanced now over at the big Morgan mare he had purchased years

19

ago off a Mormon emigrant along the Holy Road, up near Devil's Gate. He had never been sorry for the handsome price paid, nor the years shared since.

He stretched within his warm cocoon of buffalo robes and wool blankets, sensing the first far-off hint of coffee on the wind. Rubbing sleep from his gritty eyes, Shad sat up, his nose leading him now as it had across all the years past to find food or avoid brownskins. But this morning it was Indian coffee he'd drink, with a heap of army sugar to sweeten it.

Standing to shake out the kinks from those ropy muscles slower to respond these years on the downside of fifty, he pulled on his moccasins, then slipped over them another, larger pair sewn from the neck-hide of an old bull by his Cheyenne wife. How he missed Shell Woman at times like these, pulling on the clothing she had fashioned for him, or smelling in the wind a certain whiff of sage and wildflower—any of it too easily put him in remembrance of her.

And her so far away to the south now, where he hoped she would remain safe from the flames of all-out war threatening to engulf the central plains.

His toes dug into the sandy soil as he skirted through the gray sage, heading for the nearby lodges of loafers, those Brule Sioux who camped in the shadow of Fort Laramie rather than follow the herds back and forth across the plains in their seasonal migrations. The white man had come first to take the beaver from the streams, next to lead others west through the mountains to Oregon and California, and finally to plant himself here and there with his farming and his settlements. So by now there were a number of Indians who hugged the fringes of forts such as these, where flour and sugar and coffee and bolts of calico or gingham could be had—rather than chasing after the buffalo season after season.

Winters were dull here with the soldiers, but they were damned well more secure for the loafers as well.

He had tried loafing himself of a time, when the price of beaver fell through the floor and what traders took in plew didn't know prime from stinkum. When the end came to those glorious, shining times, after following the beaver in their retreat farther and farther into the recesses of the cold mountains, some of Shad Sweete's companions as well retreated back east to make a living at one endeavor or another. Fewer still of those veterans of the heyday of the twenties and thirties moseyed on west themselves, some to the valleys of California. Most to timber-shrouded hills of old Oregon.

Sweete himself had followed the elephant to the Northwest, where many former employees of the Hudson's Bay Company, as well as American Fur and Rocky Mountain Fur, all attempted to put down what roots they could, now that there wasn't all that much for a rootless man to make a decent living at.

"Coffee," he said in Lakota, handing the Brule woman his battered tin cup with the rawhide-wrapped handle. He broke off a chunk of the tobacco twist and dropped it into the cup before she took the huge tin from him.

She flicked her tired, red-rimmed eyes at him, then dug the tobacco wad from the cup with two fingers. The others were stubby, chopped off in some past mourning. The woman plopped the tobacco quid in her mouth and began chewing noisily.

After she had poured him coffee from the small kettle on the smoky fire and disappeared into her lodge, Shad settled to the ground beside the tiny flames, and grunted his own prayer to the Everywhere Spirit for this blessing of coffee on cold spring mornings such as this one.

The woman was back, carrying a small burlap sack at the end of her arm. She stood over him, opening it for the white man's inspection. From it he scooped a fistful of sugar and poured it into the steamy coffee with a smile for her. She disappeared again. He pulled one of the two knives from his belt and stirred while he drank in the heady aroma that did so much to arouse his senses of a morning. Quickly he dragged both sides of the blade across his leather britches long ago turned a rich brown patina with seasons of grease and smoke, then stuffed the skinner home in its colorful porcupine-quilled scabbard.

After the first few sips, Sweete pulled free a tiny clay pipe from the pouch ever present beneath the left arm and crumbled some tobacco leaf into the bowl. With a twig from the Brule woman's fire, he sat back and drank deep of the heady smoke, drawing it far into his lungs as an elixir stirring the cobwebs from his mind.

Coffee and tobacco and the cool, clean air of these plains of a spring morning . . . If he could not have his wife with him, at least a man like Shad Sweete had everything else worthwhile in life.

First one winter, then a second, he and his wife had survived in Oregon—then the trapper had no choice left but to admit that Oregon was not for him. He hungered for the far places, the wide stretches of the mountain west where the purple peaks hugged the far horizon in one direction, and in turning in almost any direction, a man found more peaks raking the undersides of the fluffy clouds. Such was the land more to the liking of Shad Sweete.

While some of his kind, former trappers all, were content to drag a plow behind a mule through the rich soil of Oregon, others were content to do nothing at all—hunting a little, loafing a lot. Staying as long as they wanted in one valley before moving on.

He was not cut out to do either, neither a homesteader nor a layabout could he be.

In remembering that morning he had announced they were returning to the high lonesome of the Shining Mountains, going home to the great stretch of endless, rolling plains her people knew so well, Shad recalled the joy welling in the eyes of his Cheyenne wife.

"I no more belong here in this Oregon country than Gabe Bridger belongs eating at the same table with Brigham Young himself!" he had cried out as wife and young children scurried about their camp, packing what they owned in parfleche and rawhide pouch, loading everything on a groaning travois inside of twenty minutes, the time it took for the sun to travel from one lodgepole to the next.

They moved east and south, until the ground beneath their moccasins felt more akin to home. But in the traveling itself, Shad Sweete once more felt the peace that came from the tonic of wandering. While most men wandered in search of a place to set down roots, Sweete was himself a born nomad.

In joy they had returned to the central plains, where years before he had found, fallen for, and purchased his Southern Cheyenne wife, Shell Woman, whom he promptly named "Toote" Sweete, commemorating a fragment of the French language he had learned from bandy-legged Canadian voyageurs in the north country. He thought the name fit her nicely, what with the way she could whistle him in for supper or their handful of ponies out of the village herd. Toote loved him every bit as fiercely as he loved her, and gave Shad a son back in the summer of forty-five, then a daughter one terrible winter night in forty-six when something tore inside her belly with the birthing.

Toote had cried in those first days to follow, telling him of her certainty she could never give him any more children. And each time he had always cradled the infant's tiny frame within the shelter of his huge arms and rocked his daughter, telling his wife that their healthy son, High-Backed Bull, and now this daughter with the wide eyes and the mouth always curved in a smile, would be all any man could ask for. Shad Sweete could ask for no more than them.

Pipe Woman grew up doting on her father, and he made her in turn his special pet—teaching her everything he taught High-Backed Bull. Toote taught Pipe Woman everything a Cheyenne woman should know.

During those early years on the plains, Shad hired out to the Bent brothers, who traded from that huge mud fort of theirs down on the

Arkansas River in Colorado Territory. But more and more he yearned to be wandering once again. He soon gave in to that siren of the plains and hunted buffalo on his own; his wife, son, and daughter helped him skin the hides that bought bangles and foofarraw enough to make the dark Cheyenne eyes shine.

"You're Sweete, ain't you?" asked the soldier with the well-seamed face.

Shad had watched him approaching on horseback, plodding slowly all the way from the cluster of buildings that was Fort Laramie. Sweete gazed up into the early light, finished his swallow of sweetened coffee, and answered.

"I am."

"Colonel Moonlight sent me to fetch you."

"He did, did he? Why? We're supposed to be waiting."

"Don't know nothing about your waiting, Sweete. Colonel just sent me to fetch you to his office."

"Say what for?"

"Said to tell you Bridger come in late last night."

He could not deny the old tingle that made his every muscle sing at that news. "Gabe?"

Shad stood, throwing back the last of the coffee and strapping the tin cup at his wide belt decorated with dull brass tacks.

"By God! Let's go soldier-boy!" he hollered as he took off on an easy lope, leaving the horseman behind.

It was a thing Shad Sweete could do; once he hit this easy stride, he was able to keep it up for distances and time beyond most men.

But especially this morning, hearing that his old friend Jim Bridger had finally come in.

Now they would palaver of old times shared in the high lonesome, and do a little scouting for the army once more.

As stirred up as the Cheyenne and Sioux were in these parts, he figured it just might prove to be a real bloody time for these poor soldier-boys before the last dance of the night was called and played through.

At Fort Leavenworth, Kansas, Jonah Hook heard some of the first whispers of what they were headed into.

From the lips of wagon teamsters, scouts, and soldiers just in off the prairie came the word that anything west of Fort Riley, Kansas, or west of Fort Kearney, Nebraska Territory, was a trip into hell itself. The plains were afire, lit for sure by that Methodist minister turned Injun killer, John M.

Chivington himself, down at Sand Creek. The Cheyenne broke loose, headed north after Chivington had tried to exterminate them all, and in their dash for freedom the Cheyenne were spreading the flames of war among the Arapaho and Sioux.

"This ain't no Injun scare," said the men gathered at the sutler's place each sundown. "This is a goddanged Injun war."

General Grenville M. Dodge had ordered the Second Regiment of Volunteers out of Leavenworth on 1 March. The Third wasn't ready to march west until the twenty-sixth. On muddy, rutted roads, accompanied by a few mule-drawn wagons, they trudged on foot, bound to the northwest for Fort Kearney across the wide, rolling plains that threatened to swallow Jonah wherever he cared to cast his eyes.

The stinking, hulking cottonwood-plank barracks like forgotten monuments on that Nebraska prairie beckoned the footsore Confederates turned Indian fighters after 350 miles of bone-numbing march.

"You Johnnies're now under the command of General Patrick E. Connor, Department of the Plains!" hollered a mouthy lieutenant the next morning at assembly on the Fort Kearney parade. "General telegraphed us his wire last night when he learned you boys'd made it in. Two companies will be assigned to stay here," the officer started to explain.

Hook glanced at others up and down the line, not knowing if the Fort Kearney assignment was blessing, or curse.

The officer went on, "Two more companies assigned to garrison each of the following: Cottonwood Station, Fort Rankin, Junction . . . and the last companies to report on to Fort Laramie. General Connor is establishing Fort Rankin as regimental headquarters. You Confederates—inside of a month, you'll be guarding six hundred miles of road."

Leaving companies A and B at Fort Kearney, then depositing companies C and D at Cottonwood Station, the rest of the regiment marched on into the northeastern corner of Colorado Territory, arriving at Julesburg on 25 April.

Without delaying, two days later companies I and K were formed up and marched north, leaving the rest behind to garrison the South Platte stations and to build the new Fort Sedgwick to replace the aging Fort Rankin. Captains Henry Leefeldt and A. Smith Lybe had their orders minutes after arriving at the sprawling Fort Laramie, like a beacon on those far plains.

"We're to push on west," explained Captain Lybe to his I Company that night as the men sopped up the last of their white beans with hardtack, supper in bivouac in the shadow of the Laramie barracks. "K Company will drop off at Camp Marshall, sixty-five miles west of here."

"So where we going?" asked one of the Mississippi boys Jonah had been captured with at the battle of Corinth.

Lybe turned slowly on the speaker, pursing his lips for a moment in concentration. "We been handed the toughest row of all, boys."

Some of the Confederates muttered among themselves. Others just stirred their fires with sticks or stared at the coffee going cold in their cups.

"I won't bullshit you none. We're all gonna count on each other out there—so I don't want to start by telling you this is going to be a cakewalk. You all have those down south at Sunday socials, don't you?"

Lybe smiled, trying to drive home his joke as some of the Confederates laughed self-consciously.

"Those of us what lived close enough to a church!" hollered someone behind Jonah.

The rest of them laughed now. Lybe too. Hook liked the Yankee for trying. The captain just might make this company of ragtag Confederates work, and keep them alive to boot.

"Well, now—we've got our orders."

"Going where, Cap'n?"

Lybe cleared his throat. "We'll push on to Three Crossings, where we'll build our post."

"We all gonna stay there?"

"No such luck, boys. We're being spread thin along the telegraph. To keep it open."

"How thin is thin?"

"This company's got us three hundred miles to watch," Lybe answered, wiping his palms on the tails of his tunic.

"Jesus God!" someone exclaimed.

"We'll be spread out from Sweetwater Station, St. Mary's, and clear up to South Pass itself."

"The mountains? We going clear up into those goddamned mountains?" squeaked a questioner.

"No. South Pass isn't in the mountains. You wouldn't know you had crossed the Rockies if you didn't pay attention and see the creeks and streams flowing west, instead of east."

"Don't say," muttered the fellow beside Jonah. He smiled at Hook and went back to licking coffee off his finger.

"We won't be alone though."

"Hell, no. We'll have all kinds of redskin company I bet."

Lybe laughed easily at that. "No, boys. The Eleventh Ohio is out there, waiting for us to come on west."

"Ohio boys?"

"Yes. I hear they've already got a few galvanized Rebs of their own on their rosters. Mostly Kentuckians who served under General John Morgan."

"Kentucky boys are all right," Jonah said. His voice carried loudly in the sudden stillness.

"Yes, soldier. I think Kentucky boys are all right. Just like the rest of you: Mississippi and Georgia, Virginia and Tennessee."

"Don't forget Ala-by-God-bama!" shouted one of them.

The rest hooted, singing out their home states.

Jonah watched Lybe drag a fist under his nose, not knowing if the man was touched by the homey kinship of these Southerners suddenly getting used to the ill-fitting blue uniforms and these far-flung, wide-open plains dotted with high purple mountains, or if the captain might truly be worried for what he was leading them into.

3

WHEN CRAZY HORSE and Little Big Man rode in at the van of the long procession leading many fine horses swaybacked under all that fine plunder taken in the raids along the Platte River, the eyes of the Bad Face Oglalla warriors grew big as Cheyenne conchos.

By the Moon of First Eggs, Old Man Afraid could no longer talk his people into staying out of the way of the white man. Instead, both Red Cloud and the Old Man's son were convincing more and more of the Oglalla that the time had come to make war on the white man. Raiding the Holy Road had never been so profitable, nor so easy—what with so few soldiers strung out along the road and the talking wire hung above those deep ruts pointing toward the setting sun.

Beneath the spring moon, Young Man Afraid of His Horses and Red Cloud called for an all-out effort to drive the white man and his soldiers from the North Platte by midsummer. Until then, small raiding parties would strike here and there along the Holy Road, feeling out the strength of the enemy, keeping the soldiers in a turmoil like a wasps' nest stirred with a stick, and forcing the army to dart here, then there, with what strength the bluecoats could muster.

"These soldiers do not fight like men," Young Man Afraid told the great assembly of more than fifteen hundred warriors. "We marched north from our raids along the Holy Road. Tell them, Crazy Horse—what happened to those soldiers sent against us."

The Horse stood, his young frame and light unbound hair etched in firelight. "Southeast of the fort the white man calls Laramie, the soldiers tried to attack us as we crossed the North Platte with our families and herds. There were only two hundred Blue Coats sent against us—a powerful force of Lakota and Shahiyena more than one thousand warriors strong!"

"We pushed the soldiers aside like they were troublesome buffalo gnats!" added Young Man Afraid to the laughter of the Oglalla.

"The next day the soldier chief brought more soldiers riding from the fort, but this time we attacked him," Crazy Horse continued. "The Blue Coats forted up inside a ring of their wagons and made it hard in a day-long fight to steal any of their American horses. We lost no warriors in either of those battles before moving north once more into the Sand Hills, on farther to the Paha Sapa."

"This march made in the teeth of winter," Young Man Afraid reminded the assembly.

"I think that is why Spotted Tail left us and returned to Fort Laramie to join the Loafers," said Crazy Horse. "The Arapaho went their way as well."

"But now with two full moons of the young grass in the bellies of our ponies, we are ready once more to ride after the buffalo and lay in the meat our warriors will need for the war trail," Young Man Afraid said. "Then once we hold our sun dance, we can march south to drive the white man out of our hunting land, for all time."

"Man's gotta be careful sitting alone out here," Shad Sweete said quietly as he came up out of the dark behind the young soldier sitting at the edge of the hill not far from the camp fires, but far enough that only the old plainsman's experienced eye could make out the dark shape blotting out a piece of the spring nightsky.

The soldier turned to the scout with a withering look. "Didn't hear nobody make you my nursemaid, old man. Why don't you go on back with them others and let a fella have some peace to himself out here."

Shad stood there, staring down at the soldier he took for half his age, measuring the size of the chip the man carried on his shoulder. The scout tried to place the inflection to the stranger's voice. It had been so many years. He settled down a few feet from the soldier.

"You from Kentucky, ain't you?" Sweete asked.

Again the soldier regarded him like he was meat gone bad. "No, old man. Virginia—for all it matters to you."

He pulled at some sage, rolled it between his palms, then drank deep of it into his nostrils. "Don't matter, I suppose. Just come from southern Ohio myself. So long ago I figure it don't really matter after all."

"I could've told you."

He held out his hand to the stranger. "Shadrach Sweete. I didn't catch yours."

"Didn't give it."

Shad withdrew the hand. "I figure someone foolish as you sitting alone out here in the middle of Injun country ought to have himself some company."

"I ain't alone—not now," the stranger replied, and threw a thumb over his shoulder. "Got all the company I can stand back there."

"Oh, you best understand you arc damned well alone out here, son."

The stranger snorted a quick, humorless laugh. "What—some Injun going to come pluck my hair off here in sight of those fires yonder?"

"Possible."

"You been out here under the sun and straining at them mountains for too long, old man. We ain't seen a feather one on this march from Laramie."

"That's when you best be watching for brownskins."

"No, old man—that's what you're being paid to do. I'm just here 'cause I gotta put in my time till I can go home to my family."

Sweete sighed and leaned back on his elbows, watching the dusting of stars overhead, counting two shooting stars before he spoke again to the young soldier.

"Why you come out here anyway, son?"

"You gotta be a fool, you know? I came here to get myself out of that stinking prison where men was dying every day."

"Anything to get out, that it?"

"Closer to home."

"Where's that, son?"

"You're sure a nosy old woman, ain't you now?"

"Figure a man what sits alone by hisself out in the dark needs at least one good friend."

Sweete watched the stranger regard him carefully, then went back to staring at the dark canopy overhead. In the east the big egg yolk of a yellow moon was rising off the horizon.

"Missouri."

"What's that?"

"I said—I come from Missouri."

"Thought you said you was from Virginia."

"Original. Moved few years back with my wife and oldest child to southern Missouri."

"That where you got caught up in all this, I'll bet."

The soldier hung his head between his propped knees. "Yeah."

"You wanna go home so bad you taste it, don't you?"

"I don't figure I'm any different from any of the rest of them back there in camp."

"No, I bet you ain't," Sweete replied quietly. "But you're here now. And if you don't take a notion to watching out for your hair—you'll never get home to see that family of yours again."

"What's it matter to you, old man?"

Shad sensed the chip suddenly back on the shoulder, as if the soldier had realized he was dropping all that veneer of bravado. "Matters only 'cause I've got family myself I'm worried about."

"Back east?"

"Down in Indian Territory. Cheyenne."

"You're a squaw man, ain't you?"

"Suppose you could say that. But there's a war going on out here too. And it can be every bit as messy as what's happening back across the wide Missouri."

"Didn't come here looking for a fight," the soldier explained. "Just putting in my time till it's over back there. And I can go home and pick up where I left off."

"Sure hope you can pick up where you left off, son." He held out some of his twist. "Care for a chew."

The soldier regarded what the scout held in his hand. "Might taste pretty good about now. Yessir. I thankee."

They chewed together for a while before Shad spoke again. "You keep your ears open—you'll learn a lot more about this land than you will flapping your jaws."

"You're one to tell me," he said. "I don't need to learn about this wide-open desert, old man. I'm going back home when I'm done here."

"Believe I'll turn in," Shad said minutes later. He got to his feet and was ready to stroll off the hilltop when the soldier stood.

"Figure I was a little hard on you, Mr. Sweete. Maybe you'll forgive me—it'll make me feel better."

"No harm done."

"We both got us family we're worried about, don't we?"

"I figure we got that in common, son."

"It's all I think about these days."

"Weren't no different in prison, was it?"

A shapeless grin moved across his wolfish face burled with a new beard. "Think about it all the time."

"You watch yourself out here, son. You'll make it back to that family of yours."

Shad Sweete took two steps before the soldier tugged on the sleeve of the buckskin war shirt the scout wore on the chill of evening. Turning, he found the young man holding his hand out.

"Glad to meet you, Mr. Sweete. Man needs a friend out here I suppose."

He smiled, pine-chip teeth glimmering in the new moonlight splaying silver across the rising tableland stretching to the spine of the continent itself. "I can always use a friend, mister."

"Name's Jonah Hook."

"Let's go find our bedrolls, Jonah. These bones hollering for rest something fierce."

"I sleep better out here, Mr. Sweete. Better'n I ever have—if it weren't for the nightmares about my family."

"Don't you let 'em spook you. Don't mean a thing."

Shad wished he meant it. But as he walked down the slope into the soldier camp, the old scout shuddered with the chill in remembrance of his own recurring nightmare—that burned and gutted camp of Black Kettle's on Sand Creek.

And how damned lucky his own wife and daughter were to escape the butchery of madness unleashed.

Our scout recommends you ride on in with us." Captain A. Smith Lybe dragged a dusty hand across his cracked lips. He had just ridden up to Willow Spring Creek with his platoon of I Company, along with six horsemen from the Eleventh Ohio, to find the wagon train and its Kansas escort making an early camp of it.

"I figure we're safe enough here," answered Sergeant Amos Custard of the Eleventh Kansas Cavalry, swinging an arm around their camp. "That scout of yours is a nervous old woman, you want to know what I think."

Lybe glanced at Shadrach Sweete perched atop his Morgan mare. "When you left Sweetwater Station ahead of us this morning, I was hoping you'd get more ground under you before you stopped for the night."

"You take care of your own galvanized Johnnies, Captain," Custard replied. "We're going home, and we'll mosey if we wanna."

Jonah Hook pulled his head back from the cool water of the spring where the rest of Lybe's small detail had been guzzling, in time to watch the old scout nudge his mare forward until he stood above the sergeant.

"The Sioux been hitting this line regular, Sergeant. But I ain't telling you anything you don't already know."

"That's right," Custard said. "If you're so damned nervous, go on and take the rest of these Confederates with you to Platte Bridge."

"The farther we come since this morning," Lybe explained, "the more I feel like I want to make a night march of it into the stockade at Platte Bridge."

Custard gazed at Sweete a moment more. Then he turned to Lybe. "He suggest you make a night march of it?"

"He did. And I agree. Something's up, Sergeant."

"You put in your time out here—like I have, Captain—you won't be so damned nervous about every shadow or flap of an owl's wing. And you won't be so ready to take the word of a squaw-man scout either."

Hook watched Shad Sweete gently rein his mare away.

"Let's be going, Captain," said the scout.

"See you at the station tomorrow, Sergeant Custard." Lybe put heels to his horse and brought it around. "Let's mount up and move out, men!"

Jonah wanted one last drink of that water as he corked his canteen and caught up the reins to his mount. He had to admit, his butt was growing accustomed to the riding when for so long he had either been languishing in prison or walking across the plains. Far better to ride.

And ride they had. Ever since arriving at the Sweetwater Station near South Pass, Lybe's I Company had been busy almost daily, inspecting the emigrant road for telegraph line needing repair, replacing sections at times a mile or more in length dragged down by the hostiles.

Wire pulled down. Poles burned in blackened scars along the road, the scene blotted with tracks of Indian ponies and moccasined warriors. Yet Jonah Hook had yet to see a warrior. Some of the others in I Company had been blooded in skirmishes. One killed and one dead with First Sergeant William R. Moody. But for all of the excitement, Jonah had never been in the right place at the wrong time.

He kept counting the days until he would be shet of this land and back in the bosom of family in Missouri.

This short trip back down the road to Fort Laramie was just the sort of diversion to keep his mind off so much of the yearning. Captain Lybe needed supplies the Eleventh Ohio and Eleventh Kansas had used up prior to being replaced by the galvanized Yankees of the Third U.S. And the Confederates were owed a payday as well. Lybe said he would accompany some of the Kansas and Ohio troops east to Laramie where he could pick up rations, forage, and pay vouchers.

"Watch yourself, Sergeant Custard," said the Captain as Sergeant Moody led out the mounted Confederates. "Reports of heavy activity between this spring and the bridge."

"We'll take care of ourselves, Captain. We're strong enough to hold off anything these red bastards can throw at us."

4

B LOOD WOULD FILL every boot track the white man made as he fled this
sacred hunting ground of the Lakota and Shahiyena.

Crazy Horse lay in wait behind the low hills with the others gathered
beneath the dark sky as the moon eased down into the west. And with the
rising of the sun, the Horse would lead nineteen others to entice the soldiers
from their fort walls, pulling them seductively into the trap set beyond the
sand hills where the many others would spring from hiding to swallow the
white men like nighthawks swooping down to gobble up moths on the wing.

They had been preparing for this attack for some time—ranging out in
small parties and large, probing up and down the Holy Road. Once the
Lakota had even lured out the soldiers from Fort Laramie under their soldier
chief the Loafers called Moonlight. Instead of turning back with his
horsemen when he failed to find any warriors to fight, Moonlight kept on
marching west, right to the bank of Wind River—while the Lakota and
Shahiyena joyously plundered the road behind the soldiers.

With twenty-four winters behind him now, Crazy Horse remained thin
and sinewy, slightly below average height for a white man of the time and
hardly 140 pounds in weight. So what was most remarkable about him was
not only his lighter skin color, but a hair color much fairer than most Oglalla
warriors. Behind his ear now he wore the pebble medicine made for him by
a medicine man named Chips. The stone dreamer had made his young

34

warrior friend a charm that had already proved itself potent, protecting the warrior through the many skirmishes of these past spring moons.

Crazy Horse shivered slightly beneath his blanket, wishing now for the warmth just the sight of Black Buffalo Woman gave his loins. The short summer nights in this high, flat country nonetheless grew cold when all heat seemed drawn from the land. Yet he shivered every bit as much from the remembrance of the horror suffered by the two Lakota men whose bodies still hung from chains lashed over a scaffold at the edge of Fort Laramie.

Early in the Moon of Horses Fattening, two minor Oglalla chiefs had purchased a white prisoner the Shahiyena had captured in their winter raids along the Holy Road. Although two of the woman's older children had been taken from her, she was allowed to keep a suckling infant by her Cheyenne captor. In an attempt to win themselves some presents from the soldiers, the Lakota chiefs named Two Face and Blackfoot bought Mrs. Eubanks and her infant from the Shahiyena, and delivered their white prizes to the acting commander at Fort Laramie.

But instead of rewarding the two Lakota chiefs, the drunken soldier had ordered the pair shackled with heavy ball and chain, then strung up on a scaffold with more chain about their necks.

Even now the Horse winced at the horror—this terrible death for a warrior, chained and strangled, with no way for his spirit to escape through his mouth.

The bodies of the two chiefs had swung in the spring wind, guarded by a soldier with a knife on the end of his rifle, until the weight of the heavy balls pulled a leg from each of the rotting corpses. Legs too heavy for snarling, hungry dogs to drag off into the brush by the river.

With sad eyes, Spotted Tail's Loafers at the fort related the story to the Oglalla who came and went among them until the army finally determined that no Indians should be camping next to the fort during an Indian war.

"Instead of making wolf-scouts of our warriors," Spotted Tail had explained to the Oglalla, "the stupid white soldiers decided to send us east to the fort they call Kearney. Early in the Moon of Horses Fattening, the soldiers will make us begin that march."

It was not long before word of the terrible journey spread among the bands living in freedom. Time and again small parties of Oglalla scouts dogged the trail of those two thousand Brule, guarded by more than one hundred soldiers led by a soldier chief named Fouts. With their own eyes, these scouts saw the soldiers tie up young boys to wagon wheels, where the children would be whipped for disobedience. Other, smaller children were thrown into the spring-swollen Platte River, where they would struggle and thrash in the water to make it back to shore while their parents screamed and cried out, held helpless at gunpoint on the bank.

Crawling near each night's camp, the young warrior scouts with Crazy Horse could hear the cries and sobbing of young women repeatedly taken from their families and forced into the unspeakable by the arrogant soldiers of the Seventh Iowa Cavalry.

"You must help us," Spotted Tail had begged at that camp near the mouth of Horse Creek, whispering to Crazy Horse and his warriors, who had crept into the Loafers' camp after darkness had taken the land whole.

"There are many of us to help you now," the Horse had replied there beside the Platte. "We are just across the river, on the north bank. Tonight we will mark the crossing place with tall sticks, for the women and children to follow. Make your run for freedom in the morning—leaving lodges and belongings behind."

"It will be hard to leave everything behind," Spotted Tail said sadly.

"What if the soldiers attacked our camps—you would leave everything," Crazy Horse replied. "Better to have your lives and freedom than those lodges and blankets and iron kettles the white man sold you."

The next morning when the Brule women failed to pack up quickly enough and instead moved slowly away toward a crossing of the Platte in a retreat that was covered by some of their warriors, the soldier chief rode up with a dozen men, cursing and shouting. The soldiers began shoving among the warriors with their knife-guns when Crazy Horse suddenly appeared from behind a lodge, leveled his old cap-and-ball revolver, and shot the soldier chief in the head.

Like snow gone before an August sun, the rest of the soldiers melted into the earth.

The Loafers escaped across the Platte, the last of them pulling up the tall sticks marking the shallow ford as they went. Crazy Horse and He Dog led their warriors in holding back the soldiers, preventing the white men from following the women and children and old ones in their frantic escape. On what old mares and sore-backed travois ponies they had, Spotted Tail's people would soon swell the ranks of the Lakota bands free-roaming in the north. Yet many times did the women look behind them, wailing and keening in grief that first day of flight. Oily smoke smudged the summer sky. The soldiers were burning everything Spotted Tail's people had.

Everything but their lives and their freedom.

Now they joined the Oglalla, Miniconjou, Sans Arc, along with the

Arapaho and Shahiyena led by the powerful war chiefs Roman Nose and High-Back Wolf. It was a time few could remember: so many lodges, so many songs ringing of war medicine, so many feathers brought out and powerful medicine made for the coming fight along the Holy Road. Runners had even been sent to Sitting Bull far to the north, in hopes the bands could coordinate their attacks with the Hunkpapa's attacks on Fort Rice beside the Missouri River. Perhaps the Lakota could cut off the soldiers' far-flung posts and thereby drive the white man back from the western plains.

Now after three long days of march south from the Powder River country, the great warrior bands arrived at the North Platte just below the stockade the soldiers built themselves on the south bank to protect the bridge crossing the river. It was here that the white man's Holy Road had to cross to the south side because of the crowding from the mountains along the north bank.

Moving off some distance from the fort, slowly so as not to raise a cloud of dust, the warrior bands went into camp as the summer sun set upon the cooling land. While some in that grand council held that night argued to attack the fort in force and overwhelm the soldiers, others argued for burning the bridge and killing soldiers as they came out to repair it.

Yet it was Crazy Horse and Young Man Afraid who gave voice to the battle plan that pleased most the warrior spirit of these fighting men.

"We will strike them in the open! Give these soldiers a chance to fight us like men!" Young Man Afraid had said only hours ago now at that council.

"Draw them out with our decoys and make them fight on open ground!" Crazy Horse had added.

Trader Bent's half-breed Shahiyena son George would be one of the decoys, joining Crazy Horse and eighteen others who would lure the soldiers across the bridge and into these hills north of the river.

Yet some doubt remained in the Oglalla war chief's mind if the *akicita*, the camp police, could keep a tight fisted rein on the eager young men until the moment had come to spring their thousandfold trap.

As the sun stretched itself in a bloody line along the east, then blinked over the horizon, a bugle was blown inside the soldier stockade.

Young Man Afraid nodded to his nineteen. Crazy Horse and the others discarded their blankets and robes, shifting quivers of arrows over their shoulders in the chill dawn air. While others shook out war clothing and freed medicine bundles from hiding, the Horse stood in prayer for the moment, facing the east. In ritual this morning, as he had done before every battle, the Oglalla warrior scooped up a handful of dirt from a gopher hole and tossed it over his head. Some of the sprinkling of dust clung to the earth pigment and bear grease smeared in a jagged lightning bolt from brow to jawbone. Another handful of dust he now scattered over the back of his pony before leaping atop the animal.

Wearing no more than a breechclout and his moccasins, a single feather tied so that it pointed downward at the back of his unbound hair, the Oglalla warrior rode around the base of the hills with the rest. Encircling his sinewy chest was a thin strip of soft buckskin that secured another small pebble beneath the left arm of Crazy Horse. More powerful dream medicine from Chips for this day.

"Look at the American horses!" shouted one of the eager young ones, pointing for the others to see as they neared the bridge.

"They will soon be ours!" Young Man Afraid answered.

"Bring out your blankets!" Crazy Horse shouted.

The twenty unfurled wide strips of blanket or pieces of noisy rawhide to startle the soldier horses into stampeding—just as the gates of the wooden stockade burst open and out poured some soldiers in dusty blue uniforms. Before the decoys could reach the river, the soldiers raced across the bridge to the north bank with a clatter of iron-shod hooves across the cottonwood planks—then suddenly stopped.

As planned, the twenty whirled their ponies for the hills, holding their mounts with a secure rein, while furiously whipping the ponies as if to show they were retreating in panic. The soldiers had far-shooting rifles. Spouts of earth erupted at his pony's hooves.

"Man Afraid!" Crazy Horse shouted, pointing to the rear. "The soldiers do not follow!"

"We must make them angry as the hornets to follow us!"

Several of the warriors dropped to the ground, aiming their rifles captured along the Holy Road at the soldiers.

With a sudden roar, the big-throated wagon-gun on wheels the soldiers had pulled across the bridge erupted in flame. A moment later the ground near Crazy Horse exploded, spewing dirt clods in all directions. A second round was loaded and fired—then a third roared among the stunned, confused decoys.

Those loud reports from the mountain howitzer were all it took for the hotbloods in hiding behind the hills to burst past the camp police attempting to restrain them. First a handful, then by the hundreds, the warriors tore down off the sand hills, spreading in growing numbers like puffballs that cover the prairie after a spring thunderstorm, charging toward the surprised and frightened soldiers at the end of the bridge.

The white men were turning in a confused, milling mass of rearing horses when Crazy Horse spotted a small separate party of mounted soldiers returning to the fort along the timber on the south bank.

He was angry—his stomach boiling now that the decoy and trap had been spoiled. Perhaps his warriors could still count some coup before the sun rose from the edge of the earth this day.

"Come! Let us make sport of these soldiers!" he shouted, pointing.

A dozen horsemen followed the Oglalla war chief plunging into the river, streaming up the south bank, yelling, screeching as the soldiers put heels to their mounts in a mad race to reach the walls of the post before they were cut off. At the same time, another group of cavalry bolted from the yawning gates, hurrying to the aid of those five soldiers about to be surrounded on the riverbank by the thirteen blood-eyed warriors.

In a matter of heartbeats, Crazy Horse, He Dog, and the others were among the frightened five horsemen, touching with bow and staff, striking with the flat of tomahawk blades, whipping the soldiers with their quirts— laughing at the great sport of this coup-counting while galloping right for the other soldiers riding to the rescue.

Ahead at the walls of the fort, several soldiers appeared. These knelt, shoving their long-barreled rifles against their shoulders. They were about to fire into the faces of the screeching red horsemen.

High-Back Wolf called out in his loudest voice for the rest to follow him to the wall. In that wild race he struck first one, then another of the soldiers with his quirt. Roaring in laughter, for he possessed a powerful medicine that made the white man's guns shoot only air.

Bullets screamed among the warriors. Crazy Horse turned at the grunt from a nearby horseman.

High-Back Wolf, the powerful Cheyenne war chief, spun from his pony. Three others wheeled away from the skirmish in a spray of sand, a pair of them swooping low to try recovering the warrior's body.

But the soldier bullets were barking and snapping too quickly now. Even for Crazy Horse. His mount spilled him as it went down, a leg seeping blood. As quickly, the war chief was out of the dirt and back atop the frightened animal shuddering on the riverbank. The Horse was much too close to the soldier stockade now.

With growing rage Crazy Horse and the rest of the decoys retreated and turned, watching the soldiers escape toward the wood walls of their fort, knowing his warriors could not attempt to rescue the body of High-Back Wolf without risking more deaths.

He reined up atop the hills on the north side of the river, quickly looking over the wound his pony had suffered along a foreleg. A grazing only—no doubt a painful wound, but one that would heal. Then he looked up, his attention captured by the eerie keening.

And found the Old Cheyenne chief, Blind Wolf, wailing for his dead son, left below near the walls of the soldier fort.

"I will go at darkness to help you, Blind Wolf," Crazy Horse declared in sign as he led his pony to the old man's side.

"You will help me regain my son's body?"

"I will not ride from this place in shame—knowing High-Back Wolf lies in the shadow of that fort, knowing I did not bring his body out."

For the rest of that day, the soldiers stayed hidden within their tree-trunk walls, not venturing out. At times the soldiers fired random shots at the warriors racing back and forth along the north bank of the Platte, without success. In return, the Shahiyena and Sioux shouted back at the soldiers, who were not brave enough to come out and fight on open ground.

"They stay burrowed like field mice, away from the claws of the badger!" Crazy Horse shouted in frustration to his friends.

"But even the badger will have his day," promised Young Man Afraid.

Beneath the first streaks of gray presaging the very next dawn, Crazy Horse joined the old Cheyenne chief in slipping silently across the waters of the North Platte, padding quietly to within feet of the soldier walls, to reclaim the body of High-Back Wolf.

Platte Bridge Station did not appear in any danger of being overrun after one full day of fighting. At least from what Jonah Hook could see as Captain Lybe's command arrived shortly after two A.M. on the morning of 26 July.

Surrounded by a pine-and-cottonwood stockade standing fourteen feet high, 120 soldiers of the Eleventh Kansas Cavalry were busy molding bullets or watchful at the walls when Lybe's soldiers showed up out of the summer darkness.

"You're damned lucky, Captain," announced Major Martin Anderson, Platte Station commander, "running the gauntlet of those three thousand warriors roaming those hills."

"Didn't see a sign of hostiles, Major. My scout, named Sweete, got us through in one piece. But there's five wagons and a handful of soldiers under a Sergeant Custard still out there," Lybe explained as he saluted the post commander.

"Why the devil didn't you bring them in with you, Captain?"

"Custard's a cocky one. Said he knew best for his men, staying the night at Willow Spring."

Anderson shook his head as Jonah led his weary horse toward one of the fires that tiny knots of soldiers ringed on what there was of a parade at Platte Bridge Station.

"Damned fool—always has been, that Custard," growled Anderson. "He's been a pain in my ass ever since we came out to this godforsaken land. He'll be wolf bait by sunup . . . if he ain't already."

5

"G ONNA BE SUNUP soon, Jonah."

In the chill of predawn, Jonah Hook turned at the dry rustle of the old scout's whispered words. "What you figure the Injuns will do—try to run us over?"

Shad Sweete shook his head. "They don't fight that way. Not like what you was used to back east."

"Drive a man crazy—this waiting."

"You get any sleep, son?"

"None I can own up to."

The old scout gazed over the walls at the graying along the east. "Don't matter how long you're out here in this country. Man never does get used to this."

Sweete settled against the wall, his back to it as unconcerned as if he were waiting for one of the hot-tin louse races to begin back at Sweetwater Station. How Jonah admired the scout for it now, wishing he could be as unconcerned as Sweete.

Over the past few weeks of working along the Emigrant Road that climbed toward South Pass, Jonah had spent more and more stolen minutes with Shadrach Sweete. Not that there was any lack of things needing doing, but there were long gaps of boring idleness interspersed with moments of frantic activity or bone-grinding labor. Everything that made the young

42

Confederate look forward more and more to those times spent with the old scout and his tales of a glorious bygone day.

Back in the early 1850s, Sweete spent some months off and on working for an old friend, Jim Bridger. Shad's old friend was at that moment helping the Plains Department Commander, General Patrick E. Connor, ready his troops and supplies for a major push into the Powder River country coming later in the summer. Sweete and Bridger went back to their younger, piss-and-vinegar days. And both were now much mellowed by their forty-some years in the far west.

Shad had been working for his old friend at Fort Bridger in southwestern Wyoming twelve years before when Mormon prophet Brigham Young had up and decided the mountains weren't big enough for both him and the venerable mountain man. Young dispatched his Salt Lake City sheriff and 150 Avenging Angels to arrest Jim Bridger and to confiscate all the property in his fort and trading store.

"Never met no Mormons," Hook had said when first told the story. "Don't know if I'd know one if he walked up to me. Didn't have much cause to know such things back in Missouri—or where I grew up in Virginia."

"Pray you don't ever have cause to run onto these henchmen Brigham Young sends out to do his dirty work. You'll ne'er forget their passing, son."

As Sweete had told it, a matter of hours before the Mormon posse came riding in, Jim and Shad got word the Angels were on a mission from their Prophet, and coming on hard. Together the pair escaped northeast into the mountains, hoping things would cool off.

But Young's Angels burned half of Bridger's fort and rustled off all his stock the old mountain man had acquired over the years of trade with emigrants along the road west. Then the Angels pushed on east to the well-known ford of the Green River. It was there the Mormons killed Bridger's employees and Shad's co-workers before burning the ferry buildings to the ground. Their work complete, the Angels turned about and rode back home to Brigham Young's Deseret.

Late that fall of fifty-three, when the Prophet ordered his Angels back to the half-burned Fort Bridger, intending to occupy it and to intermarry with the neighboring bands of Shoshoni, Jim and Shad were ready. They had gathered ten other former trappers and frontiersmen, hard cases all, and though they were outnumbered more than twelve to one, the hardy plainsmen cowed Brigham Young's Saints and sent them fleeing through the snow.

As the decade of the fifties grew old, Shad Sweete watched the white man rub more and more against the plains tribes. If it wasn't emigrants moving west along the Holy Road, it was miners punching into the Colorado Rockies for the new gold strikes. The new decade of the sixties thundered open with war in the East, while tensions increased in the mountain West.

"By last summer," Shad told Jonah, "I knew enough to read the sign, plain as paint."

"Writing was on the wall, eh?"

"Manner of speaking. What with the way the Territorial government in Colorado was going at things. They ordered a fella named Chivington to raise a volunteer army to quell what all the loudmouthed white settlers and businessmen was calling the Indian problem."

"Was there a problem?"

"Damn right there was. But neither me nor the old chiefs could convince the young hotbloods to stay at home in their camps—or go off and hunt what few buffalo was left instead of going on the war path."

"The young bucks left—and raised hell, didn't they? Like they're doing now. The reason we soldiers're here."

"Them warriors really let the wolf out last year—off stealing, raping, killing, and looting . . . only to ride back to their villages where the old ones, the women and children could be caught sleeping by the white man and his army."

"That the way you're supposed to fight the Indian—catch him in his villages?"

"Some think so, Jonah. But not for me. Early last winter, I left family with Black Kettle's village down south in Colorado Territory. I come north to Denver to find work with General Connor. Learned he'd moved his headquarters—was up at Laramie, so I rode north a ways farther. When I got to Laramie, Connor told me it was up to Jim Bridger to hire me or not. So while I waited for Bridger to come in last winter, I got word that some Colorado volunteers had nearly wiped out Black Kettle's camp on the Little Dried River." He hung his head as he told it, snorting back the sour taste in his throat.

"I rode south fast as my mare could carry me, Jonah. Found what was left of Black Kettle's band camped on Cherry Creek—along with a bunch of Arapaho and Sioux. They was all itchy for making war, even on me. But that old man Black Kettle come up, with Toote at his side. Wasn't a happier man than I was right then. Once Black Kettle decided not to have a hand in the fighting the other bands wanted to do, and started off for the south to the Territories with my family along—I turned back to skedaddle north to

Laramie. A week later I was passing through Denver City and stopped at a opera house in the town. Hate towns, I do, Jonah. And in that opera house, I watched the crowd cheer some of the proud heroes of that Sand Creek fight as they showed off their battle trophies."

"Cheyenne scalps."

"No. Hair cut from the privates of the squaws they had raped and butchered."

"From what we been told—the Cheyenne and Sioux been doing their share of raping and butchering as well."

"That's the shame of it. There damned well ain't no end to it once the wolf is let out to howl."

"We gonna put an end to it this summer, ain't we, Shad?"

"No, Jonah. What's set fire to this country out here is gonna take many, many a winter to put out."

There came some renewed activity among the soldiers as gray light spread across the small open compound of Platte Bridge Station, enough noise to yank Hook from his brooding reverie.

"Lieutenant Collins!" a voice called out across the way.

"Here. Who wants me?"

"Major Anderson, Lieutenant."

The slightly built young officer strode into the dark shadows of the station commander's office, lit only by smudges of yellow lamplight.

For the first time since arriving in darkness at two A.M., Jonah could look about and see the makeup of this Platte Bridge Station with the coming of dawn's light. The telegraph station itself stood flanked by warehouses on one side, troop quarters on the other. In addition, there were rooms for the few officers, a modest stable, a blacksmith shop, and a small mess hall behind the fourteen-foot-high pine walls and iron-mounted gates.

"Look at that, will you?" a fellow soldier asked as he nudged Hook. "Something, ain't it?"

The morning mist was steaming off the river as the air began to warm, showing for the first time the full thousand-foot span of the magnificent bridge crossing the North Platte. Huge peeled cottonwood stanchions sat atop monstrous handmade cribs of stone.

"I hear there's nothing like it this side of the Mississippi River."

"Wish we was on that old muddy river now," Jonah said. "And not out here waiting for Injuns to cut our nuts off."

What early light there was showed a few hundred warriors bristling the tops of the far hills across the Platte, some on foot, others mounted. None moving. All of them waiting.

Less than a half hour later, the twenty-year-old Caspar Collins reappeared. He started to put the cap back on his head, then stopped at the edge of the open compound. For a moment he stared down at the hat. Collins turned and handed it to a friend of his serving with the Eleventh Ohio.

"Came up here with a mail escort. And now I don't like what I've been ordered to do, Captain Lybe," Collins explained to the fellow officer.

"Can't Captain Bretney countermand the order? You're not part of Major Anderson's command here."

"Bretney tried, sir. Anderson won't hear of it—wants me to go bring that wagon train in. Something says I won't be coming back. So there's no need for those warriors out there to get this new hat I just bought at Laramie."

"You'll be coming back, Lieutenant. Just going out to bring that wagon train of Custard's in, aren't you?"

"Yeah," Collins sighed.

"Keep the hat, Caspar. They won't get it from you," Lybe said.

"Something's out there—got a bad feeling. You keep the hat for me, Captain. Bretney gave me his pistols." Collins pointed to the two weapons he had stuffed into the tops of his boots.

Lybe shuddered. "Gives me the creeps, Caspar—you doing this."

"Keep it."

Collins turned away, resplendent in his new full-dress uniform recently purchased at Laramie. He strode over to his platoon, where he quietly ordered the twenty-five men to saddle up for their ride.

"I don't like the idea of that boy riding out into them warriors on that skittish gelding the lieutenant's got him," Shad said quietly.

"Spooky gray animal, ain't it?"

Shouts came from a handful of the pickets along the walls, announcing that a dozen or more warriors on ponies had splashed across the river downstream from the bridge.

Hook immediately joined Sweete at the banquette along the top of the wall, watching the warriors lope up the south bank no more than a mile from the fort, where they threw several lariats over the telegraph wire, turned their stout ponies about, and succeeded in pulling down the link to Fort Laramie.

"We're cut off from all reinforcements now," moaned Major Martin Anderson.

"God bless us," whispered Lieutenant Caspar Collins as he turned away toward his waiting platoon.

· · ·

"*Major Anderson, sir!*"

"Yes, Captain Lybe?"

"Respectfully request permission to cover Lieutenant Collins's rear, Major."

Anderson regarded the officer dressed in dusty blue a moment. "Your men got in here in the middle of the night, Captain. How many do you have to take with you?"

Lybe blinked. "Fourteen, sir."

"I understand they're all volunteers—galvanized Rebs, aren't they?"

Lybe stared straight ahead without blinking this time. "They are, sir. And fighters too—every one."

The major cleared his throat and scratched his chin. "Permission granted. Cover the lieutenant's rear."

"Thank you, sir." Lybe turned and galloped off to gather his Confederates at the wall.

"C'mon boys! We've got us some skirmishing to do."

"We going to fight those Injuns?" one of the Southerners asked as the fourteen formed up into two columns of dusty, bearded men dressed in blue wool.

"Men, we're going to protect the rear of that troop leaving with Lieutenant Collins."

In the predawn light, most of the warriors had crept out of the hills down to the riverbanks, where they hid themselves in the brush and timber. The Lakota upstream from the white man's bridge. The Shahiyena down.

They did not have long to wait.

With a rustle of movement, tongues buzzing up and down the riverbank, attention was drawn to the noisy yawning of the fort gates. Counting almost three times all the fingers on both of the Oglalla war chief's hands—the soldiers galloped free of the wooden stockade in two columns. Without slowing, the soldier horses approached the south end of the long bridge, then clattered across, iron shoes thundering over the cottonwood planks, echoing loudly up and down the valley.

The soldier chief leading the horsemen turned left coming off the bridge, heading upstream.

As the last bluecoat thundered off the north end of the cottonwood planks, Roman Nose stood within the brush and raised a lance to which he had tied a colorful pennon, signaling his Shahiyena warriors, who were now downstream of the soldiers. With a loud cheering shriek, the Shahiyena rose as one, as if sprouting from the ground itself, exploding from the brush and timber in a mighty phalanx that sealed off the bridge as an escape route for those white men trapped on the north bank.

The soldier chief waved his arm—ordering his men forward sternly. For a beat of his heart, Crazy Horse admired this soldier who courageously led his men away from the bridge and safety.

A moment later, as the soldiers turned in their saddles, shouting among themselves with a clanging of hardware and weapons, Hump and Red Cloud gave their own signal. The Oglalla burst from the riverbank, adding their voices to the war songs reverberating from the nearby bluffs.

Crazy Horse kept his eye on the soldier chief leading his men. Long ago he had learned that the white man fought very differently from a warrior. While Lakota and Shahiyena went into battle as individuals, taking orders from no man once the fighting began—the white soldiers took their commands from one or two of their number, acting in concert.

The Oglalla warrior was not disappointed this morning. The soldier chief signaled, shouting into the noisy confusion of his own men while the warriors shrieked up and down the riverbanks on both sides of the bridge. Waving with one arm that held a pistol, the soldier struggled with his horse—a tall, beautiful gray animal that pranced, spun, and reared repeatedly.

It is good, Crazy Horse thought. The soldier's horse is wide-eyed and frightened, smelling death come so near.

With no real form to their charge, the soldiers bolted into a gallop, heading up the road, toward the hills and away from the Lakota breaking from riverbank.

But more Sioux warriors appeared at their front. The horsemen skidded to a ragged halt, then began firing their guns.

The Lakota swept forward, shouting, "Coup! Coup!" and shooting what few rifles they had, no more than one for every hundred warriors. Most released arrows in a short arc toward the cluster of white soldiers.

There came a momentary lull in the flight of the arrows as the Lakota surged closer still, more warriors sweeping down the slope on horseback. The soldiers seized that break in the assault, whirling their mounts and surging back toward the bridge in ragtag fashion.

A soldier grabbed the rein of a warrior who drew close enough, pounding the Lakota in the face with the barrel of his pistol as they struggled, racing along beside one another in a rising dust cloud.

Lakota warrior, White Bull, drove his pony into the fray, waving a soldier saber captured in a recent battle. With it he took off the top of a white man's head as they neared the north end of the bridge. The spray of bright crimson in the dawn light drove him blood crazy.

And for a moment, a gust of wind dissipated the swirling dust, parting the horsemen so Crazy Horse could catch a glimpse of that brave soldier chief who had reached the bridge, just as the Shahiyena came up to swallow the soldiers whole.

The soldier wavered in the saddle—an arrow fluttering just above his eyes, deeply embedded in his skull.

He was shouting at the warriors in Lakota—saying he was a friend.

Like a cold stone, the shrill sound of that voice struck the heart of Crazy Horse. He knew that soldier. Caspar. His friend.

Already many of the Lakota were drawing back as the soldier hollered at them atop his frightened mount.

"Go back, Cas-Par! Go back now!"

"It is our friend—Cas-Par!" hollered an Oglalla.

"Let him pass! Let the soldier chief onto the bridge!" yelled another.

Hump and Crazy Horse and several other war chiefs were shouting now, ordering their warriors back once they recognized their friend. Through that widening gauntlet, even as the Shahiyena bore down on the soldiers, the white horsemen began to retreat in panic, clattering across the bridge.

Seven white men lay dead or dying on the north bank, each one surrounded by a growing knot of enraged Shahiyena warriors, each warrior with blood hot at yesterday's killing of High-Back Wolf.

The fighting with the rest of the soldiers grew so close that few of the Shahiyena used the guns they had captured in the southern country. Instead, they were like a pack of water moccasins, in among the soldiers with their long lances: jabbing, pulling the weapon free, bright with blood in the growing sunlight, then plunging the weapon into horse and soldier alike in a screaming, screeching nightmare of dust and death.

"Don't leave me!" shrieked a soldier as he fell to the ground. "Oh, God—"

Around and around in a tightened circle the big gray horse pranced while the soldier chief tried to shoot at the strangling noose of Shahiyena— then the hard-mouthed animal suddenly bolted off with its wounded rider, heading not across the bridge with the other fleeing soldiers—but galloping off toward the ridge, into the nearby hills, directly for the Shahiyena who were pouring down into the valley.

With a loud, throaty roar, a wagon-gun sent its load of canister shot across the river. The charge exploded just above the ground, raising a huge spout of dirt clods and dust, shredding the willow and alder on the north bank as the warriors scurried back. A second wagon-gun roared on the heels of the first. Its charge landed farther from the river, against the bluffs.

Crazy Horse joined the rest as the warriors slowly flowed back from the riverbank. Nowhere was his soldier friend in sight. Out of the mass of Shahiyena one warrior emerged, leading the nervous gray horse by a rawhide lariat, struggling with the frightened animal. The cold stone inside his belly grew taut, and never more cold.

He had little time to study the riverbank, wondering which body might be Cas-Par's, for the soldiers at the fort walls set up a barrage with their far-shooting guns. Each time those rifles roared, brownskinned horsemen dropped from the backs of their ponies, then slid back atop them to jeer and call out, slapping their bare backsides at the soldiers so far across the river for missing them.

"Your mothers are bitch dogs!"

Crazy Horse stared along the hillside, finding George Bent, the old fur trader's half-breed son. He was shouting in English at the white men in the fort.

"Shoot that loud-mouthed son of a bitch!" a soldier cried out.

Again and again the soldiers fired, trying to hit the bare-chested Bent, who kept on cursing the soldiers in every vile English word he had learned in his years among them. From time to time he rose from the back of his pony, pulling aside his breechclout, exposing his genitals to the white men.

During the whole time, those Shahiyena gathered around the half-breed shook eight fresh scalps—further inciting the frustrated white men clustered behind the walls of their log fort.

6

N O SOONER HAD Jonah Hook and the fourteen soldiers reached the bridge than the Cheyenne and Sioux were sprouting from the far bank as if by magic.

"Skirmish formation!" Captain Lybe hollered. "Off left! Off right!"

Seven men swung out to the left. Hook turned with six other soldiers to the right. Shoulder to shoulder.

"Forward at a walk!"

As they started across the bridge to help Collins's harried troops, Lybe's men had to bunch together more than Hook liked it. This was not the way to have to come face-to-face with those screaming warriors less than a thousand yards away, across the river, at the other end of this long bridge.

By now Collins was plainly hit, his mount whirling wildly. The rest of his outfit were breaking and racing for the north end of the bridge. The first army mount clattered onto the cottonwood planks.

"Prepare to fire!" Lybe shouted. "Make it good boys—empty some ponies now. . . . *Fire!*"

The fourteen rifles spurted orange, engulfing the Volunteers in stinging smoke as the single mounted soldier surged into their midst, burst through them to the safety of the fort. Another horseman clattered onto the bridge. And a third, pounding the hollow-sounding planks as Hook rammed the ball home onto the powder. He thumbed a cap onto the nipple and brought the big hammer back to full cock as the wide, smooth buttplate slipped into the groove of his shoulder.

By damn, this is what he was out here to do, if he was going to be out here at all—and that was to kill Injuns.

Lybe was barking now, his pistol busy. "Fire your weapons at will— reload and fire at will!"

Jonah squeezed back on the trigger. The gun roared. Through the smoke he thought he saw a warrior reel and grip his pony's withers, loping out of the scramble of men and animals. But with all the confusion, Jonah could not be sure if it was his kill.

In a matter of ragged seconds, every one of Caspar Collins's squad who was going to make it out of that horde of warriors had reached the bridge—frantic in their flight, tearing through Lybe's Volunteers in panic.

"Where's Collins?" demanded the captain as each one of the troopers shot past.

One slowed, then stopped, his horse prancing when Lybe snagged the bridle.

"Don't know where the lieutenant is!" His face was ashen with fear. He turned back, pointing, the horse trying to rip itself from Lybe's firm grip. "He went back to help one of the . . . one of the men what was down. Lemme go, Captain!"

Lybe freed his grip and slapped the mount, before he turned to see Captain Bretney emerge from the gate at the lead of another twenty foot soldiers, coming on at double time. They too were ordered to spread out in a wide skirmish line that halted at the riverbank, where they commenced firing.

Lybe shouted into the noise of the gunfire, "Reload and follow me."

"We going on across, Cap'n?" Hook asked.

"By damn we're going to find out what happened to Collins."

Jonah read the determination turning the man's jawline to stone, and admired the Yankee officer for it. He was on Lybe's heels, glancing behind him once as some of the rest slammed home their ramrods and joined the captain.

Bretney signaled his men on the south bank to form again. The captain led his squad, following Lybe across as the first howitzer round whined overhead. It exploded just above the ground, spraying shot and ball into the air, kicking up dirt and brush.

With wild shrieks, the Indians retreated up the sides of the hills and atop the bluffs, leaving their victims lying stark and white as fish bellies against the summer-cured grass. Lybe stopped at the north end of the bridge, watching Bretney's squad come up to join him as the warriors jeered and slapped their bare asses at the soldiers. Taunting, leering, luring the white men on.

"No chance to make it to that wagon train now, Captain," Lybe shouted as Bretney came up with his patrol.

Bretney squinted to the northwest and pointed. "There's the lieutenant's horse."

They all watched the big gray animal being led away, into the hills by a warrior using a buffalo-hair lariat.

"He might be . . . one of these," Lybe said, visibly choking down the bile.

"Damn that Anderson!" Bretney roared, whirling to shake his fist at the Platte Bridge Station on the far side of the river. "I'll have your oak leaves for this, Anderson!"

"He may have your bars for that—"

Bretney whipped around on Lybe. "Colonel Collins will likely think I'm responsible for his son's death—because I didn't get Anderson to countermand his own order sending the boy out. God*damn* you, Anderson!"

"The colonel can't hold you responsible, Henry. Calm yourself before you're up on court-martial before Anderson's charges!"

Lybe ordered the regulars and his Volunteers to stay behind for the moment and cover the bodies of Collins's men while he escorted Bretney back to the post. In minutes a squad of soldiers came through the gate, leading a double-hitch team pulling a wagon. Into its empty bed the mutilated and scalped corpses were unceremoniously thrown.

Jonah stood, transfixed over one body. He had seen the bodies of his dead comrades, torn by grapeshot or dismembered by exploding canister. But nothing like this. He suddenly thanked God that there was nothing left in his stomach to heave up.

Both hands were hacked off. The large, white thigh muscles were cleaved open like hams from hip to kneecap, pink and rippling in glistening crimson. Four deep lacerations marked each upper arm. The belly lay open, the purple pink snake of intestine wriggling out into the summer heat, already attracting the buzzing of green-backed flies. The head lay darkened from eyebrows back, completely scalped, ears missing.

But it was the castration, along with seeing the scrotum and penis hung pendant over the young trooper's chin that caused Jonah to gag on nothing more than his revulsion of fighting this sort of enemy who would desecrate its victims with such complete and utter abandon.

"Get that body over here, soldier!" shouted a sergeant, stomping toward Hook. "We ain't got all day to lollygag here while them Injuns come down to stuff your cock in your mouth, Reb!"

"Sir?" he asked weakly.

"Grab his arms," the sergeant ordered, hoisting his weapon sling over his shoulder. "What's left of 'em anyway. I'll get the poor bastard's legs, boy. You know him?"

Jonah shook his head. About all he could do.

The wrists were sticky with blood, blotted with sand. That grit was about the only thing that kept Hook from losing his grip on the severed wrists until he reached the back of the wagon where the rest of the soldiers huddled, watching the taunting, jeering warriors shaking the bloody, still-warm scalps at the white men.

"About face!" shouted the sergeant. "Let's keep it together, men. Easy . . . easy now. Don't run off. Stay together, and we'll all make it back!"

Jonah felt no relief back within the walls of Platte Bridge Station.

"You're past the worst of it, Jonah Hook," said Shad Sweete as he came alongside, placing his big ham of a hand on the Southerner's shoulder. "Ain't nothing ever gonna be as bad as seeing your first."

Hook continued to stare into the icy blue of the scout's eyes, unable to find any words to say. They were all choked down below that ball of bile and foul-tasting phlegm he could not hack up.

The shrill call of "Assembly" on the bugle yanked him back, hard. Captain Lybe waited for the last Kansas regular to shuffle into formation.

"Major Anderson has put me in charge of the defense of this post. I want details assigned to dig rifle pits. Another detail to pile up an embrasure of earth in front of our howitzers. Any questions?"

When there weren't any, the captain went on. "Be at your assignments, men. We don't know how long we have until they make a full assault on us. Dis-missed!"

"Captain Lybe," called Major Anderson. "I've just been informed by our telegraph operator that we're now completely cut off."

"The Indians have dragged down the wire going east?"

"We've sent the last word of our desperate situation to Laramie." Anderson turned to his adjutant. "Lieutenant Walker, I want you to mount twenty men, well-armed. I want the east line repaired. Take what supplies you need and depart in ten minutes."

"Yes, Major." George Walker saluted and was gone. To his dismay, instead of twenty, the lieutenant found only sixteen horses still fit for duty, what with exhaustion and battle wounds.

As the adjutant's small repair detail cleared the post gates, Lybe climbed down the ladder from the banquette, signaling his Volunteers to form up.

"You men stay ready. Check your weapons. See that you have ball and caps in your kit."

"We gonna be ready for them Injuns when they come?" asked a Georgia man.

"No, Private. We're going out to cover that repair detail."

"We ain't been ordered out by the major," grumbled an Alabaman sourly.

"I'm going to fix that right now," Lybe snapped.

The captain was back in less than three minutes, a grim smile on his face. "Major wants us to proceed to that sandy mound overlooking the ford where the repair detail will be working. Let's march, double time to catch up with those horses."

The fifteen-man squad trotted in ragtag fashion from the post gate, moving down the Laramie Road to the east about the time the dust from the sixteen horses was settling.

Hook swallowed hard, his nose caked with the alkali silt stirred up by hooves, his stockings hot and itchy inside his boots. Then he chuckled to himself quickly. Glad to have a pair of boots after all. For the last few months of the war, he had fought barefooted, never lucky enough to be the first to come across the Yankee dead. Stripping what he needed from the blue-belly's carcass.

Better hot, sticky feet than cracked, cold, bleeding feet.

The Indians stayed on the north bank, most remaining on the slopes of the nearby hills. Watching. A few loped their ponies up and down on the flat near the river timber, gesturing obscenely, shouting their oaths at both the horsemen and the foot soldiers. While Walker led half his men on east to the far end of the break in the wire, Lybe led his small platoon up on the rise that overlooked the ford and the hills across the North Platte.

The Kansan Walker had just ordered out three pickets of his own and reached the end of the thousand-foot break of wire flopping in the breeze when the roar of a howitzer echoed over the river valley.

"That's the major's signal the Indians are coming, boys!" Lybe shouted to his Confederates on the knoll.

Down below, Walker's soldiers remounted so quickly they neglected to leave behind horses for the three pickets the lieutenant had put out. The squad retreated in wild disorder.

"We can't stay here, Cap'n!" shouted one of the fourteen Volunteers.

"Look at 'em comin' now—we'll get eaten alive for sure!"

"Form up! Column of twos, men—double time, march!"

At a brisk trot, Lybe led his galvanized Rebels off the hill for the fort. As he was closer to the stockade, he hoped he would reach the walls about the time Walker made it with his horsemen. As it turned out, Hook and a young Alabama boy dragged in the body of one of Walker's wounded horsemen. Another of the lieutenant's men slumped in his saddle, severely wounded as they poured back through the gates, the screeching of a thousand warriors loud in their ears.

"Captain!" Walker turned, his neck swollen, face red. "Respectfully, sir—you almost got our nuts cut off out there!"

Lybe shook a finger at the lieutenant. "You damned addle-brained jayhawker! Wasn't for me—you'd been on your own out there. I volunteered these men to come cover you."

"Why the hell didn't you cover us then? I've got one dead and one dying right now."

"Neither of us got the chance to fight today, Lieutenant. You decided to run instead!" Lybe turned away. "You're dismissed, Walker!"

"Dismissed?" he sputtered.

"Unless you don't understand the meaning of that order, Mr. Walker."

The lieutenant sputtered furiously for a moment, then turned on his heel.

Lybe sighed deeply, his eyes squinting. "All right, the rest of you— Kansas, Ohio, and U.S. Volunteers—get back to digging those goddamned rifle pits. We must be ready when those red bastards come!"

"*There comes the* train!"

Shad Sweete turned at the call from a picket above him along the banquette.

"That's Custard, I'll bet," he said to Jonah Hook.

Jonah stood, wagging his head in amazement. "I would've figured he'd be buzzard bait by now."

Shad shook his head. "Not with every Injun for a hundred miles gathered up here for this shivery. Likely Custard ain't seen a war feather till now."

"The major better send some men out to make sure that wagon train makes it in."

"Anderson ain't the sort can make that decision."

"Bretney?"

Shad grinned. "The captain with real guts is under arrest."

He looked around for Lybe and found the captain arguing with Anderson at the far side of the open compound pocked now with rifle pits, each one like a fresh scar on the pale, foot-hammered earth.

"Lybe won't do no good with him either, Jonah." Shad pointed at the hills across the river. "Likely it's all over for the sergeant's men anyway. They just been spotted by the warriors."

On the far hills, hundreds of warriors were leaping atop their ponies, kicking them furiously downhill toward the river. They had spotted the tops of the wagons not long after the fort had seen the incoming train, inching along the road on the Indians' side of the North Platte.

"How many's with Custard?" Shad inquired.

"I remember him having ten soldiers and fourteen teamsters," Hook answered.

"Say!" shouted a picket above them. "The Injuns just cut off five of our boys from the rest of the wagon."

"How many warriors following those five?" Shad flung his voice up the wall.

"More'n a hundred, mister."

Hook felt helpless, knowing some of those men out there by face, if not by name. Knowing they had families back home, waiting for a husband or father or brother to come marching home. "Ain't nothing we can do to help 'em?"

"Ain't a damned thing now, Jonah," Shad whispered. "Not a damned thing."

The best Major Anderson could muster in the way of relief for Sergeant Custard's wagon train was to fire the howitzers at the swarming horsemen heading west from the bridge.

The warriors caught the wagons in a shallow ravine some five miles west of the post. Far out of range of his artillery, and much farther than the major desired to dispatch a relief escort from his stockade. To everyone who asked, demanding action, Anderson justified sitting on his thumbs by saying he needed every man he had for the coming assault he expected from the gathering warriors.

For close to four hours the men in Platte Station kept their eyes on the distant smoke rising above the shallow ravine where they had last seen the wagon tops disappear. Then the firing grew intense for several minutes and gradually tapered off as if someone were damming an irrigation slough.

It wasn't long before puffs of dark, oily smoke billowed into the sky from the far ravine and the faint sound of wild screeching was heard carried on the incoming breeze from upriver.

Much later in the day as the sun eased over into the last quadrant of the sky, there came a flurry of activity along the banquettes as soldiers shouted that they had spotted three men running in from the west.

"What's your name, soldier?" Anderson demanded as he met the first of the trio of grimy, smoke-blackened survivors at the middle of the rifle pits, near Jonah Hook. Others clustered around the three as well.

"Corporal James Shrader, sir. Company D."

"You with Custard's outfit?"

"Was," he gasped, eyes wide and every bit disbelieving he had made it in. "He ordered me to take four men out in advance and probe the trail in. We heard the howitzer fire back yonder—and Custard sent us in to find out what was happening here."

"I ordered the field piece fired to warn the sergeant."

"Yessir," Shrader said, self-consciously. "When the Injuns rode down on us, we got cut off from the rest."

"What happened to those who remained with the sergeant?"

"Don't rightly know. We was more downstream from Custard and the wagons. But we could hear. The men put up a fight of it for a long time. And another bunch was close on our tails—about to find where we'd taken cover. Then a big, ugly Injun come riding down the edge of the coulee we was hiding in. He waved his rifle and called out to the rest. And they followed him like a swarm of hornets for the wagons down the ravine. That was the last we heard of any firing from Custard's bunch."

"You three hid all afternoon?"

"Yessir—five of us in the brakes near the river bottom. Private Ballew was knocked out of the saddle, and they swarmed over him there in the ravine. Private Summers was coming up the bank with me when he was hit and fell. We three is all that's left."

"Lieutenant Walker, take these men and get them something to eat and drink. You've done well, Corporal."

"We got out with our hair, Major. And right now—that's good enough for me. "

7

Moon of Cherries Blackening

AMONG THE SHAHIYENA of the North, he had long been known as Sauts, meaning the Bat.

That winged night animal swooping down on unsuspecting prey was his medicine helper.

But because of his huge beaklike nose, over the past few years more and more of his own people had taken to calling him what the few white men who came among the bands called him: Roman Nose.

So it was that this towering, muscular warrior became Woquini, or Hook Nose, to his own people. Above all, the most powerful war chief of the Northern Cheyenne.

Up and down the length of the hills overlooking the soldier fort on the south side of the river, Roman Nose passed by small groups of warriors, Lakota and Shahiyena both, sitting and talking, smoking their pipes and eating jerked meat, discussing the fight of yesterday when they had killed the soldier chief on the gray horse, perhaps talking of driving the soldiers back into the timber walls earlier today.

Warriors waving blankets on top of their lookout posts to the west caught his attention. More soldiers coming. Wagons.

This time the Shahiyena would show the Lakota how to kill all the white men. Roman Nose was still angry about the fighting yesterday. The Lakota had allowed too many soldiers to escape back across the bridge. Only eight

59

scalps taken. It was not enough to pay for the horror suffered by Black Kettle's people on the Little Dried River.

The white man's bridge would have to run red with blood before Roman Nose had avenged the deaths of the many in that cold winter camp stinking with butchery.

By the time the Cheyenne war chief arrived at the scene, he found his warriors had already forced the five white-topped wagons to halt in the sandy bottom of a shallow ravine. The white men had circled the wagons in a crude oval, freeing the mules from their hitches about the time a hundred Lakota under Crazy Horse rode down on them.

It made Roman Nose laugh to watch the frightened white men release their mules and go bounding back across the sand to the shelter of the wagons. Some of the Lakota drove the mules off to camp while others chased after five horsemen who raced for the soldier fort.

On the hillside above the timbered ravine, Roman Nose dismounted, spread his small blanket and took out his short medicine pipe. Filling the bowl with tobacco taken in the raids of last winter, he smoked, watching his warriors begin firing at the soldiers and civilians trapped in the circle of their wagons. Time enough to watch and enjoy.

But the white men poked loopholes through the sides of the wagons, and killed a few of the more daring warriors who attempted to ride close enough to hit a soldier or count coup.

So as the afternoon dragged on, and the sun grew hotter, like a white eye in the sky that seemed to be scolding him, Roman Nose grew restive, watching the lack of progress while the Cheyenne dead mounted.

Knocking out the burnt tobacco into his palm, the war chief tossed four pinches into the winds, another toward the sky, and one dropped on the earth. A last pinch he smeared across his forehead before he tied on a special headdress made for him by a feather shaman named Ice.

It was time the powerful medicine of Roman Nose ended this fight with the handful of white men burrowed in their wagon corral.

Riding slowly down the slope, he called his main lieutenants to his side and told them his plan. They left to order others to crawl in close and keep the soldiers occupied and hunkered down behind cover while Roman Nose himself prepared the grand charge.

When all was in ready, the war chief shouted his signal. The snipers who had crawled close to the wagons opened up a deadly barrage with their white-man guns taken last winter along the Platte and yesterday at the bridge.

The Shahiyena had many more rifles than did the Lakota of Young Man Afraid of His Horses.

Then Roman Nose turned atop his pony, waving both his arms for the charge to begin. The others raced behind him, like swallows following a hawk. As they neared the snipers, the Shahiyena riflemen ceased firing.

With the quickness of a striking snake, the red horsemen were among the wagons in a slashing, noisy blow, leaping over wagon tongues, shooting down at the white men who hid behind saddles and barrels and kegs. Without their chief saying a word, the warriors leapt from their ponies at a dead run, clubs or tomahawks in their hands, killing those who rose to fight to the last. Hacking at the wounded who could no longer raise themselves in defense.

In a matter of six heartbeats—their fury was spent.

With a wild screech from his powerful chest, Roman Nose announced to the white men in the fort and to the Lakota in the hills that he had been victorious. While some of his warriors stripped, scalped, and mutilated the dead soldiers, he ordered others to plunder the goods in the wagons, then set fire to the wagons themselves once everything they could carry on their ponies had been carried off into the hills north of the river.

Along with fourteen more rifles taken from the bloody, frozen clutches of their white victims.

The following afternoon Shad Sweete and two Shoshoni half-breeds led some reinforcements back to the Platte Bridge from Deer Creek Station. It had been quite a ride.

After the Cheyenne had swarmed over Sergeant Custard's wagon train, Major Anderson called for volunteers to carry a message eighteen miles east to the soldiers stationed at Deer Creek. Anderson selected three men, paying them fifty dollars each for their dangerous ride. Under cover of darkness the three slipped out separately and took different routes down the North Platte.

Anderson needed men badly: he had nine men seriously wounded, and twenty-five had been killed.

Among the mutilated dead retrieved at the far side of the river from the previous day's fierce fighting, a note was found attached to one of the bodies—more like a scrap of paper torn from a soldier's personal diary. Word of that note spread quickly among the men of Platte Bridge Station, most choosing to believe that it was in fact written by a former Confederate serving with the Eleventh Ohio for the past year.

"It says he was captured down on the Platte some time back," Jonah Hook said.

"Note don't say a damn thing about a *he*," Shad grumbled.

"It says the Injuns don't want peace, and they're expecting another thousand warriors to join up to fight us. And you don't believe it was writ by the soldier?"

Sweete shook his head, then whispered. "The Injuns don't keep a soldier alive, Jonah. That's pure addle-headed thinking."

"If it ain't a soldier, who then?"

"A woman."

"Woman?"

"Lot's of 'em got took in those raids down on the South Platte. What I saw of it—"

"You seen the note?"

"Anderson wanted me to look at it," Shad admitted. "It don't look like the hand of a man. More like a scared woman's hand wrote that note."

"Damn their black hearts!" Hook cursed not quite under his breath, his chest heaving. "Nothing more evil than these savages dragging off women and children into the wilderness—for God knows what outrage."

"Injuns ain't the only ones. White or red—we all done our share of evil to one another out here across this big land."

Sweete found Hook staring at him, eyes narrowing.

"Old man—it sounds to me like it don't bother you to think of that woman being alone with all them savages—raping her."

"It bothers me, Jonah!" he snapped. "But, goddammit—I'm telling you the Sioux and Cheyenne ain't the only sonsabitches out here. Evil bastards come wearing all color of skin. I saw for myself how Colorado Volunteers showed off the private parts of Cheyenne women they killed and raped and cut up down on the Little Dried River."

"You seen that with your own eyes?"

"Several fellas held up them privates for show at a opera house in Denver City last winter."

Jonah's mouth worked a moment, trying to form some words.

"I pray my woman and child are safe down in Indian Territory right now, where no soldier going to touch 'em, Jonah."

Hook swallowed hard.

"Lord, Shad—it's like all this is a big hole gets opened up in me, and I can't fill it or close it no way I try. Lord watch over me, but how I wish I was home with Gritta and the young'uns. Home."

Shad turned away to stare at the sky when he saw the tear tumble down the young soldier's dirty cheek.

The next day, after Sweete and the Shoshoni had delivered their urgent dispatch and the hostiles had apparently cleared out, Captain Lybe led his detail of Third U.S. Volunteers on down the Laramie Road. They had pushed several miles east of Deer Creek Station when Shad spotted a cloud of dust ahead of them.

"Indians?" Lybe inquired.

"Don't think so. Leastways, not down there. Don't make sense—them bringing a big camp with women and children this close to Laramie. Sioux and Cheyenne like to fight the soldiers off and away from the fort."

The captain wiped the back of his hand across his cracked, rosy lips. "Go see for yourself, Sweete."

Shad came back a half hour later to find Lybe's men sitting in what shade they could steal among the alder and cottonwood, escaping the late July sun.

"Soldiers, Captain," Sweete announced as he rode in among the anxious soldiers.

"Thank God," Lybe said.

"Thank General Connor and Jim Bridger," Shad replied.

"Connor?"

"Bridger's leading him this way."

"How many troops?"

"A shitload."

"Bet he's coming this way, loaded for bear. For certain he's heard of the attack on Platte Bridge Station."

General Patrick E. Connor was indeed marching upriver to bolster what forces he had left along the upper North Platte. There was some considerable cheering when the general ordered his troops into a short halt there with Lybe's men bound for Laramie.

"Going in for supplies, General. And the men haven't been paid since they were assigned posts in May."

"You've got reason to celebrate then, Captain Lybe," said Connor as he knocked dust from his blue tunic with his gauntlets.

"Getting out of that scrap against the hostiles with our hair?"

"Perhaps that," Connor said as Sweete and Bridger walked up to the soldiers. "Perhaps because the war's over."

"War's over, General?"

Connor was smiling. More soldiers surged around him suddenly. The troops with the general from Laramie were joyously informing the upriver boys of the news as well.

"Lee surrendered to Grant in Virginia."

"Lee surrendered?" Jonah Hook croaked, unable to believe it.

"War's over, son!" Shad Sweete pounded the Confederate on the shoulder. "You'll be going home soon."

"Soon as I get mustered out," Hook said, his eyes moist and his voice colicky with emotion, "that's where I'm heading, straight off. Home."

Her eyes smarted with the stinging sweat.

Gritta Hook stopped her hoeing and took the tattered bandanna she wore around her neck to swipe across her forehead, leaning against the hoe handle.

"You go get us another bucket of water from the well, Zeke," she said to her youngest, six and a half years old now, and more help in these fields with every week.

Without a word he pitched his hoe aside and went galloping past the other two children, Jeremiah and Hattie. It was hard enough raising these three on her own without Jonah, but with the added burden of working the fields behind the mules twice a year, clearing the irrigation sluices, and chopping the wood all added to what she had done before Jonah took off to ride with General Price to keep the Yankees out of Missouri—some days she just ran off to the cool cellar her husband had dug down by the spring and there she cried where no one would hear her.

And it always made her feel better, stronger, able to walk back up the slope to the cabin once more and face her three children and what she had to do alone to hold this family together. More and more during the hard seasons like this, Gritta found herself falling asleep at night as her head hit the feather pillow, her arm by rote going over to Jonah's side of the rope-and-tick-mattress bed. Dropping immediately into sleep before she could even whisper her prayer for Jonah—and for herself and the children.

But standing here beneath the hot sun of late July, Gritta prayed, for the strength to remain in her thin body until her man came marching home. The war had been over a few months and she dared not think about him never coming home—just pushed that thought out of her mind the way she had learned to shove and muscle the mules around in the corral, or shoulder over the milk cow when the old girl did not particularly want to give up on a morning.

No, she had decided Jonah was still alive, and he would come walking down that road one of these days before the fall colors came to these hardwood hills that reminded her more and more of back home to Virginia. Besides, weren't but a few of the others who had marched off to war had already coming walking back home yet. She wasn't the only woman in this narrow holler with a man gone and children to raise and crops to tend.

"Mama!"

She turned at the sound of little Zeke's call, finding him shuffling her way with the bucket. Jeremiah and Hattie were coming toward her as well, dragging their hoes, looking beyond her and off in the direction where Zeke kept turning, and pointing.

Old Seth, the rangy, ribby blue-tick hound they had brought with them years ago from Virginia set to barking and howling, as if pricked by some faraway danger.

Gritta sensed the cold prickle of fear slide down her spine in a single droplet of sweat cascading beneath the layers of her cotton clothing that gusted with a sudden hot wind forcing the bonnet ribbon hung loosely around her neck nearly to strangle her.

"Someone coming, Mama," eight-year-old Jeremiah said as he came to a stop beside her. "You want me go and fetch the gun?"

She thought on it, shading her hand and watching the worm of movement as the horsemen eased their way over the far hills at the north end of the valley. Then she glanced at Hattie for a quick flickering moment that brought more moistness to her eyes.

"They don't rightly look like Yankees, Jeremiah. Leave be the gun for now."

The riders were inching down the slope into the narrow valley, on the far side of the Hook place, beyond the cabin and what barn Jonah and his uncle had been able to throw up by themselves. How she wished either one of them were here now, not gone off to the war. So late in coming home.

Perhaps these were just some soldiers coming home. They sure didn't look like Yankee soldiers.

Her heart leapt instantly with bright hope, and she swallowed it down as quickly, still shading her eyes against the hot July sun as she watched the horsemen reach the edge of the yard there between the cabin and the barn.

No, not blue-bellies these.

The tall, hulking man in front with the big, black, dusty slouch hat shading his bearded face waved and said something to the others. She could hear his voice, but could not make out the words as he directed men to cover the cabin with their weapons, another bunch to surround the barn.

Then he nudged his horse forward, with three of his men on his heels. Slowly moving into the rows of mature crops, the tall, lathered horse bobbing its head, flecks of foam at the bit. He reined up before her and the children.

"That water in your bucket, ma'am?" he asked as he crossed his wrists over the saddle horn.

Gritta decided he didn't sound like a Southern man—but, then—a lot of folks come to Missouri didn't all talk the same neither.

"It is. You care for a drink, sir?"

"I would be dearly grateful for such refreshment, ma'am." He removed the hat from his head, and she was instantly struck with the long, flowing black curls that fell past his shoulders. He bowed his head. "Whom do I have the honor of addressing?"

Gritta's eyes flew to the other three waiting behind the big man. Then she took a step forward, hoisting up the bucket at the end of one arm, the hand still shading her eyes as she studied him for that instant.

"Gritta Hook."

"Mrs.?"

"Yes. My husband is Jonah."

"He hard at work today, ma'am?"

For a moment she thought, but could not conceive how better to answer. "He's away—gone to fight the war. Coming home soon."

The man pushed the big slouch hat onto his head and then dragged a hand across his lips as he plunged the dipper into the bucket. After he had handed the bucket back to the three behind him, he turned once more to Gritta.

"Lots of men won't be coming home, Mrs. Hook. Shame, a downright evil shame of it. War's like that, though. The Lord has seen that so many were cut down—like winnowing the wheat from the chaff."

He turned to the three. "You there, Major—finish your drink quickly and get on back to the others. See what stock we can take along while the others are to go through the cabin. I want everything we can use."

Her heart in her throat, she lunged for his tall boot, caked with dark red dirt in the stirrup. "Don't steal from us! Dear God—the Yankee soldiers already come through and left us next to nothing."

He gazed down at her as two of the men turned their glistening horses away, tromping straight across the field, hooves digging up some of the rows of ripening crops.

"My dear woman. We haven't come to steal from you. We are merely appropriating what is rightfully ours by terms of the covenants the Lord has commanded us to follow in this war against the Gentiles."

She felt fear rising in her, like a thick ball of something that was bound to gag her, make her spill her scanty breakfast on the ground right here in front of the children.

"Take it and go, then . . . if you must." Her heart pounded in her ears like the thundering of water over the falls back in the Shenandoah. How she yearned now for—

"Mrs. Hook, don't be so rude. We have no intention of merely taking from you and riding on." He reached inside his long black duster and pulled forth two pistols with white handles.

The smile on his face reminded her of the way old Seth would grin, baring his yellowed teeth, that low rumbling growl troubling his throat when danger lurked near.

The guns were pointed at her and the three children. "We're inviting you, and your little ones along as well."

8

GENERAL GRENVILLE DODGE had early on asked General Ulysses S. Grant for five thousand Union troops to protect the western frontier. Grant sent him ten thousand.

Yet most of those began to grumble and mutiny as soon as they arrived at Fort Leavenworth, Kansas. Protesting that the war with the South was over, most bowed up their backs and said they had joined up to fight the Confederacy—not to fight Indians.

Back east, powerful political pressure was already being exerted upon the War Department not only by some governors, but by the senators and congressmen of those protesting states. During the first half of 1865 alone, thirteen regiments that had reported for duty at Leavenworth and were ordered marched to Fort Rankin at Julesburg were mustered out before they reached the high plains by official orders from Washington City: seven regiments of cavalry, three each of infantry and artillery.

To fill this aching void at this critical juncture, General Dodge turned to his battle-proven U.S. Volunteers. Trouble was, most of the Confederates had signed on for a one-year enlistment. General Patrick E. Connor had to act, and fast, if he was to have enough troops to accomplish his aim of subduing the war-loving bands taking refuge in the Powder River country north of Fort Laramie.

"I'll come find you when Bridger and me get back from up north," Shad

Sweete told his young Confederate friend as they stood among the bedrolls and supper fires at twilight near the barracks of Fort Laramie. "Trust in that, Jonah."

"May not be here no more," he replied. "Lybe says we're going back to protecting the road and the wire hung over it—back up on the Sweetwater. But I swore this Yankee army only got their hands on me for a year—and that year's up the end of September."

"That's only three weeks off, Jonah."

"I'll go back and watch that road and wire for 'em. But any way I figure it, Shad—you can't possibly be back from that north country in time to see me light out for home."

"It's for sure you're heading home, you ain't here—right?"

"First and only place I'm going, once this army musters me out."

"Then I'll find you there—in Missouri."

"What for?"

Shad slapped the young man on the back. "Because friends just don't ride off without saying good-bye. So if I can't see you off to home when you go, I'll come find you after you've gone back to Missouri."

"Thought you'd be heading down to the Territories—see your family."

"Ain't no reason why I can't swing on down there and bring 'em with me, can I?"

"You got a Cheyenne wife, son, and daughter." Jonah shook his head. "That'll be something, it will. My kids seeing their first real plains Injuns—and what they'll make of you too."

"I may not be too pretty, Jonah. But I do make a fine impression on civilized folks. Can even eat with a knife and fork, I have to."

They chuckled together, then Jonah turned toward the big man, holding his hand out stiffly. He wasn't accustomed to showing his sentiment, Shad figured. The handshake would have to do.

But Sweete pushed the hand aside to wrap the young man in a fierce embrace.

"I'll miss you, Shadrach Sweete."

"I'll miss you too, my friend."

"Company I!"

Both Hook and Sweete turned at the call. Something about the way Captain Lybe was trotting up, his pistol holster slapping his left hip, told Shad he did not like what was coming.

"Gather up, men. I got some good news."

"Cap'n—whenever you tell us that," replied an old Georgia soldier, "I get feared we're in for bad news too."

Lybe said, "Ain't no use in me fooling you, is there, George? He's right. I just come from General Connor's headquarters. For the time being, men—word's come from Washington City that we have to delay mustering out any of you one-year boys."

"What the hell!"

Lybe raised both his hands, attempting to calm his angry Volunteers.

"Cap'n—we volunteered for a year. No more'n one year I'll stay!" Jonah Hook protested.

"He's right!" cried another. "We even put on Yankee uniforms to come west and fight Injuns. And we've fought Injuns for this goddamned army."

"We fought 'em up and down this river, Cap'n," Hook continued. "It's time the army lived up to its promise to us."

Lybe cleared his throat, pursing his lips in agitation as the sun sank behind the far Medicine Bow Range. "Army doesn't have enough soldiers out here for General Connor to get done what he needs doing with this expedition of his heading north in a few days. If he musters the lot of you out, you must remember he doesn't have any replacements for you fellas guarding up and down the road west of here, all the way to Camp Douglas."

"We signed on with that promise of a year's duty!" Jonah growled. "I'm fixing to head home when my time's up."

"Private Hook—we're pulling out tomorrow. For Sweetwater Station."

"And if I don't?"

"You'll be considered a deserter."

Shad could tell Jonah was thinking on that hard, the way a child would roll and roll a mud ball in his palms.

"How long we have to be back at Sweetwater?"

"Till Connor comes marching back here to Laramie."

The Georgian stepped forward. "And how long that gonna be?"

"Could be November—maybe December."

"Shee-it!"

Shad inched forward to attempt calming things as the galvanized soldiers milled and muttered, clenching fists and kicking dust up with their boot toes.

"Captain Lybe?" Sweete called. "With Bridger leading Connor north, I'm sure the general will be getting back here before November. Sure as hell he won't be out to December."

"Weather, Mr. Sweete?"

"Damn right, Captain. Where Connor's going—the weather can for certain turn around on him by the end of August."

"It's a rainy month, I'll grant you that—"

"Captain, rain on the northern plains this time of year can spell trouble. What starts out as a little pitty-pat of a rainstorm can overnight turn into a blazing blue norther of a blizzard."

Lybe straightened as if chastised, then smiled. "Mr. Sweete should know, men. See, we don't have to worry about Connor being out too long before we can be rotated out and you can be heading home."

"So what's the good news you was meaning to tell us, Cap'n?" asked the Georgian.

"Yes—General Connor has ordered that the whiskey be opened for his troops to celebrate one last time before they march out for the Powder and the Tongue. And since we're here picking up rations and forage, the general agreed Company I could join in the celebrating."

There was a cacophony of cheering and backslapping as Company I, Third U.S. Volunteers, threw hats into the air and danced around the fires with one another.

Shad was surprised to find Hook not joining in.

"Where's the whiskey being served, Cap'n Lybe?" Hook asked.

"Why, over there at some tables they've set up between the barracks and Old Bedlam. Bring your own tin, boys. It may be the last hurraw we have for some time to come."

It would prove to be the last celebration of that sort Shadrach Sweete wanted to have himself for the rest of his days. He had gone and had his fill, then wandered back to his bedroll, pleasantly warmed within. The next thing he knew, Bridger was nudging him with his toe, calling softly to Sweete. And everything was black when he opened his eyes.

Shad pulled the robe back from his face. It was still black. No more than a few stars blinked their muted light overhead.

"C'mon, Shad," urged Bridger. The old trapper had asked Sweete to sign on with General Connor for the impending expedition then assembling at Fort Laramie. "General wants to palaver with you."

"Can't it wait till morning, Gabe?"

He dug a bony toe beneath the blankets and jabbed at Sweete's ribs. "Connor told me to tell you it has to do with that young rebel what's a friend of yours."

Shad bolted upright. "Jonah?"

"The one called Hook. Connor wants to see you now."

"Middle of the goddamned night," he muttered, clambering out of the robe and blankets he kicked himself free of. "What'd Hook do now, Gabe?"

"A heap of trouble from the way Connor's acting—like a nose-stung honey bear. But I don't know no particulars."

By the time Shad Sweete stood red-eyed before an angry General Connor, the story had emerged full-blown and fleshed out.

"I figured some of the boys would become rowdy if I opened up a whiskey barrel for them," Connor explained, tapping the top of his desk with the point of a knife, "but never figured it to boil over like this."

It seems Jonah had poured down a lot of whiskey, and quickly, intent right from the start in tying on a big load.

"He got a bellyful of puggle—then what happened?"

"Sergeant, tell Mr. Sweete," Connor said, gesturing to the sergeant of the guard at the door.

"The Rebel picked him some fights, busted some heads—then announced he was taking off tonight for home. Hollering out that if any others was of a mind, they could come along home with him. He was done with the army and . . . and—"

"Say it, Sergeant," Connor ordered, staring at Sweete.

"The army and its lying, whore-banging ways."

"That's what got you riled, Sergeant?"

The old noncom glared back at Sweete. "This army been good to me, mister. And long as I'm serving this army—ain't no man going to desert if I got anything to say about it."

Shad turned back to Connor. "You really think Hook was trying to desert?"

"Said he was heading out."

Sweete slapped both palms down on Connor's desk. "But—do you believe he was going to do it, in the cups like he was?"

"I can't have any men deserting now—or even bragging that he's going to do it."

"Man what brags he's going to do something while he's got a bellyful of saddle varnish, is only letting his whiskey do his talking for him, General," said Bridger.

Connor sighed, then looked back at the tall mountain scout. "That's why I called you here, Sweete. You're his friend. I don't plan on shooting him for desertion—lord knows I should make an example out of him."

Shad sensed a flicker of hope fill his cold belly right about then. "So here you sit, General, cogitating on how can you still make a point of him—but get him out of your hair?"

"Right, Mr. Sweete. I can't send him back to his station with Captain Lybe. He's a poor influence, shall we say."

"How 'bout if I take him under my wing, so to speak, General?" Sweete asked.

Connor flicked his eyes at old Bridger, who smiled back with only his eyes.

"You're heading out with me in two days, Mr. Sweete, are you not?"

"I am, General. And that boy can go with me. I'll keep him out'n your hair. Just ask Bridger. He's trained some of the best—like Mitch Bouyer, who's going along. Right, Gabe?"

Bridger nodded.

"All right, Mr. Sweete," Connor sighed, laying the knife down and sinking into the horsehide chair behind his desk. "He's your responsibility. And if he gets one step out of line—it'll be your ass hanging over the same fire that Confederate's is slow-roasting over."

No man could really blame the general for being on the edgy side these last few days as the summer mellowed. The supplies he had begged of Department Commander General Dodge had still not arrived by the first of August after Connor had assembled his troops at Laramie. It seemed that with every day of enforced waiting there since the beginning of July, Bridger had reminded Connor that the army's campaign season was growing old. The high plains had a way of turning on a man come the autumn of the year. Better get, Bridger told the army—while the getting was good.

Connor decided he was going to wait no longer.

Through all those weeks of waiting he had been planning his expedition, deciding to assemble the campaign in three wings, all of which were to rendezvous the first of September in the Tongue River country.

The very heart of prime Sioux and Cheyenne hunting ground.

The two additional wings of Connor's assault were already pushing their way across the plains. Colonel Nelson Cole was at the head of two regiments already moving west from Omaha without incident.

Not so with the other wing commander.

After his Sixteenth Kansas Cavalry had become disgruntled because they were forced to serve past the end of the war and threatened to mutiny to the point he had to order artillery turned on them, Colonel Samuel Walker finally got his troops under way and marched north for the Black Hills country of the Sioux.

While Cole and Walker forced their reluctant soldiers into that unknown of the northern plains, Connor could himself boast of marching north at the head of the finest cavalry then to sit a saddle in the West. Besides having enlisted such proven guides as Bridger, Sweete, and Sioux half-breed Mitch Bouyer, Connor also had along a newly formed battalion of Pawnee scouts under the capable Major Frank North, as well as Captain E. W. Nash's contingent of Omaha and Winnebago scouts.

Using stout discipline each long summer's day of the march, the expedition covered ground quickly. Despite the problems encountered by a train of 185 wagons, Connor was on the Powder by 14 August. It was there he ordered the first trees felled for what would be a permanent post he christened Fort Connor.

"*I'm going away,* I'm going away, but I'm coming back, if I go ten thousand miles," sang the auburn-haired horseman as he and the rest let their animals pick their way through the timber-studded hills of northern Arkansas, heading south and west for what they had long known was the security of Indian Territory.

He loved to sing—especially this one, a popular song of the Confederacy.

Lemuel Wiser was a handsome man. Most might even say he was more than that: a devilishly handsome man. Striking in every way, from the slate green eyes above a perfect nose, those bow-shaped lips that made every young woman want to be kissed by him, even the long hair hung in ringlets over his ears and the collar of his canvas mackinaw.

Of medium height, Wiser made most folks forget that he was not all that tall, surely not standing beside Jubilee Usher, the leader of this company of freebooters staying two days ahead of the Union troops who had been tracking them for the better part of three weeks now. But in looking at Wiser, most folks simply forgot his height. He was just so damned handsome, women flocked to his side, and most men wanted to be around Wiser, for that was where a fella could find the bees. Circling the hive.

Even his hands were attractive. How he kept them so clean, especially under the nails, living off the land the way Usher's outfit was—it amazed most of the others, who stayed away from water and Wiser's bars of lye soap like the combination had the mortal scent of the plague on it. And no matter what, Wiser always had a splash of some sweet-scented water to pat on his freshly shaved cheeks every morning when he was about his personal toilet.

While many of the rest joked each morning before mounting up how good Wiser smelled, how much they wished they could have something so fragrant to curl up with in their bedrolls at night, Wiser went right on the way he went on.

And he figured that was something Jubilee liked about him. And one of the big things that set him apart from the rest of Jubilee's bunch. In fact, Wiser was Usher's right hand. The one who passed Jubilee's orders down to the rest, the one who loved the fact that he drew the lot of whipping those who broke Jubilee's "Orders of the March." It was as if dealing out punishment to the rest of the ragtag band was some reward for faithful, unquestioning service to not only Jubilee Usher—but to Jubilee's wrathful God.

Yet as Wiser stood there this morning, wiping the soap scum from his straight razor, looking over the busy camp of Jubilee's faithful Danites, Wiser wondered why men like he and Usher had to consort with the likes of these rogues and desperadoes—the unclean vermin it took every bit of his strength of will to control at times.

Jubilee was emerging now from his tent, his long coat freshly brushed by the Negro manservant he had carried along these last few years of wandering the midlands, just off the frontier itself. Usher turned and gave orders to have the tent struck.

"Once you have the woman dressed, mind you. Let's be quick about it now."

How Wiser wished Jubilee would tire of that captive woman and cast her aside as he had cast so many others aside. This woman with the light-colored hair and the sun-burnished skin. But even though it had been only a matter of weeks, Wiser brooded that Jubilee would likely hold on to this one. A real prize she was—this other man's wife Usher had claimed as his private spoils.

Her, and the three children off that hardscrabble farm back in southern Missouri.

With a course hand towel, Wiser wiped the soap residue from his cheeks, gazed back into the smoky mirror, and admired the sharply defined face, its long, bushy sideburns of reddish brown, sweeping down into the meticulously waxed and curled mustache.

Each time he stared into a mirror, it was as if the sinking feeling returned to remind Lemuel Wiser of why he had taken this path in life, each day finishing this ritual by looking away from the attractive reflection in the mirror, and having to stare once more at the crude, handmade black boot that covered the stub of his left foot.

While the right was stuffed into a shiny cavalry officer's boot, the left was but a terribly deformed clubfoot with which he had been born.

In days gone long ago, children had been cruel. So young Lem Wiser had grown up to be every bit of that and crueler. But by the time he had reached his early teens, Lemuel had taken to allowing himself to be called the nickname that poked fun at the ugly clubfoot that looked every bit like a pig's hoof.

Jubilee was striding his way atop his long legs, smartly dressed in silk vest and long-coat. He was tugging on the points of that brocade vest as he asked, "You are ready for the day's march, Boothog?"

"I am, Jubilee. Soon as I finish my toilet."

Usher walked off, whistling and carefree without another word.

And Wiser was left once again to watch how gracefully Jubilee strode across the leaves and fallen branches of the forest floor, ultimately left to stare at his own deformed foot. Knowing he would never walk but with an ungainly lurch-and-drag.

He silently cursed his mother once again, wherever she might be now. It was she who had handed down her curse to him, this single deformity on such a beautiful man.

"Boothog . . . ," he whispered, slapping lilac water on his freshly scraped cheeks.

9

T HE DAY AFTER they had killed all the wagon soldiers along the North Platte River, the warrior bands had begun to wander off to the four winds.

No chief could hold together such a great gathering. It was time to prepare for another buffalo hunt, perhaps follow some of the antelope herds. After all, it was a time of celebration that had begun that very night as they danced over the scalps Roman Nose's Shahiyena had taken near the white man's fort. Many of the dancers wore the fine blue tunics with brass buttons taken off the soldier dead.

By now the young Oglalla war chief had become a shirt wearer among his people. To put on the white, brain-tanned shirt that reached his knees meant Crazy Horse pledged his life to his people. For their safety he would die. His was a sacred vow, much respected, and with it coming much medicine power.

"H'gun! H'gun!" the old ones had shouted out the Lakota courage-word as he took his oath as shirt wearer.

This brave one who thought so little of himself, who had offered his body as a decoy time and again to lure the white walking soldiers into traps.

Yet in this rich season, Crazy Horse sensed the stab of something intrude upon the celebration of his life—like the piercing pain of a lance point.

Runners had come, bringing word from those bands who had stayed close to the Holy Road and the fort called Laramie.

It was there, the young scouts reported, that the soldiers were growing in number, every week more numerous, like puffballs sprouting on the prairie following a spring thunderstorm. Only then they had struck their camp of tents at the fort—marching north as quickly as their mules and wagons would allow once they had crossed the North Platte.

"Who is this man bellowing that all Lakota and Shahiyena males over twelve summers will be killed by his soldiers?" Crazy Horse demanded as the scouts told their story to the war-band leaders: Red Cloud, Young Man Afraid, and High Backbone.

"He is the one who leads his army toward our hunting ground."

"We must show this soldier chief that we will not stand for his army shoving its fist down the throats of our people," Crazy Horse vowed, eyes narrowing. "Instead, we will make this soldier chief choke on his own blood!"

"*H'gun!*" howled Young Man Afraid. "First the soldier chief must find us—and that is not going to be easy."

But the young scouts had sobering news to tell the warrior chiefs. The soldiers were guided by Indian trackers.

"Tell us of these trackers," Red Cloud demanded.

"Scalped-heads," the scout leader replied. Pawnees. "Ten-times-ten. And some mud Indians from the great mud river." Omaha and Winnebago. "They lead the soldiers into our hunting ground."

"Our ponies are strong," Crazy Horse said as the others fell silent. "They have their bellies full of summer grass, and the winds are cooling in their nostrils. We can ride circles around the soldiers and their scouts—and poke our heads up where the white man will not expect us to be. Let us go drive the white man from our hunting ground this one last time. Let us go make the white man bleed!"

"*They're paying you* how much?" Jonah asked, disbelieving.

"Five dollars a day," Shad Sweete answered. "Bridger's getting ten. He's chief of scouts."

"I never seen that kind of money in my life."

"Scouting pays well. Bad thing about it, you got to eat army food."

"Why can't we hunt?"

"You wander off to hunt, likely it will be your scalp hanging from some brownskin's lodgepole."

"I think your brain's been boiled by the sun, Shad. We ain't seen a feather since we left Laramie," Jonah said.

"Don't you ever doubt it, son. They've been watching us ever since we crossed the North Platte."

"Connor ready for 'em?"

"Damn right, he is. That little redheaded Irishman is taking the war right to the Sioux and Cheyenne up there in the Powder River country."

"He sure as hell is a fighting man, for a Yankee," Jonah agreed.

"You liked the way he formed his outfit back at Laramie when Walker's men refused to march, eh? Connor gave them sunshine soldiers five minutes to fight or get walking."

"That was some show when those guns and field pieces were turned on Walker's men."

"This bunch with Connor all think this trip is a lark for 'em," Shad grumbled as they rode along, the entire column of cavalry, infantry, and 187 wagons strung out for more than two and a half miles. "Some of these greenhorn soldiers lay eyes on antelope or buffalo and go off running their horses to death, like this was some Sunday social."

Jonah said, "Every Injun in fifty miles knows this column's coming, don't they? The way that platoon set fire to the grass day before last. Smoke cloud that high had to tell them we was coming."

On north from the four columns of Pumpkin Buttes, the pebbled bottom of the murky Powder River became a welcome sight that fourteenth day of August, after Connor's soldiers had crossed so much dry country north of the North Platte. But while the general had his troops making camp on the level benchland between the sharp bluffs and the river, right where he would soon order Colonel J. H. Kidd and his 250 men to begin building his Fort Connor, Jonah Hook followed Sweete downstream.

Two miles from the soldier camp, the scout stopped, listening, eyes scanning the river bluffs. "Look there, Jonah. And remember it well."

"What you want me to see?"

"Those circles, all over—where the dried grass been trompled down."

"Who?" Then he caught himself. "Injuns."

"Lodge circles, son. A fire pit in every one. And each circle likely means three warriors of fighting age. You remember that too."

"Those little brush shelters there by the riverbank. That for the children to play in?"

"Hell, no," he said, smiling, some of the nervous watchfulness gone from him. "Those the places where the young warriors sleep when they're too old to stay with their families, but don't have a squaw of their own yet. They lay brush and blankets over the top of those wickiups to keep out the rain."

"How many warriors was here, Shad?"

He wagged his head. "More'n that little Irishman can cut his way through in a day—if they decide to ride down on us."

Two days later, Jonah heard his name called and turned to find Sweete riding up to him, leading a second horse through the scattering of tents.

"C'mon, Jonah!" he huffed. "We're going scouting."

He didn't need a second invitation. Hook took the reins and climbed aboard. "Where to?"

"Riding out with some of North's Pawnee. North by west. See if we can scare up some sign."

The Pawnee trackers were not long in doing just that.

By midmorning, they came across a fresh trail of some two dozen hostiles, including at least one pony dragging a travois. The Pawnee immediately grew excited. They halted and milled about a moment, talking excitedly among themselves, then dropped to the ground to tie up the tails of their ponies. Each one prepared himself for the coming fight by performing his personal medicine.

Hook watched, wide-eyed, as most stripped off their army tunics. Others adorned themselves, smearing paint on face and chest, tying feathers in hair and the manes of their ponies. When all was ready, the group leapt atop their ponies and rode on with a single wild cheer.

That cry sent a chill of anticipation down the Confederate's spine, like a ghost from Platte Bridge Station.

Yet for the next four hours as they dogged that enemy trail, the entire Pawnee battalion led by Major Frank North fell eerily quiet.

"They're moving fast," Sweete whispered to Jonah.

"We're gonna have to move faster, aren't we?" He watched Shad nod. "Who are they, this bunch?"

"Can't tell for sure. But my money would lay on them being Cheyenne. If I know any tribe, it's the Shahiyena."

"Shahiyena," he said the word, rolling it around on his tongue the way a man would a quid of chew. "They're the bunch you said killed Lieutenant Collins at the bridge."

"Had to been. Sioux liked the man. Cheyenne still carrying a mean heart for what happened down on the Little Dried River last winter. They ain't giving no quarter to no white man—and they ain't expecting none either, Jonah."

He wasn't sure if it was the late-summer heat, or if it was the pinched look of determination on Shad's face, but Hook sensed a rumble of apprehension troubling his bowels. He caught himself gazing about at the other riders, Pawnee all except for North and Sweete and himself, hoping these Indians would know how best to fight other Indians when the time came.

Trouble was, Jonah wasn't reassured. It was one thing to march out to fight Indians with a group of soldiers around you and a mountain howitzer backing you up—not that it was anything like the heavy field artillery both sides battered one another with at Corinth and on up at Brice's Crossroads. And it was an entirely different matter when you were riding out with Indians to fight Indians.

"You stay close," Shad whispered, his great hand gripping Jonah's arm in a sudden lock, then releasing the hold. "We're going to a gallop, son."

The words were barely out of the scout's mouth when the trackers hammered their ponies into a run behind North and his Pawnee sergeant. Hook figured they had decided to eat up ground faster, chew away at the hostiles' lead.

Steadily up, then down, the swales of the rough, rolling land bordering Powder River, the Pawnee tenaciously clung to the trail as the sun eased down behind Cloud Peak in the faraway Big Horns. Twilight came over the high land, and with it North halted his Pawnee. The trackers had a quick, animated discussion with their white commander. Sweete came back to find Jonah sitting in a small patch of grass, where he was watching their two horses graze.

"North's sending about half of his bunch back."

"Why?"

"Their ponies are done in. They'll go back and tell Connor what we've found—and tell him we're going on in to find the enemy."

He swallowed. "Then you figure to stay on the trail?"

Sweete knelt in front of Hook. "You don't have to come, Jonah. I came to tell you to ride back with the Pawnee."

Something pricked his fierce pride of a sudden. "Sure—so the rest of you can say I didn't have the balls to ride with you after those Cheyenne warriors—that it?"

Sweete smiled. "That mean you're coming along with me?"

"Damn right it is, old man," he snarled, getting to his feet. "Anyone gonna say Jonah Hook ain't got the bottom to chase these red savages down, better be ready to eat his words."

"No one said you ain't got the grit, Jonah," Sweete said, backing up with a huge smile. "Figured there was fire in you when I met you, first off."

Later that evening after half the trackers had headed back to Connor's camp on their played-out ponies, North and Sweete pushed the rest on down the Powder until total darkness made it impossible to pursue the hostiles any longer.

"North's sending two of his best ahead on foot to stay with the trail." Sweete settled onto the cold ground beside Hook, their horses nearby, jaws grinding the dry, brittle grasses with a reassuring crunch. "Get your saddle off and wipe that horse down with some grass, son. We'll pick up and move out soon as it gets light enough to follow in a few hours."

As far as Hook was concerned, it was still too damned dark to do anything but sleep when the old scout rousted him from the warmth of those two blankets he had wrapped himself in beneath the whirling stars overhead. So he was amazed that by the time he had tightened the cinch and remouthed the bit he had loosened while the horse grazed, the sky along the east had grayed enough to allow a man to pick out nearby landmarks and just barely make sense out of the trail that hugged the bank of the Powder River.

It gave him a newfound respect for not only the Pawnee trackers, but for Shad Sweete as well.

"One of these days, you get to Missouri like you said—I want you to teach me everything you know about tracking the enemy."

Sweete smiled slowly. "Don't have to wait till I come visiting you and your family down in Missouri. We got plenty time to get started on your lessons while we're here."

Just before sunrise, they came up on the two trackers North had sent ahead. Unable to understand either the Pawnee tongue or the sign language used in that gray dawn, Hook nonetheless sensed he understood the import of their talk. Especially when he looked on down the direction the trail was taking and spotted what the trackers were indicating.

Thin wisps of smoke rising slowly into the still, cool dawn air. Behind the bluffs not that far downriver.

"They're Cheyenne, all right!" Sweete whispered with fiery excitement. "Northern—and that means they'll fight like the dickens, Jonah. You loaded and ready for bear?"

"S'pose I'm ready as I'll ever be, Shad. We gonna follow 'em again till we catch 'em?"

"Shit—we've caught 'em. Them two hurried back to meet us along the trail—to tell North the Cheyenne was already packing up to move out."

As North and Sweete led their forty-eight Pawnee around the base of the bluff toward a thick stand of alder bordering the Powder, Hook caught his first glimpse of the quarry they had chased for a day and most of the night.

"Watch out for the women, if there be any, Jonah," Shad instructed at the Confederate's side. "But just remember the squaws can be as deadly as the bucks. They'll fight hard as their men—God bless 'em. *Heya!*"

Hook watched as the old trapper licked the pad of his thumb, then wiped it down the bridge of his nose. Wetting his thumb again, Sweete made a cross just below the brim of his old hat, swiping across the eyebrows. As North kicked his bunch into a gallop with a wild screech, Shad opened his eyes, having made his private medicine. He grinned over at the startled Hook and added his voice to the wild calls of the Pawnee and the not-too-distant cries of the Cheyenne.

"*Hopo!* C'mon, Jonah—it's a good day to die!"

With the surge of his own hot adrenaline, the sweep of the charging horses kicking up dust and clods of yellow soil into his nostrils, the wild cries of both Pawnee and the retreating Cheyenne, who now understood they were being attacked by Indians and not white men, Hook fought down the bile of fear for the unknown.

His hands were sweating on the reins and as he thumbed back the hammer on the carbine, finding the cap securely hugging the nipple. A trickle of cold ran between the cheeks of his ass as they burst past the stand of alder where the Cheyenne had camped for the night. The odors of their fires were strong in his nostrils as they shot through the grove. Something foreign on the wind as well—it made him think he was actually smelling the warriors who had spent the night on that ground.

Bullets sang through the air, their music brutally yanking him back to surviving in battle once more. But there was no clear battle line. The Cheyenne had spread out on their front, half heading toward the riverbank, and the others hurrying toward the low, chalky bluffs. Already among them were the first of the Pawnee, cutting off the escape of those Cheyenne who stayed atop their ponies.

Most of the enemy had dismounted and were turning their animals loose before wheeling around to find cover and return the Pawnee fire.

The cries of animals and men were loud in his ears—nothing new, for he had been blooded all the way from Pea Ridge to Corinth where the Yankees found him in that scooped-out depression he had crawled into when he could not retreat—not with that bleeding leg wound that seeped his juices in a greasy track across the forest floor.

The Yankee army surgeons had told their prisoner his leg would have to come off. But he had refused their suggestion of help by knife and saw.

"Better to die soon with two legs, than to die the slow death of a cripple prisoner of the Yankees, with no hope of running for it," he had told them, gritting his teeth on the pain that tasted like sucking on a rusty iron nail.

Instead, Jonah had requested whiskey and got brandy instead, along with sulfur to pour into his own wound. Two days later he dug the Union minié ball out while the surgeons watched, unashamedly amazed at the Rebel's grit. Pinching that smear of lead bullet up between his fingers, and slowly opening the pink purple muscle with slow strokes of a surgeon's straight razor, Hook swallowed down more and more of the pain with each heartbeat. Along with more of the brandy he asked for, and poured into the wound when he finished—then promptly passed out.

Jonah found a target ahead, climbing the low bluff just in front of him. Lining the warrior in his sight, a sudden rustle of brush made him glance to his left as a warrior sprang from the alders and willow, yanking up his captured rifle.

There was no time to think, or aim. Jonah whirled and pulled the trigger as he saw the warrior's muzzle spit a burst of orange. Like jagged teeth scraping across his flesh, the bullet stung his upper arm at the same instant the Cheyenne was catapulted backward into the underbrush.

Jonah stood there, breathing deep, slowly climbing down from the saddle, gripping his bloody arm. Never had he killed anyone so close. The Indian lay there, not moving while Hook quickly glanced at the long, bloody track parting the sleeve of his blue army tunic. He didn't like wearing Yankee blue anyway.

"Arrrggghhh!"

He had time only to spin, finding a second warrior leaping over the dead body, a small-headed tomahawk held high in the air. Hook met the charge with only his muscle, pushing the weapon into the air with his empty rifle. Both men tumbled, the warrior falling forward, Hook collapsing backward with the force of the collision.

The warrior sailed on over, sprawling on his back as Hook arose, swung the carbine, and connected in the Cheyenne's rib cage full force. Air exploded from the warrior as he reeled backward, clawing for the knife at his belt.

With a shrill growl that rose to become the Rebel yell, Hook charged the ten feet separating them, driving the rifle butt into the Indian's chest. The knife dropped. Hook smashed the butt into the Indian's jaw.

The warrior collapsed, his mouth spurting shiny crimson across his yellow face paint, splattering his chest. He growled back, like a wounded animal, dragging feet under him, preparing to rise.

Taking the rifle barrel in both hands, Hook swung it just as he had battered axes at trees in both the Shenandoah Valley back in Virginia, and on that land he cleared to build a home for Gritta and their children. That quiet, narrow valley back home.

Blood splattered on him as the buttstock cracked against the skull.

The Cheyenne collapsed like a damp lampwick.

Jonah Hook stumbled backward one step, then two. And on the third, he collapsed as the creeping darkness washed over him.

10

"GREAT GOD A'MIGHTY, Jonah—you blooded yourself in this scrap!" Hook blinked his eyes, things watery at first, then slowly swimming clear. Up there blotting out a big chunk of sky hung Shad Sweete's gray-bearded face.

"Take 'er easy. Looks of it, you had yourself a real tussle."

Jonah sat upright with a jerk, wincing at the wounded arm. Near his feet lay a warrior, blood drying on the side of his head and face.

"He dead?"

Sweete smiled. "As dead as he can be. You whacked him hard enough to drive him on into the Other Side."

"Other Side?"

Sweete poked his hands beneath Hook's arms. "Where the Cheyenne go when they die. After taking a long walk in Seyan—that star road up overhead in the nightsky."

His knees felt weak. "Sweet heaven."

"You got the idea, Jonah."

"I didn't mean heaven like that." He looked at the second warrior lying still, collapsed in the underbrush, a bloody, bluish hole in the middle of his chest.

"Don't make no difference," Shad replied.

All around them Hook heard that the shooting had stopped. Replaced now with yelps and laughter, hoots of joy and wild cheering from the Pawnee, who were scattered over every one of the Cheyenne bodies.

"How many we get, Shad?"

"Twenty-four," he answered. "Every last one of 'em."

"We . . . we killed 'em all?"

"And you got two for yourself. They yours—scalps and plunder both."

"Plunder?"

"Guns, knives—whatever you want off'n the bodies. Along with the hair."

He glared at Sweete, suddenly angry at something, perhaps the cold knot in his stomach. "Ain't got no use for the hair."

"You better let me take it for you then, Jonah," Sweete said quietly as a half dozen of the Pawnee ambled up, shaking their black and bloody trophies, showing some interest in the white man's victims. "This bunch will think your yellow if'n you don't scalp them two bodies."

"Told you," Hook snarled, pushing away from the old scout. "I don't want the goddamned scalps."

"Then I'll take 'em myself," Sweete snapped, grimly pushing past the young Confederate.

Jonah watched as the Pawnee scouts closed in a tighter ring while Sweete stopped beside the first body. The old trapper yanked a short knife from his scabbard and kicked the Cheyenne over with the toe of his moccasin. As the young soldier's eyes widened, the old plainsman pulled the black hair back, set the blade at the brow line, and dragged the knife around, over and behind the ear. Lifting the long, loose hair adorned with feathers, Sweete continued the knife's path down to the nape of the neck, back up and around the ear to the brow line once more. Wiping the knife off on his buckskin britches, he stood and placed a hand on the back of the warrior's neck. Tugging carefully at the bloody edges to start the scalp ripping from the skull, the dark skin finally gave way with a sucking pop.

"Here, Jonah—you best hold it for me."

"I can't. Told you I won't."

"Goddammit!" Sweete growled. "You'll never hear the end of it from these Pawnee sonsabitches you don't hold this scalp for me. Leastways, it'll make 'em think I'm showing you how to scalp even though you don't want the goddamned thing." He held it out, shaking some of the gore and blood from it onto the yellow sand. "Now, do it."

Glancing quickly at the gathering Pawnee, loaded down with their own scalps and plunder, Jonah found a few of them whispering to one another, grinning behind their hands. He burned with resentment.

"Won't do you no good, son—though you likely feel like punching one of those faces to a bloody pulp."

"Gimme that scalp!" Hook snapped, surprised that the old man knew how badly he wanted to pummel some of those arrogant faces. "And your knife!"

Sweete handed them over to the Confederate, who promptly turned on the closest tracker who was laughing at him. Stopping almost on the Indian's toes, Jonah glared into the dark Pawnee eyes, reading the sneer on the tracker's face. Hook held the scalp up right in the man's face, then slowly inserted Sweete's knife blade between the Pawnee's neck and his long hair, slowly raising the braid with the knife.

The smile on the dark face faded like August snow. The dark eyes widened. Boiling inside, Hook rubbed the knife up and down the Indian's neck.

"You laugh anymore at me, you bastard—I'll gut you like a Christmas hog and hang you up to bleed to death," he snarled.

"I figure he got the gist of your message, Private," said Major Frank North as he appeared on the scene. "Better you take that knife from his neck now—before one of these others decide that you really do mean to kill Half Rope here."

He turned to North, not removing the knife. "I would, you know. Half Rope, you call him?"

"He's a good tracker," North replied. "Just got him a sense of humor gets him in trouble a lot. But the rest of these are stirred up. Their blood's hot from the fight—and we found the scalps of a few white men on some of these bodies. Likely from the soldiers killed by the Cheyenne at Platte Bridge a month ago."

"I was there," Hook said, not taking his eyes off the dark pools of the Pawnee's.

"Major's right about their blood being hot right now, Jonah. Best back off now. You made your point—these boys see the elephant for sure," Sweete said.

"All right," Hook eased the knife away, then turned quickly and parted the Pawnee as he strode to the second dead Cheyenne.

There he did as the old trapper had done on the first body, then popped the scalp free, holding them both aloft to the yelps and wild keening of the Pawnee—old enemies of the Cheyenne.

"You satisfied, old friend?" the young Confederate asked of Sweete.
"You'll do, Jonah Hook. By bloody damn—you'll do!"

Major North's Pawnee scouts rode back into Connor's camp brandishing the fresh, coal black scalps at the end of their coup sticks and from rifle muzzles. They howled like wolves and chanted their war songs. That night they began their ritual dancing around those twenty-four scalps, accompanied by the incessant beating of their small hand drums. The celebration went on for long past midnight and kept so many of the soldiers awake that General Connor had to order North to end the festivities.

For the next six nights, the trackers repeated their noisy dance, ending their celebration, however, by ten each night.

Only a week after that first skirmish with the Cheyenne, the Pawnee reported to Major North they had come across a large trail. North took word of the discovery to Connor.

The next morning, the general detached two companies of Ohio infantry, along with a troop of Seventh Iowa Cavalry, led by both the Pawnee and Omaha scouts. Bringing up the rear of the march was a pair of field pieces—six-pounders. This force would accompany Connor to the Tongue River in search of the migrating hostiles.

Into the rough badlands dividing the Powder River drainage from that of the Tongue, the general marched his trackers and troops. On past the Crazy Woman Fork, drawing ever closer to the bounty land of the Big Horn Mountains, where the men found not only an abundance of game, but fat trout as well in those clear-running streams far different from the alkali-tainted creeks in the Powder River country. The long column skirted the west side of a lake surrounded by ocher bluffs brilliant beneath a bright, summer blue sky.

"Water's unfit to drink—thick with alkali. Years back, during the shining times of the beaver trade," Sweete explained to Jonah as they rode past the long, narrow body of water, "this lake was named after the first Black Robe to come among the Indians of these northern plains."

"What's a Black Robe?"

"A priest. Name of Pierre-Jean De Smet." Then Sweete laughed, as if enjoying a private joke. "I remember how Gabe used to tell pilgrims heading to Oregon about the thick oil spring you can find on the far side of the lake. Loved to get those pilgrims wide-eyed and gape-mouthed by telling 'em there's a vein of coal under that lake they could set fire to, and by stirring up the oil and the alkali—make one hell of a batch of soap!"

It was here as well that they came across their first buffalo herds.

That first evening at the base of the foothills, Shad Sweete and a half dozen Pawnee trackers rode out to a nearby herd grazing near Connor's evening camp and drove fifteen buffalo back toward the soldier's bivouac, where the huge beasts were killed after they had been driven into a corral made of the expedition's freight wagons.

"You still got your shooting eye, don't you, Shad?" commented Jim Bridger as he walked up among the soldiers celebrating and butchering the shaggy buffalo.

"Bet I do, Gabe. Best you dive in now and claim one of them tongues for us—or we'll be left with poor doings, certain," Shad replied.

They shared a fat, juicy buffalo tongue that evening, cooked to a rosy, moist pink down in the glowing coals of a fire pit in the shadow of the Big Horn Mountains while Bridger told his old partner they would be taking some Pawnee ahead in the morning.

"Leave the Rebel behind this time, Shad."

Sweete felt something seize up inside him. "Gabe, you and me been friends a long time."

"We have—and that's why I figure I can talk straight to you."

"What stick you got to rub with Jonah?"

"Pawnee and me never did get along."

"I don't like 'em particular either, Gabe. What's that got to do with Hook? Something Connor say to you?"

Bridger gazed at Sweete a moment in the firelight. "You stand by this Rebel?"

"He'll do to ride the river with, Gabe."

The old trapper wiped his knife across the top of his leather britches and finally smiled at Sweete. "All right. He's your'n to worry about. I got enough to do keeping Connor's balls out of a Lakota sling and his hair from ending up on a Cheyenne lodgepole."

The next day as the sun rose and then fell, Shad and Bridger led Hook and a handful of the Pawnee north by west from the land of the Pineys, descending at last into the valley of the Tongue. They stopped, waiting a moment to enjoy the view of the Big Horns off to their left, waiting for Bridger and Captain Henry E. Palmer, Connor's quartermaster, to come up.

"You see what lies along the horizon, yonder?" Sweete asked of the small gathering, his eyes resting a moment longer on the face of his old trapping partner.

While Bridger squinted his blue eyes into the hazy distance, Hook turned to glance behind them at the distant column winding its way through the broken land. Then he looked on up the Tongue, to the northeast among the Wolf Mountains, straining to make out what might be something out of the ordinary.

"Smoke. Plain as paint, Shad," Bridger answered.

"Smoke?" Palmer asked, a touch of skepticism in his voice. "Where?"

"Look up yonder," Bridger said. "Far off there between the cut in those hills."

"Those far hills?" Palmer huffed, sounding incredulous. "That's a full forty—perhaps as much as fifty miles if it's a two-day ride for this column."

"Agreed," Bridger said. "There's smoke yonder. Best sign of any we've run across, right Shad?"

"Aye, Gabe. A heap of brownskins for sure, Captain Palmer."

The soldier's eyes measured the two buckskinned scouts for a tangible moment. "You like to have your fun with me, don't you, Jim?"

"We ain't funning you none, Captain."

Palmer considered it a minute more, then wagged his head. "I'll go let the general know."

Minutes later Palmer returned with Connor. The general gazed off to the northeast with his field glasses. After a moment, he wagged his head.

"I can't make out anything like smoke up there, Bridger."

Sweete prickled with disgust. "You're doubting our eyes, General? We've both spent two lifetimes out here in these mountains and plains. Smoke's smoke and Injuns is Injuns."

Connor turned to North. "Major, take a half dozen of your best trackers and scout in that direction where these two say they spotted the smoke. Report back when you find some positive evidence of the hostiles."

"Damned paper-collar soldiers," Bridger grumbled as he reined his horse about angrily.

"What was that, Bridger?" Connor snapped.

Shad straightened in the saddle, angry at the arrogant soldier himself. "He said you and your bunch was nothing more'n paper-collar soldiers."

"I can tell 'im myself!" Bridger growled at his friend.

"You can, can you, Mr. Bridger?" Connor flared with Irish temper.

"If you go and decide to stop trusting in your scouts—ain't nothing for Shad and me to do, so we'll just collect our pay now and be on our way."

Connor's eyes narrowed. "You're not resigning, Bridger. I won't have it!"

"Then you best start believing what you're told!"

"Major North will be back in a couple days with some good news—if there's something up there."

Across the nearby hills, the shadows were lengthening and coyotes beginning to yip and yammer.

"North'll find that camp—right where Shad and me say he'll find it."

Two days later just past dawn, a pair of the Pawnee came tearing into the soldier camp, bringing back the news Major North had sent to Connor.

A big enemy camp had been located, the trackers explained in sign. Nearby stood Bridger and Sweete, completely vindicated. But there was no apology, nor recognition of the abilities of the white scouts, forthcoming from the general.

"Ask them how many lodges?" Connor asked his chief of scouts.

Bridger wagged his hand at the Pawnee to signify asking a question. With two fingertips he formed a triangle. "Count the lodges."

The Pawnee pinched his face in thought, then shook his head.

Bridger smiled. "These Pawnee are horse thieves, General. They only count ponies. Ain't much interested in a count of the lodges." He turned back to the Indian and signed, "How many ponies?"

"Big herd."

"That's enough for me," Connor replied brusquely, turning to bark orders to his officers, preparing to move out on the attack. "No loud voices, no bugles from here on out. Talking at a minimum, and it must be at a whisper."

"General, I want to go along," Palmer requested.

"Captain, you will be in charge of the guard left with your supply train."

"Begging your pardon, General—I respectfully ask to accompany your assault force. There are several officers who are ill this morning."

"Ill?"

"Bad water, I suppose, sir. So one of them would gladly stay behind with the train, and I could accompany you."

Connor wagged his head. "Very well, Palmer. Make it so."

For the rest of that day and through a night of stumbling struggle, fighting the darkness of that yawning, broken wilderness, Bridger, Sweete, and North led Connor's troops northeast along the Tongue River. By the first streaks of dawn, North informed the general that his troops were still some distance from the enemy's village.

"We'll just have to hurry the troops along," Connor said. "In the meantime, North, take your scouts ahead and be sure the hostiles don't bolt on us. Let me know at the first sign that they are fleeing."

Shad rode with North and Palmer as the Pawnee spread out onto a wide front, carefully picking their way across country. The sun had risen close to midsky before the enemy camp was once more discovered by the scouts inching their way along, staying down in the safety of a streambed, their unshod pony hooves moving quietly on the pebbles beneath the clear surface.

Inexperienced and unaware of the danger, Palmer had allowed his horse to surge ahead of the rest and found himself following a game trail that emerged from a brushy ravine. Suddenly on the flat tableland, Palmer discovered the enemy camp spread before him, a sizable pony herd grazing between him and the lodges. By some stroke of luck, the camp appeared too busy to notice the soldier as he quickly grasped the muzzle of his horse in one hand and reined about, back into the ravine, where he slipped from the saddle.

"I found the camp!" he whispered excitedly as Sweete and North came up.

"Get on back there and tell the general," North ordered.

Connor quickly issued battle orders to his officers, then formed up two columns before he spoke personally to the enlisted men.

"This is our day! Should we get in close quarters, you men must remember to form by fours and stay together at all costs. Use your rifles as long as possible to defeat our enemy, and under no circumstances are you to use your service revolvers unless you are out of rifle ammunition and have no other choice."

He took his hat off and swiped a finger inside the headband, preparing to lead the charge himself. "You must endeavor to make every shot count, but each of you must be ever mindful of leaving one shot for yourselves. Rather than fall into the hands of the hostiles, use that last shot for yourself—as it will be preferable to falling into the hands of these savages who have killed up and down the length of Dakota.

"Very well, men. This is our day!"

11

As HOOK FOLLOWED Sweete out of the ravine behind the hundred Pawnee scouts, the level ground where Wolf Creek poured into the Tongue River sprouted close to three hundred lodges, most already nothing more than skeletons bare of buffalo-hide lodge covers.

"They're breaking camp a'ready!" Sweete hollered as the pony herd began to whinny alarm. The frightened animals bolted in all directions as the soldier columns poured out of the ravines like columns of black ants across the brown landscape.

The village erupted with the shrieks of women, cries of children, and shouts from warriors hustling for their weapons. Every throat rang with alarm as ponies were caught up. Dogs barked and howled, a thousandfold. A frightening cacophony more fitting to hell itself.

Connor's battalion burst from the ravine, wheeled left into line.

"*Charge!*" shouted the general.

Up and down the long line of 250 troopers, officers echoed the order. Now the soldiers raised their throaty roar to the sky, matching that of the warriors waiting to take the blow of the coming charge.

At four hundred yards officers ordered the first volley.

"Look at all them sonsabitches!" Hook muttered, just loud enough for Sweete to hear.

"These soldiers are outnumbered, Jonah. We best hope Connor can put the fear of God in these Injuns."

"Bunch of 'em running already." Jonah pointed to the north where those on ponies and on foot were struggling up the bluffs into the surrounding hills along Wolf Creek.

"Mostly old women and young'uns, Jonah. Scattering whilst the warriors cover the retreat. You're gonna find a lot of the younger squaws hanging back in the village—fighting 'longside their men as these soldiers charge in—"

"Shad!"

They both found Bridger reining for them at a gallop, his bony, arthritic hands gripping the reins like life itself.

"This is Black Bear's bunch!" cried the old trapper as he came alongside the two horsemen. The three reined up in a swirl of dust as the Pawnee surged on, yelling their own war cries.

"Arapaho? You sure, Gabe?"

"You never questioned me afore, you idjit!"

"You always been right as I recollect. But this bunch can't be Arap."

"They are—and Connor's making him one big mistake."

"How you gonna get him to stop?"

"No way. Blood's spilled now," Bridger groaned.

"What's the difference?" Hook asked. "This bunch made trouble for the settlers and soldiers, haven't they? Time they paid."

"This is a ragtag band compared to the Bad Face fighting bands we ought to be hunting down," Shad said.

Ahead of them the first soldiers were now among the lodges, forced into a fierce firefight with the warriors and half again as many squaws who shot rifles, pistols, and bows, then ran and dodged before they would wheel and fire again behind another lodge or some concealing brush. The ground lay littered with robes and blankets and bodies of those men and women who had fallen in their fight or flight.

A light rain of arrows fell short of the trio's horses, some sticking in the ground, others clattering against brush and rocks noisily.

"We can't be sitting here!" Bridger shouted.

"You figure to fight now?" asked Sweete.

"If we don't—it's our hair, you old pilgrim!"

"C'mon, Jonah!" Sweete hollered as Bridger tore off into the fray, flailing the sides of his army mule with his moccasins.

In the time it takes the sun to move from one lodgepole to the next, the Arapaho were driven from their village, into the rough, brushy country upstream along Wolf Creek. For ten miles Connor and his men pursued the fleeing band. Yet with every mile more and more of the soldiers were forced to drop out and turn back, their horses exhausted from the forced march of the past two days.

"General!"

Connor finally turned, clearly surprised to find only Sweete, Bridger, and Hook—along with no more than a dozen soldiers still capable of maintaining the chase. He threw up an arm and ordered a halt.

"Bridger! My God—where's the rest of my command?"

"You damned well outrun 'em, General."

"What man among you has paper and pencil?" Connor inquired. A corporal raised his hand, patting his tunic. "Good, soldier. Take the names of every trooper here who was capable of keeping up with the chase. I want a commendation written for each man."

"You ain't got time to take names and hand out your congratulations!" Sweete warned in a blistering tone.

Connor twisted in the saddle. He and the rest of the soldiers saw them coming.

It hadn't taken the Arapaho long to realize the soldiers had slowed their pursuit. The warriors doubled back on the trail and found the soldiers greatly outnumbered. In a screeching, angry mass, like a disturbed nest of hornets, the warriors swarmed back down the creekbank in a rattle of rifle fire and the hiss of stinging arrows.

"Let's get—"

A soldier yelped in pain as an arrow caught him in the leg.

Jonah felt his horse jerk, then wheel suddenly, around and around in a wild circle. It collapsed on its front legs as he dismounted to keep from falling, yanking free the carbine from its shoulder sling.

"Up here, son!"

He turned. The old mountain man held out a hand. In a fluid leap, Jonah was atop the big Morgan mare behind Sweete, who whirled the horse about as the last of the soldiers lit out.

As they raced downstream, Connor picked up more and more of the soldiers who had been forced to turn back. Slowly, by adding small groups of troopers here and there along the way, the white men were able to hold off the counterattacking Arapaho.

By the time they reached the mouth of Wolf Creek where the rest of the general's men were mopping up the defenders, the Arapaho held back from pushing their attack. Instead of pursuing into the village, the warriors fought from long-distance, and when they didn't fire at the soldiers, they flung their curses and rage at the white men preparing to put the village to the torch.

"Burn it—all!" Connor ordered.

Lodges, blankets, buffalo robes, clothing, abandoned weapons, kitchen goods, and a winter's supply of dried meat—all of it sputtered into fitful flames, eventually rising twenty feet and more into the sky, puffs of oily black smoke climbing heavily into the hot summer haze.

"I s'pose we all have to admit it when we're wrong, Gabe," Shad said as Bridger wagged his head beside him. "You had no way of knowing this bunch was Arapaho—or that they'd been raiding down on the Platte with the Sioux."

"Come out on the lucky end of the deal of these cards, didn't we, Shad?"

"Since these soldiers found some greenbacks and other plunder stole off the ranches and the Holy Road—I'd have to say this bunch of Black Bear's needs taught a lesson."

"Lucky for me, nigger," Bridger growled. "I don't like killing Injuns just for the sake of killing Injuns. Gawddamned, Shad—you and me is married to Injuns!" The old trapper turned and shuffled off, muttering to himself.

"The Pawnee having themselves a grand time of it over there, Jonah," Shad explained, pointing to the far side of the camp. "The Arapaho warriors know they haven't a chance of getting anything from the village now—but, by damn, they sure do want their ponies back."

"The Pawnee good fighters?"

He squinted in thought. "I never had much use for 'em. Neither did Gabe. Pawnee didn't turn friendly toward white men till they saw the writing on the wall. Besides, I think they figured out they could get more plunder by raiding enemy camps with the soldiers behind 'em instead of fighting the Sioux and Cheyenne in the old way—on their own."

By middle of the afternoon, Connor's officers had convinced the general it was time to cash in their chips and make good their escape. As for casualties, the general's own orderly and bugler had been seriously wounded in the first charge on the village. A lieutenant and a sergeant with one company had been wounded in the thick of it. A young soldier had been hollering at his comrades, goading them on into the village when an arrow had entered his open mouth and pierced the back of his tongue. For the longest time his friends debated cutting the soldier's tongue off to free it, until an old-line sergeant came along and held the tongue down, slowly slicing away at the red meat until the glistening iron arrow tip was freed.

"General's given orders to pull out, Shad!" hollered Bridger as he came hobbling up, snagging the reins Sweete handed him. "He's got some wounded . . . and he's taken prisoners. We best get too."

"Let's ride, Gabe. This place's getting a mite too warm for my way of thinking."

As Connor pulled his forces off, the Arapaho became bolder. Not only had they watched the destruction of their village and seen sixty of their fellow warriors killed by the soldiers, but they were now forced to watch as eight women and thirteen children were herded into the wagons and driven off, surrounded by soldier columns. Using what few ponies they had taken with them at the time of the first charge to flee the village, or what they had recaptured during the soldier retreat, the warriors now dogged both sides of the army's backtrail down the Tongue River.

At the head of the march rode a hundred Pawnee, driving before them a herd of more than seven hundred rangy Indian ponies they claimed as the spoils of battle.

"Don't fire your weapons at the hostiles!" shouted a lieutenant riding down the long columns. "General's orders: preserve your ammunition!"

"Don't shoot? How the hell does Connor expect us to keep 'em off of us if we don't shoot?" Jonah asked.

"You heard the man, Jonah. Keep your weapon ready—but don't use it."

"I don't use it—what good is it to me?"

"Right now the Arapaho don't know we're desperate short on ammunition," Bridger explained.

"If they stay afraid of what they *think* we can do to them—they won't get too bold," Sweete added.

For the next five hours of march northeast along the Tongue, the Arapaho warriors harassed, dogged, and deviled the retreating column. But as soon as the sun sank behind both the Big Horns and Connor's soldiers, the warriors trickled off and disappeared. In a matter of minutes, all that could be heard above the squeak of leather and the jangle of bit chain was the distant howl of wolf and cousin coyote floating in from the nearby hills.

Connor rode ahead to catch up with his advance scouts near twilight as the warriors drifted away into the evening.

"Bridger, what do you think of my volunteers now?"

He unloaded a stream of tobacco juice and smiled. "General, your boys done good today. Riding hard the way they did, on no food for so long—and fighting near six hours steady was something too. They didn't buckle like I was afeared they would. Rest assured, your soldiers acted like men today."

"I'll take that as a compliment, Mr. Bridger," Connor replied.

"Well, ain't you gonna compliment me and Shad here on finding that camp for you, General?"

Connor chuckled mysteriously. "You can't be serious, can you, Mr. Bridger? You don't expect me to swallow that you two actually saw smoke from this camp from fifty miles away, do you?"

Sweete and Bridger glanced at one another, both growing angry.

"We spotted that smoke and told you where to send North's trackers," Sweete growled.

"A lucky hunch. Why don't you two old trackers just admit it and stop trying to pull the wool over my eyes?" Connor reined back to his place in the column, riding with his staff.

"If that don't beat all," Bridger hissed.

"Careful, Gabe."

"Yeah—if that don't beat all," Jonah echoed. "Goddamned stupid paper-collar soldiers."

Bridger's expression slowly changed as he gazed at the Confederate. "Yeah—couldn't say it better myself, Jonah."

Connor's trail-weary, battle-ragged command did not reach its wagon camp until about two A.M.

Every man had been in the saddle riding and fighting for the past thirty hours.

Two days later, Connor ordered a pony given to each of the Arapaho prisoners and set his captives free with gifts of hardtack and a little tobacco. Along with Bridger's sign-language instructions that should the Arapaho chiefs now be interested in making peace with the white man, they should come to Fort Laramie in the Moon of Leaves Falling for a big parley with the soldier chiefs.

For the next week, the general's massive column inched down the Tongue, hoping each day to make the scheduled rendezvous with his other two wings. Then on the morning of 1 September, as the troops were preparing to break camp, the advance guard heard the distant boom of a howitzer. Because of the confusing and broken texture of the land, no two men could agree on the origin of the sound.

Yet the boom of that distant cannon was enough to remind the general that today was the date he himself had chosen for the planned rendezvous with both the Missouri cavalry under Cole and the Kansas cavalry riding under Walker. The general ordered Major North and a detail of twenty Pawnee to ride out with an escort from Captain Marshall's E Company, scouting to the northeast for the missing columns.

By the sixth of September, growing concerned about the fate of both Cole and Walker, Connor received the discouraging news from North and his Pawnee scouts. No sign of the missing troops.

Disgusted, Connor finally gave the order to turn about and begin a march back up the Tongue to find a place with sufficient graze for his sizable herd. On the morning of the eighth, the general again ordered North's Pawnee out toward the Powder River, while Captain J. L. Humfreville would take his K Company to scout toward the Rosebud under Shad Sweete.

Four hours out, a light rain began to fall. Two hours after that the wind shifted, shouldering out of the north and bringing with it a taste of winter. Within another hour, a wet snow was plastering man and mount alike with a thick coating of ice. They pushed on into the mouth of that storm quickly becoming an early plains blizzard and reached the Rosebud late on the afternoon of the ninth.

After four days of struggling through the blinding, swirling snow, Shad led Captain Humfreville's men back to Connor's camp on the eleventh. He reported to a dejected general they had found no sign of the other two wings of the Powder River Expedition.

Yet not more than a handful of hours later North's Pawnee scouts rode in with news not in the least welcomed by any of Connor's command. The trackers had run across a large recent encampment of white men. The ground was littered with hundreds of dead horses, some of which had been shot. Most, however, had evidently frozen to death on their picket lines, their carcasses lying as orderly as they were.

North gravely informed Connor, "General, each of those dead horses looked like it had been damned near starved to death before that blizzard came in to finish them off. Animals run hard and not given time to graze or forage. When that norther hit—wasn't a owl hoot of a chance any one of those mounts had enough fat on its ribs to keep from freezing."

12

"SOME OF THOSE men offered me five dollars for a single tack," Jonah Hook said in wonder to Shad Sweete. "Even up at Rock Island where most of us was rotting away—never saw a man in that bad a shape."

"More'n just hunger, Jonah. That bunch of raggedy beggars was lucky to get out of Injun country with their hair."

"All had to walk out—some of 'em in boots falling apart."

"Never knew a boot anywhere as good as a Cheyenne moccasin, son."

For days before the Pawnee scouts had finally discovered the location of the desperate columns, the Walker and Cole battalions had been under a constant state of siege, able to move very little on foot, able to do nothing more than hold back the thousands of Sioux and Cheyenne warriors by judicious use of their mountain howitzers.

"Injuns hate those big wagon-guns," Shad had explained. "They call them the guns that shoot twice: once when they are fired and a second time when the shell explodes."

Once he had the demoralized, ragged remnants of the two lost wings rejoined with his own command, General Patrick Connor had turned his force south and returned to Fort Connor on the Powder River to recuperate the men, arriving the last week of September. But the second day of that much-needed recuperation brought an early end to the Powder River Expedition.

"Connor's madder'n a wet hornet." Bridger settled in the riverbank shade where Sweete and Hook had been watching the lazy ripples of the murky river.

"Why's that redheaded Irishman mad now?"

"Got dispatches up from Laramie, Shad." Bridger sighed. "You remember hearing that wolf-howl days back."

Hook watched the two old mountain men exchange a mysterious, knowing look.

"Howl like that always means some bad medicine coming, Gabe. Sure didn't think it'd hit this soon."

"What's this you two are saying about a wolf-howl means bad medicine?" Jonah asked.

Sweete looked at Bridger. "We aren't exactly talking about a real wolf-howl, Jonah."

"Go 'head and tell the lad," Bridger prodded.

"It's downright ghosty, Jonah. A cry of a wolf like what me and Gabe heard few nights back—means only one thing. Spirits. Bad medicine. And a man in his right mind best be getting clear of these parts. Something fearsome always happens after a man hears that ghosty howl. Always has. Always will."

"Whoa, Shad. You saying that wolf call you two heard some time back meant to tell you those soldiers were starving?"

Sweete shook his head. "I can't say. Just that as long as we been out here in these mountains and plains, both Gabe and me learned to trust to what the critters tell us. Animal spirits can smell a lot more'n what any of us can."

"That wolf smelled something bad coming?"

"Like death on the wind," Sweete replied matter-of-factly. He turned back to Bridger to ask, "What's doing with Connor?"

The old trapper sighed. "The stiff-necks back in Washington City putting an end to all Injun fighting for a while."

They both sat upright, but Sweete spoke first. "The devil, you say? What's the army supposed to do—sit on its thumbs? Dumb idjits, expecting they can talk peace to these war-loving, free-roaming bucks."

"None of them back east understands the one simple rule—that the only thing a warrior understands is blood and brute force." Bridger shrugged. "Connor says that bunch of politicians back east is cutting the army down to size now that the war back east is done with."

"'Bout time, it is too," grumbled Hook. "Cut it down far enough for this boy to go on back home to his family and farm."

"Shame of it is, Connor's been relieved of command and this expedition is done," Bridger confided. "General's heading back to Utah."

"Utah?" Hook asked. "Ain't that where all the Mormons went to settle?"

Sweete nodded. "Some of these boys marching with Connor been serving out to Camp Douglas in Utah. Hell, the general himself served as military commander out there till the army called him up for this expedition."

That enviable western post, Camp Douglas, stood on a bluff above the City of the Saints in the Valley of the Great Salt Lake. A paradise duty is what the soldiers called the place, for well-groomed plots of grass and flower beds surrounded the huge parade of packed, stream-washed gravel taken from the mountain stream diverted for irrigating the post's own fields. Connor himself had seen the post raised as his first duty upon arriving in the land of Brigham Young back in October 1862.

While the general publicly told Young and his elders that the post was being built to protect the Overland Stage route and the Pacific Telegraph line from Indian depredations, the Mormon suspicion was that the army had been sent into the heart of their State of Deseret to keep an eye on them. Because most Mormons rankled at the recent bevy of laws Congress had been passing to outlaw polygamy in the states and its territories, Utah declared itself neutral once hostilities broke out between North and South in 1861.

"As far as Patrick E. Connor was concerned, in the Civil War, if you weren't with him, you were against him," Bridger went on. "The general took a special interest in keeping a close watch on the Mormons. And the dealings of that Mormon chief, the one called Brigham Young."

"Shad's told me about how he sent his private army out to get you of a time, Gabe."

Bridger grinned, but with a coldness that made a drop of sweat slip down Hook's spine.

"That's right. One of these days, Jim Bridger would like to have him a chance to look that puffed-up prairie cock eye to eye and see just what he's made of without standing behind his hired killers."

"You never will, Gabe," said Shad. "Young's the kind who'll never be a big enough man to stand on his own."

Both he and Sweete chuckled when they went on to tell Hook how Connor marched into the land of the Mormons and never once worried about ruffling Mormon feathers. He was the chief political and military officer representing his government in the territory, and as such he took his job serious.

"From the first day his men started building that post up on the bluff,

Connor ordered a cannon pointed down the hill at Brigham's pride and joy—his tabernacle."

From the walls of Camp Douglas, soldiers could look down not only on the lake itself, but the neatly platted streets and outlying farms of the Mormons where crops flourished and livestock abounded in the narrow valley. In excess of twenty thousand Latter-day Saints called it home, with more arriving every year.

"When the general started to replace his wooden buildings with stone from nearby quarries, just like the stone the Mormons had used for their own tabernacle, Brigham howled!" Sweete continued. "He came stomping up to the camp to protest to Connor that his fort was looking a mite too permanent for his liking, that the soldiers were harassing honest, God-fearing citizens, and that the army's horses and mules were fouling the city's water supply."

"After the way he's now been treated by the politicians and peace-loving turncoats back east, I'll bet Connor will damn well welcome getting back to the land of the Saints," Bridger said.

"Sounds like you got a chip on your shoulder for them Mormons," Hook said. "Not that I blame you, I s'pose."

"Me? I ain't got a problem with a Mormon—if he keeps to himself and doesn't stomp on what's mine. It's when a thieving, yellow-backed bastard like Young sends out a hundred of his Angels to burn my fort and steal my stock, murdering my hired help in the bargain—yeah, that's when you might say I get a mighty big chip on my shoulder, young'un."

"It ain't the Mormons, Jonah," Sweete went on to explain. "It's the goddamned leaders they follow, eyes closed, swallowing all that cock and bull about every threat made to their beloved Zion."

"What's Zion?"

"What the Mormons call Utah," Sweete answered.

Bridger scowled. "Zion is what the Mormons call the place that God give 'em special. 'Cause they're special people. Like Brigham tells it—the rest of us is supposed to stay out of Mormon country."

Boothog's cheek burned with the fires of hell where Jubilee Usher had slapped his huge flat hand across it.

"Let that be a warning to you, Major Wiser." Usher's voice rocked the limestone cave in the forest where they had taken refuge from a pursuing detachment of soldiers for the past week. The rain fell noisily outside the musty cave. "I never want to catch you talking to the woman again."

Boothog glanced quickly at the fair-haired woman, her own lips swollen, bruised, and bloody—knowing Jubilee had battered her too. Behind the purple bruises and swollen lids, her eyes were like some frightened animal's— almost willing to take a chance in trusting the handsome Boothog, to trust anyone and anything rather than continue with the daily abuse she endured from Jubilee.

"If you give me the girl, Colonel," Wiser declared, using the honorary title Brigham Young had awarded Usher among Young's Danites.

Usher stared incredulous at his second in command. "You are a crude animal, Major. Here for so long I had considered you above the level of these others. It is they I must watch to be sure the girl remains a virgin until the time we return to the City of the Saints."

His breath still shallow, the burn at his cheek slowly fading. "You have what you want, Jubilee—gimme the girl. Why's she so special to make it back there a virgin?"

Usher took one sudden step forward, instantly shutting Wiser up. "She'll fetch a much handsomer price from a wealthy man looking for a new, young wife." The big man turned toward the woman and began stroking her long, disheveled hair. She tried to push his hand away at first, but he caught her wrists and held them in one big paw while he went back to stroking her golden curls.

"Besides, Major Wiser. There are plenty of opportunities for you to find yourself a suitable traveling partner. The girl is just that—a girl—and I won't stand for you copulating with her like some evil, bestial tool of the devil."

He wanted to scream out that Usher himself was a hypocrite—but Wiser didn't have the nerve. He could cower any of the rest of their sizable band of freebooters, either with his fists or with his quickness at the handgun he kept resting just forward of his left hip. But try Jubilee Usher? Wiser was a far smarter man than that.

Boothog swallowed his words, mumbling as the damp, fetid smell of this place invaded his nostrils once more.

"What was that you said?" Usher demanded, turning from the woman.

"It just ain't fair, Colonel."

Usher went back to stroking the woman's hair, caressing the side of her face with a single finger. "No one ever said earthly life was fair, Major. It's just up to men like you and me to make things a little more even for ourselves, and our kind, don't you see?"

"I want—"

"Find yourself a woman, Mr. Wiser!" Usher snapped, whirling on his subordinate. At his sharp words the woman jerked back, the harsh sound echoing from the low, dripping roof of the dank cave.

"I'll do that, Jubilee."

"And you'll do well to stay away from both the woman and the girl, I mind you."

"As you order, Colonel."

"This one," Jubilee sighed, cupping the woman's chin in the palm of a huge hand and gripping it hard, "she is a pretty, pretty thing. A fitting gift from God, handed exclusively to one of his most trusted servants, can't you see? It was His will and His will alone that guided us to that farm, Major. She was waiting for me there."

Wiser wanted to tell Usher that he was crazy—but he didn't have the nerve. While Boothog realized he would be nothing more than a common thief and murderer with a devilishly handsome face and a charm that had lifted more petticoats and unbuttoned more bodices in the last three years than most men did in a lifetime—Jubilee Usher was something else altogether.

A drop of cold cave seepage splattered on his forehead.

The big man, the "Colonel," really believed in what he called his divine mission, believed in his continual revelations from God, believed he alone had been chosen to wage war on any and all Gentiles in the West whom he saw as a threat to his prophet, Brigham Young.

And it was Jubilee Usher's unshakable insanity that made him the most dangerous animal Boothog Wiser had ever known.

In the last days of summer and the first days of fall, the Shahiyena told of fighting two groups of white men who had attempted to force their way into the Black Hills country and the hunting ground north and west of the sacred Bear Butte. One group corralled its wagons, then offered one of those wagons filled with coffee and sugar and flour to the warriors if the white men were allowed to pass. The Shahiyena had allowed the white men to go on their way, knowing they were heading into Lakota land, where Red Cloud and Young Man Afraid would make things hard on them.

The Bad Face band of Oglalla did make it hard on those stupid white men. And on the two groups of soldiers groping their way around on the Rosebud and the Powder, slowly starving themselves and their horses until the great snowstorm came howling out of the north and left the riverbank littered with the stinking carcasses as soon as it warmed days later, snow melting beneath the incredibly blue skies of Indian summer.

Crazy Horse had to admit he liked this time of year the best. A season of change. It was the last time he and the other young ones had to raid and ride and romp before the coming of winter that would put the high land to sleep for many moons. Not only would the mountains be shrouded in snow, but for weeks at a time, the valleys and bluffs, the ridges and coulees would be choked with it. Rivers and creeks, springs and streams would be frozen.

And he would find himself restless and agitated, prisoner in the winter lodges once more—his spirit yearning for the freedom of the high plains.

Here in the final days of the Moon of Black Calves, the Lakota scouts had returned with news that the great soldier encampment along the Powder had finally turned south and were heading back to the fort called Laramie.

"The time has come," Crazy Horse said, having waited for his turn to speak to the great council of warriors and advisers. "The soldiers are fleeing with what horses they have left and what wagons they can pull out of our hunting ground. I agree with Man Afraid—we no longer have to keep our warriors here to protect our villages from them. These white men are going home. Let our young men go raiding on the Holy Road one last time before Winter Man seizes the land and chokes us with cold for many moons!"

"My young friend makes sense," agreed Young Man Afraid. "Our women already have many hides to tan, and the meat is dried for the winter moons. No more do we need to hunt. Our young men itch for one last ride. I say let it be a big one!"

Slowly the wild calls for war and raiding and white blood faded away. And eventually all faces turned toward Red Cloud's. A proven chief, his face only beginning to seam with the lines of age and wisdom, this undisputed leader of the Bad Face band of Oglalla chose his words well.

"We will wait until the soldiers are three days' ride south of Pumpkin Buttes."

Crazy Horse could feel the swelling of excitement growing in the huge council lodge as Red Cloud gave his pronouncement.

"Then our warriors can sweep around the tail end of the soldier column—assured they will not turn and attack our camps as they attacked the Bear's Arapaho village."

"They will not," Crazy Horse declared, watching many of the dark eyes turn his way. "The soldiers are beaten—once and for all. The white man's army will not dare attack our mighty villages as they destroyed the Arapaho camp. The Bear was not wise, my friends. It is a very careless thing for a man to embrace peace when all around him the countryside is filled with those who hunger for war!"

13

"I'LL MISS YOU, Shad," Hook said in a husky tone that scraped past the hot knot in his throat.

"Here," Sweete said gruffly, holding out his hand. "Promised I'd give you a going-away present."

Hook glanced at the lines of troops shuffling into formation, teamsters easing themselves down onto plank seats and the columns of cavalry escort going to saddle.

"What is it?" he asked, studying the small rawhide-wrapped ring in his palm. It had been divided into quadrants, at its center was encircled a small, smooth pebble. The rawhide strands were wrapped with flattened porcupine quills of greasy yellow, robin's-egg blue, and a light moss green.

"Toote's people call it a medicine wheel. This is one she made for me some time back. A pebble spoke to me beside a stream near the place where I first laid eyes on the woman. Injuns believe rocks and such things are creatures too, and talk to people."

"You believe that?"

"I'm here to tell you that's the certain of it."

"This is something she made special for you—I can't take it."

"That's why I'm giving it to you. Among these Indian people, everything sacred is a circle. Life itself is a great circle: from borning to dying. I'm asking you to keep this, 'cause one day you'll return."

"I ain't never coming back, Shad."

"You keep telling me that, Jonah. But there's a great circle of all things out there—and you don't know what will ever bring you back. All I know is, this pebble talked to me again last night. Ain't talked to me since I first picked it up and heard it say I ought to take some ponies to a particular Cheyenne warrior so I could ask his daughter to be my wife."

"It told you to marry Toote?"

"And this morning, after all those years, it spoke to me again. Telling me it was time for it to go with you on your journey home."

Jonah held out the medicine wheel in his palm, self-consciously, and more than a little concerned about all the mysticism.

He swallowed, anxious to be on the road to Fort Leavenworth where his unit would be mustered out, from there on his own to southern Missouri. But not anxious enough to rip himself from the warm security this big man had offered during Jonah's brief sojourn on the high plains. This, he felt, was something to be done carefully. He stared down at the medicine wheel.

"You can wear it round your neck—or keep it in your plunder. Its power will be with you no matter what, son," Sweete explained. With the scuffing of boots on wood, his eyes flicked over to watch the officers emerge from Colonel H. E. Maynadier's office, turn, and salute in leave-taking.

Jonah felt suddenly like hugging the big man, but such a thing just wasn't his way. Things were too much of a rush for him at the moment. Instead of embracing the old trapper, he held out his hand, reaching for Sweete's, hoping he would not become moist-eyed as he said his farewell.

"I'll remember you, Shadrach Sweete," he said as he dropped the big man's hand and started off toward his company, who were hollering for him to join their ranks. "You come to Missouri soon and look me up—you know where."

He smiled at the old trapper, waving as the dusty column was ordered to face about and into a march, pushing off the parade and past Fort Laramie's stone guardhouse, heading down the North Platte for the east and home.

"I'll find you, Jonah Hook. By glory, I'll find you."

Hook was damned well relieved that the sun had made a glorious rising this crisp fall morning. Its brightness meant he and the rest had to squint as they marched into that brilliant sunflower yellow orb. Because now no one would see the moistness come to his eyes as he shuffled along in cracked ankle-boots he hoped would last him long enough to make it home to Gritta and the children.

Crying was all right. But it sure as hell wasn't any other man's business.

Jonah glanced around him, on both sides of the column of fours, cavalry escort up ahead, wagons loaded with provision for the homeward-bound march at the tail end of the line.

As much as he had tried to deny it the last few weeks, there was something about this place that he was going to miss—although he had admitted it to no man.

At first Hook figured such thoughts rumbled around inside him merely because this was such new country to his eyes and ears and tastebuds. And for the longest time he had figured that newness would wear off. But with the rounding of every new green hill or ocher ridge or yellow-tinged bluff, the scenery never went stale to the eyes. With each new mouthful of buffalo or elk, mule deer or antelope, the tumbling, endless plains of the West became something to be savored with all his senses. With every new scent and sound, or shape to the clouds in the incredibly immense sky that always hung just beyond arm's length overhead, Jonah had slowly come to accept that his affection for this place was not merely because of its newness only.

Yet lingering still was the doubt that he would ever return to this wild, untamed land where there was no law, and certainly no church for his Gritta and the young'uns. The ache for home and family was far too strong.

It lay heavy on his heart as he moved east across the plains—this doubt he carried with him that he would ever again lay eyes on Shad Sweete's face in this lifetime.

Yet that medicine wheel lay in the palm of his hand for the rest of that day's long march. And the next day's. And the next . . .

Boothog's father and uncle had both known Jubilee Usher's father, one of the original twelve apostles who came to believe in prophet Joseph Smith and his gold tablets dictating the formation of a new church, under a new people: the Latter-day Saints.

So it had been the natural, expected thing to do out in that western kingdom of Deseret to join Brigham Young's special, handpicked military arm. With his Avenging Angels, the Mormon Prophet smote those who threatened the sanctity of the State of Deseret. Citing ancient precedent, Young empowered his hundred handpicked Danites, these Avenging Angels, to right all wrongs done the Saints, or the Mormon state.

They were vigilantes, self-empowered men who saw things through their own self-righteousness. Justice in this broad, big western land skewed to their side of the pew.

Year after year, young Lemuel Wiser had come to know the tall, imposing figure of Jubilee Usher, who was rapidly rising in influence among the more militant and self-protective of the Saints. As Wiser grew to manhood, he found the immense tower of a man all the more a capable leader of men, able to inspire and motivate, cajole when needed, threaten when necessary—but always able to get his men to do exactly what he wanted, if not exactly what Brigham Young himself desired as well.

Boothog remembered now when Jubilee first began to lose his hair, early in life for a man. Before one of those first trips east with the Mormon handicrafts for sale in Missouri and other points east. For a time, Usher felt ridiculed for this early receding of hair, then eventually learned to admire his balding head himself. He took to growing what hair there was down past his shoulders—thick and black as sin. And only in recent years had he begun to wear a mustache that curled down into a neat Vandyke beard every bit as glossy black as the boots he had one of the men shine with lampblack and grease each night in camp.

Young Wiser had yearned to take his horse and carry his new rifle along with Usher's military escort that each spring accompanied a great wagon train of two hundred, even as many as three hundred Saints, rolling east with Mormon-made goods to sell and barter for what Brigham Young's faithful could not acquire in their own land of Zion. And with each year's trip east, the Church Train found more and more immigrants from the States and other countries anxiously waiting for this annual journey, so that the newcomers could join in the return trip back—an anointed gathering of Israel in Brigham's holy valley.

In 1857 Boothog had taken his first trip east since childhood. Already tensions had blossomed again among the people of Missouri, requiring Usher to exercise a firm hand on his Mormons, reminding them that these same proslavery Missourians had been the very Gentiles to turn their guns on Mormon brethren.

"We must have nothing but the most limited contact with these sinners," Boothog had explained to some of his friends, unaware that Usher had been near enough to overhear his admonition during that trip east in fifty-seven.

That night Jubilee Usher had called Wiser to his tent and proposed to take the young man under his wing. *cop. 2*

"You will make a capable officer, Mr. Wiser. More than that—" Usher stuffed a slice of game hen into his huge mouth. "You might even take over the reins of this operation from me one day."

"I could never . . . never think of ever being as good as you."

Usher had smiled. "That's good, Wiser. Affecting the modesty as you have done comes off as quite genuine. It is good that you play the role so effectively."

"But I—"

Usher waved his hand. "We have more important things to concern ourselves with than your sincerity. What matters most is your faith in Brigham and his prophecies from God Almighty. And how well you obey, without question, the orders of his military commanders. Don't you agree, Mr. Wiser?"

"Yes, sir."

So it was that every day Boothog had grown more convinced of the rightness in Usher's might. No matter the cruelty of the man—Usher carried not only the seal of the Prophet, Brigham Young, himself, but Usher claimed he had been chosen by the Prophet to lead a rebuilding of Zion's defenses.

Most Mormon men still smarted at the military occupation of Utah by Union troops under General Albert Sidney Johnston from fifty-eight to sixty-one, ending only when the war broke out and Johnston resigned his commission to fight on the side of his beloved Confederacy, and most of the Union troops were recalled east to fight the rebels down south. Never again, the Mormons vowed, would they allow anything like that immoral and illegal occupation.

Usher was all-consumed with rebuilding the might of Deseret's army when he led Wiser's military escort for the Church Train east in sixty-two. It was to have been Boothog's sixth round trip. But in south central Missouri, the great wagon procession was surprised and stopped by an imposing force of proslavers operating under a self-appointed general named Sterling Price. The Confederates moved among the disarmed Mormon men, looking each one over and selecting the best as conscripts in Price's guerrilla campaigns against the Union.

Price reminded the surrounded Mormons that his Missouri Confederates had not forgotten the problems caused by the Mormons in years past: "My men would love nothing more than to leave you all bleeding here on the road. But let's see if you *Saints* are men enough to fight the Yankees invading from the North."

With his new draftees and his ragtag army in tow, Price marched south from there, heading for a place called Pea Ridge, leaving behind the Church Train stripped of its mules, horses, firearms, and ammunition, along with supplies and every able-bodied young male.

It was with that army of Missouri proslavers that Boothog had learned to play poker. A game to this day that he loved to play with some of the men who rode with Usher's guerrilla band raiding across postwar Missouri. Jubilee called many of the recent converts to Mormonism his cannon fodder. Boothog liked many of the simple, ignorant, fiery Southerners for no other reason than they provided some temporary diversion while the small army waited for Jubilee to decide on moving.

They always did a lot of waiting.

The cold rains of late November were turning to sleet outside the series of limestone caves where Usher's advance scouts under Captain Eloy Hastings had found them a place out of the weather three days before. In the back of this main cavern was a long, dark drop at the end of which a man could hear the faint splash of any rock he threw off the ledge to amuse himself. Without a lantern to guide him to the edge, he might fall into what hell no man knew waited at the bottom of that deep, black cavern.

Picketing the horses in a nearby grove and stowing their supplies in another cave, Usher's men had settled in for what they knew would be days of restless inactivity, waiting out the passing of the first winter storm rumbling across southern Missouri.

It wasn't their first winter in this country.

And they weren't new at waiting either.

"Who's next?" asked one of the Danites as he emerged from a side cavern, buttoning the fly to his britches, yanking on his belt.

A man quickly stood, jostling the crate they were using as a card table these days of waiting. "Me. I want a poke."

Just after leading Jubilee Usher's band to this series of caves, Hastings's scouts had been ordered back out into what was then a drizzling rain to ride farther south and see what they could rustle up in the way of women on the nearby farms.

"The men will need a little something besides cards to keep them happy," Usher had reminded Wiser and Captain Hastings.

"Nigger or white, makes no difference to my loins right now," Boothog had replied, that devilish grin crossing his handsome face.

So it was the scouts had found a black slave girl no more than sixteen and hurrying toward a Creek Indian farm located close by when the horsemen had surrounded her. From the moment she had been dropped from the horse at the entrance to the cave three days ago, the unkempt sprigs of her black hair dripping with diamonds of sleeting rain, the girl had had little rest.

Boothog had ordered her carried to an adjoining cave, where under lamplight a few of the soldiers stripped her, staked her out, and proceeded to rotate themselves on her body—Wiser claiming first go at their skinny captive. At first she had screamed and thrashed about, until gagged. No man among Boothog's army minded the nigger girl thrashing in the least. It only added to a man's fun, and enjoyment.

Wiser looked up from his cards and glanced over his shoulder as the man disappeared into the chamber where the captive lay.

As his eyes came back to the crate table, Boothog thought he caught a flicker of movement from the hands of another player.

He smiled grimly. "Lay your cards down, Billy."

The man's eyes grew wide as the rest of the players eased back from the oblong rifle crate.

"I didn't do nothing wrong, Boothog. Major Wiser, sir."

"Put the goddamned cards down."

"Yessir." He laid them down in a neat stack.

"Count them for us, Billy Baker," Wiser demanded as he slowly pulled the pistol from his waistband.

The rest of the card players arose suddenly and backed away as the solitary man left at the crate chewed on the end of a finger. With his thumb, Boothog drew back the pistol's hammer.

"I said—count your cards."

"Just playing a little poker with you, Major. I fold. See? I fold. Hand's all done."

Baker started to shove his cards under some others when Boothog slammed his hand down onto the man's wrist. With the pistol shoved under the soft underside of Baker's chin, Wiser slowly spread the cards.

"One . . . two . . . three . . . four—and five."

"See, Major? Just like I—"

"What's this, Billy? Why, it's a sixth pasteboard," Wiser declared sinisterly as he slowly pulled free the extra card.

Things became a blur in that next heartbeat as Baker attempted to bat the pistol barrel aside and the hammer fell, sending a bullet into the card player's mouth, crashing on through the brain, and splintering out the top of his head with a wet, slimy explosion of blood and gore.

The body fell backward from the crate of hardtack, trembling in death throes.

Boothog rose after glancing at the rest, their eyes wide and hollow with shock. He walked over, held the muzzle of his pistol inches from the victim's heart and pulled the trigger a second time. Baker's shirt grew damp and shiny. Wiser knelt and picked through the dead man's pockets, pulling out what little money there was.

"Bring me his bedroll," Wiser commanded. "I get first call on the bastard's things."

"Get the body out of here," Usher's voice boomed from the roof of the cavern. "It's beginning to smell a bit in here already."

Wiser turned, smiling. "It is, isn't it, Colonel?"

"Men die a violent death like that—they're apt to fill their britches with shit," Jubilee replied. "Dispose of the body now, Major."

Wiser turned to the other players. "You heard the colonel. Take Baker's body back to the far end of the cave and throw him down."

One of the players who had hold of Baker's leg snarled at the others. "I got call on his boots, I do."

"Hurry up!" Wiser snapped. "Throw him down in that cave and get on back here. I got money to win. And then I want to dip my stinger in that nigger gal's honey pot again before I take me a nap."

Book II

The
Search

14

H E HAD BEEN nearly three months getting here from Fort Laramie. Cold and wet and scared most of the way. Knowing that in the next few minutes when he finally stood on the hillside overlooking the homestead, he would at last feel a lot different.

God, how he wanted to hold Gritta. Just hold her. And hug his children. Until they cried for him to stop.

Then sit in front of the fireplace he had built with his own hands from rock quarried at the nearby creekbank. Drink the sweet milk they always kept cooling down in the limestone springhouse in the woods behind the cabin. He hadn't had a drink of cow's milk in . . .

Jonah couldn't remember now. That's how long it had been.

Drop after drop of sleet sliding off the stringy strands of oily hair at the back of his neck made Hook all the colder as he huffed to the crest of the hill where the north wind greeted him full in the face.

He drew a long breath of it, not minding its cold. For in the near valley he would finally see his home. Snowflakes lanced straight down from the icy clouds, then danced momentarily on the cruel gusts of wind cutting through the bare trees. He startled a flock of black-winged crows from their roost. They went cawing over him with a noisy clatter of wings and protest. And then it was quiet once more, except for the moaning sigh of the wind tormenting the skeletal branches brushing the underside of a low-belly sky.

He stood on one foot a moment, shaking the other. The side seam on each boot had split weeks back, just before reaching Fort Leavenworth, where he and the rest had to wait, and wait some more while the army got around to mustering them out. Because the Confederates were being discharged, the Yankees who were turning their army into Indian fighters weren't about to issue any new shoes or boots to those soon-to-be civilians who needed them.

"G'won home barefoot, for all I care," snapped a quartermaster's sergeant at Leavenworth. "I'm saving these boots for Injun fighters. Not Yankee killers."

What Jonah had left of stockings were now drenched and incapable of keeping his feet warm where the rain and mud and snow crept in through the split seam. It did not matter now. Just another mile or so was all they had to last, these boots, his feet, and he. His good broughams awaited him down there under their bed.

That made him worry of a sudden just how he would be with Gritta tonight when the lampwicks were rolled low and the children's rhythmic breathing was all the two of them could hear from the loft overhead. That, and the reassuring crackle of a hardwood fire from his stone fireplace. How would she respond to his great appetite for her? After these years without a woman, and finally able to push that need aside of late . . . only to stand here now on the hillside above their farm and know he wanted that one woman like he had never wanted her before.

He'd be twenty-nine this spring, yet still felt his cheeks go hot now at how randy he felt. Like a stud colt for the first time snuffling the moist heat of a mare in the breeding corral. His eyes sought to penetrate the low clouds and wispy fog sticky among the bony hardwoods in the valley below.

Perhaps some of that's smoke from the stone chimney—

But the more he squinted through the swirl of a few darting snowflakes, Jonah grew more certain that none of it was smoke rising from the chimney he had laid stone by stone.

"Maybe they gone over to Uncle Moser's place," he said to assure himself as he emerged from the trees.

Almost by feel beneath last autumn's great dropping of leaf and the winter's wet snow still clinging to the ground in icy slicks, his feet located the game trail that would take him down to the spring behind the cabin, right where he had built the limestone root cellar—there by the clear, cold spring where the deer and the other critters came to drink of a morning. A long-used game trail, worn by his feet across the many years he and Gritta had built their life together here in Missouri, at the far end of the same valley where his mother's brother, Amos Moser, had homesteaded years before Jonah ever stood tall enough to climb atop a plow mule by himself.

Of a sudden he stopped. The cabin was clearly in view for the first time. Unsure if he should believe his eyes. A section of corral posts busted down and no animals to be found.

Two more steps and he stopped again, now able to see the yard between cabin and barn where one of its big doors lay in the icy mud like a sawyer in the river, the other door mournfully creaking with a ghostly whisper on its cracked leather hinges, ready to give up and join its brother on the ground.

Beyond, the fields were overgrown. Uncared for . . . for months now.

She's gone to live with the Mosers, he told himself. I been so long getting back—what with her having to care for the children alone, the work and all. Maybe, goddammit, she give up on me ever coming back and went back to her family in Virginia.

The fear struck him more cold than any wind-driven sleet could at that moment.

He was cursing his luck, the Union, and the frontier army that had galvanized him out of Rock Island Prison and sent him off to the plains to fight Injuns—

But then his feet stopped him again, staring at the two windows he had been able to afford putting into the front of the cabin. What with the high price of glazing, he and Gritta bought only two when they raised the cabin from the valley floor. Both were broken, on either side of the dark, gaping rectangle where the door had once held out the cold Missouri winter.

From both holes fluttered the curtains Gritta had made years ago, looking now like the petticoats kicked up and swirled around pairs of plump knees on those chippies who worked the soldiers for all they were worth, night after night in those watering holes and brothels down in Dobe Town just outside Fort Kearney in Nebraska Territory.

That's when he saw the carcass in the yard, not yet gone completely to bone. Decomposed by time and merely tormented by robber jays and crows content to sup on carrion. Not one of his stock—a small animal. Standing over it, he recognized the carcass as the dog who had followed him and Gritta from Virginia, tongue lolling as it loped alongside their cart, before darting into the dark forest, scenting a rabbit.

Kneeling slowly, he touched Seth's skull, gently placing a fingertip into the big bullet hole.

Who'd want to kill an old, half-blind dog and leave him lying in the middle of the yard anyway?

But the tiny shred of gray denim still clinging between the skull's canines made Jonah wince in imagined pain.

Seth had him a good hold of somebody when he was shot.

Jonah stood, sensing the cold now fully seeping into his marrow like no loneliness and despair ever had. Even sitting out day after day in Rock Island, waiting . . . waiting.

No one was going to tell him to move. No one ordering him now. He was a free man again, at last. So he had to order his own feet ahead of each other, one at a time—inching toward the barn. He had to know.

And then Jonah became suddenly conscious that he was not breathing.

The barn was empty. Even the pegs where he hung tack and bridle and hackamores. Just the moldy hay in the stalls gone too long without mucking. The wild stench of it—gone to rot now.

Jonah pushed himself hard toward the cabin, certain now he would not be surprised. Certain he wouldn't find a body. They had gone. But that still did not explain the dog. And the denim of someone's britches Seth had a death hold on when he was killed.

Hook stood at the door, listening to the rustle of the field mice as they suddenly recognized some sound other than their own and scurried off the table and out of the dry sink, off her sideboard Gritta had carried in the back of their little cart from the Shenandoah Valley. The cold had made him numb, and with a shudder he remembered now too what some of the Union guards at Rock Island had told him about how that Yankee general Phil Sheridan had made a wasteland of the Shenandoah in the final summer of the war.

About like this, he sobbed quietly.

Nothing, nobody to come home to after all that praying and counting and hoping that had kept him alive and putting one foot in front of each other, marching from Illinois to Kansas and on to the Dakota Territory where he had to fight Injuns just to keep his hair and stay alive so that he could get back home to Gritta and the children but no one was left anymore and he had counted so much on them being here he didn't know what to do next but sit here in the broke-down chair where he collapsed beside the wobbly table, lay his head down on his forearm and cry.

The nature of the light slipping through the broken windows and door frame had changed subtly over the afternoon that he wept and dozed off into some unconscious state then awoke to sob some more, all without ever raising his head from his arm laid on the dusty tablecloth Gritta used to shake free of crumbs out the front door after every meal.

The same arm grazed by a Cheyenne bullet so long ago was numb now. His feet had gone so cold he could no longer recognize them as his own inside the soaked stockings and cracked, dry-split boots. He shivered, realizing the need for fire. If he was going to live, he'd have to stay warm tonight.

And just get through till tomorrow.

The wood box beside the stove was still filled. He pushed the trivet aside and grabbed a chunk of wood, from which he shaved some kindling. On the top of the stone mantle, he found the small wooden box that contained the fire-steel and char and flint and in minutes had a fire beginning to crackle as soon as the chimney heated enough to draw.

For a few distinct moments from the rest of the whole day, the sun dipped below the leaden clouds and shot its rays obliquely through the gaping windows and door hole.

The place had been looted, everything in shambles. All of it—too damned much for a simple man to absorb all at once.

The whispering feet of mice came alive in the rafters overhead and at the far walls. Perhaps not mice at all, but more so the whispering voices of someone or something that could tell him what went on here and where they had gone.

For the longest time Jonah had clung to the hope that Gritta had taken the children and left. But with Seth in the yard and some things took and more things left here in the cabin, belongings Gritta would never leave behind, Hook grew certain that something—or someone—had claimed his family.

A great weariness overtook him. With darkness coming on quickly as the foxes who came out to hunt the low places by the creeks at dusk, Hook decided he would stay the night here, although there was no food and nothing but a gaping despair threatening to swallow him. No matter, he wasn't hungry. And in the morning when the gray light nudged him awake from their dusty, abandoned wedding bed, Jonah would push on up to Uncle Moser's place. There to find some answers.

He could sleep here by the fire, he finally decided, going to the table and tipping it over, dishes and pots clattering to the plank floor. He dragged the table over by the fireplace for a windbreak. Jonah then brought the dusty blankets and the old tick prairie mattress into his windbreak and settled down to watch the flames dance in the stone fireplace.

And feed on bitter loneliness.
There was nothing else for him to eat.

Artus Moser was heading north along the rim of that same valley, while the sun sank from that same sodden, gray sky.

He was hoping to find some answers, some help, maybe a warm meal up at a neighbor's place. Skirting past the farm where Jonah's wife and children had evidently waited for his cousin's return. Then given up and most like gone on back to Virginia, where the Mosers had put down some tough taproots. Gritta came from such stock.

But it was getting too late, Artus told himself, too late for him or anyone else to expect Jonah to be coming home from the war. Couldn't blame Gritta for taking the children east. Any man coming home from the war or the Yankee prisons was already back among family by now. The rest was already laid in the ground, stacked three and four deep, most likely too. The ones blessed enough to have themselves a grave on so many of those unnamed battlefields.

Three days ago Artus had walked over here to Jonah's place for the first time since he had himself come back home, to tell Gritta that his daddy had gone. But instead of Jonah's family, he had found the place empty, and eerily silent. Artus had turned about and run most of the way home. Afraid of the ghosts that he was sure haunted that place now.

For two days now, he had been sitting inside the house where he had been born and raised, where he hoped one day to raise his own children. Waiting for what, he did not know. Only that this afternoon he had finally decided to start walking. To leave this tainted soil and start walking out of the valley. Find someone north of here who would have warm food for his belly and an ear to listen to his laments.

It had taken him months of walking to get home from the war to southern Missouri. Hiding out, stealing food where he could, getting arrested many a time for vagrancy. Even Southern folk didn't take all that kindly to a lonely Rebel making his way back to his kin. Everybody all had their own problems.

Day after day on that long, barefoot walk Artus had hoped that each night he would find someone kind enough to offer him a half a loaf of old bread, perhaps a potato or an apple set by last fall.

And when he got home to his daddy's place back there in the southern end of the valley after that long walk away from the war, Artus found a cross leaning like a stoop-shouldered old woman over a grave gone to weed out to the side of the house, finding his daddy terrible sick and taken to his bed inside the cold cabin. No telling how long the man had been in the musty bed reeking of age and sickness, his flesh going cold and his whole skinny body racked by a fluid-filled cough that reminded Artus of so many who had died of typhus or diphtheria or pneumonia during the war trying to drive the Yankees back out of the South.

His daddy had been such a strong, vital, filled-out, and fleshy man of a time.

Moser almost didn't recognize his father, eyes half-lidded, black, and sunken, like the skin of his cheeks sinking away below the high cheekbones, sallow, waxlike skin like a rumpled tablecloth that rattled with each noisy breath the old man took.

The thirty-year old Artus tried to feed his daddy some broth he'd made, more hot water than anything. But the old man was plumb gone, and everything Artus poured into the slack mouth just seeped back out from the old man's lips, onto the pillow and sheets and that patchwork comforter.

Lord, how cold his daddy's skin was.

For seventeen days, Artus stayed there beside his daddy's bed, day and night. Then rose at last to dig a grave beside his mama's and finally laid the old man to rest. A new cross standing beside hers.

All those years of war, with every step along every mile of icy or dusty or muddy or summer-blistered road he had marched, across every field of waist-high grass he had charged, muzzle loader out and bayonet gleaming in the sun, Artus Moser had promised himself he was fighting for his daddy and mama and the rights of folks back home in Missouri and for that little farm that would one day be his when at last the war ended and he could return home to help his family on that place that was his and he was its.

Artus had dropped the spade at the foot of the fresh earth he had packed over the body. Dusted his hands, and turned away. Not sure if he wanted this place now. Of a time he might decide different. But there were two ghosts here already, and he didn't want his soul to be a third, captive, made prisoner and left on this ground, a'mouldering.

So deep in his need for human contact was he that when Artus saw the firelight below through the broken windows, he bumped into a tree in dumbfounded surprise, splitting his forehead. The warmth surprised him as well, as he dabbed his fingers in the swelling, moist flesh.

No matter the pain, he had to find out who was in the Hook cabin, firelight flickering through the two yawning, paneless windows. Inching up from the side of the barn like he'd learned to hunt fox and coon and squirrel and hare, Artus saw that over the door, somebody had hung a blanket or some such. Blocking the light and the wind and hiding who was inside.

Slowly, his breath clutched in his throat, Artus sidled toward the cabin, wishing he still had that old gun he had cradled and loaded and carried and dragged through years of fighting and starving and sleeping and crying and feeling homesick beyond relief. If it was any of the freebooters he'd heard tell of raiding up and down the countryside, their kind would have horses stalled in the barn or picketed outside by the cabin.

No horses here.

"You there! Turn around—slow!"

Artus felt his heart leap to his throat. His hands shot into the air. Always had been a good one taking orders.

Hoping whoever it was would see his arms up, if not the telltale color of his tattered butternut gray uniform.

The figure moved out of the darkness, inching toward the dim light spilling out one of the windows. Then the man stopped, a black silhouette framed by the firelit window. Holding a rifle.

Moser swallowed hard. "Didn't mean no harm—"

"Artus?"

That confused him of a moment. The stranger knew his name. Then the man inched from the window, coming his way from the corner of the cabin, into the yard. Drawing closer.

"Yeah? Artus Moser."

"It's me, by damned, Artus!" shrieked the stranger as he dropped the rifle in the icy mud and dashed forward, arms outstretched.

"Good God in heaven above—it's cousin Jonah!"

15

T HE TWO OF them spent that night talking, remembering. The empty hulk of the Hook cabin was for a time filled with glorious warmth between the two. With dawn come creeping gray out of the east, they lay down on that old tick, back to back to share their warmth, and slept through much of the next day.

In the golden dusk that night Jonah and Artus hunted together, bringing back to the cabin a small doe they fed on, jerking the rest of the meat before the fire.

As the sun rose the following morning, Hook and Moser set off on foot, intending to walk in one direction, then another, until they found a neighbor who could give them both some answers.

Or would.

At the Hosking place, north out of the valley on the way to Cassville, the pair was met by three rifles as they approached the house.

"It's Jonah Hook, Mr. Hosking!" he called out across the yard splashed with January sunshine. Steam rose from the ice-slicked ruts running from all directions toward the barn, where old man Hosking and his two hands held guns on the newcomers.

"You remember us, don't you? I'm Artus. My daddy was Amos Moser."

"I know who you are, Artus. Your daddy grieved real hard after your mama passed on suddenly."

125

"You know anything about my family?" Jonah asked, anxiously. "You remember we have the place just down the road from Artus—"

"I know who the living hell you are, Hook!" the man snapped. "Heard about you from some fellas got out of Rock Island." The old man turned partway to address his hired men. "Boys, just look at that Yankee blue he's wearing for his homecoming suit!"

The hired men laughed as the ground warmed around them, steam lifting from the moist, rich earth.

"He was out west fighting Injuns for the army—just to get out of prison," Artus tried to explain.

"I been set free from a hellhole of a Yankee prison—Rock Island. Only joined the army to get out and fight Injuns."

"There it is!" Hosking roared. "The truth comes from his own damned mouth."

"Never did once raise my gun at a white man in a Confederate uniform," Jonah said.

Hosking decided to amble a bit closer, his tall boots splashing across the muddy yard. "Way I figure it—that uniform of yours makes you a turncoat, Hook—folks took you in their hearts when you and your'n come to this valley. So why don't you be a good boy and get on out of here before we have to fill your Yankee-loving carcass full of buckshot and leave it set for my hogs to grit on?"

"Lot of men died in that prison, Mr. Hosking. I didn't want to be one of 'em."

"Good men, I'll bet they were—'cause they stuck it out. Now, kindest thing I can do for you and your loyal cousin there is to tell you to scat. It's for him I didn't open up on you first sight I got of that goddamned uniform."

"It ain't fair—what you're doing," Hook snarled, taking a step forward before Moser snagged his arm.

"Keep your gun down, Jonah!"

The rifles held by the hired men came up level, then Hosking waved his hand.

"Hold on a minute," he ordered the pair. "I don't want no blood on this ground. Been enough already. Lost my oldest boy at Pea Ridge, not far from here."

"I was there, Mr. Hosking."

The old man took another step closer, appraising Hook. "You was at Pea Ridge too?"

"I rode on from there with Sterling Price and didn't give up till I was took prisoner at Corinth in Mississip."

Hosking appeared to struggle within himself. He spat a stream of brown into the icy-scum puddle at his feet. "Lost both my boys in that war—killed by men wearing the same uniform you got on. I don't much take to Yankee blue on a man. Nothing's changed. Like I said, you and Moser best run on now."

"I can't go, Mr. Hosking."

He wagged his head. "I'm telling you—get off my place, bastard traitor!"

"I ain't no traitor!"

Moser stopped Hook as his cousin lunged for the older, bulkier man. Jerking Jonah around, holding tight to his wool coat, murmuring low to Hook about how foolish it would be with two other guns and them all Yankee-hating and shut-eared anyway. Hook kept twisting, making Moser dance as Jonah kept his eyes on Hosking.

"Let's just go, Jonah. There's others'll help us."

"I doubt that, Artus," declared the old man. "You go dragging along that traitor in that Yankee suit with you—I don't figure a soul in these parts is going to help you none."

Hook relaxed, his heart still like thunder in his ears. Artus stayed close, but eventually freed his grip on Jonah's coat.

"Just tell me," he rasped, weary, afraid, angry. "Tell me what happened to my family."

Hosking wagged his head. He glanced at the other two, who likewise shrugged. "Don't know. From the talk going round, it's been some time since anyone seen life out to your place. Don't have an idea where your family went."

"They didn't go nowhere." Hook balled his fists again, so filled with despair he would hit anyone just to feel the crunch of his knuckles against their cheek and jaw and nose. "They was took."

Hosking regarded him a moment, stepping closer as he brought his rifle up. "How you so sure they was took, boy?"

Jonah watched the wariness of the man, moving his hands from the holster where rested the .44-caliber army pistol he had been allowed to keep with him when the army bade him farewell back at Leavenworth, Kansas.

"I'm sure. Just know from the looks of the place."

"It will give a man the willies just going there, Mr. Hosking," said one of the hired men with a jerky nod of his shaggy head.

"It will, eh?" Hosking replied.

"Things left there my Gritta would'a took, had she been of a mind to leave on her own. Up to the loft, the children left things belonged to them. Special things a child don't leave behind if they're moving out for good."

"And down at the springhouse," Moser said as he jumped in, "we found milk and butter gone sour and dried in the churns—left like someone was never intending to leave such victuals behind."

Hosking licked his lips, his eyes flicking the hillsides on either side of them.

"I did hear of 'em coming through here some time back."

"Who?" Jonah asked, taking a step forward that caused the old man to snap the rifle up.

"Keep your ground, traitor!"

"I—ain't—no—traitor," he growled each word as menacingly as he could. "Tell me who come through here?"

"They was like a army," the hired hand volunteered.

"Shuddup!" Hosking shouted at his man, his eyes flicking into the hills again.

The old man's furtive look now meant something to Hook. He recognized it for what it was. "You're afraid they'll come back—whoever it was. Ain't you, Hosking?"

"We got no way of knowing, Hook. Now—for your own sake and your cousin's hide—just turn around and get!"

"I ain't leaving till I got me some answers."

He wagged the muzzle menacingly. "You're gonna get—and you ain't never coming back."

"C'mon, Jonah," Artus pleaded, pulling, yanking. "We go on and find someplace else . . . somebody else what can tell us."

Over Moser's shoulder, Hook called to the hired man who had let too much slip from his tongue. "What army was they? Reb, or Yankee? How many, goddammit! Where was they headed?"

Hosking raised the muzzle of his rifle and fired it into the air, shocking both unwelcome visitors.

"C'mon, Jonah! Now!"

"You best listen to your cousin, boy," Hosking's voice followed them doggedly down the lane. "Get your ass outta here—and forget you ever had that family of your'n. Just g'won and count 'em gone 'cause your people is good as dead!"

Sometimes Jonah Hook could downright scare a man.

Even his own cousin.

Artus Moser shook his head over the smoky fire where they were roasting five squirrels. Thinking maybe he really didn't remember all that much about Jonah, like he thought he did. What with the way he had acted down at Hosking's place yesterday, it had given Artus the willies.

Like what Hook had done out west fighting Injuns or maybe even something that Moser couldn't begin to figure out—something had gone and made Jonah different from the man who left this valley with General Price back in sixty-two. Jonah sat on the far side of their little fire cleaning and recleaning those guns of his.

"Yankees let you keep your pistol?"

Hook looked up, squinting through the smoke as a gust of breeze snuffled it toward him. "You carried yours home, didn't you, Artus?" He pointed his cleaning rod at Moser's hip.

"Yeah," Artus answered, still uneasy and unable to know why. "But that don't explain the rifle. Yankees don't give away rifles, Jonah. Been meaning to ask—"

"No, the goddamned Yankees didn't go and give me this rifle. I brung it here all the way from Virginia," he replied quietly, shutting his cousin off.

"Lord, how come them raiders didn't—"

"Gritta kept it hid for me. Under the stones of the hearth. I put in a special place there for hiding things when I built the fireplace."

"Thank God you got your hands on it, Jonah."

"Thank me for putting that hiding place there." He wagged his head, dragging the cleaning rod and oil-soaked rag up and down the full length of the barrel. "Maybe if she'd had the rifle out to use—wouldn't she and the kids be gone to who knows where now."

"Then again, Jonah—Gritta might be dead."

Artus watched that jerk Jonah's head up, a hateful, glaring look smeared across his thin, wolfish face. About to leap across the fire at Moser, if not say something stinging. But in a moment he went back to wiping the oilcloth around the percussion nipple and hammer on the rifle's action.

"I thought of that myself," Hook finally admitted. "She used this gun when those riders come through, chances are her bones be laying down in my yard where I come across what was left of old Seth."

"Least you got family to find. They ain't dead like mine."

"I know they ain't dead. In my gut—I know all four of 'em is still alive. Somewhere. For sake of us both right now, you remember your daddy and mama was my family too, Artus. I grieve 'em bad as you."

"Didn't mean no offense, Jonah. Just that—if it weren't for you—don't know what kin I'd have."

"We're riding the same horse, cousin. We both got to shuffle back to the Shenandoah down under Big Cobbler Mountain if we're to look up any kinfolk of ours now. That"—Jonah nodded into the growing darkness of the hardwood forest thick around them—"or out yonder."

"Lord, how I'd like to believe strong as you that we'll find Gritta and the young'uns."

He looked hard at Artus across the smoke made a sickly orange color as it rose from the coals. "I gotta count on finding 'em. Every last one of 'em. I'll keep looking till I do. If I didn't believe I could do it—I'd curl up and die inside and couldn't go on."

With his belt knife, Hook picked a string of meat from one of the squirrel haunches. "I'll find every last one of my family—and them that took 'em—if it takes the rest of my life."

Moser rolled himself in his blankets that night after eating. Hook turned away and settled into his bedroll without having said a word while they ate. Both knew morning would come soon enough. And the silence between them was all right.

The gray of dawn nudged both awake, scraping tongues around the insides of their mouths. Without saying it both men realized they shared a deep desire for the heady taste of a cup of coffee. The two men pulled at scraps of meat on the squirrel carcasses and sucked at the bones to satisfy the gnawing they likewise shared in their bellies.

"I hope we don't have to go all the way to Neosho," Artus said as they started north and east down the rutted road toward Cassville.

"You counting on us not getting any help in town?"

Moser said, "No. We got to get you some other clothes."

"Goddammit—folks round here oughtta know me for what I am—not for wearing this Yankee uniform."

"I wanna shet myself of this raggedy old uniform myself."

"Then we gotta do it in Cassville."

"They know you there."

"That's what I'm counting on. That, and sneaking into see Boatwright without being seen."

"What you wanna see him for?" Moser asked, his suspicions pricked.

"He's sheriff, ain't he?" Hook waited a moment. "He'll know about who come through here in the last few months—any bunch looking suspicious and up to no good."

But when they found Boatwright, he was no longer sheriff.

They had slipped into the small town, hugging the treeline until they got to the man's house, tried the back door, and found it unlocked. Figuring to let themselves in and wait until Boatwright came home, they instead walked into the kitchen and found the old peace officer sitting in a chair, pointing a double-barrel scattergun at the intruders.

"Sounds like there's two of you bastards," Boatwright said, his milky eyes blinking in the gloom of midmorning. "That's why lil' Ethel here has two barrels: blow the balls off both of you."

"Eldon? That's you, ain't it?" Moser asked.

The man's face twitched a little, as if placing the voice there in the dark of the hallway separating the two rooms of the small house. "I know you?"

"Artus Moser."

"Who's with you?"

"Jonah Hook."

"Jonah?"

"It's me, Eldon."

"C'mere and give this old man a hug."

"You ain't gonna shoot us?"

"I hear better'n I ever have these days," Boatwright said. "Don't see so good no more."

"Jesus God!" Moser exclaimed as he moved closer to the old man in the chair. "What happened—"

"Let's say I got burned."

"Your eyes, Eldon," Hook whispered.

"Sit. You boys come and sit," he said, easing the scattergun off his lap and motioning for them to go into the far room. "No thankee," he replied to the nudge of help from Hook at his arm. "I know where everything is."

"Then—you're blind," Moser whispered.

"As a cave bat."

"Fire, you said?" Hook asked.

"Freebooters."

Both of them rocked forward from the bench where they had plopped.

"Freebooters? How long ago?"

"Not long. A few months. End of summer as I can remember. Hot as hell."

"Why'd the bastards do this to you?"

Boatwright chuckled. "You don't see no star on my shirt no more, do you, boys?"

"What's that got to do—"

"They took it." Boatwright sank back into his chair. "Don't matter none. I don't really need it now after all. Just me in this house, waiting for someone to come bring me something to eat, help me out. Jesus Lord! But you boys both been gone a long time—"

"Tell us about the freebooters and what they done to your eyes," Hook said impatiently.

Boatwright turned toward the sound of the voice. After some thought he began, his scarred, whitish eyes seeping the moisture that no longer stung his fire-battered flesh.

"They had me tied down, not far north of your place, Artus. I had been down to call on your daddy and was heading out of the valley by way of Jonah's place. That's when I spotted a bunch of horsemen on the Hook farm. Sat there awhile, watching them gut your place for what you had, Jonah—and then I figured I'd better get back to town and get me some help. But I never made it into the saddle again. That bunch must've had guards on their backtrail, 'cause they came out of the woods on me."

"How many of them was there altogether?"

"More'n thirty I'd say—by what I could see moving around on your place. I don't figure I ever saw 'em all."

"Why'd they tie you down?" Moser asked.

"Hold me down is more like it—'cause when their leader come up from behind where I was staked out, all I heard was his voice. Never saw his face. But he told the others I'd have to die 'cause I could identify 'em. I told him I wouldn't dare—just let 'em get on out of the territory."

"And what then?"

"He laughed some at me. Said that if I didn't want to die—he'd make it so I would beg him to kill me soon enough. But . . . I didn't ever beg, boys."

"He burned your eyes?"

"With a hot poker."

Something inside Artus curled up in a tight ball and would not loosen.

"We need clothes, Sheriff," Hook asked.

"Told you, I ain't sheriff no more."

"You always will be to us. You stake us a couple sets of clothes?"

"Ain't got much, but what there is—you're welcome to it. You going after them?"

"They got my family, Boatwright."

"Too many of 'em, Jonah."

"How many guns you got in the house, Sheriff?"

It was as if by some unseen power, Boatwright's smoky eyes behind the scarred lids and cheeks were staring right into Moser's tall, skinny cousin for the longest time.

"Back there, behind that sideboard. You'll find what you boys need. Just leave me the pistol and this here old bird gun. I do fine by them."

"I'll pay you back," Jonah said, pulling the old sideboard away from the wall. "Don't know how or when—but I'll pay you back for everything you done to help me get my family back."

16

Early February–Late April, 1866

JONAH HOOK KNOCKED the damp earth from his hands, then finished brushing them off on the worn clothing Boatwright had given the two former Confederate soldiers as a homecoming gift. They had both hurried back to the valley south out of Cassville.

The work in the dark Missouri loam had been more than Jonah had thought it would be when first he decided to dig in that spot back of the cabin. After finding a small bit of lamp oil left in the cabin, Jonah and Artus burned their old clothing out at the edge of the fields now gone to weed. Jonah didn't stand there long, watching the oily smoke rise into the cold winter afternoon air.

"We got work to do, Artus," he had directed.

And work they had.

Four holes, a good six feet long and some two feet wide. Another six feet deep. All lined in a row behind the cabin he had built for Gritta and Hattie, and the two boys yet to come when first they settled in this narrow valley. Now something had made him return to the homestead for this final ceremony. His digging of the four graves was some dark journey into the deepest recesses of his rage, and the despair he suffered at ever finding them again.

The cousins had spelled one another at that single spade, cursing the hard ground wrought of winter, thankful for the recent cold rains that had soaked some softness into the unforgiving flintlike, and frozen soil. Now they rested, gasping over the fourth and final hole.

"You understand, don't you, Artus?"

Moser swiped a streak of dirt across his cheek, smearing sweat off with his dirty hand. "No. I don't."

"You got two graves up there to your place. That's your family buried there."

"But, Jonah—you don't know what's happened to your family."

"That's why I'm leaving the graves open." He dropped the spade beside the last hole and turned away toward the cabin. "Maybe it's like old man Hosking said it—they're good as dead. Until I find 'em. And find who dragged 'em off."

"Jonah!"

Hook turned, finding Moser pulling his misshaped hat from his head.

"Man never walks away from a grave without saying a few words."

"What you mean?"

Moser waved a hand helplessly, searching for the words. "This is some like a funeral to you, ain't it?"

He thought a minute. "I suppose it is."

"We ought to say some special church words over these holes afore we leave."

Hook came back, then dragged the floppy slouch hat from his long hair. "You're right."

Jonah stood there a few moments, sorting through a lot of thoughts. Mostly struggling to swallow down the rage and despair so that he could speak some of those few church words he could remember now without making them come out like he was flinging his anger up at God and the heavens.

"I really ain't any good at this, Artus," he whispered as if some-one or some-thing near might overhear.

"We gotta say something."

"All right," Hook sighed. "This is tough, Lord. The worst it's ever been inside of me. Feel damned near gutted—I'm sorry for swearing. Do too much of that, I know. I'm not always what you want of me, I suppose. Never been much of one to get down on my prayer bones and taffy up to you, God. Hell, you know what's in my heart better'n anyone. No sense me telling you what you already know's inside me. All that's left inside me now."

Jonah knelt and picked up some of the fresh spoil beside the last grave.

"This is for little Zeke. Born and baptized as Ezekiel before you, Lord." Jonah tossed the moist clods into the dark hole.

Moving to the next hole, he spilled some loose soil through his fingers. "This is for Jeremiah. Until my boy and me can fill this damned hole up together."

"You ain't supposed to swear when you're talking to the Lord, Jonah."

"I'm sure He's heard me swear enough that he thinks nothing of it now, Artus." Hook stopped by the third grave. "And dear little Hattie—until you and your daddy can plant some wildflowers here on this spot."

He felt it welling and didn't know how to make it stop as he stepped to the final hole. And stared down into its emptiness, much like his own center, except for the anger and the despair—nothing else there but black emptiness.

It shook him a moment, right down to those old boots Boatwright had given him.

"Sometimes I curse myself, dear woman," he began, quietly. "Ever bringing you out here from our home at the foot of Big Cobbler. Curse myself for wanting to make a home that would be ours—not your family's or mine. Something that could be ours alone."

As he began to sob, some of the tears fell on the back of his dirty hands he held clasped in front of him, trembling as they crimped a hold on that slouch hat.

"This never would happen back in the Shenandoah. Out here—in this land where there's no law to speak of, where the guilty can ride in here and murder and steal, then run and hide in the Nations—" He stopped of a sudden, feeling out of control as he let the words spill.

"Pray that I find you, Gritta. Wherever they've taken you and the children. For the sake of them. For the sake of what we could be again—pray that I find you."

He turned away suddenly, unable to go on, the last words choked with bile. Angrily he wheeled and kicked dirt into the last grave, then spun again and set off toward the cabin.

It was long after they had started out, on foot, south toward Fort Smith, that Jonah finally felt like he could talk again. The sky had cleared the last two days, and winter's cold had gripped the land with an unrelenting hold. Their breath formed frosty streamers behind them as they moved along at a brisk pace, not only to cover ground, but to keep warm as well.

"Someone's gonna have to prove to me they're dead. You put your daddy in the ground—so you know he's dead. Me—I ain't got none of that. Not for the children. Not for Gritta."

"Don't have to explain it to me, Jonah. Just tell me why we're headed south. I figured we'd be heading west, into Kansas where them Yankee jayhawkers always came from before."

"No, not this time," he shivered with the cold. "We're going someplace else."

"The Nations?"

Jonah stopped, dragging Moser to a halt. "How'd you know?"

Artus shrugged. "You said it there at the graves—about the Nations."

Then Jonah remembered. "Yeah. I gotta watch that—getting angry and spilling things like that. Always done it."

"Why there?"

"I figure that's the best place to start looking."

Moser wagged his head as they started walking again, both grown cold from the standing. "Still don't get it. You must have a good reason to wanna—"

"Boatwright told me."

"Told you what? When did he tell you anything like that? You gotta be getting crazy about this—"

"I'm not crazy!" Hook growled. "Boatwright told me while you was pulling out the clothes for us. Whispered to me that he had good information that was give to him—about that bunch come through here end of last summer. They was talking about heading south and west into the Nations."

Moser smiled slowly. "Shit, Jonah—if that don't beat all! This pair of country boys got us something to track now!"

I don't believe I heard what you said, Sullivan," growled Boothog Wiser at the man standing ten feet off as the entire guerrilla camp fell to silence around them.

Mike Sullivan glanced about him for a moment, then drew his shoulders back. "I said: you don't always got first right to every woman we take."

"That's what I thought you said." Wiser shuffled over to stand beside the frightened dark-skinned Creek woman they had captured earlier that spring morning.

April was half gone, and the men sensed the warmth in their blood, making them randy and ready to mount the first female they had come across after pulling out of the streamside camp, riding on into the timbered mountains in the foggy eastern stretches of Indian Territory. Boothog himself had grown weary of a long and cold winter. And the nigger girl.

They had left her body somewhere back among those limestone caves.

Now Wiser became acutely aware of the way the men stared at his left boot, which concealed the deformed foot. Whenever he caught a man staring, they looked away quickly, almost ashamed. More so afraid.

"Whenever you're ready to take over, Sullivan—just let me know. I'll step aside, you think you're man enough to be second in command to Colonel Usher."

Wiser slowly stepped behind the frightened, trembling young woman, her broad nose and thick lips betraying her mixed blood. Creek Creole. Black slave blood tainting the Indian purity, he thought, as he ran his hand down the curve of her neck, pushing aside her dress so that he could feel along her smooth shoulder the color of milk and coffee. As he did it, his left hand slipped unseen to the inside pocket he had sewn into his wool mackinaw.

Sullivan appeared buoyed by the clear hostility for Wiser he believed he saw some of the other men show. He took a step forward.

"I figure I'm ready to tell you to step aside, Major. I'm man enough to take over from you—and the rest of the men figure you've had too long a turn at the reins on us."

"They do?" Boothog asked, not looking up, content still to stroke the young woman's bare shoulder, sensing her shudder with his caress. Like a frightened bird in the palm of his hand . . . the way he remembered it as a boy, before crushing the life from the tiny bird, sensing the strong muscles and bone resist his grinding crush in those last seconds of fight.

"Go 'head—tell him, fellas." Sullivan looked from side to side at the rest, almost twenty strong now, and more gathering, curious. Wiser had a few out scouting. "You got tongues—tell the major he's done and I'm the one to take over for him."

Wiser looked up. "This true, gentlemen? You all are of one mind with Mr. Sullivan here?"

None of them spoke. Most could not hold Wiser's gaze as he touched each one of them with his hard, cold eyes.

"You said for me to tell you." Sullivan took another step closer to Wiser. "Move aside if you don't want to get hurt."

"How do you figure I'll get hurt, Sullivan?"

The big, hard-muscled man laughed, shrill and short. "Every man here knows I'm the best with fists there is. You don't stand a snowball's chance in hell of beating me. You're . . . you was just raised with fancier folks, Major. I'd lick you too quickly."

"I don't stand a chance, is it?"

"If you want to fight to prove it, so be it," Sullivan said, starting for Wiser, bringing his hard-boned fists up.

In a blur the pistol hand came out of the coat and fired beside the Creek woman's elbow, making her shriek as she jerked herself away from Wiser in terror. The black-powder smoke made an ugly stain in the clearing beside her, the way Sullivan's screech of horror made a blot on Wiser's ears.

But Boothog had hit the man right where he wanted. He was marksman enough never to miss what he pointed the pistol at.

Sullivan was down, with both hands clamping his thigh where the bullet had plowed through meat and bone. Bright blood seeped between his fingers as he grimaced in pain.

"You there!" Wiser ordered, pointing the pistol. "And you. There, and there. You four—tie him down." He waited a couple of rapid heartbeats, his own blood pounding in his ears, then hammered back the pistol once more.

"I told you, *tie him down!*"

Rope came out with hands that struggled over Sullivan.

"Drag him over there," Wiser commanded. "Tie his hands to those two trees. No, spread him out. Get two stakes for his feet and hurry about it!"

Wiser turned to more than twenty men who were standing, staring at the wounded Sullivan being trussed and shackled.

"You—six of you, get my tent set up now. When I finish with Sullivan, I want to relax in privacy with the squaw." He waved his pistol and a half dozen bolted from the pack to immediately set to work pulling the canvas wall tent from the back of the high-walled wagon. Wiser turned back and shuffled over to Sullivan.

The man spit at Boothog, then went back to shrieking, begging for help, someone to stop the bleeding from his leg.

"When are you going to learn, Sullivan . . . or any of you for that matter? When will you learn that it is foolish for me to compete with some of you on the physical plane? I am smarter than all of you put together, and there will never be any question of that. Will there?"

The group muttered their grudging agreement.

"And any of you who ever thinks of trying to prove yourselves smarter than me should come and take a look at Mr. Sullivan."

Wiser moved closer to the man, stopping at Sullivan's head. He knelt and pulled a knife from a beaded sheath. It wasn't a particularly long knife, rather short compared to the bladed weapons the rest of the men wore on their hips. But it was a slightly curved Green River skinning knife, the sort the old fur trappers had used during the heyday of the beaver trade. And Wiser kept it expertly honed.

With a quick flick of his wrist, before Sullivan or the rest realized it, Wiser slicked off a fair-sized chunk of the end of Sullivan's nose. Blood oozed immediately as Sullivan struggled, shrieking for someone to pull Wiser off.

"An amazing weapon. Centuries old, gentlemen. Man has made himself long knives and short ones, cutlasses and foils and sabers. Yet nothing has ever come along to take the place of one small but well-honed skinning knife."

Roughly he pushed Sullivan's head to the side, clamping the man's cheek down into the dirt with a knee. As the man screamed and thrashed, he delicately sliced off Sullivan's entire ear. The ground below Sullivan's cheek was blotting with the free-flowing blood.

"Do you think he's had enough, gentlemen?"

No one dared answer. He laughed, knowing they were afraid, not knowing how to answer his question. If they said yes, he's had enough, likely they might be forced to trade places with Sullivan. If they said no, that their fellow freebooter had not yet had enough—then they themselves became accomplices to the bloody torture.

Wiser drew the knife down the length of Sullivan's chest, slicing open his shirt and opening a narrow ribbon of bloody flesh at the same time. Sullivan's screeching and thrashing was rising in volume, matched only by the stunned silence of the rest of the onlookers.

"These Indians in this western country have some unique and rather beautiful methods of making an enemy suffer. And, gentlemen—any man who says he is going to disobey me, or thwart my control, is an enemy of mine. Mark my words—the next man who attempts what Mr. Sullivan has tried will end up in far worse shape than what you will see exacted upon this frail mortal. Watch, gentlemen—and heed well the lessons taught you this day."

With a snap, Wiser turned Sullivan's head over, grinding the bloody stub of the ear into the dirt while he carved off the other ear. He then went first to one wrist, and the other, gently slashing open the veins just below the hemp rope lashing the man to the trees.

"This where I shot you?" he asked, scooting down to the bleeding thigh wound.

Sullivan was whimpering, occasionally cursing, then begging again for mercy. Just to be left alone.

"I can't leave you be," Wiser explained. "You will serve far greater

purpose in this moment of pain than the worth of your whole miserable life."
With a balled fist, he smacked the bullet hole, causing Sullivan to arch his
back, and thrash the leg in agony.

"Exquisite pain, isn't it? A lesson, this is—that all pain is itself a lesson,
Mr. Sullivan."

Wiser pricked open the bullet hole in the man's britches, slashing up and
down the trouser leg. Then with the tip of his knife, Wiser began slowly to
burrow the knife into the bullet hole itself while Sullivan screeched inhu-
manly.

He dragged the knife blade from the bullet hole, which now pumped
more vigorously.

"The Indians will cut off a man's balls too, Mr. Sullivan." He cut at the
man's belt, slashed off the buttons at the fly and yanked up the penis and
scrotum, hearing an audible gasp from the rest of the onlookers, wide-eyed
and ashen all.

"Are you man enough to live the rest of your life without your
manhood, Mr. Sullivan?"

The victim writhed, mumbling incoherently, tears mingling with the
blood and dirt smeared on his face.

"I didn't think so, Mr. Sullivan. You may talk a good game—but you
aren't really as brave as you would make out to be, are you?"

With a quicksilver movement, Wiser dragged the knife blade across
Sullivan's windpipe, watching his victim's eyes widen as Sullivan began to
gurgle and froth.

"That sound is your last breath of air before you die, Mr. Sullivan. I don't
think you worthy enough to live—hardly worthy enough to ride with Jubilee
Usher and his chosen Angels. So I'm not going to cut your balls off until
you're dead. Then I'm going to feed them to Colonel Usher's hounds. And
leave you right here for the crows who roost in these trees."

Wiser wiped the knife blade off on Sullivan's trousers as the thrashing
slowly ceased. Then the victim lay still, silent.

He stuffed the knife back in its scabbard and turned to the group. "Is my
tent ready? I so feel like making sport with that nigger squaw now."

Book IIII

Comes
the Wolf

17

"WHAT YOU FIGURE on us doing now?" Artus Moser asked his cousin. Jonah Hook's lips were drawn across his sharply chiseled face in a thin line he dared not break just yet.

Moser swiped a damp bandanna down his face in what had become an automatic gesture here in late July on the southern plains, deep in the eastern part of Indian Territory, also known as the Nations. They stood on the crude covered porch of a trader's house, one of those who by government license could legally trade with both the civilized and warrior bands assigned reservations here. While he had been glad to see white faces and hear English, the trader to the Creek tribe had nonetheless been less than forthcoming with information.

Here among the gentle timbered hills that formed the Kiamichi Mountains, Moser and Hook had wandered for days, asking their questions, growing more and more frustrated that so few understood their words, even less understood their attempts at crude sign language—anything to make the Creeks understand they were looking for a large band of white horsemen who were carrying along with them a light-haired white woman and three children.

"We can't stay here, Jonah."

"What you want from me?" Hook snapped, his cheeks red with more than the sticky heat. Even the leaves of the hardwood trees seemed to seep a damp, oppressive warmth into the heavy air.

"I come here with you—to help you find Gritta, dammit." Moser kept his voice low as he glanced back through the open doorway, his eyes finding the trader behind his long counter, stirring a breeze before his face with one of those paper fans.

"C'mon—we gotta get away from here." Hook stepped off the low porch, heading out.

"Where, Jonah? Back home?"

Hook whirled. "We ain't got no home back there now. Not you. Not me."

Moser turned as he heard the scrape of the old trader's stool on the wood floor. The man was coming out of the steamy darkness of his store, then stopped and leaned against the doorjamb, as if he would go no farther into the heat.

"Didn't realize you boys was on foot. Come all the way down from Missouri, walking, did you?"

"Most of us walked home from the war—lot farther'n that," Moser replied. He watched the droplet of sweat creep down the old man's bulbous nose, wondering when it would fall. Instead, it seemed to cling tenaciously there, pendant like a clear jewel the old man wore.

"Man who walks on foot, and goes off searching for someone who rides a horse, can't really expect to get anywhere."

Hook came to the step but did not mount to the porch. "Don't you think we thought of that? They may be ahead of us—way ahead of us . . . but that don't mean I gotta give up just 'cause they're moving faster'n us."

The trader fanned himself a bit more, moving the clear drop of sweat back and forth until it fell. "I suppose I wanted to be sure of my first impression of you fellas—that you weren't here to stir these folks up. Enough of that going on, what with the Cheyenne and Kiowa and those Arapaho pushing up against these Creek from the west. Creek just wanna be left alone, you know."

"We told you why we come here," Hook said. "And now, since you can't help us, we'll be on our way." He turned from the porch again, but stopped when the trader's words yanked him around.

"You got any money on you—we can talk about you boys buying some horses."

Moser nodded, starting to speak, but Hook opened his mouth first.

"What we need horses for, old man? No one knows a thing about this bunch we've been trailing out of Missouri. Ever since we crossed the line into the Territories—seems these bastards just up and disappeared like smoke."

"Wish I could help you there, truly do. But took me years to get the trust of these people. You gotta understand, these Creek been chivied all the way from Alabam' by white soldiers not that many years ago. Any white man come in here don't see a welcome sign hung out."

"Didn't expect to stay round here long enough to have no one hug me," Hook said.

"So you won't be needing the horses, is it?"

"We could use 'em—we just don't have no money."

"Neither one of us come home with anything," Moser replied, knowing it was a lie. He had seen Jonah dig up those few dollars from under that stone in the hearth. But Artus also knew that money had to last them as long as they could stretch it on the necessaries. Right now, a horse was a luxury. But in glancing at his cousin, Moser saw the light had changed in his eyes.

"I didn't see no horses out in the corral when we come up," Hook said suspiciously.

"I won't keep them out where someone can walk off with them," the trader explained. He pointed the fan off in a general southern direction. "My wife's people keep them with their stock. Down by their place, a few miles off."

"That your wife in there, the Injun squaw?"

"She's Creek—yes."

"Handsome woman."

"Give us twelve children through the years. We almost stopped count on the grandchildren," the trader said with a smile.

"Her people trade for horses?"

"Only if they know you."

"They know you, don't they?"

The trader fanned himself, studying Hook over the top of the fan. "So tell me, what you got to trade if you don't have money?" He eyed their weapons. "That rifle of yours be worth two horses any day, son."

"I'll bet it would, old man," Hook replied caustically. "It ain't for sale. How you expect a man to survive out here if he don't have a rifle?"

"You both hefting around big belt guns—"

"The rifle ain't for sale."

"Nothing else you want to trade, like them belt guns?"

"You take 'em for two horses?" Moser asked hopefully.

"I've got an old mare, fifteen years she is. Give you her for them two belt guns of yours."

Hook laughed humorlessly. "You're crazy, old man. We ain't interested. C'mon, Artus."

"Maybe there's something we can—"

"C'mon, Artus." He kicked off through the red dust that stived up into the heavy, damp air broken by shafts of unrelenting sunshine that broke through the thick-leafed trees.

Moser wanted to say something to the old man, but could not think of anything. He shrugged and leapt off the porch, following his younger cousin. Artus caught up with Jonah at the trees where they penetrated the cooler, heavy air of the forest, following the trail that had brought them here.

"Where we going now?"

"You're always asking me. Why don't you tell me where we ought to go."

Moser thought hard on it, unable to feel right about anything he might suggest. "I don't know where, now that we lost that bunch."

"Then you ain't a bit of help to us, are you?"

"S'pose not."

"How 'bout if I suggest something then?"

"All right, Jonah. Where we should go?"

"Get us some horses."

"Where we gonna get some—" He stopped, remembering. "You ain't thinking of trying to trade them Creek nothing for a couple of horses, are you?"

Jonah shook his head, a crooked smile growing on his face. "I been thinking. We need to find work. And up to Nebraska Territory they've got work. But—I also been thinking we can't walk up there."

"So how you gonna get horses?"

"We're gonna borrow 'em."

His throat seized up as his heart leapt. "You mean steal 'em. That's what you mean!"

Jonah grabbed him. "They got plenty. They won't miss two."

Moser swallowed hard, trying to figure it as Hook grabbed his shoulders, bringing his face close.

"Artus, it'll be all right. We'll wait until way past moonrise, then go in and lead a couple horses out."

"How we gonna do that? We ain't got any tack—"

"The old trader back there. In his barn. We'll go back after dark and get us bridles and what we can carry off."

"Bareback?"

"If we have to."

"Them Creek, they'll shoot horse thieves, you know that."

"Shit, Artus." Hook smiled. "You been shot at before."

"If you boys plan on doing any harder work than lifting that whiskey glass and poking whores," announced the army major, "I know where a man can earn good money."

"Thirteen dollars a month and two squares?" hollered a dirty civilian from the back of the watering hole the major had just entered, leading an escort of four privates.

There came an immediate burst of laughter from those in the room. Jonah Hook grinned and turned back to his drink. He and Artus Moser, like so many others, knew all too well what hard work soldiering could be.

"Slave work—that's what it is, Major!" yelled out another of the civilians.

The officer waited for the group to quiet itself. "I've come to offer enlistment in the frontier army. General William Tecumseh Sherman has already dispatched a large body of troops from this department to Indian country."

"Injun country? What the hell you think that is right out that door, Major? The cobble-paved streets of St. Louie?"

More laughter followed the jeering catcalls from the civilians long at working on their thirsts in the dimly lit, mud-floored saloon that passed for a barroom in Dobe Town, just beyond the boundaries of the Fort Kearney military reservation in Nebraska Territory.

"Colonel Henry B. Carrington recently departed with hundreds of foot troops to protect the Bozeman Trail for emigrants heading to the mines of Idaho and Montana."

"Now that's where a man can make him some money," Artus whispered into Jonah's ear.

"If he makes it through Injun hunting grounds with his hair." Hook watched Moser absently stroke a palm over the back of his head.

"Colonel Carrington's mission in protecting the Bozeman Road has depleted this department's manpower strength. General Sherman hopes we can enlist what we need in the way of good soldiers right here on the prairie," the major went on.

Down the rough-plank bar from Jonah a man with a hawkish beak of a nose turned about on the major and leaned his elbows back on the bar.

"Major, maybe you should just take your enlisting outfit on outta here. Most of these boys already had their fill of soldiering—for either Uncle Billy Sherman or Robert E. Lee."

The major turned toward the speaker. "I take it you fought for the Confederacy?"

"I did not, Major. From The Wilderness and Gettysburg, Cold Harbor and Manassas. And I fought at the siege of Atlanta under Sherman hisself." He turned back to the bar. "I had enough of soldiering. I can make more at a poker table in a week than I can in a month of Sundays as a buck-assed private, digging privy holes and shining officers' boots."

"You, sir—are the sort of soldier the army needs on the frontier at this moment in history. With the great rebellion subdued back east, our Republic can now turn its attention to the matter of pacifying the plains."

"Go tell that to the goddamned Sioux!" yelled a faceless voice from the smoky recesses.

"No one is saying it will be easy," said the major, hurling his voice into the barroom once more. "What say you now? Any of you ready for adventure in the Army of the West? I'll have enlistment forms ready at this far table when you've thought it over and want to join those who will fight to bring peace to this land, once and for all, now that the Rebels lost."

Jonah turned. "We didn't lose."

The major turned back to find the tall, thin rail of a man who had flung his words at the officer's back. "The South lost the war more than a year ago—in case you haven't heard."

"I heard, Major. And I was there. But—the South didn't lose." Jonah listened as the barroom behind him fell still again. The Union veteran at the bar had turned around once more, this time to study Hook.

"If the South didn't lose, mister—what would you call it?" asked the major, slapping his gloves across the front of his britches, sending sprays of fine dust into the smoky, oily atmosphere.

"We was whipped."

"Damn right you were whipped," shouted one of the major's escort.

"I don't see any difference," said the major.

"Big difference. If a man loses, that means he give up. And I don't know of many who gave up fighting until Robert E. Lee told 'em he was done and wanted his soldiers to go on home."

"You lose or you're whipped. Same—"

"No it ain't, Major. When a man's whipped, it means his enemy's got more strength, better rifles, more rifles. But it don't mean he lost. It just means his enemy whipped him."

"The man's right, Major," said the Union veteran as he inched down along the bar toward Hook. "It would be about like me and the Johnny here taking on the five of you soldiers because your damned big mouth won't stop flapping."

"I won't be talked to like—"

"And if the two of us get whipped by the five of you—which ain't really likely, me taking a hard look at your escort here—then we get whipped. But we didn't lose the fight." He turned to Hook. "Isn't that what you're trying to explain to this dunderhead of a major?"

Jonah smiled. "You said it just fine for me, mister. Just fine. I'd buy you a drink—but I'm afraid my cousin and me are a shade light."

"No matter," replied the Union man, turning his back on the major and escort. "Let me offer you two a drink on me." He snagged the neck of the bottle being held by the barkeep. "Put it on my bill."

"They wanted to see the color of our money before we got a drink," Moser apologized.

"It's like that out here. There's a lot of worthless scrip floating around these days. Gold will always do the trick. That, and army money."

"Always army money," Jonah replied. "Ain't no other work for a man what needs a job to eat."

"Take heart, friends. The army isn't the only good money on the plains," said the veteran. "I'm Eli Robbins."

They shook hands and introduced themselves, then helped themselves to Robbins's bottle.

"You look like you ain't hurting for walking-around money," Moser said.

Robbins smiled. He stood taller than Moser and almost as tall as Hook, but with a good thirty pounds on the whipcord-lean Confederate from Missouri. "I suppose I'm not. Work when I have to—never really want to. When my poke gets short, I know where to go looking. What brings you two Southern boys all the way out here to the middle of Nebraska?"

"Jonah come through these parts a couple times while he served out here—fighting Injuns."

The stranger's eyebrow lifted. "You was with one of them galvanized outfits, eh?"

"Third U.S. Volunteers," he answered. "Kept the telegraph up and the roads open when we could."

Robbins chuckled. "That was a job of soldiering. Outfits like yours cut their teeth on Sioux and Cheyenne I hear."

Hook wiped his bushy black mustache with the back of his hand. "What you said before, Eli—you got any ideas where we could find work?"

"I'm fixing on moseying south myself in a day or two. Hear the K-P needs hunters."

"What's the K-P?" Moser asked.

"Kansas Pacific Railroad. Word has it that the track gangs have reached Abilene."

"Down in Kansas."

He nodded. "They need hunters to supply meat for their bed gangs and riprap as well."

"Bed gangs?" Moser asked.

"Level the road where the track will lay. Riprap cuts through timber and brush, crossing water with bridges."

"I've shot mule deer and antelope before," Jonah said, pouring himself another glass of the red whiskey. "I figure I could do that."

Robbins chuckled. "You won't be shooting no mule deer or antelope out there, Jonah. Them gangs get real hungry."

"Why no deer or antelope?"

Robbins snorted with a chuckle. "Didn't you ever see 'em while you was soldiering out there in Dakota Territory?"

"See 'em—see what?"

"Buffalo, goddammit! The K-P needs buffalo hunters!"

18

"HE THE ONLY skinner you got?" came the question from the big man perched behind the table crowded with paper and whiskey glasses in the Abilene saloon.

Jonah glanced at Moser. "Yeah. Just him and me."

This central Kansas town on the great Smoky Hill River was only then starting to boom. Ever since the 1862 Homestead Act had begun to bring settlers fleeing the war that was devastating the east, granting them for next to nothing 160 acres of prairie grassland, towns like these had started to crop up across the central plains. But this particular town had something different going for it. Someone had seen something special when he had first set eyes on Abilene, Kansas.

Just this past summer, Illinois cattle buyer John McCoy had recognized the potential in putting up the corrals and shipping depot that would soon revolutionize the business of driving Texas cattle to the eastern markets. He was the first to see that profits could be realized by having a railroad closer to the cattle empires. Working alongside the Kansas Pacific, McCoy had erected the first of his cattle pens and would keep his crews constructing those pens and loading chutes until cold weather set in. The first marriage of cattle and the railroad was less than a year from becoming a reality.

Tracks heading east were already laid. Abilene and the K-P would be ready come next trail-drive season.

Chewing on some shag leaf tucked in a tight lump within his cheek, the big man behind the wobbly table eyed the two Southerners severely, his gaze eventually coming back to rest on the half-stock, heavy-barreled muzzle-loading rifle Hook rested on its butt between his scuffed boots. "You ever shoot buffalo before?"

"Served with the Third U.S. Volunteers out to the Dakotas during the war."

"Rebel, eh?"

"I was," he answered.

"I asked if you ever shot any buffalo, Reb."

"On Connor's march up to the Powder—Sioux country."

"You was with Connor?"

"I was."

"I think you're pulling my leg, mister. Bet you can't tell me—"

"You want to know about the Platte Bridge fight? Or when we got in there and wiped out that village of Black Bear's Arapaho."

The man sat there, looking a bit stunned by the suddenness of Hook's reply. "Don't remember you."

"Don't remember you neither. So what does that prove to us? That I kept to myself? Damn right I did. Now, you want someone to hunt buffalo for this railroad or not?"

The man smiled at last. "So you're good with that old front-stuffer, are you?"

"Jim Bridger himself always asked me how good a man got to be to kill something big as a buffalo."

"You knew Bridger?"

"Him and his partner, Shadrach Sweete. They scouted for Connor last summer. So how come you're here working for the railroad? Got tired of puny wages and moldy hardtack?"

With a sudden gush, the big man laughed. "You'll do." He pushed the pencil toward Hook, his other hand indicating the line. "Need your name, and your skinner's name there."

Jonah carefully made his letters, the only thing in the world he could write, or recognize. In handing the pencil over to Moser, Hook asked, "What we get in the way of fixin's?"

"The railroad will assign you a wagon and team. You lose 'em—you get docked on your pay. Three blankets a man and a poncho for each of you. Rope and come-a-long for pulling hides. You need mess gear—buy it yourself."

"Don't need none," he answered as Moser straightened. "You said something about pay. How much?"

The man turned the ledger page around and squinted at the names. "Jonah Hook. And . . . Artus Moser. Together, you'll earn two hundred dollars per month."

They looked at one another in shock.

"I know, boys. It's a shitload of money—if you got the makings of a buffalo hunter like you claim you do."

Jonah felt numb inside, thinking about just how much two hundred dollars was in real money. "I am. A hunter."

"K-P expects you to bring in the meat off ten buff a day. You get a bonus at the end of the month if you bring in more than three hundred for that month."

"And a bonus too?" Moser asked, his voice a bit on the squeaky side.

The big man looked at Artus. "That's right. But I personally think you got the worst of it. Him—he's got the easy job: just shooting the buff. When he gets ten of the big brutes down, all the fun's over and the work just starts. Ten buff a day will mean the two of you will be humping from first light to moonrise getting in and out of line camp with your meat."

"Where's camp?"

"Couple miles west of here now. The K-P been laying track since the first days after the war ended. The line camp moves west about once a week."

"Soon enough, I s'pose—camp will be so far away there won't be no more whiskey and women, Artus," Jonah said with a wry grin.

"Don't you count on that, mister," replied the sign-up man. "Watering holes and whores will damn well follow these gandy dancers right on into hell if that's where the railroad goes to lay track. Because gandy dancers got lots of money and a few hours of nighttime on their hands."

Jonah looked over the smoky room. "Ain't that fitting? 'Cause that's just the two things a whore and fancy card dealers like most about a man."

The man handed Hook a slip of paper. "You boys take this out to camp west of town. Past McCoy's corrals next to the tracks. You can't miss the camp. Just follow the tracks."

"Who we see there?"

"Ask for the camp foreman. He'll get you fixed up with the rest of your truck and wagon."

Hook stuck out his hand. "You know our names. I didn't catch yours."

"Billy Crowell. Good to have you boys signed on."

Jonah waved the hire-on slip in the air. "Believe me, mister—it's damn good to have a job like this!"

Those shaggy beasts could weigh as much as a ton, and some stood over six feet tall at the hump.

From far away, they looked like a black brown growth on the prairie. Up this close, as Jonah belly-crawled to the crest of a low rise beside Artus Moser, the buffalo looked all the bigger than he could remember. Then he recalled he had never been this near a buffalo, much less a whole herd.

"Maybe it's just the size of the head on the critter," Jonah whispered to his cousin, who was dragging the extra pouch containing an additional powder horn and cast balls.

They had spent the better part of the previous afternoon heating bar lead and pouring it into hand-held ball molds. Each of the .62-caliber balls weighed a lot in Jonah's pouch, along with powder horn and caps. And Artus was dragging another shoulder pouch full of them up the slope on his belly beside Jonah.

Once the pair had picked a place to begin, and if they were careful, the camp foreman instructed them yesterday, the Southern boys would be able to stay right where they were until they dropped ten buffalo. If they weren't careful and failed to read the wind, the rest of the herd would likely spook and take off.

"If that happens," the foreman had explained with that aggravating smile, "then you two have to hightail it back to your wagon and trail that herd until they decide to stop and graze. Ten buffalo a day. You bring in more—there's a bonus for you come the end of the month."

"Crowell told us," Hook had said, with his own wolfish grin.

"What . . . what happens—we don't bring in ten?" Moser asked suspiciously.

"Then, boys—I get to fire you."

Jonah remembered now how Artus had stared at him while the foreman walked off. Hook vowed, "Don't you worry none, cousin. We'll drop our ten, and more."

Moser had looked like he wanted to believe, especially now that they were bellied down in the dirt and summer-dried grasses of this Kansas hill country, gazing down on a herd that blackened several acres to the south.

While most of the other hunters had pushed due west from line camp before sunrise that first morning, Hook and Moser had decided they would try their first day's luck by pointing their wagon where no one else was headed. The air grew hotter with every hour the springless, rattling wagon had lurched and bounced over the rough prairie dotted with flat buffalo chips quickly dried beneath the relentless sun. And eventually as that single white eye rose to midsky, the pair began to suffer the torture of stinging buffalo gnats.

Tiny, red-hot, troublesome insects that sneaked in underneath their eyes and into their ears, swirling around in their nostrils and finding every square inch of exposed flesh. They were both so busy swatting gnats and swiping sweat that they were upon the herd before they knew it.

"Them critters are cursed with dim eyes and dull wits to match." Hook repeated what he had told Moser the night before. "Bridger and Sweete—you remember me talking about them, don't you?"

"You talk about 'em all the time since we left home," Moser grumped.

"Well, them two taught me about buffalo—"

"I know damned well you ain't never shot one yourself."

Jonah's eyes narrowed at his cousin. "Well, we're about to take care of that right now, Artus. Best get your skinning knives honed on them stones we bought you back to Abilene."

"That's all I did last night whilst you was casting balls. These knives honed so sharp they'll slit a flea's leg up the long way."

"All right," Jonah replied, smiling briefly before it went the way of the stiff, hot breeze. "I'm fixing to have me some fun now. And fixing to put you to work for your pay."

"My share's fifty dollars a month—right?"

"You'll work for it too," Jonah said. "Just remember what I told you Shadrach Sweete taught me: buffalo may got the brains of a flea—but when they get riled, they are a mighty enemy. Shad always said, 'They get their size and their surprising speed coming at you—all rolled into one deadly punch.'"

He jammed the pair of crossed sticks into the soil and laid the long-barrel of the half-stock muzzle loader into the vee. Bringing the hammer back to half cock, Jonah took a brass cap from his pouch and seated it on the nipple. He dragged the heavy hammer back to full cock and pulled on the back of the rifle's two triggers, thereby setting the front trigger to respond to a hair's touch.

"Wait a minute," Moser whispered, touching his cousin on the shoulder.

"What's wrong?"

"Nothing. Just want to look at 'em a minute. I ain't like you. I never seen anything like this before."

This was as close to an eternal mystery as anything would ever be, but no man would likely know just how many buffalo there were in those four great herds blanketing the Great Plains at the time the Civil War whimpered to a close. There would be those who would later estimate the number at more than seventy-five million spread from the Canadian border to the southern reaches of Texas: the northern, the Republican, the Arkansas, and the Texas herds.

"There just ain't no way for us to count 'em, Jonah. Like the fish in the sea."

"You ever seen the sea, Artus?"

"That neither."

"Well, cousin—to me there's but one way to count buffalo. And that's when we have ten of 'em on the ground. Then we know we keep our jobs and made our money for another day."

Moser clucked. "I 'member something my mama said from the Bible she was always reading to me, words I think on looking out on all these beasts." He cleared his throat in preparation, then spoke as if in a new voice, "'Behold, for they are like the locusts of Egypt come to trouble the pharaoh.'"

As his cousin quoted scripture in that foreign voice filled with distant thunder, Jonah turned to Moser, a little wonder mixed with admiration on his bushy, sharply chiseled face. "You said those words like a true Bible-thumper, Artus. Sure you don't want to pass a collection plate instead of skinning buffalo?"

Moser appeared a bit embarrassed, his eyes misting as he gazed back at the herd while it slowly shifted like a rolling black sea through the notch in the low hills. "I figure on skinning buffalo, Jonah. Always do what I set out to do."

Hook nestled his cheek along the riflestock. "So do I, cousin. We need us the money."

"You figure to stay here in Kansas a long time shooting buffalo?"

"Only as long as it takes to get us a small poke, cousin."

"Then we get back to looking for your family?"

"Now you shut up for a while so Jonah here can get his mind on killing a buffalo down there."

As he started to relax his breathing, Hook brought the front blade down on the nearest of the beasts. He set the blade back in the notch on the buckhorn rear sight and let half his breath out, held and moved his finger to the rear trigger.

With it set, he inched his finger to the front trigger. The rifle went off, shoving back against his shoulder so hard it surprised him. The cross-sighting sticks fell as the smoke rolled away.

"Damn, you missed him," Moser said. "Fell short, Jonah."

"Short?" he asked in that cursing tone as he dragged the rifle back, went to his knees, and blew down the barrel. Yanking up the powder horn, he poured a charger full of the black grains down the muzzle, followed by a ball seated on a greased linen patch that he drove home with the long hickory ramrod.

With the hammer at half cock, Jonah dug in his pouch for another cap and pressed it atop the nipple. "How far short, cousin?"

"From here, I'd have to say not more'n twenty foot where it kicked up dust."

"Damn lucky, ain't we?"

"How's that, Jonah?"

Hook scrunched his belly down into the grass, spread his legs apart for a steadier hold, and closed one eye. "Lucky that shot didn't spook that buffalo, or the whole damned herd."

"I s'pose so, not knowing buffalo the way you do."

The roar of the rifle surprised them both.

Through the gray smoke adrift on the gust of hot September breeze, Jonah watched the buffalo lurch forward as if spooked. Then his breath caught as the beast collapsed, hind legs first, then fell cleanly to the side, thrashing but a moment, attempting to throw its massive head about as if in so doing it could hurl itself back to his skinny, inadequate legs.

"Lordee, lordee!" Moser was screaming as Jonah clambered to his feet.

Hook grabbed his cousin and clamped a hand over his mouth. "Now you done it. Lookit!"

"They're going—dammit all and my big mouth!" Artus groaned. "But that was downright beautiful, Jonah!"

"To hell with the rest of 'em—we got one. Our first, by damned! We'll get the other nine slick as shooting that one."

"Damn right we will!"

They embraced unashamedly, bounding around and around in a tight circle there on the hilltop as the rest of the herd sauntered away from the carcass in their characteristic rocking-chair gait.

"You got work to do now, Artus."

They looked at one another, smiling—a new kinship between them that had deepened what they already felt for one another.

"That's just fine by me, cousin. Far as I'm concerned—you just keep me busy rest of the afternoon."

"All right," Hook replied, dragging the ramrod from the thimbles below the long barrel. "You get to skinning that one out so we can butcher him while I go see to dropping the other nine for the day."

He was partway down the hill and jamming a cap on the nipple when Moser called out to him.

"Hey, Jonah! You're a real buffalo hunter now."

"By glory—I guess I am at that!"

19

ICE CRUNCHED BENEATH their boots as they plodded through the shallow puddles that lay everywhere. Ice-scum puddles and the dung from half a thousand horses and mules.

Track-end was always like this: its own shantytown of thrown-up board shelters and wall tents and smoky fires and sheet-metal stoves, men and animals all turned rump to the November wind that came down off the northern plains, invading Kansas where the K-P was shutting down for the winter freeze-up.

In long lines the men waited, stretching out from the tall Sibley tent like strings of coarse linen being threaded through the tent—in one side and out the other when they had been paid off and sent on their way. Germans and Irish mostly. The rest were a motley mixture of veterans come west after the war. Nothing left for them back home now. For most, home was gone, or something a man had no hankering to return home to after living through the horrors that had been that great rebellion.

So these men stood in line again, like old soldiers at the mess kitchens, collars turned up and hat brims pulled down as the few icy flakes lanced out of the low-bellied clouds little more than an arm's length away overhead. A sky still deciding whether to snow or sleet. And with every gust of cruel wind, the smoke from the stoves and fire pits skidded in protest and in hurried patches along the ground in company with the dancing flakes.

Roadbed, grading, riprap, and track crews along with the hunters, laborers all—paid off then sent into the unknown for a winter's respite. If the money lasted a man that long.

"Company will be back here come spring," explained one of the men at the long table inside the tent as Hook and Moser inched inside the doorway, hugging as close as they could to those in front, so to squeeze into the warmth put out by the valiant sheet-iron stove.

"When you reckon on spring coming?" asked someone up ahead in line.

"Like I've said before—there's a good chance we'll be wanting to lay rail by the middle of March. Mayhaps the end of March. You men need work then, come round. We'll start putting down track right out yonder, where the last tie section finished work yesterday."

"March. Maybe middle of March," was the whisper coming back down the line among these comrades in arms sharing that vital secret with one another.

But until then, they would be on their own once more, each man taking his money and parting from this place.

"What-cher name?"

"Jonah Hook," he answered, watching his clerk beginning to scan the ledger as Moser stepped up behind Jonah and the next man in line shifted to another clerk down the table.

"You two together, is it?" the man asked, eyeing Moser.

Artus nodded.

The fleshy man went back to his ledger, then looked up, squinting. "Don't find your name here. You a recent hire for that tie gang?"

"I didn't lay track. Hunted meat."

He pursed his full, fleshy lips in a mean fashion that reminded him of a schoolteacher he'd suffered back in the Shenandoah. She was the reason he had never gone beyond the fourth grade.

"Why didn't you say so to begin with, Hook?"

He didn't figure it was a question needing an answer as the clerk dragged up another, smaller ledger, opened it, and scanned down the page with an accusingly slow index finger. "Here you are. 'Hunter.'" He looked up at Hook. "You been here awhile. Shows here you've turned in your wagon and team and squared accounts as of yesterday."

"That mean I owe anything?" he asked, suddenly worried.

"No, Mr. Hook. But you've made yourself some money I see."

"Three months' worth coming to me."

"Good wages they are too." He pointed at Artus. "After he takes his fifty dollars per month off the top."

"All right by me." Jonah watched the man behind the table reach down into an iron-banded box stationed beside his chair. Behind each payroll clerk stood a pair of armed men, short-barreled scatterguns cradled in the crook of each elbow. Their eyes were constantly on the move—from the laborers standing at the tent flaps with craning necks, to the clerks who dipped in and out of the boxes filled with neat stacks of colored scrip.

The man licked a finger and counted through the sheets of scrip. Then satisfied, he held a stack in the air for Artus, counted out another bundle he presented to Jonah. "You fellas ever seen Union money?"

"Never. Not till now anyway." He stared down at all the money he held in his hand. "How much is here?"

"I have paid Mr. Moser one hundred-fifty dollars of your seven hundred eighty-eight."

"That leaves me how much?"

The clerk smiled benignly. "Six hundred thirty-eight. You both made a few bonuses during your stay. Now please move along, fellas."

They did, staring dumbly at what they held in their hands as they exited between a pair of armed railroad guards and out to the cold of that winter's day.

"I was hoping for a bonus myself," Moser grumped, staring at the difference between his bills and Jonah's.

"You'd complain if'n I was to slit your throat with a new knife." He slapped his cousin on the back. "Any this bonus money is ours together. You got your pay 'cause you did all the hard work."

"You was always there, helping me skin, Jonah."

"Like I told you—we hired on together."

"And we're looking for family together." Moser stopped, getting Jonah to slow up and turn around. "So what we do now?"

Hook shrugged. "I figure we could do with some whiskey to wash down the memory of all this buffalo stink we got on us. Get me a new pair of boots and two new rifles for us."

"A rifle—for me?"

"You best figure on using some of that money to outfit yourself for the road, Artus."

Moser wagged his head, smiling broadly. "Damn, won't that be something. Us having new boots and maybe a new shirt to go along with 'em—and a brand new shiny rifle too."

"We got to get our outfits before we go drinking up everything we earned."

"How 'bout some poker, Jonah?"

"Does figure that we're due some fun, Artus. Let's get into town and see what they got for us in the way of trail fixin's."

They saddled their Creek horses down in the tent shantytown and mounted. Jonah cradled the old muzzle loader across his lap as they pointed their noses east, a stiff, chill wind at their back, troubling the long, brown hair that now brushed Hook's shoulders. Icy flakes hammered them in a growing swirl of white against the monotonous brown gray world as they pushed back toward Abilene.

Hard for a man to really tell, with as thick as the clouds hung overhead, but it was midafternoon by the time they reached the new town. Within another hour, they were stepping from a mercantile, wearing unfamiliar new boots, new canvas britches, and calico shirts. With new, stiff pinch hats on their heads and new Spencer rifles cradled protectively in their arms. Hook and Moser tied their old clothes in saddlepacks at the edge of the wide street.

"What now, Jonah?" Moser sighed.

"Don't think I ever seen you smile so big, cousin."

"Never had so much to smile about, I s'pose. There was a time or two that last few months where I got to wondering if I'd make it through butchering out another buffalo. We was always bringing our meat in, and it disappeared quicker'n we could shoot and gut and skin."

"You sure had a bad mouth on you there the last few months."

"What you expect—up to my elbows in blood ever' day. Smelling like a gut-eater all the time. Even caught myself turning up my nose at my own smell, Jonah. Come a time or two the wind shifted."

"We do smell like two of the prairie's finest, don't we?"

"You reckon there's a place a man can get some of this washed off?"

He looked up, then down the one street that Abilene boasted beside the newly laid track. "One of these watering holes bound to have some water they can heat up for a man wanting to scrape some prairie stink off them. C'mon."

In minutes they were standing at a low bar, watching the approach of an ugly barman.

"Most fellas just like washing the dirt down with some of my whiskey," he told the pair of buffalo hunters. "I suppose for a dollar I could get them out back to heat you some water you two could swish around in." He shrugged and turned. "Follow me."

They pushed past a blanket hung over a crude doorway, passing into a steamy, warm room where two stoves were crackling, pumping out plenty of heat. Beads of moisture popped out on Hook's forehead, just standing there, his eyes peering through the foggy gloom.

"Hey! Get over here!" the barman ordered, then turned to whisper to the two men. "This bunch ain't bad as a lot I've seen—ugly as sin and stupid to boot. But they do what I tell 'em, and they keep the place clean."

Jonah watched two middle-aged squaws appear out of the gloom of lamplight and steam. Dark stains covered the fronts of their hide dresses, from sagging breasts to the soaked moccasins they wore on their feet.

"We take in laundry," the barman explained, then smiled as if in need of no more explanation. "And if the price is right, either one of these ugly sisters can clean a man's plow right proper. Damn, but Injun women is good in the blankets."

He reached over and squeezed a woman, one hand on her rump, the other rubbing a breast. She looked at Moser and Hook with a faint smile, as if already figuring out what they had come for.

"No, they want to wash," said the barman, loudly, as if the women were deaf just because they did not readily understand his English. "No poking now." In sign with his hands and gyrating hips, he made the women understand that it was not fornication the customers had come for—but some of the squaws' hot water instead.

"That'll be two dollars," he said.

When Jonah had paid him, the barman bent down and gave one of the squaws a sloppy kiss on the mouth, then turned through the blanket doorway, proud of himself as the woman wiped the back of her hand across her mouth and grimaced. The two squaws looked at the pair of men, wrinkling their noses slightly at the stench in the close room. Hook could tell that the smell of the buffalo hung heavy about them both. He pinched his fingers on his nostrils and made a wrinkled face to show he agreed with them.

Both old squaws smiled, then signaled the white men into the far reaches of the low-roofed back room, where they were shown low wooden tubs on the floor, filled with half-dirty water, a scum of soapsuds drifting on the surface. Jonah dabbed a finger into the water.

"Least it's warm, cousin. You take that'un."

"We gonna undress in front of these women?"

"They ain't women, Artus. They just two old squaws."

Jonah dropped his britches and hurried out of his boots. When he had his longhandles off, the rifle and the belt gun handy beside the tub, he stepped in and settled himself. "Now don't this feel good. I ain't had something like this soak in . . . last time was before I walked off to join General Price."

"You been smelling a might gamy, that's for—"

Jonah looked up when Artus stopped talking suddenly. Out of the foggy haze lit with two hissing oil lamps emerged a third woman, younger than the other two and the closest thing to pretty Jonah had seen in years. He swallowed hard, looking at the way her black hair gleamed in the saffron light as she pulled the hood from her head, her proud breasts pressed against the buckskin dress as she dragged the blanket capote off her shoulders.

"Lordee, Jonah—I didn't figure on taking a bath in front of a girl."

"She . . . she ain't a girl, not rightly." From what he could see, she was something damned closer to being a woman.

Now she flicked her shy eyes at them both, then bent to pick up the bundle she had carried in with her. Clothing, secured in a snow-stiffened canvas bag. One of the old women came over to her, talking in a foreign tongue. The girl set her bundle aside and went to a stove, where she picked up a steaming kettle. From it she poured a little hot water in Jonah's tub, warming the water for the white man.

"You out—wash clothes," she said brokenly.

Broken though they were, the words fell clearly English on his ears. Yet it took a moment more before they registered. In that time, Jonah found himself staring—absorbed in studying the way in which coming in from the cold had made the young woman's high-boned, copper cheeks glow, how her hair lay plastered against the side of her head with melted snow and the overwhelming humidity of this low-roofed back room.

Jonah cursed himself. A faint, burning tingle rumbled across his loins, stirring what had been for so long dormant flesh. He had clearly been too long without a woman.

"She wants us out?" Moser asked.

"Seems so," he replied, not taking his eyes off the woman, who put the kettle back on the stove. She then threw Moser a towel.

"I ain't finished," Artus said. "Just getting to enjoy this. 'Sides, we paid a dollar to sit and—"

"Looks like we ought to go play some cards, Artus. 'Pears our time is up lollygagging here in this soapy water." He reached up to catch a towel the woman threw him, high enough in the air that he had to come out of the tub, standing just enough.

She smiled at Hook, admiringly, then turned away to go work with the two older women.

"Thank God that squaw looked away," Moser complained. "I wasn't about to come out with no woman staring at my privates like that. You didn't tell me these Injun women are so bold they got no shame to 'em."

Hook hurriedly dabbed the damp towel over the length of his shivering body, water puddling onto the rough-plank floor with the melting snow the young woman had dragged in. "Don't know a thing about Injun women, cousin."

"But you spent time out here."

He grabbed for his longhandles. "Don't mean I ever met an Injun woman. Can't claim I ever seen a one, much less know anything about 'em. C'mon—grab your clothes. We got a poker table calling out to us."

Moser wagged his head, skipping into his canvas britches. "But I damn well know everybody we've talked to since coming out here tells us they swear by Injun women—says squaws're the best for poking that can be."

For the moment Hook longingly studied the difference in the rear ends of the three women. Two were broad-beamed and shapelessly straining against their hide dresses. So different was the young woman's rump, small and firm as it pressed every bit as much against its confining buckskin dress, clearly outlined.

"I don't know nothing about that squaw-poking, cousin. But I can tell you, I'd be less than a man if I didn't want to find out about Injun women for myself."

20

H IS OWN RUMP had that comfortable feeling to it despite the fact it was cradled upon a hard chair, that sort of feeling that came from a familiar numbness that came of being planted for a time.

Jonah Hook played cards the way he had hunted buffalo. It was not an all-consuming passion, as it was for some on this frontier, more something to pass the time.

The same could not be said for the five others around the big table. Four of them were tie-gang laborers, big men with hardened hands and dull, clearly defined moves to their physical presence. Nothing slight about them.

The last was clearly not of this place, in speech and dress and the manner in which the man conducted himself. Jonah figured he could not be over thirty—no older than he. But despite the fact that the man did not fit in with the other six players in even the crudeness of their talk, the well-groomed man was nonetheless comfortable with this table and this game of cards, and perhaps the whiskey the barman kept at the ready whenever the young, long-mustached card player nodded in his direction.

Over the hours Jonah and Artus had been planted at the table, the first hints of cold had rattled into a plains snowstorm that whistled and threw everything it had against the north side of the clapboard building. Every time someone new came or went, the door thrust open with a noisy will of its own, urged on by a chill scut of freezing wind laced with icy snow. At times the arriving patrons would require the barman to hustle from his perch behind his bar and perform another sort of commerce at his nearby barrels of crackers, boxes of dry goods and shelves piled with all those sundry items the populace of central Kansas could not live without. He was clearly a businessman intent on making a living—if not from whiskey and cards, then from hawking his general merchandise to those who had nowhere else to acquire what was here for sale.

And, as well, he took in laundry. At least that's how he had started with the three Pawnee women when the track first neared this one-street town, he was prompt to explain to anyone who would listen at the bar or from the few tables that occupied most of the floor space in the low-roofed shanty of a smoky saloon. No paintings of nudes here behind the bar, at least not yet. And no smoky mirror behind those neatly arranged bottles. No, all that was unnecessary. A man came to his establishment not to have to look at himself or to stare at a wall full of bottles. His customers came to this place to drink and play cards.

Or they came to have a go at one of his three Pawnee whores.

"Didn't know they was whores," Moser whispered to Jonah there at the table. "I figured they really was washing clothes back there."

Across the table one of the big men laughed, raising his red-rimmed eyes from considering the merits of his cards held in those huge-knuckled, well-worked hands. "You're new here, not to know them three will wash the dew off your lily, Secesh!"

Hook felt the tremble go across the flat of his stomach at the mention of that word—something unrepentant Yankees liked to call Southerners. Not like *Rebel*—something a man would call himself proudly. But instead, it had become that sort of slur a Yankee could use in polite company and still get away with. Secessionist. "Secesh" for short. Almost as bad as calling a man's family to task—questioning his breeding, his mother, and a nameless, no-count father as well.

"You fight in the war?" Jonah asked, sullen and telling himself to let it be.

"Third Michigan I was." The man smiled cruelly. "We ever fight, Secesh?"

Hook wasn't about to let the man know that word nettled him.

"Not that I reckon on knowing."

"You'd remember the Third Michigan if you'd fought us. Likely you'd not be here playing cards with me and Hiram here." He tossed his head to his partner in the next chair, every bit as big and imposing in the splash of yellow lamplight and shadow in the barroom now that the sun had made its exit for the night. "Likely, you'd be laying in some moldy grave with all your kind."

"Your outfit tough?" Moser asked.

"We crushed every Johnny outfit tried us," Hiram, the second man, answered. "If you wanna call that tough."

"I'll take two," Hook told the dealer, another of the hard-handed laborers who didn't appear willing to join in on the verbal sparring. Jonah had been struck by the faint, hard edge to the taciturn man's words, something that spoke of distant Teutonic roots.

A German like me, he had thought the first time the man spoke hours ago when the first deal was set round that table.

The blanket behind him rustled, and Jonah watched the eyes of the others around the table fix upon something pleasant. He turned to glance and found the young Pawnee woman emerging with a bundle of clothing wrapped in a canvas sheet, bound with manila twine. She stood for a moment at the bar, whispering to the barman, then finally hefted her delivery under her arm and set off toward the door as the barman disappeared behind the blanket curtain.

The first big man toppled his chair with a shattering scrape as he got out of it and lumbered toward the woman, blocking her way at the door, where melted snow and ice and mud made for a crusty, red-tinged puddle.

She tried to step around him in one direction, then the other. He stood there grinning at her, not saying a thing.

Jonah found Artus looking at him. Hook let his eyes drop slowly down to Moser's waist, where the pistol butt poked from the front of his coat like a sheep's hoof. When he looked back at his cousin's face, Hook found Moser wide-eyed with a tinge of fear at what might be expected of him in the next few minutes.

"You go," she growled in that English that wasn't readily understandable to the rest in the room filled with murky light. But with a shove of her arm, she made her meaning clear enough.

Hook admired her from that moment. Not the kind to be content with calling out for her employer. She had declared her intention to right the situation on her own. While he had clearly liked what he saw of her willowy frame and dark eyes back in the washroom hours ago, Hook was all the more attracted now.

"You hear that, Hiram? She's telling me to go." The big man grabbed her shoulders and stuffed his face down into the nape of her neck as the bundle splashed into the muddy puddle. The woman tried to batter the big man with her clenched fists.

Hiram was up and moving their way. "Looks like you need some help, Simmons. Whatsamatter? Little hellcat more'n you can handle by yourself?"

Simmons wrenched one of her wrists away from the hold she had in his hair and looped it roughly behind the woman's back. She arched, wincing in pain as he shoved her toward an empty table.

"Goddamned redskin whore," he grumbled. "Not like she ain't had my pecker in her times before, is it?"

"Maybe she don't like you much as you like her, Simmons!" Hiram joked.

They both laughed. Hook sat there, growing numb by the moment, the thunder in his ears now a roaring tumult. The palms of his hands itched, sweating, as he glanced at the other three men at the table.

Hiram turned to the players as he threw the woman atop an empty table at the edge of the lamplight. "You boys want any of this when I get done—you can have her."

"I'm next, Simmons," Hiram said huskily as he snagged the woman's flaying arms and pulled them over her head, stretching the squaw across the table on her back.

"She'll throw rocks at your pecker once she gets a fill of mine, Hiram."

Simmons savagely tore up the bottom of her deerhide dress, stepping in between the woman's legs. They were encased in deerhide leggings tied to a belt around her bare waist. A wide piece of wool cloth hung like a short breechclout from the same belt, covering that flesh left bare by the leggings. Hiram yanked on it once, then a second time before the belt snapped and the cloth fell away. She began kicking at Simmons for all she was worth, with what strength she could muster against the both of them, cursing in her own tongue.

The heat had risen in Hook's throat, knowing what was about to happen and not knowing what to do. Perhaps leave. It was not of his concern, he told himself.

Then he remembered Gritta. Sensing somehow that she too might be alone against men such as these who came and took what they wanted and all others be damned. Gritta too might be unable to fight her own fight—

"Leave her be!" Hook said, loud enough that Hiram's head snapped up.

But only his. Simmons kept on, one thing only on his mind now, blood worked up and warmed to lust as he braced one of the woman's legs against the table, the other leg pinned with his huge hand, bruising the woman's dark-haired flesh while he tore at the buttons to his britches.

"Simmons! You got trouble," Hiram snarled, wagging his head once at the table.

The big man glanced over his shoulder, squinted his eyes at Hook, then slowly grinned as he freed the last button on his britches. "Don't you want none of this, Secesh? A good Pawnee honey pot? Best you ever had out here, I'll bet."

"Said to leave her be." Jonah leaned back slightly at the same time the well-dressed dealer backed slowly from the table, arose, and walked slowly to the bar behind Hook.

"I heard you, Secesh. But I ain't gonna leave it be. She'll get paid, so she's got what's coming."

Artus eased back from the table. From the corner of his eye, Jonah could see his cousin's hand resting on the pistol.

"Let's play cards, boys," Hook said quietly, as he watched Simmons tug at the front of his longhandles, trying to free his swollen flesh.

"When I'm done here, you goddamned stupid idjit!" Simmons barked.

"Pull your damned trousers up," Hook said quietly.

Simmons turned, his engorged flesh protruding from the front of his stained longhandles, eyes flaring like glowing flints at the other two men still seated like stone at the table with the Southerners. "Shut that stupid Secesh bastard up!"

As if moving in deep, clear water, the other two tie-gang laborers turned to look in Hook's direction, then rose from their chairs. Their eyes told it—going for their guns.

Beside Jonah, Moser was no slower in getting his big hog-leg out of his coat, and stumbling backward as he pushed himself away from the chair.

Hook fired and fired again at the first of the pair, watching him crumple in half and go to the floor like a damp rag neatly folded and lying still in the muddy water. A bullet whispered past Jonah's ear, from the second man's gun. Funny to think on it like that—a whisper when the guns were roaring, rocking off the roof of this tight, closed room.

Jonah's next shot missed the second man as he dived to the side, his left arm already bloodied by Moser's ball. Then the laborer was shoved forward, clutching at his back with his gun hand, slowly turning, his eyes full of fear and question as he turned round to look at Hiram behind him.

"Shit!" Hiram cursed, his gun out, realizing he had shot one of his own in the melee.

It was all he said as Hook dropped to his knees and aimed, hitting Hiram low in the gut. The man clutched his belly. Hook fired a fourth shot, blackening Hiram's chest just as Jonah felt an intense heat and pressure in a shoulder. Spun around sideways, falling, seeing the muzzle of Simmons's gun blaze a second time in the dim light, an orange burst of quick flame, followed by a snap of breaking floorboard beside Jonah's head where the ball impacted.

Hook straightened the arm at his target and pulled the trigger on instinct, hitting Simmons high in the chest, almost in the throat. The hole opened up bright red on his dirty longhandles. Still the big man took a step forward, his manhood wagging before him, and fired at his tormentor.

Through the gunsmoke at the corner of his eye Jonah saw Moser struggling with his old pistol on his knees, snapping caps. Then Hook fired again, hitting Simmons lower in the chest this time. The big man reeled a moment and took another step forward, bringing his pistol up slowly.

Hook clicked one cylinder, then a second as Simmons came on, smearing the bright blood down his greasy shirt with one hand. Frantic, Jonah shouted. "Shoot 'im! Artus, shoot!"

Moser opened his mouth as Simmons got his pistol up and cocked the hammer.

"My play now, Secesh," he growled with a smile as a gurgle of blood poured from his lower lip.

Then the side of the big man's face disappeared in a blinding glow of pink gore.

Hook winced at the blast, like a turtle shrinking his head back into his body, whirling onto the painful shoulder in that echoing roar of a pistol behind his ear. Moser was flattened on his belly, still struggling with his own weapon.

And the well-dressed young card man gripping an army .44 at arm's length, smoke crawling lazily from the muzzle.

Hook stared, blinking, while the man walked over to him.

"You're bleeding a bit," the stranger said. "That will be a nasty one, I reckon." Then he stepped over to Artus. "Help your friend get out of here, will you?"

Moser nodded. Both of them watched the younger man walk over to the fallen laborers. He knelt and inspected one, then the others.

"Simmons is dead. So's this one called Hiram." The stranger stood, straightening his coat and stuffing his pistol away beneath it at last. "The other two are hurt bad—but they ain't dead."

"You two g'won get outta here now."

Hook turned to find the barman with a double-barreled fowler at the blanketed doorway.

"We'll go," Jonah said, rising, feeling the sharp numbness growing in the shoulder. Half his chest was burning with sharp pain already. He glanced at the young Pawnee woman as she rolled off the table and collapsed to the floor, gathering her clothing up, straightening it as best as she could.

It had all happened so quickly, sweeping them all up into the maddening swirl before any of them knew how to pull out.

"These four will likely have friends," the card man said. "I spent some time scouting for the Union during the war, and some time out here since. So I figure you ought to take my advice. You best do what this barkeep says—and ride while you can."

"Where?" Moser asked.

"Doesn't matter now," said the barman. "Just get out of my place. Out of Abilene."

Hook stuffed the pistol into his left hand already wet with blood from the shoulder. He held out the right to the young card man. "Thank you, mister. Likely saved my life."

"I'm still trying to do that. But your life ain't gonna be worth much if you aren't long gone from here in the next few minutes."

"My name's Jonah Hook."

The young man smiled. "I'll remember that."

Jonah squeezed the gunman's hand. "Maybe we'll run across each other down the road sometime."

"If you like cards and beer, we'll likely bump into one another, sometime," he said to Hook. "My name is James Butler Hickok."

21

"YOU GONNA KEEP her with us?"

Many times had Artus Moser asked that question since the snowy night he had fled the Abilene watering hole with Jonah Hook and the Pawnee woman.

And over the past nine days—or was it ten now?—Moser had grown more scared of this foreign land and the way winter settled down on them in the middle of a great big patch of nothing, a rolling prairie where fleeing west they had come upon a line shack beside the unfinished roadbed where track would be laid come spring.

Spring.

That had such a good ring to Moser's ears as he said the word to himself. And pulled the blanket much tighter about his shoulders. He had allowed himself only one in keeping warm, giving another to the Pawnee woman. The rest were for Jonah—lying there on the leaky floor of the clapboard line shack, where the wind whispered through the joints and swirled snow a'times up through the cracks. On the rough planks Hook lay shivering, his lips barely moving in an endless chatter of fevered remembering.

There wasn't much they could do for real heat in this tiny place. About all was to make it warm enough to keep the frost down on the inside of the clapboard walls that moaned each time the strong north wind attempted to

172

grunt the shack over on them. The days were gray and the nights black and starless, as if the three of them had been set down in the middle of a flat tableland and someone had overturned a bowl atop them, allowing in only the thinnest stream of light off the far horizon when the sun rose, or when it set but a few hours later.

Artus had gone and collected what Hook had called squaw wood—deadfall down by the creek less than a mile away. That creek eventually gave itself to the Smoky Hill. The trees and brush along its banks offered the only firewood for them. When it ran out, the young, flat-nosed woman went in search of more.

She was gone what seemed like an eternity for him, Moser forced to sit there, watching his own breath curl up before his eyes—having to concentrate so that he would not stare at Jonah's face barely visible for the blankets they had piled cocoonlike about him as the wounded man shivered from an internal fire.

Artus dared not think about losing Jonah. That scared him more than losing his daddy right after the war. With the squaw gone off and Jonah delirious with fever, for the first time Artus felt the pinch of loneliness and wondered if he would make it out alive. Afraid of dying.

It was then that he remembered scraps and fragments of the war—unwillingly. But the memories gave him some solace, remembering how he had felt best when they were about to go into battle, close enough to the Yankees to hear the big cannon softening things up, maybe even close enough to see the Yankee battle-flags snapping far across some grassy field, through the leafy trees, maybe up some bare slope to the hilltop they would soon have to charge, racing into the face of grapeshot and canister and wheezing death cries from the long lines of bloodied men falling on either side of Artus, crying out and falling . . .

But the hardest times for Moser had been the waiting, and the marching to wait some more as the generals moved their regiments about, intent on probing for an offensive or intent on escaping to fight another day. That's when he had time to remember, like now. Time to remember and reflect and dwell on all that he had lived through.

Artus had learned never to grow too close to his fellow soldiers in that regiment and company and squad and mess. Never—because chances were they would be ripped from him by some bloody hand cutting a swath of gore and mangled flesh through what friendship had been kindled. Best not know their names.

Now his cousin lay dying on the floor of this tiny line shack beside a graded roadbed where the iron rails were to cross the creek come spring.

Spring.

But the woman returned, clutching the four corners of the one thin blanket she had taken along when she had left hours ago making Moser feel she was abandoning him at last.

"That's right!" he had yelled at her. "Damn squaw—who needs you anyway! You belong out here . . . so run off if you've a mind to!"

So now he felt bad about screaming at her from that narrow doorway, his words flung at her back, into the snowless wind that raised swirls of old, icy snow at her feet as she plodded into the gray world away from the creek, where there was hope of finding firewood.

But she was back, dropping her blanket bundle beside the tiny one-foot-square sheet-iron stove in the corner. It was the only thing warm enough in the shack to touch, though this morning they had run out of Moser's squaw wood. There remained but a few coals. He could see their brave, red struggle as she drew back the grate door with her knife handle.

"What's that?" he asked as she crumbled something from her blanket into the stove. Then he realized.

"That's a damned cow pie!" Moser exclaimed, wonder crossing his face, sensing some instant confusion—not certain if he should feel relief just yet.

"Buff . . ." She tried the word after a moment when the first crumbled chip smoldered and took to the heat of the coals. "Buff . . ."

"Buffalo?"

She nodded. Then crumbled more of the chip, using the tiny pieces as kindling in rebuilding the fire.

"Buffalo pie," he said to himself, taking his hands from the blanket and holding them near the front of that tiny stove. "By God—you might have saved you and me doing this, woman."

But of a sudden he felt guilty for saying that, his eyes drawn magnetically to the pale-skinned, mumbling cousin of his. Artus struggled, but with the woman's help he moved Hook closer to the stove. As she fed the stove from her cache of prairie fodder, Moser watched for some sign of improvement in Jonah. It never came as another twilight brought a brief period of setting, yellow light sprayed on the snow while the sun dipped out of the low-hung clouds on its path beyond the far mountains.

"We gotta do something," he whispered to her as the light seeped out of the sky. Soon only the glow from their fragrant warm stove illuminated this tiny spot in the middle of their world here beneath the dark nothingness of the overturned crock bowl.

As if she understood, the woman nodded, her plain face filled with resignation. "We go."

He felt instantly buoyed by her willingness to try, as if she perhaps knew all the better how to get out of the hole he had dug them into. After he and Jonah had found this place miles and miles west of Abilene and Jonah said he could ride no more with his shoulder killing him the way it was and they had to stop and get a few hours rest before pushing on.

But they had never pushed on, and Moser felt he was to blame. As Jonah sank deeper and deeper into his fitful fevers, Artus fell into a darker and darker despair, desperate of ever coming out of this shack and this strange land alive.

"Morning comes," Moser said, surprised at the sudden vitality to his words, "we go when the sun comes up." His hands pantomimed the sun rising to the east, where it always did at one side of the line shack during their nine days here.

Or was it ten now?

She shook her head. "No—we—go," she said, working over every word carefully with her tongue.

He was bewildered now. "We gotta go. Get him help. Back to Abilene if we have to. But somewhere."

"Two suns."

He worked on that, kneading it with his own chilled brain, then spoke her words. "Two suns . . . you mean two days!"

"Snow come. Two suns. We go two suns."

The snow had come that night. And the storm that blustered off and on had lasted for close to the two days she had predicted. It was a wonder to Artus how she had known that, and how she kept that fire going with those buffalo chips for three long nights and two short days when it grew only light enough to see a gray swirl from horizon to horizon.

Amazing that the Pawnee woman did not run out of buffalo chips before the first faint light of dawn streaking the east with pink orange.

Somehow they managed to get Hook onto his horse long enough for Moser to mount behind him. And there he cradled his shivering cousin against him and nudged the horse away from that line shack, pointing his nose toward the rising sun.

"No," she said to him as she urged the pack animal she rode beside his, holding a lead halter to Moser's horse. The woman pointed over her shoulder at the darker horizon.

Moser shook his head, nodded to Abilene, then glanced down at the pale, damp face wrapped in the blankets.

"No. Hays," she said, pointing west again.

"Hays?"

"Soldiers."

He swallowed hard. Fighting down the gall. "Yankee soldiers?"

"Go . . . Hays."

He looked back at the face of his cousin and decided then and there. "All right, woman. You kept us all alive, you did. So I don't suppose you're about to steer us wrong now, are you?"

"Hays."

"Yes," he replied. "Let's go to Hays."

It was late afternoon by the time the little party limped past the outer pickets and entered the cluster of neatly arranged buildings that made up Fort Hays, Kansas. No walled fort this, much to his surprise.

"You've business here?" asked the sergeant of the guard.

"Got a real sick man is what I got," Moser answered.

The sergeant waved a soldier over. "Take them to the infirmary. See what the surgeon can do."

As Moser and the woman turned their horses from the sergeant to follow the soldier who strode off on foot, the sergeant called out again.

"That woman can't go with you."

"Why not?"

"What's she?"

"Pawnee."

The soldier shook his head. "No, what's she to you anyway, Southerner?"

Moser drew himself up, his arms numb with ache and exhaustion from cradling his cousin within them. "She's the one saved our lives, Sergeant."

The soldier spat a brown stream onto the new snow. "All right. She's yours to look after. I'll have her gone from here in the blink of a gnat's eye I have trouble from either one of you."

"Thank you, Sergeant," Artus replied, wishing he could have said something else as he urged the weary horse away to follow the trooper.

Hospital stewards placed Jonah on a cot in a small shanty extension off the main ward of the infirmary. They said the regimental surgeon gave orders stating he did not want to take any chances that this civilian had something contagious. At the same time he quarantined Moser and the squaw in the same small ward with the feverish patient.

"What's his name?" the surgeon asked on his first visit to the canvas-roofed lean-to built against the west wall of the infirmary.

"Jonah Hook."

In the spread of yellow lamplight, the surgeon eyed Moser with consideration, then went back to examining the patient. "You're a Southerner?"

"Yes."

"Him too?"

"My cousin."

"Good lord!" the surgeon gasped, drawing back from Hook's shoulder wound. "This man's been shot!"

"I told the others—"

"Why didn't somebody say something to *me*?" The surgeon turned, flinging orders at his stewards, then leaned over Hook once more. He rolled the patient on his side to search for an exit wound. A steward came back with a rustle of his short white tunic, carrying a wood tray laden with bottles topped with glass stoppers. "We're going to have to probe this, Higgins. You and Nisley get this man ready while I go wash my hands."

"Damn," Moser muttered to the stewards as the surgeon whirled off into the infirmary. "During the war no doctor thought of washing his hands before he worked on a wounded soldier."

"Doc Porter's a different sort of animal," said Private Nisley as he and Higgins yanked at Hook's coat, shirt, and longhandles until they had their patient stripped to the waist.

The surgeon was a different sort at that. After sending Higgins to prepare a new bed in the main ward with the rest of the soldiers, Dr. Porter had Moser and Private Nisley pin the unconscious patient down before he placed a thin metal rod into the ugly, festering bullet wound.

"There it is," Porter said quietly, glancing at Moser with his eyes smiling, then quickly looking the woman up and down. "Who's she? She belong to him?"

"No. She just come with us after Jonah was shot. That woman's the reason we both got through the last thirteen days."

Porter raised his eyes, brow furrowing in a deep crease between the thick eyebrows. "He was shot two weeks ago?"

"Yes."

"Where?"

"Abilene."

Porter nodded to the woman. "Over the squaw?"

"Not really. Just some railroad fellas was setting on abusing her."

Porter had a delicate scalpel in his left hand, spreading the pink-and-purple bullet wound between the fingers of his right hand. "You mean this man stopped them from raping the Indian woman?"

"Yes, sir."

"You don't have to 'sir' me. What part you play in this?"

"I . . ." Moser said, and stopped, swallowing, his eyes staring back at the others in the tight room. Afraid of his answer, afraid if he didn't answer. "I likely killed one of 'em myself when the gunplay started."

"By lord, man—I'll buy you a drink when we're done here."

He didn't know what to feel at that moment: relief, wonder, excitement. Mostly relief that no one was going to hold him accountable to the law.

Porter gently dragged the tip of the scalpel back and forth down into the puss-filled wound, wrinkling his nose as he did so until he made contact with the bullet itself.

"There. Nisley, bring that probe here and work it down to where I've got the blade against this goddamned piece of lead."

The steward pushed the probe into the wound, carefully, as Hook mumbled and attempted to roll away from the pain.

"It's getting to be a little too much for his brain to take," Porter explained. "Hold him. Hold him now—we're almost done."

When he yanked the flattened piece of .44-caliber lead from the ugly hole, the surgeon plopped it into a small china cup on the tray beside the bed. It left a red streak down the inside of the cup.

"You don't have to worry about a constable or peace officer out here, mister," Porter said as he turned to Moser. "The only law west of Leavenworth is the army. And if the army isn't looking for you because it has a warrant outstanding for your desertion or because you hijacked an army payroll . . . then your gunplay over a Pawnee squaw doesn't mean anyone's riding hard up on your backside." He smiled at Moser, then turned to his stewards.

"Nisley, you show Higgins here how to get some sulfur worked down into that wound. It's a nasty, smelly thing, so work it in good. Then tent it best you can so it'll drain. I'll see to him first thing in the morning."

"He's gonna make it, Doc?"

"He lasted thirteen days without my help—he'll damn sure make it now," Porter said. "Now, c'mon, mister. Tell the woman to stay here with your cousin while you and me go get that drink I was fixing on having before you rode in."

"Whiskey? Is it really . . . good whiskey?"

Porter laughed in that way that made his Adam's apple bob a bit. "You grown particular, Southerner?"

"No, sir."

"Then come share a drink with me and regale me with your tales of the outside world. By lord, I'm starved for news of something other than army doings."

They started from the tiny room as the Pawnee woman settled back in the corner, pulling her blanket about her shoulders and intently watching the two hospital stewards in their ministrations over Jonah Hook.

"You said something about the army being the only law out here west of Leavenworth," Moser said. "What army you mean?"

Henry R. Porter stopped. "Why, the Seventh U.S. Cavalry."

"Sorry, but I ain't heard of you . . . of them."

The surgeon smiled, licking his dry lips in need of a drink. "Mister, there soon won't be a man who hasn't heard of this outfit. Not if General George Armstrong Custer has his say about it."

22

C HRISTMAS HAD COME and gone, and the celebration of New Year with it.

Fort Hays had done its best to bring 1867 in with a roar, out here in the middle of Indian country, in the middle of winter, in the middle of some place no man really wanted to be.

Jonah Hook and Artus Moser vowed that they would exchange gifts once they had made it back to a town. Their plan was to take the Smoky Hill Route, the stage and freight road that ran all the way west to Denver City. It was that Smoky Hill Route that the Kansas Pacific was to follow into the Rockies: grading bed, engineering bridges, softening slopes up and down the gradual rise to that mile-high settlement spreading boomlike along the South Platte and Cherry Creek.

But neither Jonah nor Artus ever talked of returning to work for that railroad as meat hunters. Only one time in the past week and a half of convalescing had Hook mentioned it as work come spring, both men agreeing that it would be pushing their luck. Jonah felt no need to say anything more.

"What did she eat while I was out of my head?" Hook asked his cousin early in January after he was up to sitting and taking solid food.

"She ate everything you left on your plate, cousin," Moser answered with a grin. "One time that soldier, Nisley—"

180

"The fella who's good at cards."

"That's the one. He come back in sooner'n she thought he would, and he caught her scraping food outta your bowl faster'n a hen pecking grit."

Jonah looked at the corner where the woman sat, huddled in her blanket and wool capote, legs drawn up to the side, squawlike. "She been getting enough, you figure?"

Moser said, "From then on, Nisley took over duty on feeding her too. He always brought two bowls of mash or ribs or fatback when he come to feed you. And always set one bowl in front of her. She ain't yet gone to bone, Jonah. Not by a long chalk."

He sighed, his head going back against the pillow. "I owe her, Artus."

"We both owe her," Moser replied. "Likely, she figures she was just paying you back for helping her, cousin."

"I help those I can . . . until I can help those of my own."

He was slow healing, not like when he had been younger, or even when he had been winged in the war. But that festering bullet in his shoulder had taken most everything out of him during those long days; it had brought fever to his mind and an endless series of nightmares drawn sepia-toned against the back of his heated, fitful thoughts. Even now, he still dreaded closing his eyes for fear of the visions of war and guerrillas and those broken windows of his Missouri home with their raggedy curtains drifting in and out on the cold breeze. Hook had always considered himself a strong man in that way—and would not let another know of his fear. But he wondered how long he would carry this horror inside.

Jonah knew that horror would plague him until he found them all.

"Your cousin tells me you're quite a hand at cards," said surgeon Henry Porter late one afternoon as the sun began to set at the edge of a clear, cold sky.

"Never learned at home," Hook explained with a grin on his wolfish face, yellowed eyes glowing as Porter turned up a nearby lamp. "Mama wouldn't allow my daddy such instruments of the devil's work."

"You learn in the war?"

"Most times there was little else for us to do—waiting to walk here or there, either attacking or retreating. Only to wait some more after the fighting was done."

"You figure you're up to playing?"

A ragged piece of Jonah's soul leapt. "When?"

"Tonight. Some of the others—we get together every two weeks or so. Usually after the paymaster's been to the fort and each of us is feeling flush, ready to spread some of our meager pay among friends of our choosing."

"They won't mind, will they? Me being . . ."

"A Southerner? No, not at all. In fact, one of my best friends is a Missourian, like yourself, Jonah. Captain Frederick Benteen. He's always anxious to play as much as he can, as there's talk that he'll be sent farther west come spring."

"What's west of here?"

Porter wagged his head. "Between us and Denver City—not a lot but the open jaws of hell itself. Benteen hears he'll be assigned to garrison Fort Wallace out on the Denver Road."

"Tough duty?"

Porter rose from the side of the bed. "It's all tough, Jonah. Otherwise, wouldn't you be soldiering—instead of making a handy target of yourself?"

He had to admit he liked Henry Porter. There were times after Porter finished rounds in the early evening that Hook came to know the surgeon's habit of returning to his monkish cell and there pulling a bottle from inside one of his dress boots. It became a habit with Hook to thus time his visits with Porter. The surgeon had made it clear he was a social animal who hated drinking alone.

Hook liked the genuineness of the man.

"That arm and shoulder of yours are likely to be stiff for some time to come, Jonah," said the surgeon that evening as he spread a gray army blanket over a table soon to see chips and cards and drinking glasses.

"How long?"

Porter stopped, holding in his hands four small china ashtrays. "It may never be the same again. I don't want you to expect that it will respond to you the way it did before you were shot."

Hook felt the severe pinch of fear cross his chest. He looked down at the sling that cradled the arm. "But I got feeling, and I move it every day."

"I know. But—that bullet sitting in there for that long, the way I had to tear at the muscle to get that sonofabitch out—all of that took its toll. It'll be some time before you get all that strength back. And it may never come back good as new."

Jonah settled into a chair, with his right arm turning an empty glass round and round, staring at his distorted reflection beneath the lamplight. "It'll come back, Doc. I know you done everything you could for me. So it'll come back in its own time."

"That's right." Porter smiled, watching the woman settle herself in the corner out of the light. "In its own time, Jonah."

The woman was always there, wherever Jonah went. He had come to accept that, then almost ignored it, taking it for granted that she followed him everywhere. Silent.

The others came in not long after Moser showed up, gone and back again from Hays City not far away, there to see about buying a pair of holsters that Jonah wanted for the two of them. Better to carry the belt guns in them than stuffed in the waistband of their britches. They were gleaming, freshly soaped, and heavy rigs. Artus claimed he would need time getting used to wearing his.

At the table, most fired up Porter's cigars as a means of socializing, smoking the fragrant cheroots while they sipped from the glasses each man kept filled from bottles newly purchased this payday. Hands were shaken all around with the newcomers. Most already knew of the two civilians and the Pawnee woman staying at Porter's infirmary, by the grace of the surgeon's largess.

Major Wycliffe Cooper was the brooding one who said little, Hook discovered. Playing his cards conservatively and drinking twice as much as anyone else. He was not a happy sort and made a disagreeable drunk as the night wore on and the room began to stink of stale sweat and cigar smoke and spilled whiskey. Yet not even Cooper dared bother the woman once he had asked the reason for her presence and Porter had explained she belonged to the buffalo hunter named Jonah Hook.

"Yes, I've heard of you," Cooper admitted, as he dragged red-rimmed eyes from the corner where the woman sat watching the white men. "Rode in here with a bullet still in you. There's a story there, my friend. Share it with us."

"I'm not your friend." Hook said it as pleasantly as he could, yet the words possessed an edge. "And there's no story to tell."

Cooper laid his cards down, bleary-eyed from the smoke and alcohol. "I'll not play a gentleman's game with a liar."

"Major," Captain Frederick W. Benteen said, putting his hand on Cooper's shoulder. "We came here to play cards, and by God—I don't want you causing any trouble for Porter's guest here. I'm bound and determined to get some of my money back that I've lost to Hook here tonight."

Cooper sank back into his chair. "I'm done for the evening. The rest of you can stay and play with this—this civilian. I'm going for some air and then to bed."

In silence the officer saw himself out, openly glaring at the woman as he dragged his long wool coat onto his arms.

"A shame," Porter commented sourly. "I think Custer's tolerance is running a short fuse for Major Cooper's drunkenness."

There followed a long moment of silence as each man dealt with his own thoughts.

"Let's play cards, gentlemen," the handsome Captain George W. Yates suddenly suggested, rubbing his hands together. "I feel I too might be dipping into Benteen's personal coffers this night. If Mr. Hook lets me!"

The rest at the table chuckled. A few raised their glasses.

"About time too," Jonah said. "The last game of cards I was playing, I had to leave before collecting my winnings."

"That the game earned you your bullet?" asked Lieutenant Myles Moylan, adjutant to Custer.

"Yes," Hook answered without hesitation. "Instead of gold, you might say I carried away a little lead for my trouble."

That eased them some that first night, as did the way Hook carefully let go most of his winnings through the final hour of the game, losing enough of what he had won earlier in the night that no man left hard of feelings or hesitant to return come next payday.

But that payday was Jonah's last at Fort Hays. There was nothing more Porter could do with the bullet wound. The rest was up to Hook now. Besides, word had it that the regiment's lieutenant colonel was growing anxious to know why Porter had taken in three civilian boarders, feeding them from his own dwindling personal pantry.

"You'll find something useful to do with yourself for the rest of the winter?" Porter asked that February day as Hook, Moser, and the woman prepared to ride out.

"Never fear, Doctor."

"It's not safe west of here."

Moser glanced at Hook. Then away.

"We're not going west of here," Jonah replied. "Find something to do until spring comes."

"Then what? Go back to looking for your family?"

"I've got to try."

"Don't waste your life, trying to find out what happened to theirs," Porter said as Jonah went to the saddle, slowly rotating the tender shoulder once he was settled.

"I don't figure any day I have now is a waste, Doctor. Every day's a gift from here on out. Owe my life to that squaw and to you too."

"Word has it there'll be work here come spring."

"Not interested in soldiering."

"You've told me of your scouting with Bridger up in the Dakotas," Porter said, backing a few steps to gaze up at the horseman in the bright winter sunshine. "I figured you could put to good use what you learned from him and that character Sweete."

He remembered now—so long without remembering—and touched the small rawhide-and-quill medicine wheel suspended from his neck on a cord there beneath his shirt. "Shadrach Sweete."

"They'll be hiring scouts for the coming campaign. A man like you can use the work."

"And the money!" Moser said.

"Till spring, Doctor!" Hook cried out as he reined about and set his horse in motion, pulling along the packhorse. Behind him came Moser, and the Pawnee woman riding bareback on the animal that of a time had been Moser's pack animal stolen from the Creeks down in Indian Territory.

"Till spring!"

She came to him again as she had those times before, most every day when he sent the other man away to hunt or search for firewood or peel cottonwood bark for the horses to eat.

She called him Hook. And her heart had grown big and warm for him. The way she grew moist for him whenever those yellow eyes told her he must have her.

He called her by her name now, ever since leaving the soldier fort she knew as Hays. Called her Grass Singing in his tongue, unable to pronounce it in her Pawnee language. It was enough that he called her Grass Singing and held her close beneath the blankets in this dugout the three of them had made against the side of a hill where erosion had started to form this small cavern they had called their home these past two moons since leaving the soldier fort.

The three had lived as her own people had lived, she told herself whenever she began to miss the village and her friends. But then she remembered her mother and aunt, and how they had been thrown away by the tribe once their husbands had been killed by Lakota. No longer could the women live within the Pawnee circle, not without a man to care for them.

Grass Singing had a man to care for her. Hook, she called him. It made a ringing sound on the back of her tongue.

Many white men had lain atop her, but he was the first she had grown to care for before she ever received him. Looking back, she had come to care for him that terrible day the white men shot their guns at one another in the drinking place, the day she ran from that awful place, following the two white men who had helped her. Not knowing anything else to do—afraid to stay there more than she was afraid to ride into the unknown with the pair.

He had not clawed at her the way others had. Still, she sensed his overpowering intensity as he rode atop her and finished quickly, sooner than she had wanted. He had slept against her that first day, still asleep when the other white man returned to the dugout with fresh meat. She was not embarrassed, for the blankets were over them, and it seemed the other white man knew anyway what would eventually come to be between her and the man Hook.

With little of the white tongue that she could remember, the three of them mostly spoke in sign that Hook taught the other man through those long weeks of waiting for the prairie to green and the winds to come about out of the south, once more blessing this land with warmth.

She did not expect him to care for her the way she had come to feel for him in her heart. It was enough that he was here with her now, touching her body the way she had always wanted it to be touched, making her breasts and nipples alive with tension and desire, his fingers stroking the inside of her thighs before he drove himself into her moistness as she sang out in maddening fury for him.

And she came to love the way he cradled her after they were finished while his flesh grew small once more. Never before had any man done more than finish with her and pull up his britches and be gone.

Until Hook had come along, she had expected no more than what she had watched the ponies do back at her village that moved with the seasons—hunting buffalo and fighting Lakota and Shahiyena.

She did not want this winter to end, knowing when it did that he would be gone from her, perhaps never to return. But Grass Singing kept her sorrow to herself and cherished each day with the man she had secretly given her heart to . . . she would not trouble him with her love or make demands on him.

Outside the snow was melting and the prairie had begun to green. The entrance to their dugout dripped with the rhythm of the changing seasons as the buds on the willow and alder began to make their appearance. More sign each day of this prairie coming back to life after a winter's sleep.

Inside, there in the private place that was her heart, Grass Singing wept with the changing seasons.

23

"WHAT YOU MEAN you can't use him?" Jonah Hook asked the two soldiers and long-bearded, unkempt civilian seated behind the table in the shade of this fort porch.

"Your friend there—"

"He's my goddamned cousin!" Hook snapped.

The officer sighed, smoothing his waxed mustaches this early spring day and continued, "Your cousin doesn't have enough experience out in this country to warrant the army hiring him as a scout."

"What am I going to do?" Artus Moser asked in a husky whisper, his eyes telling of his fear. "You got hired on, Jonah."

Hook stared at the toes of his boots, bewildered.

They had come here counting on the both of them getting hired on to scout for the forthcoming campaign. When the chief of scouts and the officers here gathered learned of Hook's months of experience along the Emigrant Road and with General Connor's Powder River Expedition as a U.S. Volunteer, not to mention the fact that he had been employed last fall as a buffalo hunter for the Kansas Pacific Railroad, the army promptly snatched up this tall, gangly Southerner the way summer rain fell in this part of the plains: fast and furious.

Hiring Moser as a scout was a different matter altogether.

"Why can't you use him?" Hook asked of the long-bearded, middle-aged frontiersman who sat quietly chewing on the stump of a much-battered briar pipe.

"I've tried to explain that to you," interrupted the double-barred officer.

"What if he rides along with me—at no pay?"

The officer slammed an open fist down on the table. "I've told you, mister. Now—if you keep at this, you'll likely find yourself without a job as a scout."

"I doubt that, Lieutenant," said the frontiersman, speaking for the first time, and getting a stony glare from the officer for his trouble.

The soldier grimaced and said, "I've been given the task of helping you by General Custer himself—"

"And a fine job you're doing too. But I've been hired by the general as chief of scouts, and I'll hire and fire my own scouts, thank you." He turned back to Hook. "Besides, any man who went along on that Powder River campaign had to know Gabe Bridger and Shad Sweete."

Hook smiled, relief washing over him suddenly. "Damn right I knowed both—and those two taught me some on that expedition."

"That's why I hired you, Hook. You got the makings. It's just that your cousin here don't know a Sioux or Cheyenne from squat."

"He fought in the war."

"That was a white man's war." The frontiersman tried to make it come out gently, packing his smoldering pipe with a fingertip.

"If he don't get to come with me—I s'pose I gotta move along."

"Just as well," growled the officer, dipping his pen into the inkwell and preparing to scratch the name from the rolls.

The frontiersman clamped a hand around the soldier's wrist. "You're fixing to walk out on a good job if this bunch don't hire on your cousin?"

"I am. Always enough for a man to do out here. I wasn't looking for my last job when it found me. I s'pose I can always find something to eat and a place to sleep while I'm waiting for something else to come along."

"Good," the frontiersman said. "Both of you'll do."

Jonah Hook was drawn up short by that. "You mean Artus can come along as a scout?"

"No, I didn't say that. But I know the wagon master, named Grigsby, is looking for teamsters and herders for the remuda we'll be wrangling along with the wagon train. If Moser here can handle a wagon or horses—he has him the chance to work with Grigsby."

"Where we find this wagon master?"

He jabbed the air with the stem of his pipe. "Off yonder."

Hook glanced in that direction, toward the trees that lined the nearby

Smoky Hill River. Then he held out his hand to the chief of scouts. "Thank you, mister. Didn't catch your name."

"Joe Milner."

"You're the one they call California Joe?"

He beamed. "That's right."

"Shad Sweete told me some about you! Knew you up to Oregon country before he give it up and come back to the mountains."

Milner was smiling broadly, his stained teeth dull against his dusty beard. "After me and Shad helped Ol' Zach settle them Mexicans down, I got me a pretty wife out to the California diggings before moseying up to Oregon country to try my hand at settling down. Nancy Emma is her name—and she give me a passel of young'uns before I decided I had to come back to these parts just like Shad done. Something about all this open country."

"Ain't it true," Hook replied.

"I'd like to palaver later with you boys," Joe said as he rocked back in the chair again, stuffing the pipe stem between lips all but hidden beneath by his overgrown mustache. "Catch up on what ol' Sweete is up to. You both come round."

"I'll look to do that before evening."

They had made it through the worst of the winter. That was enough for any man to take some pride in. Those two weeks lost to him with the bullet-fever in that line shack, then the long time mending with regimental surgeon Porter at the Fort Hays infirmary, and finally the last two months spent getting through the waning days of winter in that dugout they had made for themselves against the side of a hill overlooking Big Creek, not many miles from Fort Hays itself. There had been some small measure of security felt by both Hook and Moser in staying those last violent months of winter near the frontier fort. At times the pair had run across small patrols of cavalry riding this way or that on one errand or another—always seen in the distance, loping along in their column of twos, rarely with a guidon or flag fluttering above their determined purpose.

Were it not for Moser's skill in tracking deer and finding antelope out on this rolling tableland of central Kansas, they might not have fared as well as they had through that prairie winter. But both men had emerged from the dark days and endless nights of that dugout renewed in some unspoken way. Clearly closer to one another.

With that time behind them both, Jonah better understood his cousin's need of him here in this foreign land, and dared not tug on that bond hard enough to snap it in two like a rawhide whang.

And without saying anything, Artus showed he understood his cousin's need for the woman through those long weeks. Hook was clearly grieving in his own way the loss of Gritta, perhaps drowning himself in the squaw's flesh in some way to numb the pain come of the loss of his family.

Moser put his own thoughts on the coming campaign, his muscles to the task, thereby finding a way to salve his own wounds brought of deep loss.

In this late March there were fourteen hundred soldiers gathering for the coming campaign General Winfield S. Hancock would lead. Besides infantry foot soldiers, Lieutenant Colonel George Armstrong Custer would ride at the head of eight companies of his Seventh Cavalry: the sword Hancock intended using to punish the Sioux and Cheyenne who had been raiding and killing, stealing, raping and kidnapping up and down central and western Kansas.

Every bit as pressing to the morale of the army itself was the news of a late-December disaster now common knowledge on the high plains. For what was still an inexplicable reason, Captain William Judd Fetterman had disobeyed the orders of his commanding officer and led another eighty soldiers and two civilians to their deaths up on the Bozeman Road, lured into a seductive trap miles from Fort Phil Kearny. Two thousand warriors wiped out the entire command in less than thirty minutes of battle.

The frontier army clearly chafed at the bit, anxious to even the score.

While the military on the plains for the past two years had labored to separate itself from the wholesale slaughter of Indians committed at Sand Creek by some Colorado volunteer militia, the leadership in both the War Department and in the Department of the Missouri were not much concerned now in any distinction between the horse-mounted warriors committing the depredations and the noncombatants back in the villages.

"We must act with vindictive earnestness against the Sioux, even to their extermination, men, women, and children," wrote William Tecumseh Sherman to his superior back in Washington City, Ulysses S. Grant.

Indeed, General John B. Sanborn, one of the commissioners appointed to interview frontier officers in his investigation of the Fetterman Massacre found that, "Army officers of high grade openly proclaim their intentions to shoot down any Indian they see, and say that they instruct their men to do likewise."

Sales of weapons and ammunition to the Indians were suspended in the Department of the Platte in July of 1866. Yet it was not until January of 1867 that General Hancock issued the same order forbidding such sales in his Department of the Missouri. Forever the one given to thoughtful deliberation, Hancock had waited until both his superiors in Washington City, Grant and Sherman, agreed on the need for keeping weapons out of Indian hands.

• • •

"*You hear the* news?" Moser asked.

Jonah Hook turned as his cousin came up. "What news?" He went back to lashing his bedroll into a gum poncho.

"About that Dakota Territory where you was last year. The Powder River country and all."

"What about it?"

"Whole fort's buzzing about it. Half a regiment wiped out by Injuns up there just afore Christmas."

He stopped, slowly looking over his shoulder at the man who cast a shadow over him this early morning. "Where?"

"Place called Fort Phil Kearny they say," Moser explained. "Cap'n named Fetterman marched off over a ridge with his men—and it was over in less'n half an hour."

Hook wagged his head in disbelief. "Where's this fort?"

"They say northwest of the Powder. Near a river called the Tongue."

"I know that country."

"That's why I come to tell you soon as I heard."

A fear suddenly clutched him in its talons. "Any civilians killed with them soldiers?"

"Word has it two was killed. They was all butchered like hogs for slaughter, Jonah."

"I don't doubt it, cousin." He swallowed hard, rising. "I had two friends up there scouting for the army."

"Bridger and Sweete?"

He nodded. "Lord, I pray they weren't the ones butchered with those soldier-boys gone off marching where they shouldn't."

Moser wrung his hands in front of him, searching for the right thing to say. "Then just what the hell *we* doing—marching off with these soldiers?"

Jonah gazed off onto the distant prairie, past the fort grounds and buildings and spring-dampened parade. "Let's just hope this bunch of soldiers is more'n those Injuns wanna tackle right now."

"Hope, hell, Jonah! I'm all for praying!"

The wagon boss named Grigsby hollered for his men to account for themselves at the wagon yard, where there was no lack of work backing mules and horses into their traces and trees in preparation for this first day's march from Fort Hays into Indian country. Off Moser went, with Jonah tying his horse near California Joe's and Jack Corbin's.

"I'll be off yonder for a bit," Hook told them.

"Hancock's got us pulling out soon," Milner replied. "We're leading his column, Hook. So don't you be late."

Jonah grinned. "Never."

He found her minutes later, where he knew he would.

She was sitting near the dugout where they had fared the winter together, squatting on a buffalo robe, her legs tucked at her side as she drove a bone-handled awl through the thin buckskin she had tanned herself that spring. The Pawnee woman did not immediately look up, though Hook was sure she had heard him draw near.

"Grass Singing," he said as he settled before her. Still she would not look at him.

Jonah took her chin in his hand, raising her face to his. Only then did he understand why she had been reluctant to look at him.

"You've been crying," he said in English.

She gently pulled her chin from his rough palm and blinked her eyes clear, then went back to poking animal sinew strung with large, moss green beads through the hole she had made with the awl.

"I don't know how to tell you this," he said, himself searching for words that would touch her as his hands moved silently before him in sign. A part of him withered when he realized she was not watching his hands, much less comprehending most of his white man's tongue.

"Hell, some of this you'll understand, I hope. The rest—well, the rest I hope you'll figure out down the road some."

He reached for her hand. She pulled it away as the first large drop of salty moisture spilled down a cheek, no longer held in check, pooled in those black-cherry eyes. Jonah took her hand in his a second time, and now she did not resist.

"I got to go, Grass Singing."

"Take me," she said, her eyes imploring him as they flooded.

"Can't. This is war."

"My people take women . . . families on war path."

"My people don't. You'll stay behind. Go find what's left of your family in Abilene." And the cold of it hit him as surely as the rising of the warm spring sun caressed the side of his face. "Maybe you can understand I got to keep moving. If I don't, I can't ever hope to find my own family."

She set her beading down, using her hands to sign. "Your family is no more."

His mind struggled with the concepts she formed with her hands. "No more family," he repeated, then comprehended. "It's not true. Who says this?"

Grass Singing said it aloud. "Moser."

"He lies, woman," he said it aloud too, forgetting to sign. "My family is alive. Somewhere. I'll find them. I'll find every one of them."

"You go on a fool's journey," she signed. "I have prayed to the Great Everywhere that it would not be your final journey."

He snorted self-consciously. "Me? No—I'm not ready to die."

Her eyes moistened more. "There is the smell of death all around you."

"That's just the blood you're smelling—"

"I talk now of the death spirits. Their stench is heavy around you, Hook." The last word she spoke aloud, as there was no sign for his name.

While the rising sun warmed his face, nonetheless a chill splashed down his spine as she said it. Afraid to admit that she might know something he did not. He chose to leave, and now.

Hook stood, reached for her hands, and pulled her up into a tight embrace.

"I will not die, Grass Singing." He spoke into the top of her head where it rested below his bearded chin. "And come the time when I ride back through this country, I'll look for you. You have helped me live—not just this bullet hole"—and he tapped his chest—"but the big hole put in my heart when my family was took from me."

She pulled away from him to sign, "You grow old looking for a few pebbles lost at the bottom of a great pond."

He caught himself before he struck her, his hand hung in midair near her cheek, looking down at her moist eyes.

"You got no right to tell me what to believe in . . . tell me what to give up on."

He whirled from her, moving to his horse.

"Hook!"

She hurried after him, flung herself, and wrapped her arms about him before he could rise to the saddle. She sobbed openly, the wild keening of a squaw losing her man.

"Grass Singing—I want to come back," he explained, crushing her against him. He kissed her gently, then held her at arm's length as she stood there, arms at her side, sobbing. "But I can't come back to you until I have this done and over with. Some way . . . you try to understand."

Hook was in the saddle quickly, hammering the horse's flanks with his boot heels, intent on hurrying as fast as he could from this place. Hoping she would in some way understand his quest.

Hoping too that she was wrong—praying now that he did not carry the stench of death on him.

24

"I HEAR THE pickings are good up there in Kansas," said the tall, long-haired, bald-topped Jubilee Usher in his soft-edged yet cannonlike voice.

Boothog Wiser longed to have the power to move men as Usher did, to wrap them up into his powerful presence and *move* them. Yet Wiser had to be content threatening this band of freebooters and cutthroats. Whereas Usher motivated through awe, Wiser maintained control only through fear.

Usher laid his big arm over the beefy shoulder of one of the band of scouts under Captain Eloy Hastings newly returned to Indian Territory from a long reconnaissance. "Fordham here tells me the country's wide open up there."

Riley Fordham smiled. Wiser couldn't blame him. Any man among them would kill to bask in the glow of their leader's bright light.

"Tomorrow morning, we're pulling out," Usher went on. "Riding north. The railroad's up there in Kansas, boys. And you know what that means."

"Whiskey!"

"Women too!"

"Yes," Usher goaded them. "All that and more. It's about time this bunch had a holiday, don't you think?"

The roar of their voices was deafening, that band of more than forty now backslapping and shoulder pounding, dancing little jigs in anticipation of the hurraw they would have themselves once up there in Kansas Territory.

"I want the harness soaped and the wagon hubs greased," Usher commanded, bringing some order to the raucous celebration. "Work first, boys. Then we play!"

Usher turned away from the celebrants, dragging Riley Fordham with him as he stepped back toward Wiser. "C'mon, Major Wiser. Let's go have a drink with Riley."

"A drink, Colonel Usher?" Fordham asked.

"Some of my best."

Fordham licked his lips. "I'd drink your whiskey anytime. Not like the rest of that mule piss the rest of us been drinking."

When they stood beneath the awning of Usher's tent, each holding a china cup at the end of an arm, Usher's Negro manservant poured the whiskey red as a bay horse from a decanter. Wiser watched Fordham close his eyes and drink in the hefty aroma of the aged whiskey.

Usher raised his cup. "To your successful journey, Riley."

"Yes, sir, Colonel."

"To Kansas, Colonel," Wiser said as he brought his cup to his lips. He savored these moments shared with Usher, especially the bonded whiskey. Moments when Usher was as smooth as old scotch whiskey.

"Yes, Riley. Tell us about your trip to Kansas with Captain Hastings," Usher suggested as he took his cup from his lips.

Fordham swiped a hand across his mouth, his eyes already alive with the potency of the whiskey. "Like a juicy fruit, Colonel. Ready to drop into our hands."

Usher smiled the benign smile that made his whole face glow. "How far has the railroad penetrated?"

"They must be starting work by now, Colonel. West of Abilene. Track runs along the Smoky Hill River."

"Headed west for Colorado?" Wiser asked.

"You remember Colorado, don't you, Mr. Wiser?"

Boothog had fond recollections of the high country and the gold camps and the women who flocked to the places where men came to dig gold from the hard earth. He liked remembering the women. Times were this flat, rolling land ate at Boothog's soul the way this running and hiding, and running again did. Times were he longed for those high places where the powdered, painted women flocked, there to do things to a man he had only dreamed of.

"Maybe Kansas has some women worth the trouble, Colonel," Wiser replied.

Usher smiled, his big teeth brilliant in that shining face. "A man can find that sort of woman anywhere, Major."

"They come west, right along with the track crews, Colonel," said Fordham. "Chippies and the gamblers and the drummers all come marching right along with the railroad."

"You see, Major Wiser. In Kansas we will find your type of woman."

"Just once, Colonel—for once in my life I'd like to spread the legs on a woman like that one you're keeping all to yourself."

Boothog watched the grin drain from Usher's face like water from a busted pail.

"She is not your kind—and you'll not entertain such thoughts ever again, Mr. Wiser. That woman is truly a different sort, meant for the likes of me. Are we agreed on that?"

Wiser realized his mouth had gone dry. "We're agreed, Colonel."

"Make this the last time we will talk on this subject," Usher said as Wiser's eyes flicked to Fordham's face with the movement of a hummingbird. "We are different people, Major. And we have different needs. Yours, well—yours are more primitive. While mine . . . what I have with that woman is something spiritual. Divine and ordained—we are truly bound to one another in the manner of the temple wed. Yet you likely don't understand. Nor will you ever."

"I'll never, never cross you, Jubilee."

"Colonel Usher," Jubilee snapped, the sharp narrowing of his eyes indicating to Wiser that there was another man in their presence.

"Yes, Colonel," Boothog replied, remembering that other passion Usher possessed: always being addressed by his rank in front of the men. No matter when he and Wiser were alone—Boothog could address him as he pleased. But whenever they were before the men . . .

Usher turned and retrieved a long leather cylinder from the field table beneath the canvas canopy. From it he pulled a series of maps, found the one desired, then laid it flat upon the table, placing lunch dishes and an inkwell at the corners.

"Fordham, come over here and show us where you were on your journey to Kansas."

Wiser watched as the two of them hunched over the map, Fordham moving his finger this way, then that, at times a little uncertain.

"I don't read much, Colonel—"

"It doesn't matter, Riley."

"But this looks familiar . . . the rivers and creeks here."

"Good. Now show us where the outlying settlements are from here, and here. With the railroad coming their way—it means gold for us. Lots of gold."

Wiser watched and listened as Fordham went on, explaining the fruits of his scout north into Kansas Territory. But Boothog listened only halfheartedly. He glanced at the nearby tent flaps, not daring to let Usher catch him looking. Yet it excited him nonetheless to know that behind those flaps was the light-haired, blue-eyed Missouri woman they had captured two years before. He had rarely seen her since—only moving from the tent to Usher's ambulance, where she rode hidden, always with a cloak hood over her head, helped along by Usher and the Negro manservant. And Wiser never heard her anymore. In the beginning she had cried out each time Usher climbed atop her. But it hadn't taken long for that to come to an end.

She rarely made a peep now.

Still, Wiser hungered for her. There was something in the woman that he had never found in the others. But then, the rest had all had many men before him. They were used, soiled merchandise. Not like the settler woman.

That was why Wiser wanted the girl, the woman's daughter—in the worst way. More and more over the last months, he found himself getting dry-mouthed just looking at the young girl. Waking up at nights, knowing he had dreamt of her. Wondering if he could wait long enough, till she was old enough and Usher would finally give her over to him. Then at last, Boothog would have one of the two things he wanted most.

Telling himself he must be satisfied with only one of them.

Simply because Major Lemuel Wiser couldn't bring himself to believe he would ever have the nerve to kill Jubilee Usher.

Shad Sweete thought he recognized something familiar about the distant, thin rail of a man at first, then put the nudge of recollection out of his mind. It simply couldn't be.

Not that the rider didn't look one whole hell of a lot like someone he knew—or had known—but that it just didn't seem likely to find the man out here. Must be the sun playing tricks on him.

No way Jonah Hook would be riding in behind Milner and James Butler Hickok, with the rest of those civilian scouts. Hook had gone back home to Missouri, and Sweete doubted there would be anything that could drag the

Confederate off his farm, what with the way he talked and talked about his family and his place all through those months they had shared out on the Emigrant Road and up to the Powder River country. Likely nothing could shake Hook loose.

"Shad Sweete!"

"That you, Joe?" he called back to California Joe Milner.

The long-bearded plainsman brought his mule to a halt beside Sweete there at the edge of the parade of Fort Harker, central Kansas. "Before you go to hugging your how-dos on me, I figured I'd better ask you if you know this young fella. He claims you do."

"Howdy, Shad," the thin one said, kicking a leg over the saddle and dropping to the ground on both feet.

"Jonah?"

"By damned," Joe said, "you do know one another!"

Shad embraced Hook fiercely. "What the hell you—"

"I don't think Joe believed me when I told him I'd rid with you and Bridger," Hook said. "Gabe here with you?"

"He's gone back east, Jonah," Shad said quietly. "Figures his time might come soon."

"He dying?"

"Not just yet. But he's give up on scouting for a time. Now answer my question, boy—what the devil brings you here when you got family back to home depending on you?"

Shad watched as Jonah glanced at Milner, and Milner urged his mule away with the rest of the scruffy civilian scouts James Butler Hickok had brought in from Hays to join up with Custer's chief of scouts.

Jonah's eyes narrowed. "They're gone, Shad."

"Dead?"

He shook his head. "I wish I knew. Not a trace."

"Up and gone—like smoke?"

"Stole."

"Took off, like prisoners?"

"Or worse."

"You know who?"

"A little. A bad bunch running through Missouri there at the end of the war. Taking what they wanted from farms and settlements."

"Heard tales there was a lot of that," Sweete replied, not knowing what else to say.

Inside were a hundred feelings felt for the young man right now—but none which Shad could put to word. Instead, he drew Jonah near again. A fierce hug.

"Damn, it's good to see you, Shad." He pulled back, dragging a hand angrily beneath his nose. "Want you meet a cousin of mine. Hired on for the wagon train."

"What you been doing since last I saw you?" Shad asked, eyeing the columns of cavalry pulling in behind the scouts, marching across the parade and preparing to go into camp on the far side of Fort Harker.

"Got back home finally, that winter. Found my place empty, almost like it was a coffin somebody had dragged the body out of." Hook described the scene, kneading the leather rein in his hands as the spring sun loped down into the west. "Run onto my cousin at the place, and we went into town to try to find out something."

"Anybody know what come of your family?"

"Only the old sheriff. Enough to send us off on the trail of that bunch into Indian Territory."

"Wagh!" Sweete grunted. "That's some. Likely that's where the trail up and disappeared."

"Nobody likely to talk to me and Artus down there. Finally run out of money and come north to work for the railroad."

"Hard doin's, Jonah."

"Hunted buffalo, Shad."

"Don't that beat all by a long chalk now!"

"Then freeze-up come, and we hunkered down in a little dugout near Fort Hays for the winter."

"Just the two of you?"

He dug a toe into the rain-dampened earth. "Had a Pawnee gal with me."

"Been some time, Jonah—you without a woman. How'd you run onto her?"

"That's a story for another time, how I come to be toting her out of Abilene. That's where I first run onto Hickok. There was some bad characters and . . . the woman saved my life." Hook yanked aside his shirt and longhandles to show the puckered bullet hole high in his chest. "Army doctor pulled the bullet out over to Fort Hays."

"Lordee," Shad whispered. "Some winter doings, weren't they?"

"When green-up come, we needed work, and run onto California Joe, said he was hired on to work for Hickok for this big army march against the Injuns."

"Hickok remember you?"

"When he found out I'd hired on to scout for this march, with California Joe, Hickok told the rest I'd do to back him up in a hot fight of it."

"Hickok's all right, Jonah. A square shoot any day. Damn! But this ain't the first time we've marched with the army together!"

"Damn well pray it's the last, Shad."

"You eat since breakfast?"

When Hook wagged his head, Sweete said, "Then come along with me."

"I'll wait for my cousin and then be along."

"We'll wait together," Shad replied.

"I'll find you, old man."

"Likely you won't, Jonah." He flung an arm southwest of the fort. "Camped down there."

"You staying with some of those Injuns down there on the creek?"

"Got the woman along. Our girl too."

"They come north with you?"

"Gathered 'em up after last winter and moseyed north, fixing to find work myself. Never would I thought that we'd run onto one another this way. And from the looks of you, Jonah Hook is needing some fattening up at Toote Sweete's kettle."

"Good vittles?"

"Does a badger ever back down? None finer. C'mon, we'll gather up that cousin of yours over to the wagon yard and get down to the camp."

Minutes later the three were among the handful of smoked-hide lodges, dogs barking, the half-wild animals heeling them as they sniffed the newcomers. A few barefoot children dashed across the sodden prairie and pounded earth surrounding each lodge.

"Which one of these is your daughter?" Jonah asked.

"Which?" Shad replied, then laughed, head thrown back for a moment. "Ain't none of these children, Jonah." He pointed. "That's my child—there."

Coming head down out through a nearby lodge door, then standing full height to a little over five feet, she was clearly no child.

"*That's* your daughter?" Moser asked, the first of the pair able to squeak out the question.

"Pipe Woman is twenty summers this year. Helps her mama around the lodge now. Too old to be running with the children."

Jonah swallowed hard. "That ain't no child, Shad. She's gotta be the most beautiful Injun I ever saw."

"Wait'll you see her mama. Toote!" he called out. Shad's daughter raised her head from her work as the men approached, her own broad smile brightening the high-cheeked face, eyes bouncing from one to the other of the two newcomers politely, then finding the earth once more in that traditional coy manner of her people.

"C'mon out here, woman—we got us guests for dinner!"

25

I T WAS TO be an expedition to show the flag.

"Hancock the Superb," they called him. He, who had been most responsible for holding the vital center of the Union line against Pickett's deadly charge at Gettsyburg. Let the nomadic warriors of the plains know that "The Thunderbolt," General Winfield Scott Hancock, had led troops into every one of those bloody battles fought by the Army of the Potomac.

Yet now Hancock had to figure out how to deal with Indians on the Great Plains.

"Looking more and more like the bands want war," Shad Sweete told Jonah on their march away from those log-and-adobe buildings that made up Fort Harker standing beside the Smoky Hill River. They were pointing their noses south by west on the Olde Santa Fe Trail, headed for Fort Larned erected along the Arkansas River. "What with the way they've been making hay on the freight roads—shutting things down flat. Hickok says that the general plans to give the Cheyenne and Sioux just that—war."

Right about now Hook wasn't all that sure this was where he wanted to be. He had been pushed and prodded and goaded from one war into another, from the Civil War into Connor's War on the Powder. And looking for some whisper of a trace of his family, Hook found himself riding at the head of a huge column of cavalry, infantry, and artillery might marching off toward what had the makings of a new war.

202

"Ain't he even gonna try talking to the Injuns?" Jonah asked innocently.

"For certain he will. Hickok says the general plans on palavering with the chiefs, first off. But damn if Hancock don't make a lot of bluster and carry a damned big stick when he claims he's just going out to palaver," Sweete replied. "Bragging that he won't tolerate no insolence from the warrior bands."

General Hancock was, in fact, forced to cool his heels at Fort Larned. On 7 April, after having arrived with a force of fourteen hundred soldiers of the Seventh Cavalry, 37th Infantry, along with a battery of the Fourth Artillery and a pontoon train, the general was informed a delegation of chiefs was indeed on its way to see him. Then, as if the weather itself conspired against the Thunderbolt's plans to subdue the tribes of the Great Plains, a spring snowstorm caught the delegates in their camp some thirty miles west from Fort Larned, up the Pawnee Fork of the Arkansas River. Five days later, only two Cheyenne chiefs came in from the snowy countryside: White Horse and Tall Bull.

"Damn if Hancock didn't give them two Cheyenne what for," Hook explained to Sweete and the other scouts at their camp fire that next morning while coffee boiled. "Like a Bible-thumping circuit rider, preachifying hell and damnation if they didn't toe his line."

Shad knelt over the fire, dragging the coffeepot from the flames, allowing the roiling water to slow itself. He pushed it toward his guest. "That's why we're marching up Pawnee Fork this morning, Jonah. General wants to preach his piece to more'n just them two."

"Something down in my gut troubles me—telling me I don't want to get so close to that many Injuns ever again." Hook wrapped a greasy bandanna around the pot handle so he could pour coffee into the tin cups the others had waiting. "What I saw up there at Platte Bridge two years back was enough to last any man a normal lifetime."

Shad grinned. "But here you squat, marching with the army on the trail of these red buggers—"

"Don't remind me how stupid I am, Shad!"

"Why the devil you sign on with this outfit, Jonah—you don't figure to get so close to Injuns?"

"Right about now, I'm wondering why I signed on myself."

"Keep your nose in the wind and your eye up there on the horizon—you'll fare through all right," Sweete reminded.

The following afternoon, Hickok and Milner had the advance party of scouts spread out on a broad front, each of those plainsmen knowing they could expect to meet warriors riding out to protect their villages at any moment. Instead, mile after mile of shimmering prairie was crossed, with no sign of the bands or their crossing.

Late in the afternoon, only the horizon betrayed a massive dust cloud.

Hickok came tearing back toward his flankers, reining up and haunch-sliding his mount around in a tight circle, his shoulder-length hair lifting in the breeze from the collar of his red waist-length Zouave jacket resplendent with gold braid. "We got problems, Shad!"

"They're running, ain't they?"

"By glory if they ain't."

"They torn down the lodges?"

"No," Hickok replied. "Just bolting off—women and young'uns."

"Warriors staying behind?"

"They'll likely guard the retreat." Hickok reined about. "I'm going to tell the old man!"

Hancock immediately growled his displeasure with the fleeing Indians and ordered Hickok around, dispatched back to the village to find one of the headmen he could parley with.

"Tell those chiefs they better round their people up and bring them back, goddammit! Make sure they understand this is a bad show of faith on their part."

"To them, General," Hickok explained from atop his prancing horse, "this many soldiers along is a clear show of what your intentions are."

"By God—if they want war, I'm here to give it to them!" Hancock snapped. "Now go do what the hell I'm paying you for, Hickok."

By the time Hickok returned to the advance of the march, the situation had soured. He rode up to Sweete and the rest where the scouts had halted on a low hillock.

"Damn," Hickok muttered.

"They aim to make a fight of it," Sweete said, nodding toward the hundreds of warriors who had spread out across a broad front before the scouts and advance guard.

Feathers stirred on the chill spring breeze. The tails of every war pony had been tied up with red trade cloth or strips of rawhide. Shields clung to every arm, a bow, rifle, or carbine held at the ready by the jeering, taunting warriors who urged the white men on.

"Fat's in the fire now, boys," Milner said, then spit some tobacco juice into the dust. "I reckon we ought'n go on down there and palaver with 'em afore ol' Thunderbutt gets up here to stir things with his big stick."

"Not a bad idea, Joe," Hickok replied. "C'mon. You and Shad come with me."

"We showing guns?" Sweete asked.

"By damn if we ain't," Milner said. "It's the only thing these red bastards understand—is gunpower."

The trio inched off that low hillock into the rolling lowland where the long cordon of warriors waited on their restive ponies. As the white men halted midway between the two lines, a score of the young warriors grew more than verbal. They raced their ponies back and forth along the Indian line, taunting, shaking their weapons in the air.

"Damn if they don't want war every bit as much as Hancock's itching for it," Hickok muttered. He straightened in the saddle. "All right, Shad. Tell their chiefs we want to parley a bit."

Sweete handed his rifle over to California Joe, now second in command of the scouts behind Hickok. Shad then held his hands up to begin signing as he spoke in the Shahiyena tongue. The white men wanted some delegates to come forward onto neutral ground for a parley, he said. For a few moments, a half dozen of the warriors conferred among themselves a hundred yards away. Then they too inched forward, ordering the rest to remain behind.

"We don't want no trouble," Hickok reminded Milner as Joe shifted uneasily on his saddle after tossing the Spencer carbine back to Sweete.

"These bastards won't mind taking our scalps," Joe muttered. "Don't trust 'em a bit."

"And right you are," Shad whispered as the chiefs drew near. "Let's smile and act hospitable, boys. And keep your finger on your triggers."

The warriors came to a halt twenty feet away, ponies pawing at the new grass flowering across the prairie. The breeze rustled feathers and fringe and the edges of blankets in that great silence beneath the cornflower blue sky while everyone waited for something to happen, someone to speak. A pony snorted. One of the warriors coughed.

"Shad, tell 'em what we want."

"What is it we want?"

"Hancock wants to talk with the chiefs."

Sweete once more spoke and signed—telling them the soldier chief wanted to talk with the mighty chiefs of the Lakota and Shahiyena bands.

One of the warriors snorted, loudly. He spit on the ground.

"Who's that?" Hickok asked quietly.

"Think he's called Pawnee Killer. Brule chief. Bad sonofabitch if it is."

"Heard tell of him," Milner added. "He's a mean one what don't know a lick of common sense."

Sweete spoke after one of the half dozen had signed. "They're asking us something, Hickok. Why we brought along the soldiers—both walk-a-heaps and pony soldiers—if all that we mean to do is talk."

Hickok shifted in his saddle. "I figure he's got us there. A fair question, but I don't know what to tell him." He glanced over his shoulder, his eyes scanning the countryside behind them for sign of Hancock's columns.

"I know what to say," Milner growled.

"I won't have you starting anything here, Joe," Hickok snapped.

Sweete watched all the dark, lidded eyes concentrating on the two arguing white men. Behind the delegates, the rest of the warriors were surging, their ponies racing up and down the long line strung horizon to horizon—galloping the ponies about in short sprints to get their second wind.

"We better tell them something . . . and now," Shad muttered. "Or our butts may be in the soup."

He inched his horse forward a few yards, away from Hickok and Milner. Then he began signing.

The soldiers come for two reasons: they come to talk to the chiefs about making peace, so that the Lakota and Shahiyena make no more war on the white settlers.

Two of the delegates glanced at one another, then one moved his hands slowly.

You said the soldiers come for two reasons. You spoke of but one.

Shad straightened in the saddle, slowly moving his Spencer carbine across his lap before his hands went back to signing.

If the Lakota and Shahiyena do not want to talk of peace, then the soldiers come to make war.

The entire half dozen warriors stirred at that.

The white man finally talks straight. Perhaps you should prepare to die.

Shad knew he could not let his eyes betray him. Never that. Instead, he let his eyes continue resting on the dark-skinned speaker.

If it is war you want, then do not wait. Let us begin here . . . and now.

When his hands finished, they went to grip the carbine, quietly moving it off his lap, held over the horse's head.

At that moment, a trio of warriors showed up from the east, appearing over the hills to Sweete's right. They were shouting, waving pieces of blanket overhead. What they said Shad was not able to pick up, only that it was Cheyenne, and not Sioux. The half dozen delegates stirred uneasily. Pawnee

Killer savagely wrenched his pony around and tore off toward the long line of warriors.

"Get ready to make your stand," Milner hissed.

"Not yet, we don't," Sweete warned. "I think they've spotted the soldiers getting close."

The big warrior glared at the white men a moment, then signed for Sweete.

You have succeeded in living this day through, Indian-talker. Your soldiers come before we can dare take your scalps.

"You are Shahiyena," Shad spoke the words in Cheyenne.

"I am," the big one answered. "You speak our tongue."

"Your name is Roman Nose?"

The war chief did not answer at first, only staring at the white tracker with less disdain now.

"I am Roman Nose."

"You are known as a great warrior, a brave leader of your men," Sweete replied. "I cannot believe a warrior of your stature would find honor in wiping out three white men so outnumbered by your own."

Roman Nose smiled, reluctantly at first, then broadly. "What is your name?"

"Shad Sweete."

"Sh-h-a-a-d Sweet-t-t," he mimicked the words with emphasis on the hard consonants. "I will remember you. As a brave man, and one who talks straight."

"Let's get," Hickok was ordering in a low voice, as calm as he could make it.

Sweete glanced at the heaving, roiling line of warriors, every one of them in turmoil now that the soldiers drew near the villages.

"Tell your soldiers to stop where they are," Roman Nose ordered.

"They will not," Sweete replied above the clamor of snorting ponies and clattering weapons, the shouts and jeers of warriors surging, throbbing across the prairie. "They have come to talk with you of peace . . . or war."

"The soldiers must not come any closer to our villages," Roman Nose demanded. "They frighten the women and little ones. Frighten the old ones."

"If it is peace your bands want—then they have no reason to be frightened."

The war chief appeared to think on that, then said something quietly to the other four headmen. They reined about and rode back to their wide front of armed warriors. Only once did Roman Nose glance over his shoulder, his eyes finding Shad Sweete.

A rattle of bit chain and a clopping of hooves arrested his attention. Sweet turned in the saddle as more than a dozen soldiers galloped up under a flutter of snapping guidons. A lieutenant held his arm up as most stopped. Two rode on, halting only when they were among the three scouts.

"Do they want a f-fight of it?"

With that recognizable stutter, Sweete glanced at the flushed, excited features of the youngest general in American military history, now relegated to the rank of lieutenant colonel in the newly formed U.S. Seventh Cavalry.

"Don't think so, General Custer," he answered. "They're blustering, but I don't figure they'll—"

"General Hancock," Custer interrupted the scout and turned toward the expedition commander, "let me throw a cordon around their village."

"Capital idea, Custer! Do it. I don't want a one of these savages sneaking out on us now."

Then Hancock turned to Sweete and the others. "You've done well, gentlemen. Well, indeed. In a matter of moments, Custer's Seventh will have this bunch of thieves and murderers surrounded. Then we can get down to the business of punishing the guilty parties."

26

H E EARNED HIS name early in life.

Pawnee Killer.

He hated them. Almost as much as he hated the white man.

And lately he had learned some of the Pawnee up north of the Republican River had not only scouted into the Powder River country two winters back, but were now hiring on to be the eyes and ears for the white man's army.

Pawnee Killer smiled. It was meant to happen.

As much as what he had been telling his band of Brule and the bands of Shahiyena Dog Soldiers who traveled with his people—the soldiers were bound to come.

Make no mistake—these were fighting bands.

Down south, the Comanche and Kiowa and a few others were doing their best against a growing tide of white men: soldiers, settlers, those who laid the tracks for the great, smoking iron horses, the traders who brought bolts of cloth and the tinkling hawks-bells that made the Indian women lust for new things. They struggled on the southern plains, with hope still alive.

Up north Sitting Bull's Hunkpapa were doing their best to stay away from the white man. Red Cloud's Bad Face Oglalla were still reveling in their defeat of the soldiers last winter at the Battle of the Hundred in the Hand, far up on what the white man called the Bozeman Road. But Red Cloud had not succeeded in driving the soldiers from their three forts in the heart of that Lakota hunting ground.

So for now, it seemed, the soldiers had turned their attention to these central plains.

Not that far north along the Buffalo Shit River, what the white man called the Platte, others were laying more iron tracks. And down here south of the Republican, what the Cheyenne called their Plum River, another band of white men labored to lay more tracks toward the far western mountains, where the sun went to sleep at the end of each day.

Pawnee Killer was sure that the white man had focused his attention on this great buffalo ground as surely as a warrior would aim the iron-tipped point of his arrow at the heart of a young bull.

And now he was sure. The army had come. With five other chiefs, he had gone to talk with the three white men who scouted for the soldiers. Quickly he had grown angry and turned about, not content to talk further with the three. Instead, he would remain with his fighting men. When the soldiers came, they would stand and fight until the women and old ones, the ones too small to fight themselves, all had escaped.

Then the great warrior bands would disappear across the mapless prairie, like spring snow before the snow-eating chinook.

Hancock did nothing to inspire the trust of those fighting bands.

He sent Custer's cavalry to surround the great village at sunset on 15 April. The lodges were still there, as were the racks groaning beneath drying strips of buffalo meat. Surrounding every lodge were staked the bloody hides being fleshed by the women. From a few smoke holes appeared wisps of smoke.

But except for a few dogs that had remained behind to enjoy an easy feast on the drying meat, the great village was empty.

"They've f-fled, General," Custer stammered as he leapt to the ground beside Hancock's luxuriously appointed army ambulance.

"By damn—tell me they haven't!"

Shad Sweete edged up, hanging onto his reins. "They're heading north and west, General."

Hancock regarded the old scout a moment. "Where's Hickok?"

"Him and some of the others stayed behind in the village."

"They're plundering it?"

"No, General. Stayed behind with some of the rest who found a little girl."

"A white prisoner?"

Sweete shook his head. "Half-breed. She was left behind when the rest took off."

"Savages used her pretty bad, General," Custer broke in.

Hancock's eyes narrowed as he brought the back of his hand to his mouth. "The disgusting—"

"You want her brought to our camp?" Sweete asked.

Custer turned to the scout, seeing that Hancock was not about to answer. "Have one of the surgeons see to her, Sweete. If not them, one of the hospital stewards."

"Custer," Hancock said as he settled back against the canvas campaign chair he had placed in the ambulance, "we'll bloody well make these bastards pay one of these days."

Jonah Hook wasn't sure why he had stayed behind with the others when Shad had gone riding off with Custer to report to Hancock that the village was empty.

But now as the light was falling from the sky, he knew it had something to do with the little girl he had been the first to find among the empty, abandoned lodges. Something to do with thinking about his own daughter. Hattie would be twelve this spring, he thought. Not much older than this little thing.

He held the half-breed child in his arms, wishing it were Hattie he were rocking. As the light faded from the lodge, so did those scared eyes he hesitated to look into.

She had fought him like a frightened animal at first, until she gave up—perhaps her hope gone, perhaps all remaining strength. Then she had collapsed into his arms as he knelt atop a buffalo-robe bed, strewn with blankets not taken in the hasty retreat.

When the others had shown up, she had explained to Shad Sweete in her broken Cheyenne what the warriors had done after the women and old ones had abandoned her.

"When the others gone off, running with what they could carry," Shad explained to Custer and the scouts who had gathered in that gloomy lodge, "a dozen or so of them young warriors rode back here to have their fun with her. She's half-breed you know. And to them bucks—it makes her white."

"You're saying that while we were parleying with their chiefs," Hickok growled, "some of those red bastards came back here?"

Shad had only nodded as Custer whirled, slapping his quirt against the top of his boot.

"You there, Sweete. Come with me—back to Hancock. The rest of you can eat what you can find here. Chances are I'll talk Hancock into freeing me to pursue these vile heathens this very night. If not to punish them for escaping us—then to punish them for what crimes they have committed against this . . . this child."

"Stay with her, Jonah," Sweete had said in a whisper before he left the lodge. "Chances are you're the only one she'll let near her now. I'll see about getting a surgeon to help her back with Hancock's soldiers."

That night there hadn't been much they could do for the girl, with the exception of washing her wounds caused at the hands of those who had repeatedly raped her. It took hours before she would let one of the hospital stewards close to her. Near morning, Jonah laid the girl on some blankets at the back of an ambulance, where she slipped contentedly into sleep, her head in the lap of the steward.

As the eastern sky stretched into a bloody pink, Jonah wearily found the rest of the scouts just then beginning to move about their fires.

"You need some coffee, Jonah," Sweete said, trudging about the low flames of his breakfast fire with his blanket draped from his shoulders, slurring the ground.

Hook settled nearby, where the old mountain man patted the ground. Jonah pulled a blanket around his own shoulders against the predawn chill. "What I need is sleep. Forget the coffee, old man."

"You'll want the coffee, Jonah. We're riding out in a few minutes."

"Not until I get some sleep, I'm not."

"Hancock's asked that I stay with him and California Joe. He plans on heading down to Fort Dodge from here."

"Good. Just as long as old Thunderass don't climb into his ambulance till I get me a little shut-eye."

Sweete dragged the coffeepot from the fire as he cleared his throat. "You ain't going with Hancock."

Hook opened one eye into the murky darkness and glared at the old trapper. "What you figure on me doing—I don't go with you?"

"Custer asked for you go with him and Hickok."

Hook closed the one eye and sighed. "He did, did he?"

"We're riding out soon as you have a cup of coffee," a new voice drew close from the darkness.

With the one eye opened again, he found the dusty, prairie-crusted long hair of normally dapper James Butler Hickok hanging disheveled about his face.

"I had my way about it—there'd been a few more of you goddamned Yankees I'd a'killed afore you put a end to the war," he grumbled.

"Rise an' shine, friend—there's a trail of Injuns we're bound to follow." Hickok ran fingers through his hair.

"Likely it's a war we're off to start, Bill."

Hickok straightened, allowing the Confederate room to kick his way out of the blanket. "You're wrong there, Reb. Wasn't us started this war."

In their hasty flight, the bands left only small trails for Hickok's scouts to mull over, deciding which to follow. But follow they did, heading north in the general direction of the many dim tracks, onto the open prairie, leading Custer and his eight companies of the Seventh Cavalry rapidly behind them.

North of Walnut Creek, Hickok left the guiding in the hands of others while he motioned Hook to join him in pulling away from Custer's column. Without a word of explanation, Hickok set a bruising pace, the rising sun constantly on his right cheek as they loped across the rolling tableland of central Kansas Territory. It was late that day when the pair reined up at a stage ranch, embers smoking still.

Hook let his eyes run over the scene quickly, then glanced at Hickok.

"You ever see something like this, Jonah?"

"I fought that war, same as you," he answered quietly.

"I know. But—you ever see anything like that?"

Hickok pointed his Spencer carbine at the blackened, bloated bodies of the two ranch hands, burned among the charred wreckage of this way station along the Smoky Hill Road.

"I've smelled this afore, Hickok—in Missouri."

Hickok nodded. "Some of the worst of it happened on the borderlands. Let's get."

No one had to drag him from that place. Problem was, it was only the first of many the two ran across over the next two days.

"Looks like everything west of Hays been hit, General," Hickok explained when he and Hook dismounted before Custer that third week of April, after they had returned from their far-ranging scout.

"All the same story?" Custer asked, his blue eyes narrowing.

"Every station . . . burned out. All the stock run off. Workers what didn't make it out, we found butchered," Hook answered.

At that moment they stood among the ruins of Lookout Station, only fifteen miles west of Fort Hays. The burned bodies of three men had just been found near the smoldering debris.

"They don't even look like something once human," Custer muttered in something close to a curse.

"Likely, they were tortured by the red bastards," growled a handsome soldier standing at Custer's elbow.

"Little doubt of that, Tom," Custer said to his younger brother. Then he suddenly turned to his adjutant, animated once more. "Mr. Moylan, pass along the order for our command to move off two miles and make camp."

Jonah stood dumbfounded as the long-haired lieutenant colonel and his staff strode off, their shadows lengthening beneath the all but gone western sun. How many could look at this scene and not have his stomach turned? And not grow angry? Not be changed?

For three days after Custer had marched off to continue the hunt, General Winfield Scott Hancock debated with himself on just what to do with the captured, empty Indian village on Pawnee Fork.

Agents for both the Cheyenne and the Brule Sioux gave it their best to convince Hancock to be a gracious victor.

"The bands fled only because of their fear of your amassed might, General," declared Edward W. Wynkoop. "They're mortally afraid of another Sand Creek massacre."

Shad Sweete had watched as Hancock's eyes grew steely. "I am a professional soldier, Major Wynkoop. In no way similar to that minister-turned-butcher named Chivington!"

Colonel Jesse W. Leavenworth attempted his own appeal. "General, to put that village to the torch as you have been suggesting would only add to the flames already scorching the central plains. You will make war certain by not staying your hand and showing the tribes your benevolence."

Hancock smiled, calling out to the old scout. "Mr. Sweete—that is a good one, isn't it? Benevolence for these warrior bands?"

Shad watched both the agents turn to look in his direction in the steamy shade provided by the canvas awning strung from the top of Hancock's ambulance. He cleared his throat. "Truth of it is, General—these bands understand only one thing. War."

Wynkoop bolted up. "I protest, General—"

"Give my scout a chance to finish, Major Wynkoop!" growled Hancock.

"And," Sweete continued, "the warrior bands fear only one thing. Death."

"There," Hancock sighed, sinking back into his canvas campaign chair. "This man's spent his entire adult life out here in these far western regions. No one understands these Indians the way Mr. Sweete does, gentlemen." He tapped a finger against his fleshy lower lip, then stroked it down his chin whiskers.

"Gentlemen, I've decided. Satisfied that this village acted in bad faith by fleeing before we had a chance to talk of peace has proved they were a nest of conspirators. This command will burn the village before we move off toward Fort Dodge."

The next morning, 19 April, as the bulk of his troops marched south, Hancock's selected tarried behind to set fire to the village on Pawnee Fork: 111 Cheyenne and 140 Brule Sioux lodges, along with robes, blankets, meat, utensils, parfleches filled with clothing, and abandoned travois.

Less than a week later, the general met with a delegation of Arapaho and Kiowa chiefs who had already learned of the destruction of the villages, though their bands roamed country far south of the Arkansas River. The moccasin telegraph rapidly spread the word.

A buoyant Hancock at last delivered his war-or-peace message he had intended on delivering to the Cheyenne and Sioux.

"I don't know if you can trust the word of that one, General," Sweete whispered in Hancock's ear as he and the general looked over the assembled chiefs, seated on blankets and robes before Hancock's table.

"What's his name?"

"Satanta."

"Which means?"

"White Bear. He's the slipperiest of the Kiowa headmen."

"But you yourself just translated his most moving and eloquent speech, claiming his people would forever abandon the road to war against the white man."

"General, you'll come off the fool if you go believing in the word of Satanta," Sweete said quietly as Hancock passed by him.

The general took a full-dress uniform, replete with gold braid and tassels, from the arms of his adjutant and strode over to Satanta. There, in a grand presentation, he handed the Kiowa chief that freshly brushed uniform as a symbol of the peace just made between the army and White Bear's Kiowa.

"You see, Mr. Sweete—how he smiles. How this grand gift makes the rest of his headmen smile. We have just forged a lasting relationship with Satanta's people."

"General, you ain't done nothing but give another war chief something to wear when he rides down on white settlements to burn, rape, and kill."

27

Moon of Fattening

N EVER BEFORE HAD Pawnee Killer been so proud of his warriors.
Stripped of almost everything his people owned, his angry
warriors were making a wreck of the Smoky Hill Route: burning, killing,
looting, running off all stock from the road-ranches. With every new day,
Pawnee Killer's people were regaining what they had been forced to abandon
in the valley of Pawnee Fork to the soldiers who had put the villages to the
torch.

For the rising of six suns now, the warriors had brought fear to the white
men who laid the heavy iron tracks that carried the smoking horses. They had
killed many of the workers and run off the rest who fled on their tiny
machines that never strayed from the iron tracks. Then the young warriors set
to work, bending rails and burning cross ties.

The real fun began two days later when a column of dark smoke
appeared on the far horizon. The smoke kept shifting. Never staying in the
same place on that bleak meeting of earth brown and sky blue.

Pawnee Killer stepped from the cross ties to the rail bed, and in so doing
his moccasin brushed the great, heavy iron rail. It trembled, ever so slightly,
but nonetheless trembled beneath his foot.

Cautiously, as one would approach a deadly snake, the Brule chief went
to his knees, bending over the iron rail. Then gingerly laid his ear to it, as he
would lay his ear on the ground to learn of the approach of enemies or

buffalo. Many of the rest had halted their destruction, watching him in curious fascination.

"It hums!" he declared, grinning, raising his head.

Others now fell to their knees along both of the long rails, yelling for quiet, bickering, shoving for a place along the cross ties. Every one of them bent over, an ear on the rails.

They laughed and shouted their joy.

"The white man comes. It is his smoking horse that brings him!" shouted Pawnee Killer. "Let us welcome him!"

There were several white men on that train comprising a belching locomotive, wood tender, and a flatcar filled with armed white men. With a screech of brakes, a peculiar and new sound to Pawnee Killer's ears, the hissing, smoking engine slowed atop its iron rails as the white men hollered out warning to one another, craning their necks from window holes in the smoking monster, spotting the torn-up tracks.

The great, heavy, belching iron horse did not slow soon enough.

It eased off its tracks like a huge, old herd bull, derailing into the burned cross timbers, striking the heated, bent rails with a loud, shrill scraping that raised the hairs on the back of Pawnee Killer's neck. Then slowly, like that herd bull settling in a buffalo wallow, the engine sank off the edge of the roadbed and eased over as the white men scrambled off the flatbed car.

Pawnee Killer's warriors swept into motion, and their own keening war cries rose to the hot, pale sky overhead.

The monstrous bulk of the engine lay on its side, hissing, spitting steam like winter's gauze over a prairie river come the Moon of Seven Cold Nights. Inside the belly of the huge monster, a gurgling, roiling, spitting rumble belched and blew while the white men dug in behind the wreckage and made it known they had come to fight.

For better than two hours, Pawnee Killer's warriors charged past the white men, burrowed like frightened field mice where the red-tailed hawks cannot get at them. A few of the warriors were winged, hit with a lucky shot when they did not drop on the far side of their ponies in time.

And when he called off the attack late that afternoon, Pawnee Killer did not even know if they had killed any of the white men who rode the iron monster now lying mute and motionless. As the war chief drew up and halted on a nearby hill, looking back this one last time, that steam engine now reminded him of some gelded stallion. Impotent and powerless.

"*Hopo!*" he yelled to the others, who swirled around him, flush with victory, three carrying the scalps of the white men who did not make it to cover quickly enough at the beginning of the attack.

"*H'gun! H'gun!*" they cheered him with the Lakota courage-word.

"It has been a good day—watching the smoking monster die!" he cried, shaking his bow at the end of his arm. "A good day for the white man to be reminded what will happen next time he follows the tracks of our people!"

The rains of April had come and gone as the central plains slipped into the warm days and cool nights of May.

And with them, Custer had led his eight companies into Fort Hays to resupply before he could even begin to consider resuming the chase of those hostile Cheyenne and Sioux who had so far successfully eluded him.

Upon their arrival at Hays, the word on every lip was talk of the destruction being made of the entire Smoky Hill Route. Stages attacked, a train derailed, and workers killed. Track crews had abandoned their roadbeds and were fleeing east to safety, demanding action from the army. The entire freight road to Denver City had been shut down. Nothing was moving, except the warrior bands who continued to harass the outlying forts.

Fort Wallace, far to the west along the Federal Road had been under daily attack. And even the nearby Fort Dodge down on the Arkansas was far from immune. Only now, reports had it, Kiowa chief Satanta himself had led a massed raid on Fort Dodge and had driven off more than a hundred head of stock, all while dressed in that pretty blue uniform, resplendent with braid and brass buttons—a gift from the head of the department, one General Winfield Scott Hancock.

"Gonna take some time to get these animals ready to go back out on the trail of those war bands."

Jonah Hook turned at the sound of the voice. Shad Sweete strode up in the falling light. The ex-Confederate stooped to snatch up another handful of grass, using it to curry his horse.

"I hear some of them soldiers give Custer a new name few days back," he said to Sweete. "Horse-Killer."

The big man snorted a quick, light chuckle. "He drove the animals hard, eh?"

Jonah's gut tightened. "He drove us and his men even harder. No graze or forage for the animals. Little water from camp to camp. A real sin, Shad. Treating stock the way he done—and all the time, coddling up to his hounds the way he does. Takes better care of those dogs than he does his own men."

The surprising cold of spring coupled with the sudden and early heat of an approaching summer had taken about all there was in the way of strength from the regiment's mounts. Yet worse still was to find upon their arrival at Fort Hays no feed and forage waiting. Traders and government sutlers had been there before the Seventh Cavalry rode in—weeks ago bartering and selling it off to the tribes.

Hundreds of horses and mules were led onto the prairie to graze as best they could on the new grass.

"Injun ponies live on the stuff," Hook said as his horse snapped off some more of the growing stalks with a crackling crunch.

"But these horses of ours never meant to live wild and free on the prairie like Injun ponies, Jonah," said Sweete. "Injun pony bred to eat grass all night and run all day. These horses of Custer's—they don't have a snowball's chance in the hand of the devil hisself."

Off in the distance, a prairie wolf set up a brief howl. Then another in the pack answered.

"There are critters live off this hard land. And some what can't, so you're telling me," Jonah said as the eerie howls faded.

"Just like the warrior bands, Jonah. They'll live off the land, running and fighting, and running again. But Custer's cavalry—these young soldiers—they ain't fit to run and fight on what the land gives 'em. They need their bacon and hardtack and beans."

"You see what they had for supper tonight?"

Sweete nodded. "Moldy salt pork. And the hardtack so full of weevils, I swear mine walked right off the plate from me!"

Jonah laughed along easily with the old scout.

"Listen, son—these traders been selling the army what a sutler calls surplus."

"Goods from the war?"

"The crates is marked with the dates it was packed—years ago, during your war back east."

"Damn. Didn't know a man could stoop so low as to send soldiers such food to eat."

"Some of the bastards back east even sending crates filled with rocks."

"Can they make 'em pay, Shad?" he asked, stuffing the last handful of grass beneath his horse's muzzle.

"Government contracts, boy. Never anything be done about it."

"So we starve along with Custer's soldiers, that it?"

"Pray you don't come down with scurvy like some already has. Cholera spreading through some of the other stations, Jonah. Pray you keep your health."

"Injuns don't get sick like that, do they?"

He wagged his head. "Not less'n they get too close, rubbing up against the white man, they don't."

For all the serious illness, for the lack of food and, worst of all, for all the lack of hope—there was one sure-fire remedy: desertion. And over the next few weeks of despair and waiting for supplies in the growing heat, a growing number of the Seventh U.S. Cavalry tried the remedy.

Yet at Fort Hays there was one officer not about to let pass the slightest infraction of rules, much less insubordination and mutiny. Not to mention out-and-out desertion. Custer vowed he would deal with every infraction swiftly, and harshly.

Without trial, soldiers who had been accused of an infraction of some military regulation or another were confined during the day to a large hole dug in the Kansas prairie, climbing down on ladders that were as quickly pulled up until sunset. It was then those soldiers still conscious from the excruciating heat were allowed to climb onto the cool prairie once more.

Drunks were quickly dealt with: given a stirring ride at the end of a dunking stool that repeatedly plunged them into the Smoky Hill River.

At first deserters were "skinned"—half their heads shaved by the regimental barber. When that did not prove enough of a deterrent, deserters were stripped to the waist and horsewhipped. Yet even then, each morning saw a few more failing to report at reveille. That's when Custer ordered sentries thrown around the entire regimental bivouac, given instructions to shoot first and ask questions later if a soldier was found outside of camp.

But as hard as he was on his regiment, Custer also gave some relief to the sickening chow his men were forced to eat. He organized hunting parties to push into the surrounding country, killing deer, elk, antelope, and bison. Along with relieving the monotony of the moldy salt pork and weevil-infested hardtack, the hunting parties Custer ordered out gave the Seventh Cavalry a chance to fire their weapons from horseback, improve their aim, and become more familiar with the countryside so different from what most had grown up with back east.

Then on 18 May, Mrs. Elizabeth Custer herself had rolled into Fort Hays, been swept up into her husband's arms, and spirited off to the privacy of his canvas-and-log shelter.

"Makes a man ache for his own family," Sweete said quietly as he watched Jonah turn grimly away from the happy reunion.

"Makes a man wanna find those who stole my family."

Hook shuffled off to find himself a piece of shade.

"When we're ready—we'll see what we can do to find hide or hair of that bunch took your kin," Sweete said as he came to the younger man's side.

"I'm ready now!" He stopped and wheeled on the mountain man. "We'll get saddled and pull out right now."

"Whoa, Jonah! Ain't as easy as all that. We signed on—"

"You signed on to stay. As for me, I can be gone as easy as I signed my name. Had me enough, Shad. You coming with me?"

He shook his head. "Not yet. Not taking off like this neither. Time comes . . . we'll track. Go clear back down into the Territories if'n we have to. Don't you ever doubt we'll come up with something."

Jonah felt the gall rising to his throat. The sudden flare of anticipation and hope warming him once more, so long buried—and now so quickly doused with the cold water of Sweete's reason.

"Damn you, Shad Sweete!" He captured a fistful of the old man's greasy calico shirt. "I'll do it alone, I have to."

"You go now—hell, you go alone anytime—them roving bands of warriors make a prickly pear of you in no uncertain way."

"I learned how to take care of myself," he snapped, turning away.

Shad snagged him by the arm just as quickly. "You watch your temper—"

"Take your hand off my arm!" he snarled at the older man who towered over him.

"Watch your temper . . . and you'll keep your hair, Jonah."

"You saying you're the one who's gonna take my hair?"

Sweete released the sinew-tough, rail-thin arm. "No. I don't figure that mangy scalp of your'n worth the trouble of cutting on, Jonah Hook. I'm just trying to make sense—"

"You coming?" He shook his arm, rubbing it where the big man had held him.

"No."

"Then I'm going with Artus." His lips formed a thin line of determination.

"He won't go."

Jonah stopped and turned on his heel slowly, hands balled on his hips. "How you so sure?"

"'Cause it's plain to me that his side of the family got all the common sense."

It flooded over Jonah, all the rage and disappointment tumbling together into one acid knot eating a hole in the soul of him, plain as the hot Kansas sun overhead.

"When?" Hook finally asked as the tears simmered in his eyes, tears he refused to release.

"When our job's done with Custer. I gave my word when I signed on. That's a bond. We'll go only when the job's done."

28

S HAD SWEETE WAS every bit as anxious to get out of Fort Hays as was
Jonah Hook or Artus Moser.

Trouble was, Custer wasn't ready to march his ill-fed, poorly equipped
command out from Fort Hays until the first of June.

And by that time, the roving bands of marauding warriors had moved
north from the Smoky Hill, Saline, and Solomon rivers—north all the way to
the Platte River country.

With Department Commander Philip H. Sheridan's blessing, General
Hancock was to have the Seventh Cavalry push north toward the Emigrant
Road, that heavily used wagon route that brought settlers and miners west to
Colorado or on to California. As well, the rails then being laid by the Union
Pacific followed the same valley of the Platte. It was nothing short of vital
that Custer's cavalry march toward Fort McPherson on the Platte, and from
there begin their sweep to clear the plains of hostiles between that river and
the Republican.

Colonel Andrew Jackson Smith's orders to Custer read:

> The Brev. Maj.-Gen'l Comdg. directs that you proceed with your
> Command . . . to Ft. McPherson, at which point you will find a large
> supply of rations & forage. . . . From Ft. McPherson you will proceed
> up the South Fork of the Platte to Ft. Sedgwick. . . . If every thing is

found to be quiet & your presence not required . . . you may come South to Ft. Wallace, at which point you will find further instructions. The object of the Expedition is to hunt out & chastise the Cheyennes, and that portion of the Sioux who are their allies, between the Smoky Hill & the Platte. It is reported that all friendly Sioux have gone South of the Platte, and may be in the vicinity of Fts. McPherson or Sedgwick. You will (as soon as possible) inform yourself as to the whereabouts of these friendly bands, and avoid a collision with them.

On that first day of June, Shad Sweete watched the long-haired cavalry commander stuff those orders inside the dark blue blouse with gold piping Mrs. Custer had herself sewn for her dashing husband, then give the word to his adjutant, Myles Moylan, to move out.

Three hundred fifty sweating, anxious, and hungry horse soldiers pointed their noses north by west at distant Fort McPherson, some 175 miles away across the shimmering, summer-seared prairie.

"We get up there close to that Platte Road, we'll find us a place to jump off and disappear," whispered a soldier to the rider beside him as they passed by Sweete and the rest of the scouts.

"That fella sounds like he's got the right idea, Shad," Hook said.

Shad didn't even look at Jonah. "You like wearing your hair—you'll give no thought to deserting this bunch. Even up there on the Holy Road, where a man might find more folks to join up with. Ain't likely any of these soldiers know what's waiting for 'em they decide to take off on their own hook."

None of them knew what was in store over the next few days of grueling march beneath the prairie sun, drinking alkali water grown warm in their canteens, breathing the stinging alkali dust that coated every nostril and caked the insides of their mouths in a gauzy swirl that rose like an ache of despair from every plodding hoof along that strung-out, head-drooping column led forever northwest by Custer and his officers.

"You ever dream of whiskey?" Hook asked as he squatted wearily with Sweete at a smoky fire one evening a week later. "Don't even have to be good whiskey. Just . . . whiskey."

"Sure," Shad answered, honestly. "Dream about the taste of it on my tongue a lot. 'Specially when I'm drinking this warm water that stings my mouth the same way whiskey does."

"Water does have a sour tang to it—"

A single shot rang out.

They both looked at one another, drawing pistols and slowly standing as the echo of that lone shot faded over the prairie.

"Pistol?" Hook asked.

"Sounded to be," Sweete answered as the camp quieted once more and men went back to preparing the supper they would force down here at the end of a long day's march. "Likely some idjit cleaning his sidearm and it went off."

More than an hour later that eighth day of June, Hickok came to their fire, passing on the story to the rest of the scouts.

"Cooper's second in command this trip out, ain't he?" asked Sweete.

Hickok nodded. "Seems the major had a problem with drinking."

"That what Custer says?" Sweete asked.

"What the rest of the officers say," Hickok answered.

"I saw the man in a bad way myself," Hook told them. "Last winter. He wasn't a drinker like a normal man. Cooper looked like he drank till it made him mad enough at himself."

"He was in a fit—not acting like himself so the talk goes," said Hickok. "But he was at times a real gentleman. With a quiet sort of normal."

"Something made him put that pistol in his mouth and blow out the back of his head," Jonah said.

Hickok regarded him. "The ride. The damn heat. Nothing else to do but ride and drink his whiskey—this campaign is getting to a lot of us, Hook."

"Man don't just go and give up like that," Hook muttered, still staring at the flames. "He leave any family?"

Hickok glanced at Sweete before answering. "Major had a young wife. I understand from Tom Custer that the woman was . . . is expecting soon."

"Damn shame." Hook rose and strode off into the twilight.

"What you figure's eating at him?" Hickok asked.

Shad pulled a shaft of dried grass from his lips and tossed it onto the small fire at his feet. "Family, Bill. He's got one—but he don't know where. And everywhere around him, Jonah's watching folks go killing off what they do have. The man's just touchy right now."

Hickok shook his head. "Jonah's always touchy."

Much more of the sad tale had become general knowledge by the time Custer led his command into Fort McPherson two days later, on the afternoon of 10 June.

Kentucky-born Major Wycliffe Cooper had served the Union with honor during the recent rebellion before his manic depression began to take its toll on his career. For months he had attempted control over his life by drinking himself into oblivion. Teetotaler Custer had eventually confiscated Cooper's supply of whiskey and ordered the major to straighten himself out or suffer court-martial.

"So Cooper put a bullet through his brain instead?"

"They're burying him tomorrow," Sweete replied. "Quiet as possible. Custer won't give him military honors. Says suicide is a coward's way out."

Hook glared at the old trapper. "You never thought about it?"

"What, Jonah?"

He stopped whittling on the stick with his folding knife. "Giving up. Just putting a end to it."

"You ain't thinking like that?"

He tossed the peeled twig into the dust of Fort McPherson's parade as the late afternoon shadows lengthened. "Man loses just about all he cares for in life—natural for him to figure there ain't nothing for him to go on living for."

"You ain't lost them, Jonah." Sweete inched closer, talking softer. "They're out there. Long as you got hope in your heart of finding 'em—they're out there."

He squinted into the far distance darkly veined with shallow, tree-lined rivers, studded and dippled with the flesh-colored, rolling, grass-covered hills.

"Why's this damned ground so all-fired important that these Injuns ready to kill to keep it? This army of Custer's ready to kill to tear it from 'em? Where'd it ever say that a chunk of ground got that important—and a human life was something you just stomped into the dust under your heel?"

"Lots of folks is coming west—"

"Damn them, Shad!" he snapped. "Don't you think I hate that about people? I was off fighting for someone else's goddamned land when I was captured by the Yankees. I was out in Sioux hell on the North Platte or the Sweetwater or the Powder River or the Tongue, fighting Injuns for a piece of ground when that bunch come in and took my family from me, dammit! What made ground more important than people anyway, old man? Tell me that!"

Sweete was a long time before answering. "Never owned me a piece of land, Jonah. What I tried out to Oregon, I never bought, never filed on. Didn't set right with me, son. So take your spurs off when you're fixing to ride me."

"By God, it's you out here leading me on this little journey of yours."

"This ain't got nothing to do with land!" Sweete snapped back. "I got me a family. Same as you. Doing the best I can for 'em. You ain't the only man ever lost loved ones."

Hook studied the old trapper a moment, finding Sweete would not hold his eyes. "You understand, don't you? I mean—you're really trying to understand."

Sweete shook his head, a sad grin growing there in the midst of his shaggy beard. "You can be a bit slow of times, Jonah Hook. Of course I been trying to understand about how it must be for a man to have his kin took from him—"

"No," Jonah interrupted. "This is something different. You lost family, Shad."

"It don't matter now."

"Tell me. It makes a difference to me."

"Sometime, Jonah. Sometime I will tell you."

Major Wycliffe Cooper was laid to rest at Fort McPherson on the eleventh, the same day General Philip H. Sheridan arrived.

Custer was able to report on his meeting with Pawnee Killer, whose village was camped a few miles from the fort, when the department commander arrived.

"While they protested most strongly in favor of maintaining peaceful relations with the white man," Custer explained, "the actions of their chiefs only served to confirm for me that they had arranged their parley with me for one purpose: to spy on my intentions and strength."

"You're learning that the word of an Indian is like shoveling fleas in a barnyard, Armstrong," Sheridan replied. "Their promises aren't worth the time it took to speak them."

"None of us like being played the fool, General."

"Indian promises are like horse apples. There's more than you know what to do with—and they aren't worth a damn. I'll tell you, Armstrong— these bands need to be taught a severe lesson and soon."

Custer scowled. "Just what kind of lesson do you and General Sherman have in mind, sir?"

"Something that will last, Custer," said the short Irishman. "This is your job, I'll remind you. After all is said and done—you're a soldier. This is the inevitable clashing of the races: what must occur when a stronger, more advanced race pushes aside the weaker."

"I take it I'm to serve as the point man for that assault on a primitive culture, General?"

Sheridan smiled within his dark, well-trimmed beard. "Nothing so fancy as that. By god, Custer—I want you to sweep this country between the Platte and Republican—sweep it clean of hostiles and show the rest of the tribes how we'll deal with them if they attempt trouble."

He saluted smartly. "With your permission, General, I'll pass the word to my officers that we're back in the saddle at six tomorrow morning."

From Fort McPherson, Custer led his cavalry west along the Platte River for less than fifty miles before pointing their noses due south.

For the next three weeks, the Seventh crossed Frenchman's Creek, then the Republican River itself, looping first southwest, following the South Fork of the Republican, then slowly turning to the northwest once more, where they crossed the Arikara Fork of the Republican. Nearing the cruel sand hills of the South Platte country, Custer turned his columns back on themselves and recrossed the Arikara, moving roughly east along its southern bank.

Twenty-three days of staring into a merciless white summer sky with eyes scoured by alkali dust. The flour-fine dust still seeped beneath the damp bandanna Jonah Hook had tied over his nose and mouth. He tasted dust. No matter what they had to eat each night—the food still tasted like the dust he had eaten on the march that day.

Everything smelled of stinging, cream-colored alkali. No matter how fragrant was Shad Sweete's coffee a'brew over the greasewood fires, all Jonah smelled with his crusted nose was the stinging alkali.

"You'll sleep tonight, Jonah," said the old mountain man, offering the young Confederate a steaming cup.

He looked down at the tin of coffee. Then reluctantly took it in hand. "Oh, for the want of a cup of some water come out of the mountains."

"This alkali water giving your bowels the tremors, eh?"

Hook shook his head. "Cold."

Sweete said, "Cold is what you want, eh? Water born of the high country."

"Yeah," he replied, his eyes squinting on those distant but remembered places. "I remember the taste of that water up there on the Holy Road. The Sweetwater, it was."

"Lord! And so cold it would set a man's teeth on edge just to drink it."

"For just a cup of that now. Just one cup."

"We've turned about, Jonah," Shad said in that confiding way of his. "I think Custer figures he's not going to find any Injuns this trip out after all."

He nodded, blowing steam from the surface of his coffee, not relishing the hot liquid here after another scorching and dust-filled fifteen-hour day in the saddle. Jonah scratched at a saddle gall, the inside of his thighs chafed and raw from the nonstop sweat and rubbing of the past three weeks in the saddle crossing the high plains.

"Some of the others, they've started to call Custer Old Iron-Ass."

Sweete glanced at some of the other scouts gathered about the evening fire. Hickok settled, knocking dust from the short leather leggings he had tied over the tops of his boots, stretching from knee to ankle.

"I heard that name too, and another. Some of them boys in Custer's outfit starting to call him Horse-Killer."

"He keeps up this pace, chasing smoke on the wind, there soon won't be many horses able to go on. And if it ain't horses Custer will kill on this march through hell," Jonah grumbled, "it just might be the rest of us."

29

T HE SKY ABOVE Jonah Hook hung suspended in that moment when night is as yet undecided in giving itself to day. . . .

—a rifle cracked the still, cool air along the Arikara Fork.

Spencer carbine, he thought as he kicked his way from his sweat-dampened blankets.

"All out! *All out!*"

Men were shouting at one another. Most ran for the horse herd as the screeching war cries suddenly on the horizon drew closer to the near edge of camp with the thunder of hundreds upon hundreds of hooves.

"They're after the horses!" hollered Shad Sweete.

Hickok was among them, both guns out, swirling darkly in the gray light. "Look lively, boys!"

Behind the handful of civilian scouts, soldiers came running from their bivouac like maddened ants driven from their hill. Yelling, confused, frightened. It was Pea Ridge and Corinth again—and Jonah remembered how the yelling gave a man a sense of courage, even if he didn't feel particularly brave right at the moment. At least with all the hollering, a man wasn't all that aware of fear boiling up inside him.

Then he was back on the high plains, blinking away the foggy mist of the hardwood forests. Here . . . damn!

More rifle shots. A bullet sang over his head. A second past his ear as

Hook followed the rest into the murky darkness along the riverbank, flanking the horse herd.

"They're in the river!" someone shouted.

To the man, the civilian scouts all stopped on the grassy sand of the riverbank and shouldered their weapons, firing at random, aiming for the inky forms looming out of the murky predawn darkness. The carbines punctuated that gray, ghostly light with orange spurts of muzzle flame. Behind him rattled more carbine fire as half a hundred soldiers appeared at the top of the bank.

In the span of less time than it would take Jonah to tell the story across those years still in the womb, the coming morning was smudged with gun smoke and noise, men crying out to one another as they fired into the hundreds of warriors like disembodied shadows, splashing out of the river, up the far bank, and into the skimpy brush and timber. In a matter of heartbeats, they were gone, become part of the plum brush and swamp-willow and the few stunted cottonwoods across the fork.

"They get anything?" Hickok sang out, easing off in the direction of camp.

"Half a dozen!" a voice came back from the dark. "No more'n that."

"Hickok!"

The scouts whirled, each one recognizing that high-pitched call from the expedition commander.

"General Custer—over here!"

The soldier came out of the darkness, dressed only in stockings and a red flannel night robe. His long, shoulder-length curls were yet to be brushed for the day, rumpled from sleep. "I hear you say the hostiles got some of our horses?"

Hickok threw a finger over his shoulder. "One of your pickets said they ran off with half a dozen."

"Blast it!" He whirled, calling out into the darkness. "Elliott—you, Yates, and Tom—double-time!"

The officers came among the civilian scouts in a matter of seconds, every one of them breathing heavily, while Custer had already purchased his second wind.

"Hickok, you and Sweete find out who that bunch is—who they belong to."

Sweete glanced at Hickok in the growing gray light. "I'll put my money on them being Lakota . . . er, Sioux, General."

Custer wagged his head. "Your gambling spirit is admirable, Mr. Sweete. But I want to know for certain. Now—find out!"

"Let's go see if we can get them to talk with us, Shad," Hickok said, waving his arm.

"You stay put, Jonah," Sweete said, a hand on Hook's shoulder. "And keep your head down."

In a matter of moments the pair returned to the spot, this time on horseback, inching past the soldiers and urging their mounts into the shallow river. They crossed, slowly—stopping on the far side, their horses standing at the edge of the sluggish river. Jonah could hear muted talk, not sure if the two riders were talking between themselves, or with one of the would-be horse thieves concealed on the far bank. Then, ever so slowly, the two scouts reined about and made their way back across the water.

"You t-talked with them?" Custer asked, excited.

"I told you they was Sioux, General," Shad said.

"Whose Sioux?"

"I figure we'll find out when you got your britches on," Sweete replied.

Custer glanced down at his red robe.

"You make a fine red target of yourself, General." Hook joined the group. "Parading up and down, here on this side of the river. All them Sioux over there know you as Long Hair. Any one of them bucks would love to place a bullet somewhere between your gullet and your gizzard."

"Major Elliott," Custer rasped, still glaring at the scout who spoke with the drawl, "you're in charge until I return in uniform. See that nothing changes here until I get back."

The general was fingering the top button into the hole in his blouse as he strode back minutes later.

"Now tell me what these Sioux plan on doing, Sweete. Do they want a fight of it?"

Hickok shook his head and took a step forward. "Appears they wanna talk—for now."

"A parley, is it?" Custer replied. "They've seen they can't whip us, can't run off our stock."

"They want the soldier chief and only six of his men," Sweete explained.

"Take me, Autie!" Tom Custer addressed his brother by the family's intimate name for the eldest brother.

"No, you and Elliott and Yates will wait here. If there's treachery afoot—I won't have us all wiped out."

"Dammit, when will you gimme a chance—"

"Tom, you are a soldier above all, and you will learn to do as I order. Like every other man in this regiment must do." Custer turned to the gathering of soldiers on that streamside slope, quickly finding his bugler and selecting three other enlisted. "You men will follow me."

"You want us come along to translate for you, General?" Sweete asked, with a thumb indicating Jonah Hook.

"He know Sioux as well as you?" Custer asked, eyeing the ex-Confederate.

"I don't know it all that good, General—but I do know the only way he will learn is by hearing it spoke and talking it himself."

"All right. We'll take pistols," Custer advised the group. "But unbelt them, and stuff the weapon beneath your tunics, men. Have them ready in the event of something underhanded."

He turned to his officers. "Major Elliott, you and Captain Yates will see that the men are deployed in the willows, up and down the streambank. If there is any treachery, we'll blow the bugle from the far side."

"And we come riding!" Tom Custer answered enthusiastically.

"You understand that, soldier?" the lieutenant colonel asked of his bugler. "At the first sign of trouble, turn and blow your trumpet."

"Yessir."

"If you and Mr. Hook are ready, Sweete—let's go parley with this bunch."

By the time Custer's delegation was at the edge of the water to welcome a half dozen warriors wading across the stream, the sun had burst full and yellow as an egg yolk at the edge of the eastern plain. The air stirred with sudden new life as insects took to the wing, and the water beneath their horses' hooves shimmered like liquid gold in the breaking light of jeweled morn.

"Pawnee Killer," Sweete whispered to the officer beside him.

Custer said, "I recognize him. Back at McPherson—he told me what good friends he was to the white man."

"He tell you how honest he was—and how he never lied to a soldier?"

"I believe I remember him saying something like that."

"Then he was lying to you," Sweete replied. "Watch his oily tongue, General. The sonofabitch opens his mouth, he's lying. White or red—his kind of snake will cheat their own mother."

"*Hau!*" came the greeting from the warrior at the center of the six bare-chested Brule when they entered the stream astride their multicolored ponies.

"How!" Custer replied.

"C'mon, General." Sweete nudged his horse into motion. "Let's go be sociable in the middle of the river."

As the soldiers came up and halted, the warriors raised their arms in greeting, then presented their hands.

"They wanna shake, General—but I suggest you don't go any closer than where you sit now."

"All right," Custer answered, making it plain to the warriors that his right hand was going to remain on the butt of his pistol. "Let's see what Pawnee Killer has to say for himself—coming to steal my horses when he said he was my friend back at McPherson."

Sweete flicked his eyes at Hook. "Get your hands limbered up, Jonah. You need to practice your sign as much as I need practice on my Lakota."

When he had the chief's answer, he told Custer, "Pawnee Killer says he'll forgive you for getting lost and crossing his hunting ground, General. Forgive you for spoiling his pony raid."

"He will . . ." Custer cleared his throat, drew himself up. "Tell Pawnee Killer that among my people we punish thieves and murderers. If any live among his people—they are the ones should be afraid for their lives."

"He says his people are not thieves and they don't murder white men. And he takes shame that you think with his warriors there are some with bad hearts for the white man."

Custer snorted quickly. "What's he take us for, Sweete? The snake just about ran off with half our herd an hour ago."

"Claims he didn't know it was you, Long Hair. Says his band will mosey on now—no hard feelings."

"They want to pull out? Just like that?" Custer asked.

As Sweete started to reply, a young warrior brandishing a war club in his left hand and an old rifle in his right appeared on the far bank from the plum brush. Without hesitation, the warrior urged his pony into the stream, sending diamond drops into the golden air as he splashed noisily toward the conference.

"*Hau!*" shouted the newcomer as he came to a halt, shaking his weapons at the white men.

"Tell Pawnee Killer I'm growing angry!" Custer demanded, watching the far bank, hearing the brush rustle. "Now more warriors are coming when he guaranteed six only."

From the plum and swamp-willow on the far side appeared a second unwelcome warrior, who reined into the stream. Then two more splashed into the water as the white men grew restless.

"Tell the chief he's violating his word as a warrior," Custer demanded.

As Shad Sweete's words were spoken and Jonah Hook's sign was made with his hands, Pawnee Killer smiled widely with big teeth in his small, feral face.

"The chief says his young warriors only wanna come say hello to the great soldier chief Long Hair. Says his men admire you—want to see you up close."

"Not too close, Sweete. Tell him that if any more come—we will start our fight right here . . . and now."

When the words were spoken in Lakota, the smile slipped from Pawnee Killer's face like a man's longhandles as he stood over a latrine trench.

"The chief wonders why you don't trust your new friend."

"Because he cannot control his warriors," Custer replied. "Like those."

Jonah and the rest watched another handful of warriors ride into the stream to join Pawnee Killer.

"That's enough of this, Sweete. It's plain they mean to do something underhanded here. Inform them there are many soldiers with repeating rifles in the brush behind me."

Pawnee Killer held up his hand, causing the five warriors to halt halfway between the bank and midstream.

"Put your horn to your lips, bugler," Custer directed, then turned quickly back to the old mountain man. "Tell the chief if any more come, my bugler here will signal the rest of my soldiers and there will be blood in the water this morning."

Sweete sighed after the Brule leader had spoken. "Pawnee Killer wonders who will be the first to fall."

"Tell him it will undoubtedly be both Pawnee Killer and Long Hair— chiefs die first." Custer inched the pistol loose from his belt.

The Sioux's flinty scowl was eventually replaced with a broad smile as he spoke once more.

"Seems they want some coffee and sugar, General. They need powder and bullets too."

"For hunting, of course."

"I figure they've got bigger game on their minds," Sweete replied.

"Tell them nothing doing."

"He's unhappy about your answer, General," Shad said after refusing the chief's demand for provisions.

"How far off you suppose is their village?"

"A few miles perhaps. And getting the jump on us as we palaver."

"They're making good their escape, while this bunch keeps us talking."

"With Pawnee Killer's warriors covering the retreat, General."

At their chief's direction, the warriors inched their ponies backward with a rattle of rawhide and weapons, and a splash of pony hooves. Pawnee Killer joining them.

"Where they going?" Custer's blue eyes darted over the retreating warriors.

"I figure they got done what they came for."

His sunburned brow knitted beneath the broad brim of his cream-colored slouch hat. "We . . . can't we hold them?"

"Unless you want to start shooting—and then the only ones you'll have hold of here will be the dead ones floating facedown in a bloody river, General."

Custer quickly studied the bank behind him, upstream, then down. "Bloody blazes! We'll follow them."

He sawed his reins around, the horse kicking up a gritty spray over Sweete and Hook. Jonah recognized the intense light behind those blue eyes Custer trained on the soldiers awaiting his orders.

"Major Elliott! Take a battalion, your company and Keogh's"—he pointed across the stream—"follow the trail of that village."

"Follow the warriors," Elliott replied, his voice bellowing. "Yessir!"

As the major splashed away, more than a hundred soldiers scrambled out of the brush, trotting up the grassy bank toward their bivouac where they would quickly saddle and mount for the chase. Custer turned back to Shad Sweete and Jonah Hook.

Hickok reined up in the middle of the stream with the group. He shook his head in resignation as he glanced over the two scouts who had been with Custer at midstream. "What chances you think we have of keeping that bunch in sight now, Shad?"

"A snowball's chance between a hot squaw's legs, Bill."

30

E LLIOTT EVENTUALLY CAUGHT up with Pawnee Killer's Sioux.
But only when the warriors had loped far enough ahead to set up an ambush for the trail-weary soldiers. Had it not been for the captain's battle savvy and a little bit of luck in sniffing out the ambush, that battalion of the Seventh Cavalry would have made history of a different sort.

As it was, they had to return to the main command, reporting their lack of success to a frustrated Custer.

"Except for bullets, this bunch is out of everything an army needs to march on," grumbled Shad Sweete as he plopped onto his bedroll between scouts Jonah Hook and Will Comstock.

"You figure we're ready to boil your greasy moccasins down for soup yet?" Hook asked, pointing at the old trapper's feet.

He wiggled his toes thoughtfully. "You don't want to even think of making soup out of these."

They laughed together. Shad had to admit it helped ease the empty gnawing of their bellies. Following the trail of the fleeing Sioux across this fire-hot skillet bottom of a prairie, the scouts had found the land cleared of game.

"What I wouldn't give now for some of that hardtack," complained Will Comstock, a veteran frontiersman. "Weevils or no."

"Meat's meat!" Shad cheered. "Maybe them weevils ain't buffler hump ribs—but they'd go a long way to cheering up a bowl of moccasin stew."

"Don't even talk about hump ribs," Hook mumbled. "Makes my mouth water thinking about them spitting grease over a fire. Instead, we're down to dreaming about moldy salt pork sold to the Yankees during the goddamned war!"

"Custer's had enough himself," Hickok said, coming up out of the darkness. "We're moving out come first-light."

Shad rolled up on his elbow as Hickok hunkered at the fire, warming his hands from the coming chill of a prairie night. "Where we bound for, he say?"

"Forced march. Sedgwick. Custer figures to get supplies over there on the South Platte."

"Glory! It's about time," Comstock whispered, collapsing back on his bedroll and gazing overhead at the stars.

"We really gonna get some decent food at this fort?" Hook asked.

"If they got any." Shad's eyes measured Hickok.

"Who knows, fellas?" Hickok rose and trudged over to his own bedroll, kicking it flat. "All a man can do is hope."

"If'n I was a praying man, I'd say *amen* to that. This bunch that Custer's leading around is about ready to bolt on him," Sweete said.

"They got the Colorado gold diggings not far yonder, that's for sure," Comstock said.

"Lure of gold is strong enough to lead men to point their noses off into Injun country anytime," Hickok said.

"Trouble is, it ain't only the lure of gold," Sweete said. "Maybe now it's the lure of some decent food, an end to this hot saddle ride, and a chance for a little piece of shade."

The next dawn came early enough, but saw the column of dusty twos already pushing northwest toward the South Platte. Custer ordered his scouts out far ahead, with orders to set a bruising pace for his command. Into that furnace of early July on the high plains, the Seventh Cavalry marched, eating up mile after mile as the sun rose off the horizon, hung at midsky for the longest time with no water in sight, and slipped off into the western half of that cruel blue dome overhead.

No water. No stopping. No rest for man nor animal. Most of the dogs belonging to troopers, which had trotted out of Fort Hays with the command weeks before, collapsed from thirst and exhaustion as the hours rolled by, mile after grueling nonstop mile put behind the Seventh Cavalry.

Sixty-five miles in one long summer day.

It was just past the first streaking of stars across the prairie sky when Shad Sweete, Comstock, and Hook stopped at the top of a hill. There they spied the beckoning glow of windows below.

"Riverside Station." Comstock pulled the floppy hat from his head and swiped a greasy sleeve across his dusty brow. His face, like the rest, was streaked with yellow alkali dust and rivulets of sweat.

"That the one Hickok's been calling Valley Station?" Shad asked, eyeing the narrow ribbon of water, lying like a silver, moonlit thread across the darker prairie land just beyond the three small shacks and a skeletal corral comprising the outpost.

"Water down there?" Hook inquired, his voice cracking with dryness.

"You'll have your drink soon enough," Shad said.

"I'm going now." Jonah ran his tongue over his cracked lips as he nudged heels into his horse's flanks.

Sweete caught the reins.

"Let go me," Hook demanded.

"We got a job to do, Jonah. Ride back—"

"You go do that, old man. Only need one to tell them goddamned soldiers to come on. I don't only smell water—I see it!"

He yanked on the bridle again, causing Hook's horse to sidestep suddenly. The ex-Confederate fought the reins a moment, then his right hand shot to his belt.

Comstock had his elk-handled quirt tacked down on Hook's wrist in the next heartbeat. "Take your hand off the gun."

His dark eyes flared. "Tell the old man take his hand off my horse!"

"We're going to ride back to the columns now," Shad said quietly, hearing the coming of hoofbeats.

Hickok was among them, out of the growing darkness, his horse lathered at the withers, foam at the bit. "Trouble here, boys?"

Sweete never took his eyes off Hook. "No trouble, Bill. Me and Jonah here set to come back and give you word."

"That must be Valley Station down there," Hickok sighed. "And—praise God—that's the Platte lying yonder." He eyed the three scouts in the silver light. Comstock removed his quirt from Jonah's wrist as Sweete released the bridle.

"C'mon, Will. You and me ride back and give ol' Horse-Killer the good news about the station and water." Hickok tilted his head toward Sweete. "Shad, you and Jonah stay here—ride on down and get yourselves a good drink and tell those fellas the Seventh's coming in to bivouac tonight."

Shad glanced at Hook. "All right, Bill. Obliged to you."

Hickok started off, then flung his voice over his shoulder, turning in the saddle. "Just don't muddy the water too much that it ain't fit for the rest of us to drink, Jonah!"

They waited a moment, watching Hickok and Comstock disappear into the starry night splayed on the prairie hills before Sweete slapped Hook on the arm.

"Go pulling a gun on me, boy—I'll break every one of your fingers in that hand I get the chance!"

"You gotta catch me first, old man!" he whooped, pounding heels into his weary horse, bolting off the hilltop.

Shad sang out at the top of his lungs as well when he set his animal in motion. There was no problem getting the horses rolling—both had been anxious on that hilltop, what with the smell of the nearby river in their alkali-crusted nostrils.

Halfway down the gentle slope, another yellow slash opened up on one of the three low-roofed buildings nestled fifty yards from the river. The short rectangle was as quickly filled with first one, then two and finally a third dark shadow, each making its way into the yard. From the glint of lamplight spraying into the dusty yard, Sweete could see the three held rifles at the ready.

"Ho! The ranch!" he hollered out.

"Who goes?"

"By damned—it's white men!" yelled a second voice from the darkness.

Shad slowed his horse a bit as they loped past the yard and the three shadows, headed for the river. "A thirsty pair of scouts for the army."

"What outfit?"

"Seventh Cavalry!" he hollered back, twisting in the saddle as Jonah reached the riverbank up ahead with a joyous splash.

"By damned—Custer's outfit. You can't be here," a new voice called out, the body framed in the lamplit doorway. "How the hell you come across that piece of country so quick?"

By that time Sweete was in the water up to his knees, slurping and gurgling. He turned and hurled his voice up the bank to the four civilians who stood looking down on the two scouts and their thirsty horses.

"By damned is right, boys. When you're chasing Sioux with George Armstrong Custer, you better be ready to ride across the fry pan plains of hell itself at double time!"

"Sweet Jesus, but you can't be here yet!" the voice muttered from the top of the bank.

Shad spread his arms out, dripping wet from dousing his hair with a hatful of water. It seeped off his mustache and beard. "Take a look, pilgrims. This ain't no goddamned ghost you got your eyes laid on."

Hook joyously flung some water his way. "No, sir. We ain't ghosts a'tall. Just a pair of poor resurrected souls come wandering in off that godforsaken prairie!"

Jonah got to his feet wearily as Hickok and Sweete came up to the small knot of civilian scouts huddled beneath the stars.

"No word waiting for Custer when we got in," Hickok told them. Beyond the station's three low-roofed buildings, the Seventh Cavalry was going into camp. The twinkling of those first few fires brightened the noisy celebration of *water*.

"Where we head from here—Custer figure that out yet?" Comstock asked.

"He wired for written orders from Sherman . . . Sheridan—anyone at this point, fellas," Hickok explained. Then he glanced at Sweete.

The old mountain trapper nodded. "That's when Custer found out the post commander at Sedgwick already sent written orders out to Custer. Somewhere . . . out there"—he flung his arm southwest—"there's a Lieutenant Lyman Kidder and ten troopers of the Second U.S. Cavalry hunting for us now."

Comstock dug a toe into the sandy soil. "Unless Pawnee Killer's Sioux already got 'em."

The group fell quiet a moment. Then Hickok spoke again.

"I figure we'll find out soon enough what happened to that patrol. As for us, grab what shut-eye you can. We're back in the saddle before sunup."

"Marching north to Sedgwick, ain't we?" Comstock asked. "It can't be more'n fifty mile up there."

Hickok shook his head. "Fort Wallace, Will."

"Fort goddamned Wallace? Why in hell?"

"Custer figures its the only place where there'll be enough supplies to ration this outfit," Sweete told them. "'Sides, I think Custer can't get Kidder's outfit off his mind."

Jonah turned toward the southwest, at his back the twinkling firelights of the cavalry camp, staring into the slap-dark of the rolling prairie grassland that had swallowed Custer's regiment and spit them back out again. He wondered if Kidder's men would be so lucky.

The next morning the entire command was moving at first-light, moving away from the South Platte, reluctantly.

Twenty . . . twenty-five . . . thirty and more miles per day Custer put behind them. Pushing relentlessly toward Fort Wallace. That night a half dozen men slipped off unheard into the prairie darkness.

And the following dawn found the rest whispering at report before they saddled up and pushed off again behind their hard-driving commander. Better than forty miles he prodded them to march.

Through that night of 6 July more than two dozen slipped away, every last man of them taking his horse with him.

Already the mad chase had covered as many miles as he had fingers on one hand.

Pawnee Killer's blood was up. His thirty warriors were warming to the kill. For this was truly fun—to have a wild chase such as this, running down each victim and killing him before continuing on the trail of the rest.

The Sioux had cut a fresh trail miles back—a dozen, perhaps as many as fifteen men. Iron-shod horses. White men.

Within minutes, his war party had been rewarded with finding the quarry in the distance. One man out in front by a few hundred yards. A leader riding in the van. And ten soldiers in a short double column.

The white man always rode like that, Pawnee Killer knew. While the Indian rode in single file.

His warriors now had four of the soldiers dead behind them in the running battle. The white men riding their worn-out horses would turn and attempt to shoot behind them at the warriors on their furious ponies.

The air crackled with sporadic gunshots. The white men cursed and cried out as the warriors drew near. But not a one gave up easily.

It was good, the Killer thought. Good that each one should fight to the last breath.

The last eight finally reined up in a frantic spray of dirt and summer-cured grass, dismounting on the run, dragging their lathered horses into a crude ring. They began shooting the animals as Pawnee Killer's screeching warriors topped the rise.

Down behind the still-quivering, thrashing horses the last soldiers crouched, laying their pistols and long banded-barrel rifles over the still-heaving ribs of the foam-flecked army mounts. And began returning a hot fire like nothing Pawnee Killer had ever seen in his fighting life.

The white men had decided to sell their lives dearly.

He ordered his warriors to stay at a distance, crawling on their bellies along the slopes of the gentle hill to the west of the white men, through the grass on the south and east. The north was open, flat land. Unusable for attack.

From three directions the Brule warriors began walking in their deadly iron-tipped hail, arrow after arrow raining down from a cruel, cloudless sky on the last survivors of that wild chase across the summer-honed prairie.

First one, then another, and a third soldier cried out in pain—a yelp shut off in fear or death. And still more arrows rained down on them while the last of their big brown horses thrashed its way into death. Behind the still carcasses the men hid, only a few firing, and only then when they had a target.

The warriors gave them no targets.

Instead, the arrows arced out of the tall prairie grass far off, sailing into the cruel summer blue and down again in an ugly flight of whispering death that caused another soldier to cry out. And another. And still another.

Until all was quiet.

"Stop!" Pawnee Killer called out, waving both his arms as he came to his knees, signaling the warriors to the east and those on the long slope to the west.

Eventually he stood and took a half dozen steps toward the far ring of silent horses. Another ten steps, his heart pounding, afraid one of them would be alive . . . alive enough to—

He fired his leveled rifle as the figure stirred.

Then went to his knees to reload. Around him the warriors cried out, swirling madly out of the grass like demons who would no longer listen to his orders.

It was time to have someone pay for what they had lost to the soldiers in the recent moons.

They were over the barricade of still-warm carcasses in a matter of heartbeats—clubbing, slashing, hammering with their rifle butts. Counting coup and stripping weapons. Claiming the white man's objects.

In a fury of bloodlust for what had been done by the soldiers to their families, stripping their women and children and old ones of their lodges and dried meat and blankets and robes, Pawnee Killer's warriors hacked arms and legs and hands and feet from the bodies.

Heads were smashed to jelly beside the stinking carcasses of their tired horses.

The manhood parts were slashed from their bodies.

Thighs were opened up like a fresh buffalo kill, from hip to knee.

Bellies riven so that slick purple gut spilled forth.

"This one, you will want to see," said one of the older warriors. "Come, Pawnee Killer."

"Yes, I know him," the chief said. "We will not take his scalp."

"A Lakota?"

The chief nodded. "Guiding for the pony soldiers."

"He should have known better, Pawnee Killer."

"Perhaps he did not know better," he replied. "These were brave men. They fought well while they could. It is the last thing we can do for him—leaving his body untouched. Scalp him only, but leave the scalp here."

"You know his name?"

"Yes. It is Red Bead," Pawnee Killer replied quietly, the wind rustling the summer-dried grass. "As children we played together in our camp along the Buffalo Wallow River."

31

T HE MORNING OF of the seventh dawned as had so many before it.

By the time the gray was gone from the sky and the bloody corona of the sun made its appearance at the far eastern rim of the earth, the command was called to horse.

Apparently on cue, thirteen soldiers from two troops rose from their fires and, without a word, turned west, never looking back. Six strode off on foot. Seven quickly, self-consciously mounted army horses and rode away. All thirteen aimed for the nearby stream—clearly away from Custer's line of march for the day.

"You boys better get back here—you get skinned alive!" yelled a sergeant, trying his best to cajole the deserters.

Lieutenant Edward Godfrey stood watching the seven mounted soldiers reach the far streambank, then the six stragglers slogged across the shallow creek on foot and clambered up the far side without so much as a glance back in the direction of the camp. Practically every soldier in camp was on his feet now, most whispering among themselves, watching the lack of action among their officers. An electrifying tension had come over the entire bivouac readying itself for the march.

Down near the streambank where the scouts had pitched their bedrolls, Shad Sweete stood watching the unfolding drama with the rest as the last straggler on foot among the thirteen slogged out of the creek, up the bank, and onto the rolling prairie.

"They taking off for the gold mines, ain't they?" asked Jonah Hook as he came to a stop beside the old trapper.

Sweete kept looking back and forth between the deserters and the bustling soldier camp, knowing something was soon come to budge. "S'pose so, Jonah. Some men can take only so much of this. Some just ain't cut out to take such a hammering that Custer hisself can take."

"Officer of the Day!"

"That was Custer hollering, weren't it?" Comstock asked.

"Sounded to be," Hickock replied.

"Major Elliott, get Tom—Lieutenant Custer—and Billy Cooke. Bring Jackson with you too. They're our best marksmen." Custer was sputtering as he reached the streambank, arms flaying the chill morning air. "I want those men!"

"Yessir," Elliott replied, turning away into the disordered bivouac halfway to being put on the march.

Shad shook his head and spit a stream of tobacco juice into the sand at his feet. The coffee in his tin cup had quickly gone cold and tasteless.

"Why don't he just let 'em go?" Hook asked. "He didn't get so worked up over the rest took off before."

Hickok glanced at Sweete a moment before he said, "This is something different, I imagine. The rest sneaked off under cover of darkness. This bunch—they just bolted off right in the bright of day."

Sweete nodded. "Right under Custer's nose. He can't let 'em do that—he won't have no soldiers left if he don't get control and get it quick."

A clatter of bit and saddle and hooves snagged their attention as four soldiers reined up beside an agitated, stammering George Armstrong Custer at the grassy bank.

"You're in charge of this detail, Major Elliott," Custer explained, his arm outstretched, pointing across the stream. "You are to perform as if these men were deserting in time of war, men! And how the army deals with deserters in time of war is to bring them back . . ." He pointed at his feet. "Bring them to me, *here*. Dead or alive."

Elliott and the rest nodded gravely. Only Tom Custer, a dull-red Civil War bullet wound still glowing in his cheek, made a comment as the four hurriedly nudged their animals down the slope toward the water.

"By God, Autie—we'll bring 'em all back—one way or other!"

Shad looked over at the rest, then stared at the quartet of officers splashing noisily out of the stream, up the far bank. He said quietly, "The general's sent off a lynch mob."

Across the next hour, it was hard for any man with good ears not to hear the distant rattle of sporadic gunfire roll back to camp on the pristine prairie air. The camp bustled with nervous energy, waiting. Waiting . . .

"Here they come!" a voice called out.

Every eye strained into the distance of those rolling, grassy hills on the far side of the South Fork of the Republican.

"They're back!"

Elliott rode at the lead. Behind his saddle slumped a body.

"By God—they killed 'em all!" someone whispered loudly as the soldiers and civilians alike jostled for a place among the plum brush and willow along the stream.

As Elliott made it down to the far edge of the stream and his horse began splashing across, the water flung up by the prancing hooves appeared to revive his prisoner. The soldier, hands and feet bound together beneath the horse's belly, raised his dripping head, cursing and thrashing wildly. The captain turned in his McClellan saddle and grabbed his prisoner by the back of the belt, readjusting the soldier and cursing back every bit as loudly.

Three of the deserters suddenly appeared on foot at the top of the bank behind Elliott. They paused there for a moment, then were nudged down the bank by Tom Custer, pistol in hand. The last two mounted officers carried restrained prisoners behind them, lashed behind their McClellan saddles. The whole sad procession plodded through the shallow creek, up the grassy bank, and halted before Custer.

"Cut 'em loose," he ordered his sergeant of the guard.

The camp guards hurried forward and cut the three men loose. Two of them crumpled to the ground, loudly complaining. A third sank to the damp sand like a sack of wet oats, without a word and not moving.

"These three wounded, General," explained Major Elliott.

"Get us a surgeon, goddammit, General!"

Custer stood above the soldier in that next heartbeat, sand flying, his pistol drawn. "By the saints—you'll not have a surgeon's care. And any man who takes a step to help these three will answer to me!" He waved the pistol, causing most to step back.

"You're refusing the men my care?" inquired an officer who broke through the curious throng, carrying a small leather-bound satchel at the end of one arm.

"Yes, surgeon. That's precisely what I'm doing. These men wanted to desert the army," Custer spat. "By God—they won't get the attention of an army surgeon for their wounds."

"You've had them shot, General! In the name of humanity!"

"That's the last I'll hear from you, Captain!" Custer snapped at the surgeon. "I'll put you on report myself if you continue." He whirled on the rest of the group. "And let this be a lesson to the rest of you! I'll shoot any man who deserts from here on!"

Custer turned on his heel. "Take these men to a wagon. Chain them up inside," he ordered his camp guards. "Tom—where are the others? I thought there was more."

Tom stepped up, scratching his chin self-consciously. "Seven more. They were horseback. Got too much a head start on us. Spotted us when we crossed the stream—and took off at a hard gallop."

"They left these six to fend for themselves," added Lieutenant William W. Cooke, a Canadian who had come to the States to fight for the Union during the Civil War.

Below his bushy mustache, Custer pressed his windburned lips into a line of utter frustration. The man looked as if he wanted to cuss in the worst way, but swallowed down the temptation. He whirled on the noisy, protesting deserters who were being led off by the guard. Stomping over to one, he jammed his pistol against the man's head.

"You shut up that caterwauling right now! Or I'll be the one to blow your head off!"

"Yessirgeneral," the man replied meekly, his eyes wide and fearful.

"Get them out of my sight!" Custer ordered his guard. "These men aren't soldiers. They're criminals!" He wheeled on the breathless assembly. "And any criminal in this regiment will be dealt with just as harshly!"

"You want the march ordered for the day?" Elliott asked.

"No," Custer answered, squinting into the new sunlight. "Not just yet. Tom—I want you to see that the three who are wounded are placed in the wagon. The other three—have them shaved completely, and then stripped to their birthday suits."

Tom was smiling, a devilish light in his own blue eyes. "We'll march 'em to the 'Rogue,' Autie?"

"Exactly," Custer answered. "Now, go do it."

"With pleasure!"

"*What's going on* over there?" Custer inquired moments later, overhearing the growing noise from the teamsters' bivouac.

Jonah Hook and the rest craned their necks at the increasing clamor from the wagon camp. He and Shad Sweete followed Custer's officers toward the men's voices.

"You can't control your employees, Watkins?" Custer asked of his wagon boss.

"They seen how the rest took off on you, General," Lyle Watkins, the contract civilian, explained. "How you treated your own men. They figure they've had enough. I think—"

"You're not getting paid to think, Watkins." Custer whirled to find Elliott nearby. "Major—these civilians who are guilty of mutiny are under arrest. I want them punished!"

Some of the civilians lunged forward. A rattle of pistols greeted them as iron cleared leather, officers and camp guards protectively ringing their lieutenant colonel.

"We quit! Ain't working for you no more, Custer!" a voice called out.

"I want that man staked out!" Custer ordered. "Some of the rest as well. See how they like the ants and the sun after a while. Who started this, Watkins?"

The wagon boss stared at his boots.

"Who, Watkins?"

Reluctantly, the wagon boss pointed out a big, burly teamster.

"Major Elliott, I want that man tied to a wagon wheel and horse-whipped. Twenty lashes."

"Twenty?" roared the big teamster as the guards approached, guns drawn.

"Make that thirty, Major. And don't be shy to lay them on!"

In a matter of minutes, the soldiers had more than fifteen teamsters striped and staked out on the sandy prairie, their sweating bodies attracting ants and all manner of crawling, flying, buzzing insects. Thirty lashes had been delivered to the ringleader who hung semiconscious against the wagon wheel, his back a mass of red welts and crimson streamers.

"We got one over there, General—a fella tried to help some of the others by pulling up their stakes after we spread 'em," announced Elliott. "You want him get the same medicine, sir?"

Custer thought but a moment. "No. Lash him up and drag the man through the stream. Have the rest watch the show. It will show both soldier and teamster alike that I won't tolerate mutiny—nor will I tolerate those who aid the mutineers."

Hook found his stomach filled with about all the gall he could take. He turned away, stalked back to the scouts' camp with Sweete, leaving the angry hollering behind.

"That how a Yankee soldier keeps order among his men?" he asked nobody in particular. "Never did a Confederate have to run off—we always had something to fight for."

Sweete grumbled. "Out here on the plains—most of these men don't know what the hell they're being asked to fight for . . . maybe die for."

They both whirled at the approach of two horses and the sound of splashing water drawing near. Hook bolted down the streambank as the soldiers drew near, dragging a civilian behind them, lashed hand and foot in ropes, arms strung overhead full length, his body bouncing through the gritty, shallow flow of the South Fork of the Republican. The man popped up, eyes clenched tightly, sputtering and gasping for air as he cleared the water. Then he hit another riffle that submerged him, spitting sand and river water, his bound legs flaying helplessly.

Hook was in the water, pistol drawn before the two mounted soldiers knew it. He snagged the reins of one rider, nearly upsetting the trooper. The far soldier tried to pull his pistol, but stopped, finding the Confederate's muzzle pointed at him.

"You gonna live, Artus?" Hook asked in a loud voice, never taking his eyes off the two soldiers who had been dragging the civilian down the streambed.

Moser sputtered, struggling to come out of the shallow stream, raising himself on elbows. His long hair sopped into his eyes as he hacked up the murky, gritty water, and he drew his legs under him. Moser slowly got to his knees, heaving, puking up river-bottom grit.

"I don't know—"

"You're in a heap of trouble, mister!" growled one of the soldiers.

"Looks to me like you're the one staring down the bore of my pistol, soldier."

"What's he to you?"

"My cousin," Hook snapped. "Now—you there, get down real easy and cut 'im loose." He glanced at the growing crowd of soldiers and civilians on the streambank.

The trooper shook his head. "I ain't a-gonna—"

"You'll do, or I'll wing you so you can't sit a saddle for a month of Sundays!"

The soldier clambered down and pulled out a folding knife. He was cutting Artus loose when some new, loud voices drew Hook's attention to the riverbank. A squad of armed soldiers bolted down the slope, piercing the gathered throng of curious spectators.

"Drop your gun, mister!" bawled a soldier.

Hook flicked him with his eyes. He wore three stripes. Red from the neck up and nervous looking, the way he chewed his lip.

"You best keep your finger away from that trigger, soldier," said Shad Sweete.

Hook quickly glanced at the bank, finding the old trapper wading into the water.

"I ain't taking my gun off these two until they cut my cousin loose," Jonah growled.

"We'll shoot—we have to," said the nervous sergeant.

"They probably will at that," Sweete said, measuring the half dozen soldiers.

"Then tell 'em to start shooting." Hook turned his back on them, again facing the pair who had dragged Moser downstream. "They want to shoot a man in the back—they can start with me. But you remind them, Shad—that this big ugly Yankee here is gonna get a lead ball in the face before I go down."

The eyes of that burly soldier who still sat his horse widened even more, flickering over the half dozen come to his rescue, then back to the bore of the Confederate's gun. "Now . . ." His deep voice cracked, a slight squeak around its edges. "Now, let's no one go getting fretful here, fellas. Sarge, suppose we just cut this man loose"—and he motioned to the kneeling Moser at the middle of the stream—"and we all call it a day. I figure he's had enough. What say, Sarge?"

"Can't do that, Henline," grumbled the itchy sergeant. "Custer ordered punishment. So punishment it will be."

"Cut 'im loose—like I told you!" Hook snarled, for a moment wagging his pistol's muzzle down at the soldier with the folding knife who stood over his cousin.

"Don't you move, soldier!"

Hook looked up to find Tom Custer loping down the grassy bank.

"There's hell to pay now, Jonah," Shad said with a sigh. "We got the general's brother in the pot now."

"This man is being punished for mutiny!" the younger Custer declared as he came to a halt in front of the half dozen soldiers, less than ten yards from Jonah and Artus.

"He's being dragged through the river until he drowns, you stupid sonofabitch!"

Young Custer flared. "Drop your weapon, mister—or there'll be a dead man in this river."

"There'll be two." Hook slowly brought his pistol off the mounted soldier and pointed it at Tom Custer. His gut told him enough—that at least it was the smart thing to point your gun at the man doing the talking. "You and me, Custer."

"What's going on here, Tom?"

The lieutenant colonel appeared in the parting crowd at the top of the bank.

"Got us someone ready to die to cut loose one of the teamsters."

"The man with the pistol—"

"I know damned well who he is," Custer snapped at the sergeant. "Hook, isn't it? One of Hickok's guides."

"That's right, General," Jonah replied.

"Tell him what's going on, Jonah," Shad pleaded.

"Don't want your goddamned soldiers dragging my cousin through your goddamned river, General. He was trying to help the others you staked out—when he was caught and your men here tried drowning him."

"I ordered the punishment for your cousin myself."

Hook smiled. "Then it's your brother going to die when your soldiers start shooting, General."

"None of this warrants any shooting," Custer said, his voice laced with strain.

"You had your own soldiers shot, General," Hook said. "I think the shooting's already started. Let's just get it finished."

"Don't threaten me, Mr. Hook."

"No threat. I just don't figure I got much left to live for but family. That goddamned war you Yankees whipped on us caused me to lose my wife and children. Far as I know—all I got now is my cousin . . . this man you about drownded in this shithole river. So—you go and kill him, I figure you might as well kill me same time."

"I don't plan on killing anyone, Mr. Hook."

"I do—and it's gonna be your brother, General."

For a long moment the sun beat down on that stretch of prairie river, while the water continued to riffle around the horses' legs and Artus Moser's bound and bloody body.

Finally. "Cut the prisoner loose," Custer said.

"Don't back down, Autie!" Tom said. "He ain't got the nerve to shoot me."

Hook leveled the pistol at the younger brother's heart, his arm straightening.

"I don't have time to find out, Lieutenant Custer," said the elder brother. "We have Indians to track and Indians to fight. Not our own teamsters and scouts. It's time this outfit was on the march. Now, Sergeant—cut the prisoner loose. Cut all them loose. We're pointing this bunch south, to Fort Wallace!"

Hook waited as Custer wheeled from the bank and disappeared among the gathered crowd in dusty blue. Some of the half dozen soldiers grumbled, most of all their sergeant as he turned his detail around and trudged away up the slope.

"You heard the general—cut my cousin loose, soldier," Hook repeated.

As the pair of soldiers led their horses out of the river, Jonah went to his knees in the water beside Artus, dragging his cousin against him, cradling his head, stroking his wet, gritty hair, wiping sand from Moser's mouth and eyes and nostrils.

"Ain't no one gonna treat my family this way," Hook said quietly. "Don't care if I gotta take on the whole goddamned Yankee army. Ain't no one gonna dare treat my family this way."

32

T HEY HAD COVERED at least half the ground from the South Platte to Fort Wallace, marching on a trail a shade east of south.

Shad Sweete was today riding point, far in the advance of Custer's columns. Alone. For three days Jonah Hook had been assigned to bring up the rear of the columns, closing file and watching the backtrail for both stragglers and lurking hostiles. At least that's what Custer called it.

Yet it was really nothing more than Custer's way of punishing the civilian scout for what had happened back at the South Fork of the Republican. Make Hook eat the dust of the entire regiment and wagon train as the command ground its way through the low, grass-covered hills of western Kansas. Every night a few miles closer to Fort Wallace and the Denver Road. That much closer to some real food and some shade.

Someone had reminded Sweete this morning that it was the twelfth. July. Just the word itself had always made him hot enough even without this midsummer sun suspended overhead. At least it was nudging off midsky now. Casting a little bit of a shadow it seemed. Not like at full high, when the only shadow a man could see was directly under a horse's belly.

It was in that bright light shimmering off the rolling prairie land that he spotted the big-winged black birds fluttering down to roost not far ahead. They were cackling, fighting among one another over their carrion—but scattered momentarily at his approach. The great buzzards came to a rest just

254

yards away, craning their great wrinkled necks at the man as he brought his horse to a halt, having first circled upwind.

A terrible stench greeted Shad when he drew close.

Trying not to breathe through his nose, he ground-hobbled the horse with the rein, then stepped up, cautiously, his eyes watering with the strong smell of death. His skin already crawled, knowing this was only the beginning of it.

"Damn," he muttered when he recognized what was left of the telltale brand on the torn meat of the rear haunch.

Without slowing, the old man snagged up the rein and did not use the stirrup to vault atop the saddle. In a tight circle he brought his horse around, hammering it with his heels. He feared he knew already.

At the top of the next hill, he was sure of it. Ahead of him, in that broad bowl of rolling country, he spotted three more . . . then a fourth . . . four bunches altogether, knots of the big-winged black birds swirling overhead, landing, *kee-raw*ing, then ripping flesh from bleaching bone.

He had seen enough and turned his horse around, pounding hooves back across the sunbaked prairie to the head of the strung-out cavalry column. Shad could see Hickok's mouth *O* up, and imagined what the chief of scouts was hollering back to Custer.

"Rider coming in, General! It's Sweete."

He brought the big Morgan mare hard around, slowing her, nostrils flaring as he matched the gait of the lieutenant colonel's mount.

"You and Hickok might wanna come have a look. Something I run onto that will snag your interest, General."

"Indians?" Custer asked, his pale, sunburned face flushing with excitement.

"Not exactly."

"Some sign of hostiles?" Hickok inquired.

Shad leveled his eyes on the young chief of scouts. "All the sign a man would care to see."

Custer turned in the saddle, flinging orders to his adjutant and to the officer of the day to continue their march at the present pace. Then he broke out Major Elliott, along with a sergeant and a half dozen men to escort the two officers behind the two scouts.

"Lead on, Mr. Sweete."

Without a word, Shad reined away from the head of the column, pointing his nose a little more east of south than the line of march had been taking.

"Buzzards?" Custer inquired as they topped the knoll where they could see the first gathering of the huge flesh-necked meat-eaters.

"Something dead down there, General," Hickok said.

Custer cleared his throat, removing one of the damp deerskin gloves and stuffing it in his belt. "Mr. Sweete will tell us if we're going to find a body down there."

"Only a horse."

He led them far around the bloating carcass of the white horse, coming back into the stinking carrion on the upwind drift of the prairie breeze rustling the dried grass. That gentle wind and the noisy protests of the scattered buzzards proved the only sound, besides the slow clop of the hooves, then the scrape and grind of Custer's boots as he got down, alone, and strode purposefully forward to have a look for himself.

He came back to his mount after but a moment, only then removing his hand from his mouth and nose.

"There's more, Mr. Sweete?"

Shad waited for Custer to swing into the saddle. "Up yonder, General."

"More of the same?"

Pursing his lips to keep from puking the words, he wagged his head. "No. It's soldiers."

Sweete and Hickok watched Custer's lips form the word, but left it unspoken as he sighed, his eyes narrowing on the middistance. "Take us to them, Mr. Sweete."

They put the miles behind them, not that many, really. But enough to see it had been a running battle. By the time they topped the last knoll and Shad reined up the entire escort, the flat, sun-shimmering bowl lay before them, populated now with only the *kee-raw*ing, noisy birds of prey.

"One of 'em had his horse go down on him back there," Shad explained. "Signs of his boots tell it. He was running hard. Iron-shod hoofprints circled back, picked the fella up, and they tried to make it double."

Custer swallowed. "They didn't make it, did they?"

"None of 'em, General. I figure that first bunch of buzzards up ahead, down there—just one horse and two bodies there—they made a hell of a fight of it."

The lieutenant colonel ground his teeth. "Let's go."

One horse. Two men. One directly in the tangle of the dead animal's legs, taking cover. The other body a few yards off. Either dragged there by the warriors working over the bodies, or by the huge, broad-winged birds attempting to drag off their stinking meal-claim.

"This the first time you've seen what a warrior can do, General?" Hickok asked.

Custer shook his head, swallowing hard. "No." He looked up at the old mountain man. "Who was it—the bunch who did this?"

"I got an idea, General. Let's go see the rest afore I say for sure."

There were two more horse carcasses, each with a man's naked, white, bloated, and sunburned body nearby—each man having fought to the end alone—until they came upon the last stand, where the eight had dropped their horses and hunkered down to make a fight of it to the last.

"Bastards didn't leave much of 'em," Hickok said, holding his bandanna over his mouth and nose.

Shad breathed through his mouth. Still the stench of it stung his tongue with a sour burn. High meat, he thought. Just what them goddamned buzzards love to eat. High meat going to soup under this unforgiving sun. He prayed to be long gone from there, but knew he would stay until the column arrived and this bunch had a decent burial.

"They were on the road to Fort Wallace?" Custer asked.

Hickok glanced at Sweete. Shad nodded.

"Yes," Hickok answered. "Headed that way."

"Likely they figured they would meet up with some sign of you between the Platte and Wallace," Shad explained.

Custer ordered three of the soldiers to ride back and bring the columns on at moderate speed. A burial detail . . . shovels . . . and some prayers were needed over these men, is what he told them before sending the trio off.

"Second Cavalry," said the lieutenant colonel.

"You know any of them, General?"

"Can't say as I do, Hickok." He pointed at the one body with long, black, unbraided hair. It had been stripped and scalped, but for the most part remained unmutilated. Something clearly evident compared to the butchery practiced on the other eleven bodies.

"Who was that?"

Hickok shook his head.

"Name of Red Bead." Shad looked away to the west where the sun would not fall for many hours yet. Too many hours, and he wanted to be far away by then. Not that he was particularly superstitious about death. But Red Bead and his soul would haunt this ground forever.

"He Cheyenne . . . Pawnee?" Custer asked.

"No, General. He was Sioux."

Custer looked up with those blue eyes of his, glaring into the tall mountain man's face. "You mean he was Sioux . . . like the ones who killed him?"

Shad nodded.

"That why they didn't take his scalp?"

"They respected him. Whoever it was killed this bunch—someone knew Red Bead and didn't want his body touched for the long trip across the Star Road."

"He died as bravely as the rest," Custer commented quietly. "I'll say prayers over his grave as well."

"You want to show your respect for how brave that Injun died, General Custer," Shad stepped right up to the soldier, "you'll wrap his body in a blanket and leave it lay right here. Don't you dare say your white medicine words over his body. It would be a mighty bad sign to do such."

"Just leave his body here? Not bury him with military honors?"

"He's already been honored by whoever killed him, General," Shad explained. "Just let his body be . . . for the wind and the birds of prey . . . and the winters yet to come visit this sacred place."

Jonah hadn't seen such savagery in longer than he could remember—if ever.

Two of the white soldiers with Lieutenant Lyman S. Kidder's doomed patrol had evidently been alive enough when the warriors reached them; then they had been tortured to death. Two small fires over which to exact some excruciatingly delicious agony on their prisoners while death lingered, hovering closer and closer.

Every nose hacked off. Faces hammered into pulp. Tongues severed at the root. Shoulders, elbows, wrists, hips, knees, and ankles all with sinews and tendons severed. Flopping loose as a wood marionette when the burial detail hauled the bodies over to each shallow grave. Other soldiers were assigned to bring along the severed limbs.

Naked, white, puffy bodies were lowered into the shallow, yawning holes and quickly covered up by the grunting, puking burial detail, each man sweating through it, some collapsing. The officer in charge had to order another man up to complete what the others could not. Few made it through without losing what they had left in their bellies from breakfast many hours before.

Each body pierced with so many arrows had reminded Jonah of the soft velvet pincushion his mother had used almost daily back in the Shenandoah, down in the shadow of Big Cobbler while he was growing into a man. Before he moved to Missouri. Before he marched off to war behind General Sterling Price. And ended up never seeing his family again.

He squeezed the thought from his mind—the way he wrung his socks out once they reached Fort Wallace. Hard, even savagely—he forced the thought from his mind every time it came to haunt him with not knowing. Trying again to concentrate on that image of his mother's pincushion—so he would not have to remember the image of those twelve bodies, each bristling with no less than forty, perhaps fifty shafts, silently rustled by the omnipresent prairie wind.

It was something he was coming to think on less and less now. Only out here on the plains was the wind always blowing. Not like this back where he was born, nor in that Missouri valley where the curtains still hung, motionless in the broken windows like the eye sockets on buffalo skulls. Out here, the wind always blew.

It cleansed the land and the air that moved over it. Without stop, he figured. Nothing lasted for long out here. But then, everything stayed the same forever here too. Funny, but to his way of thinking right now as he sat in a little patch of shade beside the limestone walls of Fort Wallace, Kansas Territory, that fit in some type of symmetry.

Nothing lasted long out here. Yet everything stayed the same forever.

Victory . . . or death. He thought often on that now. Seeing that the doomed dozen had been given little choice but to die with as much honor as each of them could muster. Dying was lonely, even with others around you. No man do it for you. It came down to it, Jonah had seen enough of the dying already. Came close a couple times himself. The coldest he had ever been. Wondering at the time if he'd ever be warm again.

And here he sat, sweating in this piece of shade as the sun settled. A Monday he was told by Wheeler, the contract post commissary agent, 15 July.

Custer strode out of the post commander's office into the easing of the sun minutes later, yanking on his sweat-stained deerskin gloves. He tugged down the big, cream-colored, broad-brimmed hat and adjusted the blood red tie at his Adam's apple, letting the breeze nudge it over his shoulder among the strawberry curls.

He was a sight, Jonah had to admit. The man who had cut a swath through one Confederate horse outfit after another. Twelve mounts shot out from under him. The Yankee who whipped J.E.B. Stuart at Gettysburg back to sixty-three. And the one who bottled up the old man himself, Robert E., in the wood down to Appomattox near McLean's new farmhouse.

Custer.

By God, the man was pulling out from this run-down motley collection of limestone buildings and adobe dugouts with an escort of four officers and seventy-two troopers, leaving the rest behind with Major Elliott and what soldiers the Seventh's own Captain Frederick W. Benteen already commanded here at Wallace. Custer was hurrying east as fast as those with him could follow.

Upon arriving here yesterday, the lieutenant colonel had greedily read dispatches wired from Fort Harker far to the east along the Smoky Hill, learning of the terrible flood that had required Harker to be abandoned. Word had it cholera was ravaging the forts of central Kansas. No other news had been received at Fort Wallace. Nothing from Sherman nor Sheridan. No letters from his beloved wife either.

Jonah cursed Custer for that, then smiled. At least the lieutenant colonel, that Yankee from Michigan, knew now how it felt not knowing where his wife was.

What's more, the Seventh needed fresh horses to continue their stalking of the plains tribes.

Food enough here at Wallace. Enough to last until Custer was back again with those horses. After the man had sworn to find Libbie and hold her in his arms for one, perfect, summer day.

Jonah watched the man with the cinnamon curls fling his arm forward and set off at the head of his detail, that crimson tie fluttering.

Damn you anyway, Custer, he thought, dragging himself to his feet as the sun eased out of the sky and the air became a squeeze more tolerable.

"You go find your woman, Custer. This goddamned campaign's over— and you ain't killed yourself a Injun one. Gone off and shot your own men though . . . and found the bodies of dozen more good soldiers killed trying to get dispatches to you. But you—you ain't shot a Injun one."

Jonah watched the backs of the last pair of the seventy-seven dusty troopers lope out of sight. Custer set a blistering pace.

Yet as much as he hated Custer, Hook understood just how a man could feel down in the private, blackened, buried pit of him—afraid for the not knowing. Not sure if he ever would know what had become of his own woman.

If nothing else, at least he shared that in common with the Michigan Yankee with the long strawberry curls.

33

S HE ALWAYS PUT her mind somewhere else.

For weeks—or had it been months? She had been afraid of allowing her mind the freedom to go elsewhere. Fearing that she might forget where she had put it. Afraid she might not even care to go back to get it when the time came.

But lately now, not really sure how long that meant, Gritta Hook had come to the not caring, or not fearing anymore.

It was a victory for her to remember her name today.

Just . . . remember . . . her . . . name . . .

To this private place where she took her mind she came each time the giant bald-headed man came close with that look in his eye. She recognized it. Every man had it when he wanted a woman in that way. Even . . . Jonah.

Yes—Jonah.

She remembered him now. In a fuzzy, outlined sort of way. Less and less every day, the picture of him in her mind growing dimmer and dimmer, shadowed more and more darkly by the big man the rest called Usher.

She hated him for pushing the memory of Jonah away. Hated Usher, and Jonah just as much for not pushing Usher away.

Gritta had given up a long, long, long time ago trying to push the man off when he got that way and hung close to her. Smelling her, lifting her long hair to sniff at the nape of her neck the way he did when he wanted her in that way.

This way.

The way he was using her right now.

But—it was like he was using someone else too.

Standing outside herself and watching, arms crossed and haughty, chin jutted, watching the two of them sweating in the summer heat. She was sure it was late summer, standing here, looking at herself sweating with her eyes opened and unblinking, staring at the shocking white of the canvas roof of the wall tent. How he grunted, like a boar planting his shoat seed in the sow back to home.

There was no more home, she reminded herself, scolding as she looked down on the woman lying beneath the half-naked man. She was half-naked herself, with her dress pulled up and her chemise torn down, breasts open for the whole world and God Himself to see.

How shameless that she should lie there and not fight off that rutting, stinking, brute of a man, Gritta thought, looking down at herself and clucking her tongue as she would to one of her errant children.

No, she did not want to think of them any longer. Her daughter—Gritta saw Hattie sometimes, but never close enough to talk. And the boys. She knew they were gone now. Usher had told her a long, long time ago . . . so long she barely remembered their faces—they were sold off for good Yankee dollars to buy bullets and beans and flour and whiskey. Usher had laughed.

And she loathed her womb for ever giving birth to her children, that they should suffer.

It was meant for her to suffer, her alone. Stand here and look down on that poor woman lying perfectly still beneath that sweating, heaving animal as he drove his hot, hard flesh in and out of her flaccid body, taking her when he wanted, how he wanted.

Long ago she had ceased to protest each time he circled her, flung back her hair, and bit her shoulder. It was the same each time. No more did she fight him with her fists and knees and teeth. Now she just fought him by going outside herself until he was done with her. She wasn't really that body, after all, was she?

She clucked again. Shameless, how that body just laid there letting the brute abuse her with his privates, doing his business on her, in her, up to her womb where she knew she must never again have another child only to have it taken from her to suffer.

They would never get her mind. Not Usher. Not any of them. She would keep coming here, out of herself. That shrinking shell of what she had been, something that seemed to dry up and fall in of itself when she left her body, each time Usher wanted it for himself.

She left her body behind and feared going far away, forcing herself to remember, and look, and still feel something. But felt something less and less each time. Afraid now the last few weeks . . . or was it months? She had no way of knowing and grew afraid of that as well. Afraid mostly that she was losing her soul.

More and more now it was like stepping first with one foot, then the other, into that wide, yawning pit of quicksand—with nowhere else to go but into the pit. Then turning, reaching out for a limb, something hanging over the pit to help pull her out.

For the longest time there, she remembered the faceless man standing at the edge of the pit. And felt, more than knew, it had been Jonah. Him—reaching out for her . . . first with his hand. Then with a stout limb . . . then there was nothing left for him to do but stand on the edge of that pit helplessly watching her sink deeper and deeper into the quicksand of insanity.

After all, if she couldn't help herself . . .

Hancock's campaign along the Republican River and Custer's campaign along the Platte had accomplished nothing but to stir the tribes to a boil.

"Like jabbing a stick into a hornets' nest," Shad Sweete had told Jonah that late August afternoon as the entire command finally marched back to Fort Hays. A hot, steamy summer evening coming down slowly on the central plains.

"There's talk everything west of here's shut down," Jonah said.

"Construction on the K-P ain't no more. Workers skedaddled back east to safety. Wagon road from track's end west to Denver City is closed down. No man willing to take the ride into Injun country now. What I was a'feared of most is just what happened."

"What didn't you want to happen?"

"I came along with Hancock and Custer to try my level best to see that the army talked with the tribes this time out—'stead of charging in shooting and slashing."

Jonah had snorted quietly, without needing to say a word.

"I know," Sweete agreed. "A foolish thing for me to think, weren't it, son? Figuring I could help these bands by going along with the army."

"Don't grumble so much, Shad Sweete. After all, you was the one talked me into going along with you."

"Should've listened to Toote all along." Sweete looked up from the lodge peg he was carving on to watch his wife hauling water up from Big Creek.

"She figure it wasn't such a good idea riding with the army?"

"Not so much that as much as she just wants us long gone from this country." He jabbed the pointed end of the lodge peg into the dry, flaky soil. "We ain't got no business staying around here where so much trouble's bound to boil over. She wants to wander on west, over the mountains again. Says we'll be safer . . . she'll be happier there."

"Maybe you should listen to her."

Shad watched Toote carry the sloshing kettle of water in through the lodge door. "It ain't like I never thought of it myself, Jonah."

The voices from inside the lodge grew louder, more strident. Sweete glanced up at Jonah's face as the angry words penetrated the buffalo hides.

"It's hard on them both," Shad explained, seeing Jonah become self-conscious when the ex-Confederate was discovered overhearing the argument. "They been doing the best they can, what with being Injun and Cheyenne and come up here to this soldier fort looking for a white man to boot."

"Ain't that many women around, Shad. And them two happen to be some of the best looking a man could set his eyes on."

"I oughtta send the two of 'em north—live up there with the Northern Cheyenne on the Powder and Tongue." He scratched at the ground with the peg. "It isn't that the soldiers give 'em a hard time here—we all come to figure on that. It's something else—something Toote or me can't put our finger on. Unless . . ."

"Unless what?"

Shad gazed at the Confederate's face a moment before answering. "Toote says it's the girl's white blood making her crazy the way she is."

He chuckled. "That'd explain a whole lot, wouldn't it? We white men seem just about as crazy as folks can get to the Injun, don't we?"

He sighed, feeling better for having talked about it. "Perhaps you're right. We don't do anything what makes sense to an Injun. Especially an Injun woman. And when you mix in my white blood with that girl's growing up a Cheyenne half-breed—it just makes things all the harder—"

The young woman burst out the lodge door, shoving aside the antelope hide roughly, storming off as Toote burst out on her tail, squawking her disapproval in a sing song Cheyenne. Pipe Woman kept right on going, headlong for the creek and the timber, where she could disappear, while mother ground to a dusty halt a few yards from the lodge, balled her fists on her hips, and stomped a foot angrily into the dried grass.

Shad rose as she trudged back toward the lodge. She plunged right past him as if he were not there. He reached for her. Toote yanked away from him angrily and dived back into the darkness of the lodge.

After a moment he shrugged his shoulders and returned to Jonah Hook.

"Seems sometimes I don't do nothing right. Got a mark against me from the first whack, just because I'm a white man. She thinks I made Pipe Woman's problem. Maybeso, I should send 'em north."

"Let 'em simmer down. Both of 'em. Time was—" Jonah paused a minute, stared off across the prairie. "Gritta and me'd go for days not talking. Better for it—getting over being mad, rather'n saying something cruel or hateful, and being sorry for it later. A woman needs her time to get shet of it, and heal what made her mad at you to begin with."

Sweete watched Jonah's eyes focus on something a long, long way off. If not in distance, then something far away in time.

"Sometimes you love a woman more for the arguing," Shad said quietly.

"I want to find her, Shad," he said almost in a whisper. "Like a hole's opened up in me and it won't close up without her. I got to find them."

Sweete reached out with one of his huge hands and squeezed Jonah's shoulder.

"Your time's coming soon."

A tall dark-skinned young man bolted from the lodge door as Jonah Hook strode toward Shad Sweete's lodge days later.

Jonah stopped, watching in surprise as the young man leapt atop his pony, bareback, and reined off, hooves spewing clods of dry soil and long, unbound hair flying.

Toote Sweete emerged into the sunlight, followed by her husband. She called in Cheyenne to the young man as Shad stood watching the rider disappear over the nearby hills. He dropped the hand shading his eyes to find Hook staring, motionless, at the scene.

"You come just in time, Jonah."

"What's that all about?" he asked, striding up to the lodge. Toote turned, fuming once more, her eyes filled more with sadness than anger as she dived back into the lodge. "Some young suitor come to pay court to your daughter?"

Sweete put an arm around Jonah's shoulder and led him a few yards from the lodge. "No one courting Pipe Woman." He stopped, standing right in front of Hook. "That's my son."

Jonah found it hard to believe. "Your son? Didn't know he—"

"Just didn't tell you." Shad turned and trudged over to a tree.

When the old trapper had settled against the trunk, Hook came over and plopped down as well.

"Pretty important thing—not to go tell a friend, don't you think?"

"He ain't lived with us for some time. Never quite did get used to the idea he's a half blood. Damn his hide anyway. Always has a way of showing up at the worst of times. Here I thought Toote might be getting over the boy—and he comes a'waltzing in on her again, making life miserable for his mama."

"What about you, Shad? He's your blood kin. Your boy."

"Don't I know. But there's something in him that ain't in either his mother or me, Jonah."

"Where's he go off to, if he ain't living with you?"

"Ah, hell—he's been old enough for some time now, twenty-one winters. He can live on his own."

"Where?"

Shad shook his head, his lips curled up in clear disappointment. "Don't have any idea most times."

"He come back to stir up trouble?"

"Just to stir his mother up," Sweete answered. "Always does him a dandy job of that too."

"Better that he's gone then," Hook replied, hoping his friend would see sense in his appraisal of the situation.

Sweete sighed. "No, this time he's really tore his mother up. Always before it was something little, but this time he's gone and made a real ruckus between us."

"Between you and him."

"No. Between Toote and me. Bull's doing a good job driving a wedge between that woman and me. Back there minutes ago, he just spit on his white blood. Then he spit on his mother for laying with a white man and giving birth to him—cursing him with his white blood."

"She'll get over it, won't she?"

"I damn well hope she does, Jonah."

"Give her time—like we was talking the other day. Better that High-Backed Bull's gone, ain't it? So's he can't go causing her no more trouble."

"But he can cause us a whole lot of trouble."

"If he just stays away, things simmer down—"

"He's run back to a band of Cheyenne he's been with for a little over a year, to hear him talk about it."

"They trouble?"

"Tall Bull's band of every outlaw and renegade and outcast from every village on these plains. That bunch ain't just warriors who will fight to protect their women and children. The bunch Bull been running with loves the stalking, the raiding, the killing just for the sake of fun. They're bad from the word go."

Jonah fell silent, not knowing what to say to the man, except that he understood. "Family is trouble when you have 'em. Trouble when you don't."

"Man comes to realize that, Jonah. But it don't stop you loving 'em as much as you do." His face brightened a moment. "Tell me about Grass Singing. You find out anything? Run across word of her?"

"Heard in Hays City she's gone back to the blanket."

"My, but you are picking up the tongue out in these parts. So she went back to her people?"

"What I'm told, asking about her in town. Gone back to her mother, and they both headed north to someplace in Nebraska to find their old village."

"Lotta Pawnee up there. You figure on looking for her?"

"Enough folks for me to look for, Shad. She's with her mama now—and I need to be finding some work while I keep my nose to the ground for that bunch out of Missouri."

"You got any idea what we're to be doing come freeze-up?"

He smiled at the old trapper. "We, eh? Well, now—for this boy, I've gone and found me a job with a new bunch of scouts being formed."

"That the bunch under the North brothers?"

"Yeah. The major remembered me from Connor's expedition to the Powder two years back. North needs help getting his Pawnee Battalion back together."

"I hear the Norths both fought on the Union side."

"Don't matter, I suppose. Long as they can use me, I figure I can learn what I can from them Pawnee. Maybeso some tracking."

"You learn what you can while there's time. Come freeze-up this fall, the army will cut you loose."

"That's when I'll be ready to ride south again—pick up that trail that went blind on me down in the Territories."

Shad nodded. "I'll be ready to ride with you. Your cousin—he going to go with us come winter?"

"Artus? I s'pose he is. Come winter, he figured he wouldn't have no more work on that crew laying track up north on the U-P."

"Nebraska?"

"Yeah."

"I wish he'd hire on somewhere else, Jonah. Injuns still making things a might hot for track crews up there on the U-P."

Jonah shrugged. "Artus, now, he's come out of that damned war back east and got through just about everything else that's been throwed at him. He'll do all right, laying track. I don't worry none 'bout Artus."

34

ONLY THE NIGHTS were cool this season of the year. The days hot, sticky, steamy. But when the sun went down, a man could feel halfway alive once more.

Turkey Leg sat with the others. Their council held outside, at the center of the great circle of Cheyenne lodges. Too warm for any of them to huddle as normal inside a lodge to debate, argue, make plans. The breeze was better out here. Besides, the stars were out and bright this night.

"If the young men want to go to investigate this smoking, noisy monster," said Burns, one of the older warriors, "I say let them."

"Yes," Spotted Wolf agreed. "We know the soldiers are back in their forts already. And they show no desire to again march after us."

"It is true, the soldiers are no longer sniffing on the trails taken by our villages," Turkey Leg said when all had grown quiet. Though he was chief, every man had his say in this warrior band. "Perhaps they do not have the heart to make war on us."

"These soldiers," spat Spotted Wolf, "they only want to make war on women and children . . . burn empty lodges."

"Then go marching off aimlessly to wear both men and animals down without food or water," Burns said.

"The white man is back where he is safe," Spotted Wolf continued. "The young men want to ride with me to see what we can of this great smoking monster making noise in the north."

"We have all heard tales of the monster, Spotted Wolf," said Turkey Leg, an aging chief. "I would go with you to see it myself."

Spotted Wolf rose before the others, all of them seated beneath the starshine. "This is a great honor, Turkey Leg. I will tell the others we ride in the morning."

Turkey Leg chuckled, nodding. Many of the rest in the group were smiling at the young warrior's enthusiasm. "But not too early, Spotted Wolf! An old man enjoys his sleep too much. Let me ride out to see this smoking monster when the sun has come to greet the day. You will see my old head come from my lodge door when the sun is rising. And no sooner!"

For all he knew, it could be the end of the world.

There wasn't a thing out here but the endless hills covered with the tall grass rustling in the incessant breeze, the white-rumped antelope who stopped, cocked their heads, and watched the two men on the handcar pumping by on the noisy iron rails, and the endless blue mirror overhead that seemed to reflect all the sun's heat back down on the rolling, swaying tableland.

The bandanna tied around his neck was soaked from the work this handle pumping had become. The shirt worn by the man on the other side of the handcar was darkened with sweat as well.

"How far we come, Harris?" Artus Moser asked. He was the lead man, which meant he was up-track and could only look where they had been. Unless he craned his neck around, which was damned difficult while you were pumping the handle.

Harris rubbernecked around his sweating partner and gazed up-track, considering. "Five mile. Maybe more."

"We ought to spot that break in the line soon enough then," Moser grumbled.

"You didn't want to come with me, did you?" Harris asked.

"No—but you needed another man for this damned handcar," Moser explained, trying to make the best of it. "And a hand with the repairs."

"We'll make it quick," said the older man. Nels Harris was in his second summer with the Union Pacific, hired on year-round for his knowledge of telegraph that he had earned during the war. He could repair a downed wire quicker than any man out here. When word came from the last station east that the wire was down somewhere between it and track's end, Harris was asked to go and see to it.

"Didn't have me enough breakfast to work all day on," Moser grumped. It was nearing sundown, and his belly hollered for supper. The muscles in his back crying out for what comfort his three blankets spread on the cold ground could give him. It was enough to wish for.

"Neither did I," Harris replied.

It was minutes later when Artus thought he smelled wood smoke and glanced over his shoulder. Looking up-track, he sniffed the air carefully. Then figured he must be imagining things. Wanting something for his growling belly so badly that he imagined the smell of a supper fire where he would be roasting juicy hump ribs. Remembering now the crackle and spit of the red, lean meat he and Jonah would carve from the huge carcasses they had provided for the track crews. A year gone now and he still remembered the taste of that red meat on his tongue.

The mind . . . maybe his gnawing belly . . . had a way of playing tricks on a man.

They were entering a short range of low, rolling hills.

"I'll bet next week's wages the break is no farther than the other side of this draw," Harris huffed.

"You're 'bout done in, ain't you, Harris?"

"I'm not a young, strapping lad like you no more, Moser." The sweat clung to the tops of the whiskers on his cheeks where it beaded, each droplet catching the pinkish, orange light of sunset. "Work like this makes a man old before his—"

Above the beads of sweat, Moser watched the older man's eyes squint with confusion, then dilate with fear. His head snapped around, gazing up-track at the faint glow of the firelight.

There was no damned good reason for a fire to be built there beside the track, up yonder a hundred yards.

"I don't like this," Moser muttered.

"I got a bad feeling myself," Harris echoed quietly.

But it was as if the handcar had a rhythm all its own once they had set it into motion on the downgrade side of the series of low hills. Both men no longer pumped hard as they had been getting it upgrade. Not really pumping at all now—but the handle kept on rocking up and down as the handcar hurtled them toward the fire glowing among the shadows come here to the hills at sunset.

"Goddamn! There's Injuns up there!" Harris shouted, his eyes now filled with horror.

Moser didn't pump for a few moments, craning his neck around to stare at the fire, watching the black figures lope off the side of the hill atop their ponies, blotting out the glow of the fire. The flames grew higher the closer they drew.

"Stop this car!" Artus growled. He was shoving his weight against the handle, but Harris started pumping with all he had.

"Don't do that, goddammit!" growled the older man. "We don't stand a chance stopping this thing . . . getting it started again back down-track. Pump, dammit—for all you're worth! Pump right on through 'em!"

Artus was pumping. Like nothing he had ever done—not driving spikes into rail ties or chopping wood with the double-bit axe. Artus was pumping, glancing over his shoulder, watching everything come upon him much faster than he wanted it to. Pumping that handle as the rush of cooling breeze and the huffing of the older man across the tiny car from him were blotted out with the growing crescendo of war cries.

"Pray we can shoot on past them," Harris was saying. "Faster. Faster!"

Moser had it figured that way too. The faster they went, the sooner they could sail right on past the Indians and their fire and be on their way toward track's end, pumping with all their might. Closer and closer to the fire and the yelling warriors and that mishmash stack of . . .

—the whole world was topsy-turvy. Moser was in the air, turning over and over. Catching glimpses of Harris sailing through the sundown sky as well, the handcar tipped over, keeling onto its side slowly as Artus came down in a heap among the grass and sage and graveled roadbed. Tumbling . . . rolling. The cries of the warriors louder now than before.

As they swirled over him, their shadows like nighthawks swooping down on a moth or other flying thing, he thought of Grass Singing. Wished he had lain with the Pawnee girl instead of Jonah. It had been so long since he had been with a woman—he could not remember how they smelled when they got aroused with him, taking his hot, hard flesh in their hands eagerly, wanting the poke as much as he.

Did Grass Singing smell like these warriors? Rancid grease on their braids. Stale sweat gone cold.

The lights twinkled before his eyes. A dull thunk echoed in his mind, like a man driving a wedge down into a resistant chunk of timber. A wedge slowly cracking the wood with the sheer power of his sweating muscle. The lights glowed once more, showering sprays of meteors.

And he realized one of the warriors was beating his head in with a stone war club.

Artus put his hand up into the blackened blindness of what he could not see. His eyes filled with something hot and sticky, blinking them did not help. Put his hands up and then felt his throat opened up.

Sensing that last good breath of air. Struggling to feel, no—struggling to drag more of that shocking air down into his lungs. Gurgling. Gasping. The cool prairie air wheezing through the huge, gaping hole in his neck.

The club sank deep into the back of his head. And as he rolled over on his belly, his legs convulsing out of control, he cursed himself for pissing in his pants, for his bowels voiding.

Realizing that wasn't a stone war club that had crushed the back of his head, driving his bloody face into the gravel of the graded roadbed.

That had been a huge, gleaming war-axe that had likely split his head open like a juicy melon. . . .

Near the small wagon that ran along the iron tracks before the warriors had tipped it over, two of Spotted Wolf's men found the two rifles.

Piling wood on the tracks had worked. The small wagon had run into the timber and gone tumbling off its tracks.

Turkey Leg watched the young warriors finish off the two white men, strip their victims, then mutilate the bodies when the two warriors came over with Spotted Wolf and the rifles.

"These are broken," the war leader told Turkey Leg.

"Broken when the wagon fell off its tracks?" asked the chief.

"Perhaps." Spotted Wolf held one of the rifles across his two hands. "I was looking at it, claiming one for myself, touching the rifle when it broke in half. Like this."

"Perhaps it is bad medicine for us," Turkey Leg tried to explain. "We are not meant to have these rifles—I am sure of it now. They are broken. Leave them here, with them," he said, pointing at the naked, bloody bodies as the last glimmer of the sun's fading light drained from the far western sky.

"We go back to the village now?"

"No, Spotted Wolf. Come morning, we will finish our work here."

The leader of the war party grinned in the deepening twilight. "To tear up these iron tracks the smoking monster rides upon?"

"When these two do not return, there will be more coming," Turkey Leg said. "We will prepare a welcome for them when they do."

In the cool before sunup the next morning, Spotted Wolf's warriors were busy over the iron tracks: building fires on the wood ties, a few yards away using two long iron bars found on the small pump-handle wagon to pry at the rails themselves, doing their best to bend the rails upward. One after another of the young warriors joined the group, grunting and struggling together as they pitted the muscle of their bodies against the iron strength of the white man's smoking monster.

They succeeded in twisting the bent rail and were whooping their joy when Porcupine hollered out from atop the nearby hill where he had gone to watch both east and west along the path of the iron monster.

Porcupine signaled east with his outstretched arm. "The morning star is rising! It is brighter than ever before."

Others turned to see. Turkey Leg did not think it was the morning star at all.

"No," the Cheyenne chief said to the muttering group. "That light comes from one of these smoking monsters we have seen with our own eyes. Not the morning star—"

"Look!" Spotted Wolf shouted. "There are two of these far-off stars. And they draw closer all the time!"

True, there were two lights, pulsating in the distance, there on the far edge of the horizon where the sun was spreading pink-orange mist before its rising for the day. Two morning stars emerging from the bowels of the earth where the sun would itself greet the morning.

"Two smoking wagons," Turkey Leg said.

"The iron monsters?"

"Let us prepare a welcome for them, as Turkey Leg has told us!" hollered Spotted Wolf.

With yelps like young coyotes ready for their first hunt with the pack, the warriors gathered up their ponies and weapons and rode behind the low hills where they would await the coming of the white man's noisy wagons.

"Send three riders east," Turkey Leg said, turning to Spotted Wolf. "When they have seen the iron monsters coming, seen that these are indeed the white man's wagons, tell them to ride back here as fast as they can and tell us so that we might be ready for their arrival."

The three eager warriors did just that. As soon as they could see that the first of the dancing lights was mounted on the front of the first smoking, belching iron monster, they reined their ponies about and headed back toward the ambush. But on came the growling monster, and behind it a second with its own dancing light spraying brightness over the graveled roadbed the white man had smoothed for the iron tracks of his noisy, wheezing wagons.

The train steadily gained on the three galloping warriors, no matter how fast they rode or whipped their war ponies. One brave rider loosened his best buffalo rawhide lariat and tried to guide his pony toward the smoking monster, where he could rope it to slow it down. But his pony would not get close enough, fighting the reins, resisting, its head jerking away from the steaming, spitting, hissing monster.

On the smoking wagon pressed into the low hills, passing the three riders on their weary ponies without slowing. And the second wagon as well. Both of the monsters disappearing into the night about the time Spotted Wolf's warriors began firing at the first smoking wagon.

Sparks flew up from the great, spinning wheels, lighting the whole of morning itself. With a wheezing sigh the sparks went out as two white men riding atop the monster shouted to one another and fired back at the warriors along both sides of the track, others racing after the monster on horseback.

The smoking wagon was slowing, gradually slowing when it hit the bent rails and burned ties. The wheels spun and screeched, trying to grab for a hold on the tracks as it heeled over onto its side. White men hollered, jumped clear at the last moment. One by one the smaller wagons behind the smoking wagon came crashing up the tracks, not slowing.

One by one they crunched into the smoking wagon and keeled over, falling, tumbling, careening off the iron tracks, spilling on one side then the other of the roadbed.

A white man burst from the smoky haze of the wreckage, waving a bright light at the end of his arm.

"Get that one!" Spotted Wolf called out. "He warns the other wagon!"

The white man was running back down the track, swearing and hollering, when the young warriors rode him down and brought him to his knees. He clawed at the arrows sprouting from his back. His bright light fell into the gravel of the roadbed as he sank slowly to his face, still clawing. The young ones were upon him as he breathed his last.

Yet the damage was done.

The second smoking monster wheezed to a halt. Loud voices from that far wagon. A shrill whistle sounded, startling Turkey Leg's warriors. Every one of them stopped what he was doing, crawling over the smoky wreckage, butchering the two white men from the wagons—every one watching the second monster as it screeched into motion—backward up the iron tracks.

Four or five white men hollered at one another. They had jumped off the second wagon and had started for the wreckage when they saw Spotted Wolf's warriors. Now they were screaming wildly, sprinting for all they were worth toward the retreating second wagon as it backed into the coming of day.

That was where the white men belonged, Turkey Leg thought to himself proudly, watching some of the young warriors race across the nearby prairie with bolts of cloth pulled from the wreckage, bright colorful streamers fluttering from their ponies.

In the land to the east. Where the white man should have stayed in the first place.

Out here—this land belonged to the Lakota and Shahiyena. Coming out here only meant death to the white man.

He should have stayed in the east, where the sun came up each day.

35

September, 1867

T HIS WAS THE only time of the day when the air cooled this late in the summer. Here when the moon finally sank from the sky.

He had waited for better than two weeks for this phase of the moon. When there wasn't so much of the moon's light to shine on this thickly wooded land—part of the Choctaw Nation down in the Territories . . . or were they now in the Creek Nation?

Riley Fordham didn't know for sure. Certain only that it really didn't matter right now as he swallowed down his heart that was choking him. Afraid of being caught as he stood and listened into the night. Hearing the June bugs scritching at one another, listening for the swoop of owls at their nightly hunting, the croak of frogs and other creatures up here in the darkness when few men walked the earth.

Only he and a dozen others guarding the perimeter of Jubilee Usher's camp.

Fordham was one of the trusted ones. That's the only way this was going to work. Boothog Wiser had put Riley in charge of a detail of camp guards. Every man of them knew they had to be extra careful now, this deep in Injun territory, what with the way they were stealing horses and borrowing squaws from the villages where the Choctaws and Creeks and Cherokees squatted, living out their miserable existences here where the white man had moved them from the east.

277

Riley swallowed down his heart, hearing it thunder in his ears as he strained at the night-sounds. Hoping none of the others were up and wandering about. He had made sure the rest of his guards were spread thin that night. He untied the horse where it grazed nearby, leading it into the thick timber along the game trail he had chosen for his escape.

Riley had been planning this for weeks now. Waiting for moon-dark, as Usher called it. And waiting to figure out a good route of escape. Earlier in the first dark of the moon's silvery rising, not long after returning here to his spot, having completed an entire circuit of the camp and finding his pickets in their places for the night, Fordham had taken the tools from his saddlebag and pried each of the four shoes loose from his horse's hooves.

Moving silently, slowly down the game trail, he knew the horse's tracks would in the morning appear to be nothing more than an unshod Indian's pony—when Jubilee's men came looking.

Usher and Wiser would mount a search to one degree or another. Simply because Riley was one of the best they had. The best marksman. Perhaps the smartest Usher had working for him now.

Smart enough to know he wanted out. The war was long over, and still Usher was not taking them back to Deseret. Instead, Jubilee had told them their God-granted work was here on the plains, not back with Brigham's people in the Valley of the Great Salt Lake. All was at peace there. It was here, Usher told them, here where the might of God's hand was needed.

Here, where Jubilee Usher would baptize the land with the blood of the lamb.

Riley had followed Jubilee east with the others that last trip, part of the Mormon army protecting the wagon train when they were all commandeered to fight the Civil War. He had been willing to fight and kill and even die for the faith—his family's faith in Joseph Smith and Brigham Young.

But this had become something different altogether.

Jubilee Usher kept the fair-haired woman to himself. And the girl. She couldn't be more than twelve now . . . and still Boothog lusted after her. It would not be much longer that Usher could keep Wiser off the girl. Riley strained to remember the girl's name. Wishing for a moment that he had brought her along. Knowing if he had, the chances were good that neither of them would make it.

Hattie.

He felt sorry for her as he plunged deeper and deeper into the timber along the game trail, farther and farther from Usher and Wiser and their insanity.

The woman was lost. She belonged to Usher now, after all this time, body and soul. But the girl. She was starting to bud, her young breasts only lately beginning to press against the too-small cloth dress she was forced to wear like a blouse over the men's britches they had given her. One of these days her beauty would drive Boothog Wiser to madness, and he would no longer deny himself her virgin flesh.

Riley Fordham had to desert—risking his life to escape north to Kansas. He knew that country, been up there scouting it with Hastings for Jubilee Usher. Up there with the westbound railroad. Up there with all the rumors of the tribes making trouble for settler and track crews alike—why, a man could lose himself among the many. And no one, not even Usher and Wiser, could track him down and make him bleed as he knew they would if they ever got their hands on him.

No man ever quit Usher's outfit. No man ever just walked off the job. To Usher, this was God's work. And God's vengeance would be his if a man just up and rode off.

But that's exactly what Riley Fordham was doing. Planning to ride until sunup. Lie low where he could just before the sun rose. Then ride again come nightfall. Day after each new day of freedom.

Fordham had to go, and now. Because he knew that come one day soon, Boothog Wiser would claim the girl for his and Usher would allow it. Them two so alike in their abuse of the women. Not that Riley didn't like pinning a squaw beneath him of a time when they had one for the men to use. That was something different. Something Brigham had said about the Indians being some animal less than the white man. Like the land was God-given for the Saints to use—and with it the use of the dark-skinned Injuns who lived here too.

Those two women weren't squaws. They were beauties to his way of seeing things. And they had belonged to a white man. A man's wife . . . and his daughter.

And if that man weren't killed in that bloody war back east, Riley Fordham knew damned well that man was pretty near crazy by now, wondering, hunting, stalking down those who took his family.

Riley didn't want to be around when that man caught up with Jubilee Usher and Boothog Wiser.

It sure wouldn't be a pretty sight what those two crazed blood-lovers would do to that poor sod-buster come to claim his wife and daughter.

The crumpled rail cars lay on both sides of the track like a child's toys. From a distance, they looked like something he had carved for Jeremiah or little Zeke. Tiny railcars scattered along the ruin of its rail bed.

With all his might, Jonah Hook hefted the memory of his two boys from his thoughts.

Enough to think on now. Knowing the chances were good that he would find his cousin somewhere out here.

For the past two days, he had asked after Artus every chance he had, whenever Lieutenant James Murie stopped his small detachment of Pawnee scouts. Major Frank North had assigned Jonah to Murie, because the ex-Confederate knew a good measure of sign language as well as some of the Pawnee tongue.

"After that time we chased Cheyenne and Arapaho with General Connor, I spent a winter learning what I could from a Pawnee gal," he had explained to North and Murie.

"You're hired, Mr. Hook," said the major.

"I can track and am a pretty fair marksman," he had gone on to explain.

"Major North said you were hired," Murie reminded.

"Just like that?"

"By talking with Bear Runs Him over there," North said, pointing at one of the Pawnee sergeants, "you've showed your worth. Now, Murie here will get you squared away with the McPherson quartermaster. We're likely to have something for you to do soon enough."

And they had. As soon as word arrived of the attack on the train, along with orders telegraphed from General Hancock, Major North dispatched Murie and his squad of fifty scouts to explore the ground near the derailment and see what they could come up with for clues to who the war party might be.

All Jonah knew was that his cousin had pumped away from the repair station the afternoon before the derailment along with another man named Harris. Bound for a break in the wire somewhere west of there. With every passing mile, Jonah had prayed the two had made it past the scene of the destruction long before the warriors had arrived to rip up the track and stage their ambush on the train. He prayed Artus was long gone west of the scene, unable for the moment to get word back east that they were safe because of the downed line. After all, Artus would have no idea that his cousin was come looking for him. . . .

The fires were out now. Likely the warriors hadn't stayed around long enough to make sure the rail cars were completely destroyed. But the autumn rains of the past two days very likely put out the smoldering wreckage. Just charred hunks of twisted, toppled—

"Over here!"

Murie was hollering at him in English. Likely found something the lieutenant wanted him to ask the Pawnee to look at.

Hook slowly turned the body over with his toe. The man was too damned fleshy, downright fat, to be Artus. What there was left of the man. It wasn't the first time he had seen work done like this.

"They say it was Cheyenne, Lieutenant," Hook explained after asking the warriors who had committed the butchery.

"The arms . . . cut like they are?"

"You're learning." Hook looked up as a trio of Pawnee riders loped onto the scene. They had gone on ahead, following the tracks to scout for prints, sign, anything worthy of attention.

"You come. Now," one of the older Pawnee said. His long braids nuzzled his cheek above the blue tunic the Indian scouts wore above their breechclouts and buckskin leggings.

"Find something?" Hook asked.

"Come."

The scout motioned, then reined his pony about as Jonah raised himself to his saddle.

Through the string of low hills they rode along the gaping iron rails pointing their way west, toward the far blue mountains of Dakota Territory.

"Two more," said the Pawnee scout, breaking into Jonah's reverie. He was pointing at the wreckage of the half-burnt handcar as he reined up near the other two Indians on the ground.

Hook slowed his horse, but he kept on, passing the three Pawnee. The first body was clearly not Moser. He sighed with little relief, the bile stinging the back of his throat. This was nothing new, no sir. Not the mutilation anyway, nor the heat bloating and the way the insects had been drawn to the blood and gore. Every wound, as well as the open mouth and eyes frozen wide in horror were now home to the wriggling maggots and larvae of the green-bottle flies . . . it was enough to turn any man's stomach. It would not be long before the wild dogs of the prairie would find this place of death.

Jonah dropped to the ground, letting go the reins, and walked slowly forward, down the side of the graveled roadbed. He spotted the second body, laying face down. The ground around the body had soaked up the blood in several spots, especially beneath the head.

What was left of the head anyway.

He swallowed down the acid taste, afraid he would lose his belly then and there beside the puffy, swollen, blackening body.

It could be Artus, he thought. He hated himself for even thinking it as he circled around the remains. Get upwind, he told himself.

He started to turn the body over with the toe of his boot, but the swollen skin burst with a sickening hiss, emitting a horrendous gas that drove Jonah back from the corpse.

Taking a deep breath, he approached once more, again using his boot to turn the body over. At first the skin slipped and tore, already mortifying out here in the elements these past few days. But slowly the stiffened body moved, leaving slime on the toe of his dusty boot.

He swallowed hard, turning away, unable to stop his belly from lurching. He lost his breakfast as he stumbled away, his head swimming, gasping, spitting bile and vomit and stinging pain wrenching the center of him. Some of it clung to his lower lip, in his beard.

He realized he would never forget the smell of this place where his cousin had died.

He knelt there, several yards upwind from the blackened corpse, his back turned to what had once been more than just family—what had been a true friend these last years since they both had returned from a damned long war.

His stomach finally heaved its last into a pool between his knees.

Jonah wiped and wiped his beard again. Thinking only on how he had to bury what was left of his cousin.

Trying to remember now the words he should say over the grave. Words of love and forgiveness and everlasting peace.

Jonah realized he knew nothing of love and forgiveness . . . and damned well would likely never know anything of everlasting peace.

It wasn't like he expected to find the warriors responsible for wrecking the train, but Shad Sweete led the soldiers north from Fort Hays anyway.

Not that he always did what he was ordered. No matter that General Hancock himself had telegraphed his dispatch sending this bunch out on the chase. Sweete could have refused. But there was no point.

That hot-blooded bunch had disappeared onto the prairie. Shad was sure of that. At least they would be disappearing like breathsmoke on a winter wind soon enough, what with this squad of Seventh Cavalry coming up from the south and Frank North's Pawnee Battalion sweeping the country clear along the Platte River itself. It was North's Pawnee who were going out to the scene of the derailed train. And likely, Jonah Hook would be with them.

Not that he was worried about Jonah either. The Cheyenne would be long ago gone from the countryside around Plum Creek Station by the time Shad Sweete led Captain Louis Hamilton and his two companies of cavalry to the scene.

There was no danger the Seventh would catch the warriors. Too far to travel for this bunch of plodding horsemen. And he doubted this bunch of cavalry had the resolve to find the guilty warriors anyway. Easier to jump the villages filled with women and children and the old ones too sick to fight. Much harder to track and follow the wild-roaming bands of young warriors ready to turn and spit in your eye.

Sweete knew his son would likely be among them. Riding with Roman Nose or Turkey Leg, Tall Bull or White Horse. Every bit as likely as the fact that the main bands of Dog Soldiers would soon be coming together for the fall hunt. Breaking up only after the first good cold snap, that first early snow foretelling of the harsh arrival of winter.

As certain as the sun rose each new morn, Shad knew his son would be in on that hunt this autumn. Like every year gone before, the bands would be laying in the meat that would see them through the winter.

Except that this year—the bands would be hunting some new game: two-legged game.

36

P *E - T A H - H A W - E E - K A T* is what they called themselves. Living Above Pawnee.

Company B, under newly promoted Captain James Murie and Lieutenant Issac Davis.

Each of the four bands of Pawnee had been formed into a formal company of scouts. Which meant that the army hired three white officers to command each company. In this case, the sergeant of Company B was one Jonah Hook.

Company B had just received orders to find the bunch that had destroyed the tracks west of Alkali Station. Hunting Cheyenne ranked right high on the list of what the Pawnee liked to do. And word had it that the Cheyenne were getting bold enough to make another raid on the track.

Frank North made it plain he felt the rumor was just that—not worthy of belief. But he determined he would ride out for Plum Creek with Captain Murie and Company B.

"I'll be go to hell," North muttered, the men around him stunned into silence.

"Sounds like you didn't believe we'd find 'em. At least not this quick," said Hook, his eyes scanning the far hills where at least 150 warriors sat their ponies, breaking the skyline.

Company B had just ridden down to the ford at Plum Creek, closing on

284

the old bridge near the abandoned stage station, in no way expecting to find the Cheyenne so quickly.

"I truly didn't," North replied. "Captain, let's get this bunch into battle order!"

Something easier said than done.

Every one of the forty Pawnee had already spotted the Cheyenne, their ancient enemies. Their blood instantly hot, the scouts were already stripping for battle, hollering at one another, working one another up for the coming fight. They checked their weapons, straightened the little bundles of war medicine each man carried tied around his neck, maybe under an arm, perhaps tied behind an ear or adorning the long, unbraided hair that stirred with each hot breeze.

Murie and Hook were among them, the captain shouting his orders in English, waving his arm to show his meaning. The ex-Confederate on the other hand rode up and down the entire line of the brigade, hollering in his crude Pawnee, getting his wards to spread out on a wide front to receive the coming assault.

"We must cross at the bridge, Captain!" North shouted, his cheeks gone flush with adrenaline.

"This bunch will cross ahead of us at the ford if we don't get moving," Murie hollered back against the din of screeching raised by the Cheyenne warning their women and children away, against the noise of the ringing war songs of the Pawnee as they tightened saddles and bound up the tails of their ponies.

"Hook—order the scouts to cross at the bridge. Warn them that the ford may be filled with shifting sand and unpassable. Everyone is to follow me!"

"Yessir, Major!" Hook reined about to deliver his order as North and Murie trotted down to the old bridge fifty yards off.

He was too late explaining the danger in crossing at the ford. Already the first of the eager Pawnee were in the water, their army horses fighting them, head-rearing, snorting, bogging down in the mud of the crossing as the scouts called out for help from those yet to enter the water.

In a mad scene of confusion, a dozen not yet gone to the water wheeled about and tore down the bank toward the bridge, crossing on the heels of their white commanders while the rest soon abandoned their horses in the water. One by one and in pairs, the rest dropped from their saddles, plunging into the creek that rose above their knees—as the Cheyenne opened fire.

Bullets smacked the water. Slapped into the old grayed timbers of the bridge long used by the stages bound east or west from Plum Creek Station along the Platte River Road. Snarled overhead madly like angry hornets.

As he reached the far end of the bridge, the Cheyenne were slowly backing into the nearby bluffs, already carrying five of their own with them. On the north bank of Plum Creek lay a wounded Pawnee calling out to the others. Nearby lay another scout, past all caring, his body lapping against the sandy mud and willows on the bank.

"Hook! Get those men to force their horses out of the river!" North shouted, pointing his rifle at the horses struggling in the creek.

Hammering heels against his mount's heaving sides, Jonah was among the scouts in a heartbeat, yelling in Pawnee, trying to make himself heard above their own courage-shouts and the rattle of their gunfire.

"We can't follow the Shahiyena if you do not have your horses to ride!" he screamed at them.

The first to understand rose from his knee where he had been firing at the fleeing Cheyenne and turned back into the creek. Then a second, and finally more rose and returned to the muddy, churning water, snagging up the reins to their frightened mounts, soothing the animals if they could. The scouts got the horses to the north bank, where they quickly mounted and swirled around Hook.

Jonah realized if he did not take command immediately, the hot-blooded Pawnee would go to fight without him. Flicking his eyes at North and Murie, Jonah found the white men waving him to advance with his thirty scouts.

But to do that did not make sense to him. Why go join the officers and their ten warriors . . . when the Cheyenne were escaping in a totally different direction?

"Follow me!" he ordered in Pawnee.

With an ear-shattering whoop, the thirty obeyed. A rattle of saddle and bit, a grunt of frightened animal, and the shriek of worked-up warrior in each of them drowned out all protests flung in their direction by North and Murie.

But instead of sitting back to watch the chase, North and Murie led their ten to join it.

The Cheyenne were not long in running, stopping after less than a mile among their women and children. The travois filled with lodges and camp plunder had been following the procession of warriors when the men blundered into the Pawnee. Now they were back among their families, where the warriors turned about on their Pawnee pursuers, shouting the courage-words to one another, here to make a stand and protect the weak ones from their tribal enemy.

With screams of panic, the women furiously tore at the baggage, freeing the lodgepole travois from most of the ponies, abandoning their camp gear, putting a child and old one on nearly every animal before turning to scatter north into the hills, away from the charging Pawnee.

Ahead of the broad line of scouts he led, Jonah watched the Cheyenne warriors swirl in among themselves, as if confused, disorganized, until suddenly they reined about with a shout and leapt away from the scene. They left the field littered with baggage torn from the travois and backs of packhorses.

It was now a race. The trail-weary ponies of the Cheyenne versus the army horses the Pawnee rode.

For better than twelve miles the scouts followed the warriors covering the retreat of their village, gaining little of the ground between them. Disappointed, North ordered a halt just past sundown. The command's horses were all but done in. Lathered and weak-kneed, the mounts quickly obeyed their riders when asked to slow the pace and turn about.

"How many we kill, Hook?"

Jonah quickly asked his men for an accounting.

"Near as they can count, seven—maybe eight."

"Along with all the camp plunder we can carry off," Murie commented.

"Or burn," Hook added.

"That's the idea, Sergeant. We'll burn what we can't carry back." A grim smile creased North's dusty, sweat-stained face.

"Don't forget the prisoners," Hook reminded the officers.

"The old woman and girl?"

"Them and a boy—maybe ten years old." Hook looked over his shoulder, watching a half dozen of the scouts bringing the three prisoners up.

At separate times during the wild chase that afternoon, each of the Cheyenne captives had fallen from a pony and been captured by a swarm of Pawnee. A young girl no more than eight years old. An old woman, her well-seamed face still haughty and arrogant in the midst of the Pawnee calling for her death. And the ten-year-old boy. Jonah looked at his dirty face, the wide brown eyes—remembering that Jeremiah would have been ten years old this past summer. He had not seen his son since . . .

Since Jeremiah was five years old.

That hurt more than any bullet smashing through his insides. The thought was as cold as any pain could be. As he stared at the Cheyenne child, he wondered if he would ever know his son, if he would even recognize Jeremiah after so long a time.

"Tell the men we're riding back toward that stand of trees, yonder," North explained. "We won't go any farther tonight to make camp. But we will send back ten men to guard the camp plunder. With instructions to abandon it if the Cheyenne double back to reclaim it."

"I don't figure they will, Major," Jonah said. "Those Cheyenne have had their fill for one day."

Turkey Leg did not like licking wounds.

Even if none of them were his own, the old chief did not like having to look over his people and see so many without so much.

They had to leave most of what they owned behind when they ran into the Pawnee at Plum Creek. Turkey Leg's band had been on their way to a second raid on the smoking wagons of the white man here in the Moon of Scarlet Plums when the Pawnee bumped into them.

So now, instead of being richer for the raid, they were poor. Huddled beneath the cold prairie night sky, gathered like beggars around their fires they would keep going until sunup. No lodges. Few blankets to go around. The little ones crying in hunger and the old ones in need of comfort. Remembering the old days before the white man and his soldiers and their great smoking wagons came to this land thick with buffalo.

Now the buffalo refused to cross the great, endless iron tracks.

Seven women keened loudly at the edge of camp, refusing to join the rest at the modest warmth of the small fires. Instead they mourned the loss of their men in the old way, outside the village circle—slashing themselves, cutting off hunks of hair, chopping off the tips of fingers, and wailing.

The seven would not stop with the rising of the moon, Turkey Leg knew. The keening would echo from the hills all night and into the morrow. He felt like mourning himself.

Spotted Wolf had been wounded. At first it had worried them all that the war leader had been shot through the body by a Pawnee bullet. But though the wound was painful, Spotted Wolf claimed he would be able to mount his pony come morning. He lay now on a blanket by one of the fires with his two wives in attendance, drinking water from a horn spoon. He complained of much thirst.

It was not a good sign, Turkey Leg knew.

The sound of hooves drew his attention onto the starlit prairie. Four, perhaps five, riders. They came on, past the outer guards, past the herders keeping watch on the last riches still claimed by Turkey Leg's band—their ponies.

"Turkey Leg! We have news!"

He watched the young warrior dismount even before his pony was at a complete stop. "Porcupine!"

The warrior strode into the firelight. "Yes. We scouted our backtrail. The scalped-heads do not follow us," Porcupine explained, using the Cheyenne term for the Pawnee, indicating their practice of shaving most of the hair from their heads.

"It is good, for we have little left to lose," Turkey Leg replied. "Tell me of the three who are missing."

Porcupine shook his head. "We found no sign."

"No bodies? Didn't you call out for them?"

"We looked carefully. We called out for the three by name. All six of us called into the darkness. There was no answer from the prairie night."

The old man felt hollow again where there had been a moment of hope. Three of his people were not accounted for when they finally stopped to build their little fires long after sundown, here in the dark. Yes, here in the dark—the despair seemed to weigh that much more on the chief.

"I was afraid we would find their bodies," Turkey Leg said quietly, careful that no one should overhear.

"It is better, I keep telling myself," Porcupine replied. "Better that we found no bodies. The scalped-heads have not killed the three and left their bodies to rot on the prairie."

"How far back did the scalped-heads ride this night?"

He pointed. "We saw the red light from their fires. A few have gone back farther—back to where we left our belongings."

"I want to know what they take and what they leave behind when they go in the morning, Porcupine," the chief ordered. "But more important, I want you to send some of your warriors to look over the main camp of these who scout for the white man."

Porcupine gazed steadily into the chief's eyes. He had a grin on his face. "You want to know if the scalped-heads have captured our people?"

"Yes—the girl, the boy, and the old woman."

"Your mother?"

Turkey Leg gazed at the ground. It was where his heart rested, cold and on the ground. "Yes. My mother fell from her horse in the chase. She cannot see, for the Grandfather Above has put the milky flesh over her eyes. She cannot hold tight to the pony reins, for her old hands are seized with spasms of pain. They are hands that once held me as a child, hands that taught me to walk. Hands that never begged anything of any person—much less her own son."

"I will find out if the scalped-heads have the three, Turkey Leg. Will you—" He paused a moment, thoughtful before he asked the question. "Will you trade our prisoners to gain the release of our people?"

"You already know the answer to your question, young one." The old warrior sighed, the cold inside him no warmer. "These scalped-heads must not ever know they have captured the mother of Turkey Leg."

37

H<small>E HAD NEVER</small> truly lost his wonder at it—how this wide and rolling land did its best to swallow a man, especially at night.

Not much of a moon to speak of overhead. But a generous sprinkling of stars well scattered in the dark dome that greedily licked every last bit of warmth out of the land like the Pawnee licked every last smear of marrow from the center of the bones they roasted in their fires.

Here Jonah roamed with the rest, eleven of North's Pawnee, digging among the baggage and folded lodge skins and camp equipment and broken travois poles abandoned by the Cheyenne in their mad flight away from Plum Creek. Much of it looking like black lumps on the prairie beneath the pale starshine—no pattern at all. More like a random scattering of buffalo chips.

With his teeth, Jonah yanked on a strip of dried jerky. Antelope or deer, he figured. One of the Pawnee had found some among the abandoned baggage. The one among them who had the best nose, so joked the rest. They were thankful for that dried meat and marrow bones, especially after darkness smothered the land. The Pawnee extinguished their cooking fires and contented themselves with waiting out the rest of the night. Talking softly among their little knots and drinking sips of cool water from canteens dipped into Plum Creek not far away, eager for the sun-coming.

Jonah leaned back against a bundle of smoked lodge skins, warmly pungent with the fragrance of many fires. It had been a long time since he felt this lonely. Something to do with the overwhelming darkness, for out here, unlike nighttime in the timbered hills back home or the high slopes of the Rockies, the plains magnified the darkness, and the bigness of the land, and hence the smallness of one lonely man.

Perhaps he was more lonely because he was the only white man here among so many Pawnee. But right now he really didn't want to have to work and strain at translating their foreign tongue to follow their conversation. So he sat by himself, off a ways from the rest as they laughed quietly, poked fun at one another, told of coups from bygone days and what feats had belonged to the day just grown old with night's coming.

Listening to the horses hobbled nearby crunching the dried grasses aroused a feeling of yearning for a time already gone from his life—of early autumn nights such as this, after the children had been bedded down, wandering outside the cabin into the moonlit yard, leaning against the barn door and hearing the animals in their stalls, working their feed hay.

It was a good sound, reassuring, a sound claiming that in some manner of thinking all things were made right at this moment in his world. But Jonah knew they were not. There were pieces of his life left unraveled, like the hem to one of Gritta's long dresses snagged on her heel and slowly unfurling with time.

Time lost. Never to have those minutes, hours and now years back again. Time.

And he didn't know how to stop it. How to repair the damage. How to make it good as new. At least make things almost as good as they were before he marched off to fight the damned blue-bellies when he should have been home to mind the fields and fight off the bullyboys who came in to tear his family asunder.

His kidneys hurt from the pounding they had taken in the running battle. Jonah slowly rolled onto his side, drawing his legs up to ease that pain at the small of his back, knowing by morning, he would be needing to relieve himself. It hurt to even think of that—what with the hammering his body had taken in the fight and the ride back. He closed his eyes and thought on that rutted, muddy road leading down among the trees, and at the end stood Gritta, her poke bonnet at the end of her arm, waving . . . waving him on. . . .

It was damned cold later when the urge to piss would not be denied. He snorted quietly, seeing the breath before his face turn silver in the late starshine. Blinking his eyes clear of grit, Jonah glanced at the east. The autumn nightsky was gray there. The land coming to life far off . . .

somewhere over Big Cobbler Mountain in Virginia it was morning now. Soon to be over the homestead left behind in Missouri. Right now it was light enough that a man could tell the baggage from the sleeping Pawnee rolled in their blankets or cocooned in the Cheyenne's abandoned buffalo robes.

He was warm enough and did not want to stir, but damn if his kidneys and bladder would let him wait any longer.

Jonah struggled to his feet, cold as they had grown in the boots. He shuffled his clothing around him and buttoned the wool mackinaw clear up to his neck, blowing in his hands as he strode off several yards. While he unbuttoned his fly and was spraying the ground, Jonah gazed at the dozen horses grazing here and there among the scattered baggage. Perhaps he could find some Cheyenne coffee to boil. Get a fire started and find a pot or kettle. As empty as his bladder was at last, Jonah figured he could drink a mess of coffee—

One of the Pawnee yelled out, falling at the crack of a rifle. As Jonah took off, his fly still unbuttoned, the scouts came out of their blankets and robes behind him. The two other camp guards were already on their feet and coming on as well. But Jonah was going to get there first.

As he drew his pistol from its mule-ear holster, the gray horizon north of their position suddenly sprouted a weaving mass of horsemen, surging down on the Pawnee. At least two dozen. No, more than that now. At least three-to-one odds, he figured. Who was to know, he argued with himself, his breathsmoke disappearing as quickly as his lungs ached with each step into the cold, seeping darkness. All he cared about was his little piece of it. Three of the horsemen were peeling off from the rest, heading for the wounded Pawnee picket who struggled to crawl backward, his hand gripping the side of his hip, dragging the useless leg.

On instinct Jonah fired. Not so much aiming into the dark, but sensing where he ought to point the weapon at one of the trio of screeching horsemen.

A yelp answered the bark of his pistol. A body tumbled backward off the rump of a pony with a thud, and air was driven from his lungs as the warrior landed on the grassy sand.

Jonah's eyes stung from the bright muzzle flash, and as they cleared, he found another target bearing down on him with a horrifying scream. A war club raised overhead. Pony knees coming up and hammering down like steam pistons. Hooves clawing at the sandy soil, sending dark clods flying into the gray light of morning coming. Nostrils swollen wide as it carried its rider closer and closer still to the white man.

Behind that faceless, formless rider came another, turning off to claim the wounded Pawnee.

Jonah met the Cheyenne horseman as he swept low off the side of his pony. He caught the warrior's arm with the war club in it, yanking so hard as the pony tore by that Jonah heard a distinct snap, a yelp of pain, and the thud of the warrior striking the ground.

Jonah whirled, firing . . . then firing again as the third rider closed on the wounded Pawnee. Another screech of surprise, perhaps pain. The pony Hook had wounded suddenly skidded to a halt, reared wildly, and spun about with its rider holding dearly to the withers.

"Stay down!" he shouted, then realized he had yelled in English. Jonah couldn't remember the Pawnee words. Even the one for down.

But the scout's eyes told him he understood. Darkness oozed between the Pawnee's fingers where he held his hand over the bullet hole in his hip. Jonah dragged him upright on one leg, the other dangling useless now. Behind them the whole of the scattered camp was ablaze with spurts of orange and yellow light. There really was no safe place, except at the center of it all, among the baggage and lodge skins.

Madness and terror brought in the new day—screaming horses and shouted curses, chanting songs and death wails from warrior throats on both sides. Bullets singing through the cold morning air. The flat putty-smack of lead and snake-hiss of iron-tipped arrow.

"Follow them!" one of the Pawnee shouted.

"Don't let them ride away!"

"Finish these scalped-heads—now!" cried a voice from beyond.

As most of the young Cheyenne circled the camp, firing into the dark lumps of scouts and baggage, the Pawnee struggled to control their horses enough to mount and pursue the enemy. Jonah marveled at their courage. Outnumbered more than three to one, they coolly went about wresting the offensive from the Cheyenne when most men would be content finding a big place in which to make themselves small. In Jonah's breast burned a pride for fighting alongside such brave men.

And in the next few moments he was not sure why he did what he did, but he remembered helping the wounded man behind a large bundle of lodge skins, then sprinting toward his horse and leaping atop it bareback, joining a handful of the rest who were charging out to break through the cordon of attackers.

The yelling grew faint in his ears as the animal carried him into the growing light of dawn, all rose and blood orange to the east, the ground a hammering thunder of noise—

—when suddenly the earth shook and came upon him, driving the breath from his lungs. Beneath his bloody cheek he heard the riders coming. Dragging his heavy head from the soil where it was warm and wet with his blood, he saw the young Cheyenne warriors bearing down on him. He did not stand a chance, he thought, his eyes rolling back in his head as he slipped away.

Two Pawnee horsemen fired their rifles again and again at the approaching Cheyenne. Then both leaned off the bare backs of their ponies and scooped the white man from the grassy sand at a full run.

Jonah started to come to, his eyes struggling to focus as his toes dragged the ground, bouncing off tufts of bunchgrass, suspended between two men and their heaving, sweat-slicked horses. He tried to look up at who carried him helpless as a newborn, hoping they were Pawnee. Then blacked out again from the pain in the side of his head.

Wondering if the Cheyenne warrior who had knocked him off his horse had been Shad's half-breed son.

Blessed, merciful blackness . . .

Porcupine looked over the young warriors as they dismounted with him, back among Turkey Leg's people.

Women and children surged forward, old ones too—each one looking for any who were missing among the war party gone to the hills beside Plum Creek where the Cheyenne had abandoned their belongings.

There were three missing. Three more carried in wounded. Women wailing anew—knowing the Pawnee would surely mutilate the bodies of their men left on the battlefield.

Porcupine looked at Turkey Leg, then walked on past the old man, leading his pony through the crowd.

"Porcupine!"

He turned, not really wanting to talk with the chief. Slowly, the warrior faced about.

"You tried, young one. Sometimes—that is all that counts."

"I could not hold the rest long enough to see what the scalped-heads would take, what they would leave behind," he said with bitterness. "They were too anxious to fight."

"In some the blood of revenge runs so hot it knows no control."

"We failed—and paid a mighty cost for it," Porcupine sighed. "There is one among us who is without control, Turkey Leg. He rides without thought into the muzzles of the white man's guns. He taunts the others because of it—and so brings danger to the rest of our war party because he is without fear—perhaps because he is crazy."

"The half-breed? Son of the Cheyenne woman who married the tall white man?"

Porcupine nodded.

Turkey Leg gazed into the distance a moment. "I remember the man well—as if it were yesterday. More than twenty winters ago, he came among us and would have no other for his wife. Now his son pays for the transgressions of his father." He looked up at Porcupine. "I fear that High-Backed Bull will one day die at the hands of the white man—perhaps his own father."

"What I fear most is that he is so crazy, so hot for blood, that he will cause the deaths of many of our finest warriors."

"If it is something that is to come to pass—it is not for us to change the will of the Grandfather Above."

Porcupine sighed. It was so. Not for him to decide who was to live. Who was to die. The recent journey of the sun and moon had brought death to this camp, which meant many left without husbands, without fathers.

"And still, Turkey Leg, the scalped-heads hold three of our people prisoners and sit on almost all that we owned."

"But there are small victories, Porcupine. Small, but most meaningful. No more do the scalped-heads hold three Shahiyena. One has escaped."

"Your mother?"

Turkey Leg shook his head, moistness coming to his eyes in the midday light. "No. It is the girl of ten summers. Somehow she escaped the scalped-heads as they were crossing the great river. She hid on an island from her captors. Because of this, the people have renamed her Island Woman. After our enemies gave up their search for her, she turned about and walked north onto the prairie. From what she told me of the time she heard horsemen coming, I believe she made herself small and hid from you and your warriors when you rode south to Plum Creek in the darkness."

"Island Woman! This is good news, Turkey Leg!" He clamped a hand on the old man's shoulder. "Now—we must free the last two."

The chief tried to smile, then sucked on a lower lip in thought before he replied. "I have little hope for the boy and woman to escape like the girl. Better that I send word to the white man that I will trade for them."

"The white children?"

"Yes."

"You will give two back to the white man?"

"I will return all six to the soldiers—if they will only free the boy and the old woman."

"You are a good son, Turkey Leg."

"No," the old chief answered finally, gazing up at the tall warrior with moist eyes. "If I had truly been a good son, my mother would not now be a prisoner of the scalped-heads and the white pony soldiers."

At the beginning of the third week of September, Major Frank North gathered his four companies of Pawnee scouts at the thriving community of North Platte in western Nebraska. It was there on the twenty-first that a commission was assembled to discuss peace terms with the various bands then roaming the central plains. Over the next three days, chiefs of some of the strongest warrior bands rode in at the invitation of the commissioners: five professional soldiers and three civilian representatives who sat at their tables, looking down at those chiefs they had called together.

Man That Walks Under the Ground, Spotted Tail, Young Man Afraid of His Horses, Pawnee Killer, Standing Elk, and others of the Sioux. The Cheyenne came as well.

Turkey Leg motioned Shad Sweete to the doorway of the crowded Sibley tent where the peace-talkers held court. The old mountain man was there to help translate for the Cheyenne when needed.

"You are the father of High-Backed Bull?" asked the Cheyenne chief.

"I am," Shad answered.

"Husband to Shell Woman?"

Shad had to think a moment, to remember her given Shahiyena name. "She is mother to High-Backed Bull, yes."

Turkey Leg sighed. "I wish to speak with you, Indian-talker."

Shad followed the old Indian out the open tent flaps stirred by the autumn breeze. Although he could not recall ever meeting Turkey Leg, Sweete knew of the man by reputation. His word was good. And right now the old trapper was figuring Turkey Leg was set on doing some wrangling over peace terms away from the soldiers.

"I don't have any power to help you in your talks with the great father's peace-talkers."

Turkey Leg raised a wrinkled hand, silencing the white man. "I did not ask you to talk to me of peace with the soldiers. Years ago, when you came among Tall Crane's village, to buy yourself a wife—I too lived in that camp."

"We have met, Turkey Leg?"

The old man shook his head. "No. But I know of you."

"I know of you as well. Among many honorable men—you are known as a man of honor."

"You speak of me like I am some ancient man, Indian-talker. I cannot have more than ten winters of life on you."

Shad liked the chief's smile. "I remember Tall Crane's camp. It was a good time in my life. A good time in our lives—before things got . . . mixed-up and confused."

"It was a good time for us all, Indian-talker." Now the chief's old eyes gazed back into the tent. "You see that one at the end of the table, seated beside the one with much braid on his blue coat?"

Shad nodded. "Major Frank North. Leader of the scalped-heads. The army's scouts."

No emotion was betrayed in the old man's eyes. "I know of him. He was leading the fight we had at Plum Creek Ford."

"Yes. You wish to meet him?"

"No. It is not necessary. I only know that he is the man you must talk to for me. I have—" He bit his lip as if it were something difficult to discuss. "I have six children this North will want."

"Prisoners?"

"They are white children. But they are no longer our prisoners. We were raising them to be Shahiyena."

Shad sighed, trying to contain his excitement at the news. "Six children. Yes. What do you wish in return for the six children?"

Turkey Leg looked up at the scout, then back at Frank North behind the table some ten yards away where the commissioners were debating points of their peace plan through the various interpreters.

"North's scalped-heads captured two of our people at that Plum Creek fight. I want them back."

"A boy of ten summers. And another."

"An old woman."

"That is all you want?" Shad asked, not believing his ears.

"We want nothing more for the six children."

Sweete was stirred. "They must be important to you, Turkey Leg."

With moist eyes, the old chief gazed up at the tall white man. "All my people are important to me."

As much as Shad wanted to touch the old man at that moment, suddenly understanding, Shad did not.

"I will see that it is done with Major North," he replied quietly at the old man's ear. "I understand how a man must do what he can to protect his family. It is this way with my own—this worry I have for my own blood."

And in the old, rheumy eyes, there came a new moistness telling Shad Sweete that Turkey Leg was thankful to the white scout for his understanding about the old woman, but that the Cheyenne chief in turn sympathized about the white man's half-breed son.

"Yes, Indian-talker. A man must always do everything he can to protect his family."

38

A T A RAILSIDE eating house in North Platte, Nebraska, the formal exchange of the prisoners took place. Three young women, two aged nineteen and one girl seventeen years old, along with six-year-old twin boys and an infant.

The Cheyenne boy of ten summers was returned to his joyous people, who promptly renamed him Pawnee in commemoration of his capture by North's scouts. In the end, Turkey Leg's aged mother walked slowly from that eating house in North Platte, gripping her son's arm, tears dampening both of their winter-seamed faces.

That exchange was the only productive thing to come of three days of haggling between the chiefs and the peace commissioners. As Jonah Hook and the other army scouts listened, the white men had again expressed that the Indians would be required to remain on their reservations south of the Arkansas River or north of the Platte, where the bands would be expected to settle down and become farmers, every bit as much as those white settlers moving onto the plains with their plows and spotted buffalo.

In turn, the chiefs listened attentively, but refused to budge from their trust in the old life as lived by their people for as long as any old man's memory—season by season following the migration of the buffalo.

But the problem was, said the chiefs, the white man was crossing the buffalo ground with the iron tracks for his smoking wagons. And the buffalo would no longer cross those tracks. Instead, the great herds that once roamed the extent of the central plains were now kept far to the south, while another herd stayed far to the north.

"Our people will starve if we cannot hunt the buffalo," Spotted Tail told the peace commissioners.

"We will go where the buffalo are," said Cut Nose.

"Even if the buffalo graze where the white man settles, cutting at the earth and raising his spotted buffalo," Whistler added.

"No, you must stay far away from the white man and his settlements," General Alfred Terry warned.

"Any time your young warriors steal or kill, the soldiers will follow," said General William Tecumseh Sherman. "We will chase your villages and find them, wherever you hide."

"You make life hard on us," said Cold Face.

"Yes," agreed Turkey Leg. "We must go where we can feed our families. Doesn't the white man understand that? Doesn't the white man now go where he goes to settle on this buffalo ground so that he can feed his family?"

"If our two peoples stay away from one another," General John B. Sanborn said calmly, "we will not have reason to fight."

Standing Elk took the speaking fan from Turkey Leg. It was his turn to add words so the peace-talkers might understand before war once more erupted. "All things are good for the white man. But our people were here first. You are not wanted here in our land. Go away, and all things will be better once more."

"We will not be leaving," Sherman sputtered. "You will have to make room for all the white families yet to come from the east. They are as plentiful as the stars in the sky. And if you do not move aside and allow them room, the army will round you up and put you on the reservations, where you will be forced to raise your crops—or starve. There will be no more buffalo when the white man finishes pacifying this land."

Young Man Afraid rose, taking the speaking fan made from the wing of a golden eagle. It carried not only great power, but responsibility as well for the man who spoke while holding it. "We have never been like you white men. Ever since I was born, I have eaten wild meat. Not one bite have I taken of your spotted buffalo."

"You will grow to like it, I am sure," said General William S. Harney, smiling benevolently.

"I think not," Young Man Afraid continued, his face taut as a hand drum at the white soldier's rude interruption. "My father and his father, and his father before him all ate wild meat. It is not for me to change our way of life now. It was good for my ancestors. It is good for my children, and their children, and the children to come after them."

"Times are changing," Sanborn said. "We must all realize progress is coming to this new land."

"I know nothing of this progress," Young Man Afraid said. "All I know is the taste of buffalo in my mouth, the sweetness of cold water on my tongue, and the way the clouds touch the earth as I look far away at everything the Grandfather Above has placed here for his children. No! Listen and heed me—it will not be my generation that will give up to the greedy white man all that has been given us by the Grandfather Above!"

The discussions, debate, and heated exchanges droned on and on for most of three days in that tent on the outskirts of North Platte. In the end, the commissioners said they were calling an end to the inconclusive hearings, but were asking the bands to attend another treaty talk, scheduled for later that same month, near the end of the Falling Leaf Moon.

"There we can come to agreement on the terms of our new peace treaty," explained General Terry as he disbanded the conference.

"You put too much hope in things changing between now and the next time we come together," Turkey Leg said as the white men rose from their chairs behind the tables.

"I put a lot of hope in each of you tribal leaders doing what is best for your people," General Harney said.

"That is for us to decide," Pawnee Killer growled. "Not you white soldiers and peace-talkers."

Fully a mile away, the young riders were gathering along the hilltops, watching Shad Sweete and the rest of his party approach along the meandering path of the creek bottom. From what the old mountain man could tell, the horsemen were mostly young boys, very likely carrying bows and quivers of arrows. No sign yet of older warriors brandishing rifles as they watched the small group of white men ride toward their village nestled among the cottonwoods and plum brush.

Sweete wondered . . . then caught himself hoping. It would be too great a gift, he figured, to find his half-breed son among those young men dippled along the hilltops, swirling away one by one on the off side of the knolls where the tall grass waved in the wind. Was he here? Shad wondered. Or was he still out with the Dog Soldiers of Tall Bull and White Horse, roaming and riding and raiding?

The old scout glanced at Jonah Hook riding beside him, finding the younger man most attentive to the distant spectacle, his eyes squinting into the bright autumn light this Indian summer day as the dried cottonwood leaves rattled in golden splendor, birds calling out in warning as the horsemen approached. Overhead a cloudless blue sky stretched everlasting to the far horizon in all directions. Sweete was adrift, as were these dark-skinned nomads he had come to visit, here on an inland sea of rolling, grass-covered surf.

More like paying homage, this visit was. To beg the attendance of the mighty Cheyenne of the central plains.

After the old mountain man had arranged the prisoner exchange at North Platte, General Phil Sheridan himself, that banty Irishman who commanded this part of the frontier, had personally asked Shad Sweete to lead this effort to assure that Turkey Leg and his headmen would come to Medicine Lodge Creek when the new moon had grown to half its full size. That's when the white peace-talkers would once more assemble with the chiefs, to forge some kind of lasting agreement with the bands roaming Kansas and Nebraska—where the white man was pushing harder than ever, bringing his plow and raising sod houses and laying his iron rails.

Shad knew exactly how the bands felt. When the stench of human offal and waste in their camps grew too much to take, the bands simply took down their lodges and moved to a new campsite. Once more allowing the land and the wind and the rolling rhythm of the seasons to cleanse the breast of the mother of all things.

Such beauty, simplicity, he thought. So simple that its beauty continued to escape the white man. For only the white man squatted and never moved on. Continuing to live where he took a shit. A quarter century ago as a nomadic fur trapper, Shad had learned a better way. Man truly was not meant to live long in one place. Better that he took his shit, and moved on. Like the buffalo.

Dogs barking among the horses' hooves announced the coming of the four white men—civilians all.

Women rose from their work at new buffalo hides that had been taken in the weeks before the village was required to move for its safety away from the white man and his Pawnee trackers. Each woman, young and old, holding an elk-handled scraper, with only the power of their resolve and muscle slowly working the flesh from the great white-and-red hides staked out like huge squares demarcating the outskirts of Turkey Leg's village.

Old men rose from their places in the warm sun that afternoon. They had been talking of days gone by when the meat was good and fleet were the ponies a man could steal from the Pawnee or Crow or Ute. Then the young horsemen were among the lodges, making a show of themselves, more weapons in evidence now. Bows, yes—but many more rifles than Shad had expected he would see.

"This bunch been raiding to get them guns?" asked Hook from the side of his mouth as the four white men entered the outskirts of the lodge circle.

The air was strong with smoked hides and grease, pungent with wood smoke and boiling meat. Fragrant with the incense of white sage. Far better were those perfumes than any meal of boiled potatoes and red whiskey and a cigar smoked after a man had himself a full belly. Shad thought of Shell Woman, then worried for their son.

With warriors and headmen spread out from him like the sides of an arrow point, Turkey Leg waited for the white men to approach, halt, and dismount. The old chief motioned forward some young boys, who took the reins to the four horses and led the animals away.

"It is always good to see you, my friend," Shad said, smiling at the old chief.

Turkey Leg smiled in return. "How is life for you, Indian-talker?"

"Some things could be better, I suppose. But, what life is worth living if it is not filled with lessons to be learned?"

"You always pose questions that this old man cannot easily answer." The chief motioned for the other three white men to follow, taking Sweete by the arm as he turned toward his lodge erected at the center of the camp crescent. "Come. We will eat. Then smoke. And only then will we hear why you have journeyed here. I suppose you want me to go listen to words of the peace-talkers once more."

"My belly talks now," Shad said, grinning. "It is so empty. Yes—we will eat, then with the pipe speak of the peace-talkers."

More than two hours passed in that lodge filled with white man and red alike. Eating first the jerked meat passed among the circle while the main course came to a boil. After every man had licked his fingers clean and finished his coffee flavored with generous heapings of sugar, the pipe was lit. It was the first time, Sweete knew, that Jonah had been witness to such a conference, held at the leisurely pace of the plains Indian, with no artificial timetable to be satisfied. Only the dictates of the old men themselves.

Turkey Leg cleared his throat. "Black Kettle comes to this talk planned for Medicine Lodge Creek?"

"Yes, he and Medicine Arrow."

The chief nodded, looking at the faces of his headmen. "The one who was once called Rock Forehead. He is a powerful chief."

"Three from the Southern Cheyenne will come. Those two and Little Robe as well."

"And of the Kiowa?"

"We believe White Bear and Lone Wolf will attend with their warriors to talk of making peace on this part of the plains," Sweete answered.

For a long time the pipe passed among those seated in a grand circle in that lodge. No man talking, only the noise of the pipe as air was drawn down through the bowl, only the music of camp life outside the lodge. Children playing, dogs barking, and ponies coming and going through the browned cones raised against the autumn sky.

"We are going south with the coming of winter," Turkey Leg began after a long, considered silence. "It is there that winter will not arrive as soon, nor will it last as long. Yes, perhaps we can raise our lodges beside Medicine Lodge Creek with the others who will speak with the peace-talkers."

"You will be there by the time the moon is half-full?" Shad asked the old chief.

Turkey Leg looked about the lodge at his headmen. No man spoke, no man gave signal that he disapproved. "We will come talk this one last time to the white soldier chiefs. Perhaps we will hear something that is good in their words."

"They want all the bands to live in peace with the white settlers."

"But the white man fails to understand that we do not want to live in peace with his people. We do not want to live with the white man at all." Turkey Leg sighed.

The expression on the old chief's face spoke something to Sweete, as if Turkey Leg understood more of what was in the scout's heart than what the white scout had ever spoken.

"There are some among us who believe we can live near your people," the chief went on. "Yet there are a few among us who will never hold anything but a bad heart for the white man."

"It is the same among my people," Shad replied. "While some want to put an end to your way of life forever, there are still many who would try to find a way for both white man and red man to live side by side, each in his own way."

"In some men," Turkey Leg came to the point, "there are both bloods at war."

Shad saw the meaning more clear in the old man's eyes than in his words.

"You would mean a young warrior who has in his veins the blood of our two peoples?"

Turkey Leg nodded. A few of the older men grunted their assent. "You have been among our people for many winters. You came among us when there were few white men. Now I am told the numbers of white men in the east are greater than the stars at night."

Shad smiled. "Sometimes I think there are more white men than there are buffalo chips on this great prairie."

Most of the old men chuckled at the analogy. Shad felt the lightening of the mood within the lodge as the sun fell headlong into the west.

"Where is it I might find word of High-Backed Bull?" he asked bluntly.

"You worry about your son, don't you?"

"As any father would, Turkey Leg."

"This is good. A son must protect his parents. And a man must care for his children."

"Your mother?"

"She is well. Thank you again."

"We speak the same heart when we talk of family, Turkey Leg. There is nothing more important than family."

The old chief knocked into his palm what ash was left in the pipe bowl after its fourth circuit of the lodge. The burnt residue he tossed into the fire pit at his feet before he removed the red stone bowl from the ash stem. Only then did he seek to fill the silence in that lodge.

"Your son, he has cursed his white blood. You must know this before you go searching to find him."

"He curses the blood I gave him?"

"Yes. He swears his desire for vengeance on any white man—even if that white man is his father."

Shad swallowed hard, as if the news were something foul. "My son, where would I find him?"

"He rides with the young warriors of Porcupine."

"This Porcupine," Shad began, careful not to sound too anxious, "he is war leader in your village?"

"He is of this band. But Porcupine is gone from us for now. He rode north to join the Dog Soldiers of Roman Nose."

Sweete glanced at Hook, who was fervently trying to follow the sense of the discussion, even if he could not understand the words being spoken.

"I know of that one."

"Yes. Many white men have heard of the Nose. But no white man has ever set eyes on this great warrior—and lived to tell of that meeting."

"Tell me, Turkey Leg—where would I find Roman Nose?"

"Where one would find Tall Bull and White Horse—the Dog Soldier bands. That is where a man could find Roman Nose."

39

October, 1867

"Your name's Hook, isn't it?"

Jonah looked up from his coffee-making chores. The tall, handsome soldier came to a stop on the far side of the small fire where supper was beginning to roast. Jonah spotted the clusters on the collar.

"Have we met, Major?"

The soldier held out his hand as Jonah rose, dusting off his own.

"Not official, mind you. Joel Elliott. U.S. Seventh Cavalry."

They shook, Hook suspicious. "I see. To what do I owe the honor of your come to call, Major? This go back to that time I was ready to shoot Tom Custer, don't it? Go 'head and have you a set, where you can," he said, waving at a nearby spot.

Elliott settled on a hardtack box, one by one slowly undoing the buttons on his tunic. As if he were searching for an answer.

"Suppose I only wanted to meet you—especially after that incident with your cousin—"

"He's dead," Jonah interrupted sharply, his suspicions confirmed.

The major appeared brought up by that, something short. "I see." Then he cleared his throat. "I'm sorry to hear that, Mr. Hook."

"Jonah."

"As much as you created a stir that day on the South Fork of the Republican . . . as much as Tom Custer has hated you ever since for

308

holding him at gunpoint, I've got to say, and will admit this to any man who asks—I admire your sense of family. Your loyalty to family in the face of overwhelming odds."

"Not overwhelming, Major," Jonah said, dusting coffee grounds from his hands after he had dumped them into the boiling water. "It was just Tom Custer and me."

Elliott smiled. "There were at least a dozen soldiers there, ready to put holes in you."

Hook smiled in return. "Important thing was that Tom Custer understood that there was only one important hole—and that was the one I was fixing to put in him if he didn't let my cousin go."

"Like I said, as much as Tom hates you, and as much as the general himself doesn't quite know how to deal with your brand of courage—I figured it was time for me to shake your hand."

"Still doesn't figure that I done something so special that a cavalry major come look me up."

"You pour me some coffee, Jonah?" Elliott asked, watching Hook pull up two tin cups. "Sounds to me like you're selling yourself short."

As Jonah poured the steaming coffee from the blackened pot, he listened to the nearby *cherk-cherk-cree* of the meadowlarks feeding among the tall dry grasses caressed by autumn's cool nights. "Man who makes something big of himself is a man I wonder about, Major."

Elliott accepted his cup. "How old are you—you mind me asking?"

"Thirty, this last spring."

"You been out here long?"

He hoisted his cup in the fashion of a toast. "Just since the Yankees brought me west to keep telegraph wire up and follow General Connor to the Powder River."

"Back a little more than two years then." Elliott sipped at his coffee. "You figure we got a chance making peace with these bands?"

"Major—you're asking the wrong fella. That's for certain. I've fought the Injuns, bedded down one winter with a Pawnee gal who taught me a bit of her tongue . . . and I've tracked around a good chunk of this territory with North's Pawnee Battalion." He speared a thick slice of buffalo hump and turned it over in the cast-iron skillet. "None of that makes me no great shakes when it comes to knowing if the army can make peace with these bands."

"I've been trying to find out if there is really much cause to hope."

"Hell—it's hard enough for most men to make peace with themselves, much less have to worry about making peace with each other."

"Let's pray the chiefs of the warrior bands aren't as cynical as you are, Jonah."

Hook smiled, liking the open, ready good humor of the soldier. "Glory be—but we might have a chance to make peace between the Cheyenne and the army yet. If all the Injuns was like Turkey Leg—and all the soldiers like you, Major."

In that second week of October, the bands had begun gathering for the great peace council along Medicine Lodge Creek, not far from Fort Larned in Kansas.

Miles to the south down on the Cimarron River were camped the bulk of the Cheyenne bands, more than 250 lodges. They waited, skeptical of the white man's good intentions and promises of presents. On Medicine Lodge Creek itself Black Kettle's 25 lodges of Southern Cheyenne camped. Below them were more than 100 lodges of Comanches. And below them stood the camp circles of some 150 lodges of Kiowa, along with 85 lodges of Kiowa-Apache. Closest to Fort Larned were 170 lodges of Southern Arapaho.

A great and impressive gathering of more than 800 lodges, all in a joyous mood, for recent hunting had been good, and word had it the soldiers at the nearby post had just received shipments of the goods soon to be brought out to the great encampment in wagons: coffee, sugar, flour, and dried fruits; in addition to blankets and bolts of colorful cloth, and surplus uniforms from the white man's recent war among himself, uniforms the War Department had in the last few months turned over to the Interior Department. And on its way was a sizable herd of the white man's cattle to feed the gathering bands.

When the white commissioners arrived at the scene on the fifteenth, they and their military escort of the Seventh Cavalry camped across the creek, on the north side of the Medicine Lodge. Row upon row of tents housing the troopers spread in grand fashion across the prairie. Next to those tents stood a long line of the freight wagons bulging with the presents for those making peace with the Great Father back east, and closest to the creek were the tents erected for the commissioners themselves. In that flat meadow between their tents and the streambank, the great council had begun its informal sessions on 17 October. Yet it had not been until the nineteenth when the chiefs began making their formal speeches.

Behind the commissioners, both military and civilian, hung a large canopy beneath which the many clerks and stenographers sat, recording the proceedings, word for word. There too sat the many newsmen here to record for their readers back east this momentous gathering with the warrior bands of the Great Plains.

On each morning the council assembled, the Cheyenne and Arapaho chiefs seated themselves on the right hand of the white men, or on the west. On the left-hand side sat the Kiowa and Comanche leaders. And in a broad crescent behind these chiefs sat the old men, councillors and leaders all. Beyond them along the stream itself the young warriors moved about in all their finery—feathers and bells, paint and totems, not shy in the least of showing off their weapons. Eager young boys at times attempted to mingle with the warriors, but only with caution, for youths were never allowed to attend councils as important as this.

That first day Senator John B. Henderson had proposed to the assembled chiefs that the Cheyenne and Arapaho bands be moved south to the Arkansas River while the Kiowas could settle on land farther south along the Red River. As soon as the head men would agree to this proposal and formally touch the pen, the army would distribute the promised goods. First the Kiowa, then the Comanche, followed by the Arapaho, and finally—after many days of debate—the Cheyenne agreed to the white man's terms.

Two days it took them to decide, two days as well after Jonah spoke with Major Elliott at that little fire beside the gurgling music of Medicine Lodge Creek, beneath the wide autumn black canopy with an egg-yolk moon rising off the horizon to the east.

Their job done after much debate and political posturing, the commissioners informed the chiefs they were leaving now, heading east to inform the Great Father of their success. In leaving, they were ordering the issuance of the promised presents. Tall side-walled army freight wagons rumbled into the meadow, emptied of everything in three huge piles: on the west, a pile for the Apache and Arapaho; on the east, a pile for the Kiowa and Comanche; and in the middle, a pile for the great Cheyenne of the plains.

There was so much there, and the celebrating was much greater than anything Shad Sweete would have ever expected, more than he had ever seen among the Cheyenne.

Little Robe, Black Kettle, Medicine Arrow, and Turkey Leg each sent their warrior societies forward to be in charge of a fair distribution of the presents among their bands. One by one the women were given kettles and axes, blankets and clothing, flour and sugar and coffee and more. Never before had any of them seen anything like this.

Perhaps the white man does number like the stars in the sky, Shad heard them whisper among themselves during that day and a half it took to distribute all the gifts placed on the prairie for the Cheyenne bands.

No man, no woman nor child rode from that meadow back to their villages. Every pony and pack animal they put to use to haul their new riches, stacked high and cumbersome and wobbly on animal backs or on sway-backed, groaning travois. Many times the poorly tied packs fell off ponies and burst open across the grass trampled with the pounding of many moccasins and hooves. Just as many travois poles snapped under the great weight required of them.

Women muttered, complaining of their plight, having to pack and repack and struggle along with their newfound wealth. But they smiled all the same. And no woman among them complained all that much.

With the days growing shorter and the nights colder, Shad watched with the other scouts as the bands moved out onto the mapless prairie, slowly marching into the four winds. Along the bank of Medicine Lodge Creek that last morning, the old mountain man found the water slicked with a thin, fragile layer of ice scum. Winter was due on the high plains. Winter would not be denied.

With the presents distributed, the women happy, and the chiefs satisfied that their hunting grounds had been somehow preserved by touching the pen to the white man's talking paper, the civilian scouts found themselves out of a job for the coming cold that would one day soon squeeze down on the land.

Sweete thought of Shell Woman. Funny to think of her not as Toote, but as Shell Woman. But then, he had found himself among her own people for the better part of the last two weeks now. And in that time had not really thought of her as being among and surrounded by his own people—where she often camped at Fort Laramie, waiting for his return to her lodge. Perhaps by now she and Pipe Woman were in a winter camp far up in the Powder River or Rosebud country.

But it hurt, thinking on them now as he watched the great cloud of dust rise into the clear, autumn-cold sky above the rear marchers—these Southern Cheyenne going off to find their own winter camps. It hurt, that thought of mother and daughter, Cheyenne both. So only natural now that he think on father and son. One a white man, happy only when he was among an adopted people. And the other a half-breed, a young man denying his white blood and swearing vengeance on all white men.

What overwhelming hate must fill the heart of his son. One day there would be no *other* white men standing between them. One day, Shad realized, there would be no gulf of time nor distance between him and the son he had long hoped for.

"You coming, Shad?"

Startled, Sweete looked up from staring at the march of the disappearing Cheyenne, yanked of a sudden out of his reverie. Jonah Hook had come up with the horses and that one pack animal they had shared between them this last few weeks. "S'pose there's no reason to be hanging on here."

He glanced over the great, empty campsites strung up and down the banks of the little creek, grass trampled and pocked with lodge circles and fire pits, pony droppings and bones and the remains of willow bowers used by the young warriors too old to live any longer with their families but too young yet to have a wife and lodge and children too.

His eyes misted for a moment as he swallowed the pain of loss. To be hated, despised, cursed by a son was a deeper wound than he had ever suffered—across all those years of trapping and freezing, of fighting Indians and grizzly and loneliness and time itself. To stand in this place and realize what with so much time gone from his life, all he had to show for it was a son who had spit on his father's name, his father's race—his father's blood.

"Winter's coming, Shad," Jonah said, slowly easing forward after he rose to the saddle. He crossed his wrists atop the wide saddlehorn. "Maybe we can go find us some work down south."

He remembered. "The Territories?"

Hook nodded. "Down with the Creek and Choctaw. Sniff around for some word."

Shad rose to the saddle and settled his rear gently against the cantle for the coming ride. How he wanted now to be plopped down in the sun, leaning back against the fragrant homeyness of her lodge, listening to the kettles bubble and smelling the pungent tang of autumn on the same winds that drove the long-necked honkers across the endless blue in great, dark vees. Going south.

Where Jonah yearned to go as well for the winter.

"Let's settle up at Larned, Jonah," he said, easing the horse away, pointing their noses east out of the meadow, toward the sun now fully off the horizon. A new day of opportunity and possibilities. Another chance to deal with fears and disappointments and pain that no man ought to know.

He glanced at the silent man riding beside him, seeing the gentle curve of a slight smile on Hook's bony face. Something tugged at Shad now—seeing the comfort it gave the Confederate to be heading down south at last. To be going where there might be some answers.

And in that moment, he felt a little peace within himself to balance out that pain. For some time it had been there, and he had chosen not to realize it—this peace versus the pain.

Now he felt it, assured by it, comforted by it. Because so jumbled up were those thoughts of father and son with thoughts of him and Jonah Hook . . . that it caused him confusion and comfort, guilt and a sense of completeness never before experienced—that left him wondering where to go for help.

Knowing the only help for Shad Sweete rested within.

40

November, 1867

"THEY WAS TRICKED—and we helped the army do it, Jonah."

Hook gazed through his own red-rimmed eyes at the moist, bleary eyes of the old mountain man across the table from him, at Shad Sweete's mouth as he stumbled over some of the words.

"For better than a day now you've been sitting here in this stinking hole, washing your tonsils with this whiskey, old man," Jonah said. "And all that time I been telling you your crying ain't gonna change a thing."

"Was hoping you cared."

"I do care, dammit." He slapped a flat hand on his chest. "But what'm I to do by my lonesome? What you wanna do, huh?"

The whiskey had long ago passed the point of warming Jonah's belly. It felt like there was a hole burned right through him, hollering for something more than the cheap grain alcohol turned amber with a plug of tobacco and potent with some red pepper. Some called it prairie dew, others stumble-foot. Jonah just called it whiskey.

"Don't know," Shad Sweete grumped.

"Damn right, you don't. Wanna go riding off and tell 'em?" he asked, feeling his belly burn for want of food. "Go tell them chiefs how they got swindled for putting their marks on that piece of paper you asked 'em to come and sign?"

"Maybe we should. Somebody's gotta tell 'em."

"What then, old man? We gonna help 'em take on the whole army? Seems they been doing just that since before we come out here. And from the look of things—these Injuns'll be fighting the white man long after our bones are buried and there's grass growing over the spot they buried us."

Sweete sighed, working the whiskey around in his mouth the way he worked the thoughts around in his numbed brain.

They had arrived back at Fort Larned and were four days all told getting mustered out. Shad Sweete released from duty with the army, and Jonah Hook bidding farewell to Major Frank North's Pawnee Battalion. Come spring, they were told at the last, there would be work for a man who was willing to guide and track, interpret and fight. Come spring, that is, after a man made it on his own through the prairie winter.

So there was money in their pockets and a thirst in their throats. But first the old mountain man had his duties, learned years before in the fur trade at rendezvous. Company trapper like Jim Bridger, or free trapper the likes of Titus Bass—either one would tell you your money had to go down on the necessaries before the money went to liquor. No matter the color of the whiskey, no matter how strong the scent of the women once you started your drinking—a man had to assure himself of the necessaries before everything was drunk up and there was nothing left. Nothing to get him through the winter and over to shortgrass time when he would again find work.

So with their pokes bulging, Shad Sweete steered Jonah over to the local sutler at his canvas-topped mercantile squatting just beyond the fringe of the military reservation surrounding Fort Larned. There they perused what the squinty-eyed clerk had to sell.

"A nervous and shifty-eyed one, that he is," Shad whispered.

"We go someplace else do our business?"

"No," he replied, grabbing Jonah's elbow. Shad looked up at the clerk. "The owner in, mister?"

"He's off right now."

"When he be back?"

"Tomorrow afternoon, most likely."

"We'll be back."

And they were—not long after the sutler returned.

"Name's Sweete. Yours?"

The man presented his hand. "Sidney Gould. What is it I can do for you?"

"Some outfitting," Sweete had replied, and Jonah remembered now that look on the mountain man's face as Shad had glanced at him, a look of warming to the haggling. "You see, we're bound for the Territories for the winter and are in need of some provisioning."

"You've got money? Gold, I take it?"

"Army scrip ought'n be as good as gold here, Mr. Gould."

The dark-haired, full-bearded sutler smiled. "It is indeed, Mr. Sweete. Show me what it is you think you need for this trip of yours."

"And we'll talk."

Gould showed more teeth, leaning across the plank counter. "Yes—we'll talk."

Shad had grunted his approval and walked over to the wood-and-glass case where the weapons were locked. "What's them three guns? Never seen anything like 'em."

"Winchesters," Gould said. "Model 1866."

"Let's look."

Gould unlocked the case and brought out one of the lever-action rifles with a full-length, twenty-four-inch barrel.

"What's the caliber?"

"Forty-four rimfire, Mr. Sweete."

"Paper, like army?"

The sutler shook his head. "Rimfire brass. Twenty-eight grains of powder behind a two-hundred-grain bullet."

"Light charge," the old mountain man grunted, used to bigger bore and bigger charges. "Must move that bullet at a good speed."

"These give a man more than one shot. With one in the chamber and a full load—you have eighteen shots."

"Eighteen, Jonah."

"Spencer's only got seven, Shad."

"These the first I've seen of them," Gould explained. "I'm told by the drummer who sold them to me he delivered the first pair to Major H. G. Litchfield, adjutant for the Department of the Platte, back in August."

"How much you want for a pair?"

Gould studied it, scratching his chin. "Considering what I got in them—"

"How much?"

"A hundred-twenty dollars."

He snorted, pulling at his gray beard. "You think a little gun like this gonna be a weapon a man can use out here on the plains, Jonah?"

Hook hefted it to his shoulder, down to look at the action, then back to his shoulder before answering. "That's a lot of shooting, Shad."

"Tell you what, Mr. Gould—I'll give you what you want for two of these rifles. You throw in two hundred rounds each."

Gould thought, then smiled. "I like a man who knows his own mind and can make a deal quickly. All right, Mr. Sweete. You and your partner have your Winchesters."

Down the counter Sweete selected goods from the shelves: coffee, a little salt, and a lot of sugar. Toote sure enough loved her sugar, which reminded him to get both her and Pipe Woman the geegaws that would make her eyes shine when he came to fetch her up in the Laramie country. Bright finger rings and hawks-bells, some trade strouding and a bolt of fancy calico cloth. Along with a new brass kettle and some tin cups. Ribbons of many colors and a handful of shells brought all the way in from the far Pacific coast. Those pale, pink shells had been a pure wonder for Jonah Hook.

Then the old man had looked down at Jonah's feet. "Them boots you're wearing got deplorable on you." Speaking to the sutler, "Show us your best boot. Hog-leg is preferred."

"Your size, mister?"

Jonah shrugged, then brought one boot up to plop squarely down on the counter. "'Bout so big."

Gould grinned. "I see." He brought forth a tall pair of high-heeled boots. "In these parts, the teamsters and mule whackers call 'em Coffeyvilles. Other fellas prefer 'em because the heel is tall enough to hang in a stirrup the way they want."

Jonah had tried them on and found them snug. "I can break 'em in all right, Shad. They'll do."

Sweete turned to Gould. "Get me a size bigger. Maybe two sizes."

"What the hell for?" Jonah had protested. "Told you I could break these in."

"I want you wearing more'n one pair of stockings from now on. Till I get you stomping around in buffler moccasins like me—least you can do is keep your feet warm this winter with a couple pairs of stockings."

It was done. A new pair of boots he pulled on by yanking up the mule ears, with a snug, comfortable fit over two new pair of cotton stockings. Four new hickory shirts for each of them, and a new pair of canvas britches for Hook. With new suspenders and some deer-hide gloves to go along, they were ready to settle accounts with the sutler.

"By damn, I even think we got us a little left over to celebrate with," Shad had declared. "We'll be back in a couple days to pick up our truck and plunder from you, Mr. Gould."

"It'll be here, waiting."

"Don't go sell them two Winchesters on us."

"They're yours, Mr. Sweete. I'm taking them out of the case now."

"C'mon, Jonah. I got me a terrible thirst and know a place down the street what sells saddle varnish they call whiskey!"

The plank floor in the dingy watering hole where Jonah and Shad sat at a corner table proved little better than dirt itself. In places the floor turned to mud and icy slop with so much November traffic. Despite the constant feeding of two wood stoves in the corners, the temperature in the place remained cold, the breath of so many like fine gauze above the knots at the tables and along the rickety bar, what with the incessant opening of the noisy, ill-fitting door.

"You mind I join you fellas?"

Jonah looked up into the haze of wood and tobacco smoke, enough to choke a man more accustomed to the clean air of the windswept prairie, finding a stranger gazing down at Sweete, his handsome face wreathed in breathsmoke. The stranger held a whole loaf of bread and an entire sausage that looked to weigh ten pounds by itself in one hand, while in the other he cradled a glass and the neck of a full bottle.

"Looks like you're drinking the good stuff," Sweete commented, his eyes coming clear enough to study the stranger's bottle.

"I'm looking to share your table and my whiskey," he said, shrugging a shoulder at the full room. "Don't want to stand at the bar, eating my supper. And this here's the last chair. Besides, you fellas look like good company."

"Don't mind company, neither of us," Sweete said.

"And your whiskey too." Hook licked his lips, anticipating the taste of the good stuff. If he could still taste the good stuff after so much of the saddle varnish.

"Got enough here to share," the stranger offered, tearing off an end of the huge loaf of dark bread. "Help yourselves." He reached beneath the tail of his calf-length coat and pulled forth a large skinning knife he put to work slicing off delicate slivers of the fragrant sausage.

It made Jonah's mouth water. "Mister, you're welcome at our table anytime. We was just talking about getting out of here and finding us something to eat."

"From the looks of it—if you fellas don't mind me being honest—you boys don't look like you're gonna be off anywhere for a while."

Sweete rocked slightly in his chair. "Damn, but I think the man's right, Jonah. S'pose we sit here and help this stranger dispose of his vittles, like he offered. Then we can work on finding ourselves a place to spend the night."

"You fellas passing through yourselves?"

"On our way out of town," Jonah answered. "You?"

"Up from Fort Dodge a few days back. Didn't find no work down there. Damn, but I thought there'd always be something for a man to do around a army post—honest money—if he was willing to work."

"Maybe not this time of year," Sweete said. "Quartermaster across the creek at Larned might find you something to do keep you fed this winter. But you keep eating this high on the hog, you'll be busted inside of a week."

"I got a little money set back," the stranger admitted. "Enough to feed on. Put me up a night or two when the weather gets bad—leastways until I can get on something regular."

"Where you been working?"

His eyes went back to the sausage, slicing, slicing slowly in careful, considered strokes like he really knew what he was doing with the sticker. Like he was weighing his answer.

"Been down south of here for some time."

"You a Yankee though," Jonah said.

"Damn—but you don't got no manners," Shad slurred. "He don't mean to be rude, mister."

"I s'pose I am," the stranger answered. "Leastways, I didn't do any fighting back east—if that's what you're asking. I figure you're from the South."

"By God, if you don't have that right," Jonah replied. "Where you do your fighting during the war?"

"Didn't. Nothing more than a civilian—working what I could during that time."

"Where 'bouts?" Shad inquired. "Out here to Kansas country?"

He tore part of a slice off with his big teeth in that handsome, well-groomed face of his. "Some time out here, yeah. The rest on the borderlands."

It snagged Jonah's attention as he stuffed a piece of dark crust into his own mouth. He vowed he would not sound anxious. "Just where . . . on the borderlands? Down to Texas? Up to Arkansas? Or just in the Territories?"

The stranger poured more good whiskey in the three short, smoky glasses. Apparently disarmed. "No. Mostly in southern Missouri. On the run to keep ahead of . . . ahead of any army wanted me to do its fighting for it."

Hook sagged back in the chair, his belly feeling more settled now for the food. His gut more settled, yet disappointed was he that the stranger had not been part of either army that might know something of that band of freebooters that had come marching through his quiet valley back of a time.

"You been south of here, was it?" Jonah asked. "Not much on south, less'n you get into Injun country."

"Injuns don't bother me none," he answered. "Now, that sausage was tasty, it was. You fellas eat up the rest. And," he said, rising from his chair, "you figure on needing a place out of the snow—"

"It starting to snow outside?" Sweete asked, turning clumsily in his chair.

"Was when I came in. Big ol' flakes, mister," said the stranger. "I got me a small room for the night down the street."

"Jenkins place?"

"That's the one," he replied.

"What's a man do to feed himself down in the Territories?" Jonah asked before the stranger was ready to push away into the crowd.

He smiled at Hook. "Whatever he can to keep himself busy, I suppose. You fellas don't finish that bottle, bring it 'long with you."

Sweete held up his hand. "By the way . . ."

"Yeah, I forgot my manners too," he replied, taking the old man's hand, shaking it quickly then letting it go.

"Shad Sweete."

The Confederate held his hand out to the stranger reaching across the table. "Jonah Hook."

"Glad to meet you fellas. Riley Fordham is my name. You come make yourselves to home with me tonight before I pull out to go talk with the quartermaster out to Larned in the morning."

"Least we'll be dry, Jonah."

Fordham smiled with those big, pretty teeth of his as he turned and was gone through the smoke and tobacco haze and the crowd. The air stirred as the noisy door opened, then closed, shutting out the swirl of wet, icy flakes that had come to settle on central Kansas Territory.

"He might know something, Shad."

"It's for certain the man knows good whiskey, Jonah."

"Dammit—I mean he might know about that bunch disappeared down in the Territories."

"Been a long time, son."

"We were fixing on going down there together."

"Been wanting to talk to you about that."

"Sounds like your whiskey's talking now, old man."

Sweete laughed. "All right. Let's talk another time about going down to sniff around."

Jonah gazed through the crowd, through that ill-fitting door, and right on through the icy, swirling mist squeezing down on the central plains.

"I scent me something, Shad. That fella—Riley Fordham . . . he smells like he just might have something to tell me about Missouri. And the Territories."

"And that bunch you got a hankering to gut real slow with a dull elk antler?"

With a crooked grin that lit up the face beneath the wolfish, yellowed eyes, Hook said, "Real . . . real slow."

41

Late November, 1867

"Yeah, I knew of a bunch like that," Riley Fordham admitted, casually. His eyes held steadily on Jonah.

Either he's telling the truth about all of this and he don't have nothing to hide, Jonah thought to himself, or the man is a downright cold-blooded liar.

"You know of 'em in southern Missouri?"

Fordham nodded. "Seems I recollect hearing they rode through down there too. Like some others. I hear Missouri was a bad place during the war. Why you so interested in that one bunch of bad characters?"

"I got family mixed up in it." He watched Fordham cleaning his pistols at the small table against the wall.

Jonah sat on the edge of the bed in the tiny room. Both of them were waiting for Shad Sweete to return from Fort Larned, where the old mountain man had been summoned by the post commander early that morning, red-eyed and plagued with a hangover, swearing he was too old to be drinking that way with young guns like Hook and Fordham. Official business, the messenger from Larned had said.

But this was family business for Jonah. Because of it he felt he was walking on eggshells with the man rubbing the oilcloth back and forth, in and out that .44-caliber pistol barrel.

"Looking for a bunch I understand rode into Indian Territory not long after end of the war come to that part of the country."

Fordham kept on polishing. "Lots of bad folks always run off to the Territories when it gets too hot for 'em elsewhere. How are you so sure the fellas you're looking for went down there?"

"I was told."

The oilcloth stopped. Then after a moment, began polishing again.

"Told, huh? Somebody knew where they were going?"

"I s'pose," Jonah said, beginning to sense a growing tension from the man at the table. "I guess they didn't figure on this fella having any reason for talking."

Fordham cleared his throat. "But sounds like he did—talk that is."

"Said the man who hurt him bragged that they was going to the Territories—where no one would find them. He said that just before his men burned my friend's eyes out."

Fordham gazed at Hook steadily, then finally looked back at his pistol, slipping the cylinder back into the frame. "Pretty cruel torture, I'd say. Knew a couple men once like that. Loved to hurt. One of 'em loved to hurt for a purpose. The other just because he loved hurting."

"You might know the fellas I'm looking for."

"What makes you say that, Jonah?"

"Those two you talked about sound an awful lot like the men who burned my friend's eyes out are the same ones you said you knowed of."

"Didn't mean to make you think that now. What makes you figure the ones I heard of are the same ones burned the sheriff's eyes out?"

Hook leaned forward, almost coming off the edge of the bed, startling Fordham. "You do know 'em! Where they've been—where they're going!"

Fordham licked his lips gone dry, watching Hook ease the pistol from its holster and lay it on the bed beside him. "How—how you so sure—"

"I never said anything about a sheriff. You're the one just come up with that all on your own. You was there when they did it to him, weren't you?"

The man stared a moment at Hook's pistol on the bed, then found Jonah's eyes.

"I damn well had to get out. You'll never understand what it was like being in that bunch."

Jonah sagged. "I don't give a damn about you or how you come clean about what you done. God knows there's enough hell for all of you to spend more than one eternity with the devil for it. All I want to know is where you took my family."

Riley Fordham was about to speak when the door burst open and Shad Sweete filled the doorway. In the next heartbeat Fordham shot to his feet, lunging toward that door, when Jonah pulled up the pistol and caught him midroom.

"What the hell, Jonah!"

"Lemme go!"

Hook shoved the muzzle backward into the man's belly, driving Fordham back to his chair. "Let's talk some more, Riley."

"What's this all about?" Sweete stepped into the room, glanced both ways down the narrow hall and closed the door.

"Fordham here was with the bunch took my family."

"Now listen, Jonah—"

"You shuddup, Fordham," Hook snapped.

Shad chuckled. "Jonah Hook. If that don't beat all. You're having some fun with this new friend of ours. But from the looks of it you got him really scared. Time to put that six-shoot away and—"

"You best believe me, Shad."

Sweete's face drained of color. "This for real, Jonah?"

Hook didn't answer. The old man looked from Jonah's face to Fordham's.

"What he say is true, Fordham?"

The deserter finally nodded. "I run with 'em. And I figure I know who Jonah Hook is now."

Shad took a step toward Fordham. "You know 'bout his family?"

"We took 'em. The others wanted to use up the woman and the girl—then and there and be done with 'em. But for some reason, Usher took a shine to the woman."

"Usher?"

"Jubilee Usher. Big fella. Every bit as big as Sweete here."

"He's got my wife and children?"

Fordham's head sank, his hands working, finger in finger. "The boys . . . Usher and Wiser sold 'em to someone down in the Territories."

"Sold . . ." Jonah swallowed hard on the pain of it. "Sold my boys?"

"Who? Where they go?" Sweete wanted to know.

He shrugged. "Someone out of Texas."

"I oughtta kill you just for the—"

"Hold it, Jonah!" Sweete said, snagging the pistol barrel.

"Don't blame you if you do, Jonah," Fordham said. "Took me long enough to decide to leave. I ain't got anyone else to blame but me for staying long as I did."

"Why did you?"

"I believed Usher, that he was the new Prophet. Believed God was talking to him—that this was part of our plan against the folks that drove our people out of Missouri."

"Your people?"

"Latter-day Saints—most of us."

Jonah looked up at Sweete, shaking his head in confusion.

"Mormons," Sweete explained. "Usher sold the boys to comancheros, didn't he?"

Fordham said, "Seems I remember that word being used, yes."

"Where's my wife?"

"You said Usher took a shine to her?" Sweete asked as he took another step and towered over Fordham.

"Yeah. He wouldn't let any of the rest touch her. Keeping her for himself."

Hook whispered then. "He . . . he using her?"

Fordham looked away to the single, small window in the room. The icy snow lanced against it noisily in that heavy silence. It seemed he could not bear to look at Hook.

"She's his now, Jonah. Maybe you best forget and—"

He was across that six feet and had Fordham's shirt in his hand, the pistol barrel shoved up under the man's chin so far it made the deserter bug-eyed.

"Goddamn you, Fordham! I never will forget. Not till I find her. Not till I find my children. And make all of you pay for what you done to 'em!"

Sweete eased his big hand down on Jonah's arm until the muzzle came away from Fordham's throat. "He's got every right in the world to splatter that ceiling with your brains, Fordham."

"I . . . I know he does. Go 'head. Kill me now. Better that way. Least I won't have to live with what I done. What I didn't do to stop all the hurt."

"This bunch brought hurt to a lot of folks?"

Fordham looked from Sweete to Jonah, whose eyes were only inches from his. "A lot. I figured I needed out—so I could make my peace with God about it."

"S'pose you start now," Sweete said. "Tell this man where he can find his wife."

"And his daughter," Fordham said quietly. "It was 'cause of her I run off.

Usher's bunch finds me, Usher will kill me for running off. No one gets out alive."

"I don't give a damn about them finding you, Fordham!" Hook snapped. "Just—tell—me—of—my—daughter."

"Hattie," Fordham said her name softly.

The sound of her name in that tiny room caught Jonah by surprise. But not nearly as much as did the look on Fordham's face, or the catch in Fordham's voice as he spoke the name. Almost with something akin to reverence.

"Yes," Jonah replied, easing back, "tell me about Hattie."

I wish you'd just quit your bellyaching, Jonah." Shad Sweete's words were louder than normal as they had to be flung into a stiff wind edged with winter's bite coming face-on out of the west. "You damn well now know you're no closer to finding Usher's bunch down south in the Territories than you are sniffing around out here on the plains."

"It's for sure we aren't gonna find 'em out to Fort Laramie," Hook grumbled.

Shad pulled up the fur collar more snugly around his face. "That's where you just might be wrong, son. You spent time out there along that Emigrant Road your own self. And that's the way any bunch like this Usher's is going to make it back across the mountains, and on down to the Salt Lake where those Mormons have settled in."

"You can't stand us Mormons, can you?" asked Riley Fordham, riding on the far side of Jonah.

"It shows, does it?" Shad asked. Knowing it did—in his eyes for sure. Maybe in the sound of his voice.

Mormons had tried to kill Jim Bridger years before, and missing out on that, Brigham Young's band of Danites had killed some of Sweete's friends who worked Bridger's ferry on the Green River. There was no love lost there, no, sir. If anything, that hatred had smoldered every bit as hot that day as it was the day he and Bridger had come down from the hills to find Fort Bridger half burned to the ground. They had found some of the stock killed and left to bloat in their pens, riding east in dread only to find the bodies of friends left to rot among the willows along Green River.

"Can't say I'm proud of everything I've done," Riley Fordham admitted.

"You wasn't old enough then to be a part of that," Sweete said, seeing the young man's eyes mist up. Perhaps only with the cold, incessant wind stiff against their faces.

"My uncle was," Fordham said. "And we always heard how heroic it was going against Indians and Gentiles—white men who were no better than savage Indians anyway."

"That's what they taught you 'bout what those butchers did up there on the Green?"

"I got my own sins to account for, Mr. Sweete," Fordham said, answering it in his own way. "Can't blame no one else for what I've done on my own."

"With the help of this Usher and his right-hand man, the one you called Wiser," Hook said.

"Perhaps that's why I chose to stay on with the two of you back when we crossed the Smoky Hill," Fordham admitted. "Because I've got my own righting of things to see to."

The deserter from Jubilee Usher's Danites had told the two stunned plainsmen all he could there in that tiny room near Fort Larned that late November day as winter came down to squeeze the central plains. Fordham told them how he had rarely seen Gritta Hook, only going from tent to ambulance and back again.

"They keep both her and Hattie pretty sleepy most of the time."

"What they using?"

"Laudanum," he answered. "The woman . . . your wife—she stays with another squad. Usher keeps the girl with a small bunch I rode with, under Wiser. That's why we didn't always know what was going on with the woman. But I was one Usher put in charge of keeping an eye on Hattie. A bright and pretty child, Mr. Hook," Fordham said with clear admiration in his eyes. "If ever I had a daughter of my own, I'd pray she'd be like your Hattie."

"Why'd you desert, leaving her in that den of animals, Fordham?"

"I knew there'd come a time when Wiser would get Usher talked into letting Wiser have Hattie for his own. It was just a matter of time. As each year passed, she grew older, prettier . . . starting to . . ." Fordham cleared his throat nervously. "She was starting to fill out, looking more and more like a young woman. I could see it in Wiser's eyes when he looked at her. One day soon—he'd get her. 'Cause every man of us knew Wiser had already laid claim to her. He'd killed before for her."

"Killed some of his own men?"

"More'n once—when Wiser figured they looked at Hattie the wrong way, or too long. Make no mistake about it—Wiser considered Hattie his already. I couldn't stand to be around when the time came. . . ."

By that next morning Sweete and Hook had been ready to pull out, heading north, with plans to make it to the Platte before turning west. They were again throwing in together to accomplish something important for each other. With that hangover yesterday Shad had learned Phil Sheridan wanted him to ride to Fort Laramie, there to meet with, advise, and interpret for the peace commissioners who had completed but a portion of their work at the Medicine Lodge treaty.

Some of the commissioners were going west, to see what they could do to bring an end to the bloodshed up in Dakota Territory. For more than a year now the army had strung itself thin along the Bozeman Road, establishing Fort Reno, Fort Phil Kearny, and Fort C. F. Smith. Each post existing day to day under a virtual state of siege, plopped down as they were in the heart of prime Sioux and Northern Cheyenne hunting ground.

But the army had put a call out to the bands to come in and talk peace at Fort Laramie. And if Two Moons' band of Shahiyena chose to come in, Shad was sure Toote and Pipe Woman would be with them. The possibility was something the old mountain man did not want to pass up.

Jonah Hook would ride along until he found some word of where Jubilee Usher's band of murderers had been, or might be going. It was for certain Sweete had been right about one thing: if Usher's bunch was heading west to the City of Saints, they would in all likelihood pass Fort Laramie. It was as good a place as any he had right now to continue his search.

This would be a journey of the heart for all three of them. Sweete to once more touch and hold Shell Woman. Hook to find some clue to where he might next search for wife and daughter. And Riley Fordham rode with the two scouts for no better reason than he had to. He had his own sins to atone for.

42

Late December, 1867

"THAT THEM?" JONAH asked the old mountain man standing beside him. The light snow swirled from time to time, but mostly it drifted down flat and fluffy. Hook and Sweete watched shadows of movement in the distance. Coming out of the north. Down from the heart of Red Cloud's country.

"Chances be, Jonah," the tall trapper replied, his eyes never straying from that distance, hopeful.

"Gotta be," Hook said. "Down from the land of the Tongue and the Powder and the Crazy Woman. As wild a country as you were a young stallion in your early days, I'd wager."

Sweete nodded. "Man thinks of nothing more'n getting his stinger dipped in a woman's honey pot when he's a young colt. Ain't till he gets older that a man learns the real value of a woman."

"He don't have to get old to learn that. Not if he's a lucky man, Shad."

Jonah felt the keen, sharp-edged anticipation of the big man beside him. Not angry at Sweete for it, when he could have been. For there was plenty of need in Hook to experience just that same anticipation of seeing one's woman again after a long separation. And while Hook realized his was a far greater separation in both time and distance, he begrudged Sweete not.

It had been Spotted Tail, chief of a large band of Brule Sioux camped near Fort Laramie these days, who had told the two white men that he had

330

reason to believe Two Moons' band of Cheyenne were coming south to the fort. Not so surprising as it might seem, the old chief had said. There were many bands coming in to Laramie to see what the peace-talkers had to say. After all, listening meant receiving presents. Fine presents the likes of which other bands had received at the talks down on Medicine Lodge Creek. Word of such splendor traveled fast along the moccasin telegraph, all the way up the Bozeman Road to Montana Territory.

Travel on the road was all but impossible this time of year, what with the Indian troubles coupled with the way winter had clamped down hard on the northern plains. Just a year ago many of these same bands had waited in ambush while a dozen young horsemen lured Captain William Judd Fetterman and eighty soldiers over the snowy Lodge Trail Ridge up by Fort Phil Kearny. And when the white men were all in the trap, killed every last one of those soldiers.

And only this past summer the warrior bands of Sioux, Cheyenne, and Arapaho had agreed to wipe out the two northernmost forts on the Montana Road in one furious day of bloodletting. As it turned out, the warriors failed in destroying Fort C. F. Smith up on the Bighorn River. It was there they failed in a day-long attempt to wipe out the few civilians and a handful of soldiers hunkered down inside a corral beside a hay field a few miles from the post.

The following August day saw a repeat of the same failure—this time Red Cloud's own, in another hot fight that saw the Oglalla chief's horsemen hurl themselves against a tiny ring of wagon boxes where some thirty soldiers held out against the hundreds, a matter of miles from Fort Phil Kearny while the sun hung high in that summer sky.

Nothing moved on the Montana Road now. Winter had come, and only the army escorted its occasional supply trains north. From time to time a solitary mail carrier slipped through, riding by night, making himself scarce by day. Men like Portugee Phillips, who were made of sinewy stuff that could take what the land and the sky and the warrior bands handed out—and still not break.

Riley Fordham had decided he would wait for spring and the first civilian train to gather on the outskirts of Fort Laramie, bound for the goldfields along Alder Gulch and Bannack and Virginia City.

"A man gets older and learns a little humility, doesn't he, Mr. Sweete," Fordham had commented one recent evening, "when he finds out he isn't so immortal."

"Gives a man a whole new outlook on life, Mr. Fordham, it does."

But the prospect of waiting out the winter at Laramie did not improve the deserter's disposition. Most of the time Fordham was looking over his shoulder, watching every new group of horsemen come riding in from the east along the Platte River Road, or south from the Colorado Territory. Always on the lookout for a familiar face, someone who might be looking for his.

The uncertainty in that waiting must surely take its toll on a man, Jonah decided. Perhaps, just perhaps, as much as the not knowing took its toll on him.

He gave Riley Fordham a grudging respect for riding away from Jubilee Usher. Better had it been that he rode away with Hattie, rather than just saving his own skin. But then again, Jonah figured, Fordham would have to deal with that ghost of failure in his own way, in his own time.

"You know that band. I can tell you do," Jonah said, the cold breeze whipping the breathsmoke from his face. The wind here came cruelly off the Medicine Bows to the west.

Sweete smiled a bit bigger now. "Ain't that I know the band so particular, Jonah. But I do recognize three of them ponies."

"You see her?"

"Yes," he said finally, pushing the wolf-fur hat back farther on his brow. "I believe I do."

It might have been difficult for some men to pick an individual out of that crowd of several hundred warriors, women, and children, along with the old ones too lame or frail to walk or ride atop the ponies. Those wrinkled ones cackled and complained from the travois slung behind many of the horses where they sat among the folded lodge skins and camp equipment, parfleches and rawhide boxes filled with dried buffalo. Man and woman looked so much alike at this distance, every one so wrapped in blanket and robe, hoods pulled up around faces, coyote and wolf and bear hides pulled down to eyebrows to keep out the blowing, stinging snow. A colorful parade this was, coming down to Laramie in a gray December snowstorm.

In the van rode the young warriors, each brandishing his favored weapon, bow or rifle. They gave the gathering soldiers and the great number of civilians employed at the fort a brief exhibition of their horsemanship; their animals kicked up great clods of the frozen snow as they tore past, hanging from rumps by one heel, hiding behind the great, heaving necks of the grass-fed war ponies recent of the buffalo hunts in the north country. Then came the old men, each one riding more stately than the prancing bucks, no longer having to prove anything to any man, white or red. On the scarred ones came, their fans and pipes and other symbols of office now on display as they arrived at this great gathering place to be counted in those discussions to come with the white peace-talkers.

At the last came the women, guiding, riding, or walking beside the ponies who packed on their backs or dragged behind them on a wide vee of lodgepoles the wealth of the band. Like the great arms of an arrow point behind their men, the women slowed their march as the young men slowed theirs, waiting now for the Medicine Pipe Bearer to show the site he had selected for their camp.

And once the word was passed that their long march south had ended, a great shout went up from the old men, echoed by the young warriors— answered and eventually drowned out by the trilling, keening cries of joy from the women and children. Dogs barked their agreement. It had been a long, long journey of many, many days. And this would be a good camp, with many presents yet to come just for listening to the words of the white peace-talkers.

"Shell Woman!" Sweete called out, flinging his voice into the cacophony of camp making as the women shouted to one another as they raised the swirl of their lodgepoles, forming the great horned crescent facing the east.

The old mountain man turned for a moment, reaching out to snag Hook's coat and pull him along. "C'mon, dammit."

"Shell Woman!" Shad cried again in Cheyenne as the two white men trotted through the confusion. Man and woman, child and old one alike turned in amazement to watch the two white men zigzagging through their newly claimed camping ground heaped with the scattered lodge skins and parfleches and bundles of private riches.

A few yards ahead, he watched a woman lift her head, then turn fully around with a jerk. Surely it was Toote. She reached out to tap the person beside her, who bent over at the bundles atop the travois they had just dropped from a weary pony. The second woman stood almost a full head taller than Toote, who began running, full speed toward her husband.

"Rising Fire!" she called out in English, her arms opening as they collided in a swirl of snow.

Surely that must be the daughter, Jonah figured, watching the second, taller woman hurry forward now, pushing back her wolf-hide hat that caped her shoulders above the blanket capote. He could claim to have seen only her back of a time, and not much of that really, when she went stalking off in anger at her mother and white father months gone the way of spring and summer and autumn now.

The three embraced, the women bouncing on the toes of their buffalo-hide winter moccasins, snow swirling up their blanket-wrapped calves. Shad glanced over his shoulder, finding Hook standing there.

"C'mere, Jonah. You remember Toote," Sweete said as the woman nodded. "And this is my daughter. You see'd her before—but never met proper. Her name's Pipe Woman."

Only then did she raise her eyes to him, capturing his attention with their almond luster. Then looked away, glancing up at her father. Asking something quietly in Cheyenne.

"Jonah Hook," Sweete told her.

She looked at the tall, rail-thin white man again for but a moment. Only as long as it took her to smile and say, "Jo-naw. Jo-naw Hoo-oucks."

This was the reason she did not like most white men.

They pawed at her with their eyes. Some of them lunged close enough that she smelled their stinking breath, the stench of their unwashed bodies. Young warriors bathed frequently. Young, arrogant white men did not.

By now Pipe Woman was old enough to know what the white men wanted with her. This would be her twenty-first winter. Long ago she had come to understand what men and women meant to one another beneath a buffalo robe, when their hands ran up and down one another's bodies, tasting, licking, kissing, feeling, sweating in rhythm with each other.

She had grown up sneaking looks at her parents across the fire pit whenever her white father returned to the lodge of her full-blood Cheyenne mother. And their union had often filled her with confusion: as much as she hated her white blood, she loved her father and all he had meant to not only Shell Woman, but to his daughter as well. He was the only white man she had ever tolerated.

Many looked at her with undisguised lust in their eyes, licking their lips, lurking close with the smell of whiskey strong about them, their blood-stained, greasy wool-and-leather britches straining beneath the rigid hardness of their flesh as they tried rubbing against her. So it was that in young womanhood Pipe Woman had learned where first to strike a man whose hands she did not want mauling her breasts or pinching her bottom. One swift, sure blow to that swollen flesh that a man ofttimes let rule him.

More than once Pipe Woman had had to fight men off. She did not understand this power of her beauty yet. As much as her mother and father told her, still she did not fully realize the power it held over men, both her own, and the white man.

This stinking gathering place was filled with them. Soldiers in their dirty, mud-crusted uniforms soaked with melting snow. Unwashed civilians in their unwashed clothing, smelling of old fires and stale tobacco and meals spilled and smeared and forgotten. Both kinds seated at the small tables in this dingy, smoke-filled room where the walls themselves reeked of whiskey and worse.

Again Pipe Woman wondered why it was that a man who came equipped so well for peeing did not take the trouble to walk outside of such places as these and pee on the ground. Instead, she remained mystified, so many of these white men chose to pee where they stood, in the same room where they smoked and drank, and traded.

That's why she was here. Her mother had sent her to the sutler's for some hard candy. Sweete had brought coffee, but had been unable to find any hard candy for Toote along the trail the three men had ridden northwest from Fort Larned. It was a special craving Shell Woman suffered, from the time she was a child and experienced her first taste of hard candy given her by a trader on the upper Missouri River. From that moment, she was hooked something fierce.

So it was this third afternoon since the arrival of the women at Laramie that Shad had come down to the post with Pipe Woman and Jonah Hook. The men turned off to see the peace-talkers, and Pipe Woman was sent on to the post sutler's place, to buy Shell Woman's hard candy before the three of them returned to the Cheyenne camp where Toote was involved with a special supper: elk loin and marrow bones and fry-bread.

"Ain't you a pretty little thing."

Pipe Woman turned away from the man as he loomed toward her out of the dingy, smoky haze. The smell of him turned her stomach. And staring at the stinking hole in his face made her all the sicker.

She stood her place at the counter, waiting for the clerk to finish with a soldier.

The foul one came slowly around to her other side, his eyes moving down, then up her body.

"I'll bet you know how to make a man mighty happy, don't you, squaw?"

She did not understand all the words he said. There was some English she knew, learned from her father. Yet the meaning of the words spoken by this smelly man got across to her all the same. Pipe Woman refused to look at him.

"Bet that body of yours under that coat is all soft and warm and willing to let a good man show you just how he can make you happy too, little squaw."

She glanced over at the side of the room where the tables and chairs sat—that part of this place given over to the white men who drank whiskey and became mad from it. They were, by and large, quiet and attentive at this moment. Watching her. Watching him too.

She looked in the other direction. The clerk nervously continued helping the young soldier. He wanted no trouble, and was doing everything he could to ignore her problem.

Then his dirty hand was on her arm, at her elbow. She stared down at the dark crescents beneath the long, cracked fingernails. Pipe Woman turned to face him as her right hand shot up, slapping him full force. The noise of that flesh against flesh weighed heavy in the smelly room where the white man drank himself crazy.

But as quickly her left arm was hurting—at both the elbow and the shoulder.

The man with the stinking breath had twisted and spun her about, pinning her arm behind her, raising it as she bent over, yelping as the stabbing pain took her breath away. His left hand now grabbed her hair at the crown of her head, yanking back slowly. He showed pleasure at the hurt he was causing her.

"Shit, fellas," he said near her ear, "I'm new in your country here. But it sure looks like these squaws out in these parts like to play with a man just the way the squaws do back down to the Territories."

"These are Sioux, and Cheyenne Injuns out here, mister," one of the others said, all but his voice obscured by the murky, smoky haze. She did not know what face spoke. The pain was so great in her shoulder now that she saw stars blink before her eyes.

"What the hell that mean?" asked her tormentor.

"Just figured you'd wanna know these Injuns don't just lay down for a white man out here the way they maybe done for you down in the Territories."

"What you trying to say, mister?"

"Nothing," replied the voice quietly.

"Just so you know," her attacker said, dragging Pipe Woman away from the counter toward the smoky part of the room, "them squaws back down there don't always lay down and spread their legs just 'cause a white man wants to rut on 'em." He smiled wickedly. "You just gotta convince 'em how bad they want what you got to give 'em!"

He took his hand from her hair and reached around to tear open the flaps of her capote, the colorful woven sash falling to the floor at her feet. His long-nailed fingers dug at her firm breasts. With her heels, Pipe Woman tried kicking backward at his shins. He yanked upward on her arm, making her cry out, and dug his fingers into her breast brutally. So hard the first tears came to her eyes. Pipe Woman cursed those tears for betraying her.

"I'm used to taking a squaw where I want her," the man said.

"Take her outside," someone suggested. "Least do that."

"All right," he hissed at her ear, breathing heavily behind it. "Yeah, that's the least I can do for you fellas. Since I am new out here. I'll call you when I'm done—and any the rest of you can have what's left when I am."

She could feel him now, that rigid hardness pressing in behind her, near the tops of her buttocks. He was a tall man, and younger than her father.

He lifted her off her feet, starting her backward for the door when a sudden blast of cold air told Pipe Woman that someone else had come in.

"Say you! Hold that door open, mister!" her tormentor called out.

He shuffled her toward the cold draft that said he was drawing her closer to the door.

"Pipe Woman?"

Thinking she recognized the voice, the young woman was only sure when her attacker turned slowly.

"You know this squaw, mister?"

"Yeah," answered Jonah Hook, taking his eyes off her face and looking into the man's.

"She any good?" he rasped, then laughed humorlessly.

"Doubt she's been with a man at all."

She could feel his entire body tense at that. "How you so sure?"

"Cheyenne women like that. Go 'head. Put your hand down there between her legs. Yeah, down 'round her waist. Feel that rope. That's a belt she'll cut off for the man she'll marry."

Pipe Woman could feel the man's breathing go shallow, hard and shallow. He was growing more than excited.

"She's a goddamned virgin!" he said greedily. "Let's go, sweetheart."

Hook put out his empty hand. "I guess I didn't get it across to you. She ain't for you to use."

The stranger stopped shoving her toward the door, his attention on Hook. "Where you from, Reb? You one of them poor white trash we whipped in the war?"

"You didn't whip me, mister. I'm still standing here—waiting for your yellow-bellied kind to show me how you fight a man. You're pretty tough with a woman. But your kind gets all yellow and runs when you gotta fight a man."

"I figure I'll take care of you—then have my fun with the squaw here."

"Your kind never learned any manners around a woman, did you, Yankee trash?"

"This red slut ain't no woman. She's a goddamned Injun whore—and I'm just lucky enough to be her first man. Now—if you know what's better for you, why don't you just wait in line when I'm done, you ugly Gentile."

"Gentile," Hook repeated. "Seems I remember some folks calling me that before."

"Chances are—you rubbed up against Mormons. And come out losing against the power of God. Like I said, Reb—I'll whip you good tonight and leave you for the dogs to chew on come morning."

"You're a lot of talk with a Injun girl between us, Mormon," Hook said.

Pipe Woman watched Hook pull open his coat, the big handle of his pistol sticking out now, looking huge like a deer hoof.

Her attacker was silent for a few moments, breathing hard, probably considering. Then he shoved her forward a step, closer to Hook.

"Something about you bothers me, mister."

"Maybe because I come to hate Mormons."

The man shook his head. "Naw—it's them eyes of yours. Swear I seen eyes like that before. Yeah—almost like you could be kin to some other poor Secesh trash we burned out down in Missouri."

She watched Hook swallow hard, his eyes narrowing as he asked, "Missouri?"

"You know the place, do you? Well, let me tell you about this hardscrabble farm we come on," he hissed. "Folks there without no man to take care of 'em. Years back. Kids all got the same yellow eyes like yours, mister. Especially the girl. What's she now? Maybe ten—eleven years old. Just about prime for rutting, don't you think?"

"Maybe you ought'n hold your tongue, before you get it cut out of your throat."

"Oh, you is it? It's you gonna do the cutting? I don't think so. So let me tell you we took that girl and her mama and two young boys and—"

"Let the Injun girl go now." Hook breathed out slowly.

"You want her for yourself, mister?"

"I want to know where you got my daughter and wife. Then . . . I'm going to kill you."

He laughed, like the quick, high bleet of a sheep. "You better be real good with that hog-leg you got stuck in your belt—because I'm quick."

"Let the girl go now."

"Yeah," he breathed heavily, almost in a curse of a whisper. "I'll let her go."

His hand came away from her breast, with a sudden rush of blood to her flesh after so long beneath his clawing grip. Then he released her wrist and her arm fell, limp, tingling with the rush of circulation returned to its entire length.

"G'won now, Pipe Woman."

"Nice name," the Mormon said, pulling apart the flaps of his coat.

"Take it outside!" yelled someone from behind Hook.

"Go now, Pipe Woman!" Hook repeated, urgently, motioning toward the open door where the snow swirled.

She saw that Hook never took his eyes off the one who had grabbed her, so she was not sure he would know she had left. Only when she stepped through the doorway into the darkness filled with cold, icy, dancing snow . . . and slammed the door behind her.

She was running, running through the deep snow, sprinting through the patches of darkness and lamplit brightness—heading back to her mother's lodge, breathless, hurting, scared—

—when she heard the gunshots throb profanely into that winter night, behind her.

43

O NLY THE WIND keening outside the lodge.
Nothing more than that.

Shad Sweete closed his eyes again and rolled over, his bare back warming as he snuggled against Toote. He sighed in contentment, the air in the lodge cold, yet still fragrant with that night's supper.

His eyes shot open again.

Sweete was certain now—sure that what he had heard was something more than the winter wind. Almost like the whimper of a man . . .

His ears strained, picking up the first sounds of footsteps across the icy snow. Two sets. Two men. No, not really . . . the second man was being dragged along by the first. And whoever was doing the dragging had that second man begging for his life.

More noise to it now on the old, icy snow.

As he bolted up, yanking his wool shirt over his longhandles, Shad's ears picked up the sound of camp dogs snuffling around outside, their own paws padding across the icy crust atop the four-day-old snow outside.

Quickly he yanked on the two buffalo winter moccasins, sewn hair in, and snatched up his long winter capote. He was out through the lodge door, pulling the coat over his arms as Jonah Hook appeared from the backside of the lodge.

He was dragging a man across the snow.

In the pale moonlight that gave a dim, morning luster to the snow, Shad could see the thin, greasy trail of blood beneath the man as he was hauled along behind Hook. The dogs were busy over that track of warm gore, muzzle deep.

"What in glory is going on?" Shad demanded in a harsh whisper, his shoulder-length gray hair and beard brilliant beneath the winter starlight.

"Wanted you to meet somebody, Shad," Jonah rasped, short of breath.

Sweete recognized a cold light in the young Confederate's eyes. Something so cold it caused the old mountain man to shiver there in the snow spilling over his ankles that he found himself having to glance away, down to the stranger.

"Who's this? What the bloody hell is going on?"

Hook knelt, jabbing his fingers into the man's hair and yanking the head back. The eyes rolled up, attempting to focus on Hook a moment, then flickered toward Shad Sweete. A wild sheen came over them of a sudden.

"Help—help me, mister!" he called out weakly. "I'm bleeding to death, dammit."

"I can see that," Sweete replied. None of this made a tinker's bit of sense. He knelt beside Jonah, the stranger too. "How—"

"This bastard shot me!" the stranger explained, reaching out his hand to Sweete.

Hook brought his pistol barrel down on the back of the man's wrist with a brutal snap.

"He's gonna kill me—for sure," he whimpered. "You gotta help me!"

"You shoot him?"

Hook nodded. Silent in the moonlight.

Then something struck Shad, and his eyes opened a bit wider in its recognition. "This is the one Pipe Woman told us about when she come back to the lodge tonight—"

"He was about to rape her, Shad," Hook explained, his voice emotionless.

Sweete looked back at the man. "She's my daughter." He snagged hold of the man's throat himself, fingers on one side of the trachea, a big, powerful thumb pinching the other.

Gurgling with some feeble, small animal sound, he flailed with his arms at the grip the big mountain man had on him.

"She came running back here from the sutler's all worked up, Jonah. I never made much sense of it, from the way she was going on about something happened up there while you and me was over talking to

Maynadier at post headquarters. I just figured it had something to do with you—a fight of some kind you got into when I headed back here and you said you'd mosey over to the sutler's to walk her back to camp."

"What else she try to tell you?"

"Something about a fight. Toote finally got her calmed down. Talking about guns and blood and you and somebody hurting her. Figured we'd find out come morning. It didn't make no sense—till now."

"That ain't but the start of it, Shad," Hook said. "I brung him here for us both to hear him talk before I gut him."

"Bad medicine. Not near the lodge, Jonah."

"No. I'll take him off a ways when I do it." Hook paused, his head coming up, ear cocking as if listening.

Shad heard it too.

A shadow stood ten yards off, a dark monolith punching a hole out of the nightsky, the outline of a riflestock very plain.

"Gimme your pistol, Jonah," Shad whispered.

"You won't need it, Shad," came the voice.

"Fordham?"

"It's me. Now, just let me come on in, easy."

"What business you got down here this time of night?" Shad asked.

"Got business with Jonah."

The deserter came up and stopped as Sweete stood, watching the man's eyes, and his hand on the action of that rifle. In the moonlight, Fordham gazed down on Hook, his rifle pointed in the Confederate's direction.

Shad saw Jonah's pistol pointed right at Fordham's belly.

"You know 'im, don't you, Riley?" Jonah inquired at last, in a quiet whisper.

He took another step up, slowly moving the rifle barrel toward the stranger as the bleeding man's eyes grew bigger. Fordham jammed the rifle muzzle against the man's jawbone and pushed the face more into the light.

"Yeah. Now I'm sure."

"You gonna help me, aincha, Riley?" the man begged.

"And he sure as hell knows you, don't he?" Jonah asked, his eyes narrowing.

Fordham finally dropped the angle of the rifle. "Yes."

Shad began, "What's this all about?"

"They worked together," Jonah interrupted, not taking his eyes off Riley Fordham's face. "Tell 'im, Riley."

"What he says is right. This bastard being here can only mean one thing:

they're tracking me. He's found me. Meaning that the others can too. I'd best be going, fellas. Pushing on to make the trail cold as I can before the rest come."

Shad snagged Fordham's arm as the deserter started to turn away. "You're staying—least till this makes sense."

"That man there," Fordham said, pointing his rifle at the bleeding man. "He's got two of Hook's bullets in him. And near as I tell, Jonah's likely got one of this bastard's in him."

"You hit, Jonah?" Shad asked.

Hook pulled aside his coat to show a dark stain at his right side, just above his hip. "Grazed me. A wild shot he got off when I hit him the first time."

"How you two ever work together, Riley?" Shad asked. "Unless this one was with Usher's bunch."

"That's what I tried to tell you. Now I gotta go. No telling how many out there now—coming."

"There's a way to find out." Jonah handed his pistol up to Shad then and pulled out his skinning knife, laying the edge against the stranger's jawline. "You remember his name, Riley?"

"Called Laughing Jack. Never knew his last name."

"All right, Jack. S'pose you tell us how many there are here at Laramie."

"O-only me," Jack coughed his answer. "God! Don't—"

Hook dragged the knife across the skin, opening a thin laceration that beaded with dark blood in the silver light.

"Goddammit—I beg you!"

Hook yanked back on the man's head. "I'm gonna keep cutting down, slow . . . real slow—while you tell me who all came with you."

"No one, for the love of God!" he sputtered, coughing up a little black fluid. "I'm alone. Though I am in the presence of mine enemies, may my hand be strong to smite the—"

"You believe him, Riley?"

"You gotta believe me, Riley!" the man pleaded. "Usher and Wiser—sent out a few of us they trusted. Some went on north, into Nebraska country. Others down sniffing around for you at Denver City . . . out to the forts in Kansas. You was there months back—they figured you'd . . . so some are asking around the railroad. I'm alone, goddammit! You can't let this Gentile . . . get this crazy bastard off me and find me a doctor—I'm bleeding to death!"

Fordham knelt beside Laughing Jack. "What's Usher gonna give the man who finds me?"

Jack's eyes grew even more frightened. He swallowed, realizing now, then gurgled some on the blood dribbling from the corner of his mouth. "Usher's gonna give 'im the girl. She's a virgin—"

Fordham drove the back of his hand across Jack's jaw. "Hattie—"

Hook yanked Jack's head back, bringing the blade down in that heartbeat until Fordham put a hand against Jonah that stayed the Confederate's. "All right, Jack. How 'bout you telling me and Hattie's papa just where we can find them."

"I don't know where now—" Jack started, then screeched as Jonah dragged the knife blade deeper into the flesh of the man's throat. It was pink and white, the neck turning bloody now, right across the rings of cartilage that formed the windpipe.

"Get back in the lodge!" Shad hollered as the two women started out the door with a rustle of frozen hides. They obeyed without question in a swirl of blankets. He heard their voices whispering in fear between themselves.

"Take the son of a bitch someplace else, Jonah. Away from this lodge—my family."

"I'm leaving now," Fordham said, rising to his feet.

"You're coming with me, Riley," Hook said firmly.

Fordham looked down at his rifle, then at Sweete with the pistol, and finally back at Hook.

"All right. I owe Hattie that much."

"You owe me that much for not killing you the first time I found out back there in Kansas."

Hook yanked on the front of Jack's shirt, straining to pull the man. Sweete at last saw the two holes: one in the chest, the other low in the belly. Bleeders—both of them. A man drowns in his own juices, gut-shot that way, Shad thought.

"I'll be back, this is over, Shad," Hook said quietly as he started off, dragging Jack, with Fordham bringing up the rear.

Sweete watched them hobble through the snow toward the nearby cottonwoods and willow, listening to the whining of the dogs sniffing the blood on the snow where Jack had lain, hearing the whimpering of the man as he begged Riley for his life, begged his God for help, begged for anyone to put him out of his pain—quickly.

"Soon enough."

Hook's whisper went the way of smoke on that cruel, winter wind.

"You won't feel no pain soon enough."

• • •

"*They come north,* Shad," Jonah explained, blowing the steam from his coffee. His first cup that morning. Always better in the gray of predawn like this, when it was the coldest time of day. Especially after a sleepless night.

"Out of the Territories?"

"Yeah. Course, Fordham told us Usher was planning to do that eventual."

"Riley—he gone now?"

"Must be. After we . . . finished with Jack: dragged his body a ways down the bank, rolled it under the ice in the river over yonder—Fordham lit out. Said he had to get moving or his scent would stay around for the next one come along."

"He's probably right. This bunch with Usher found Fordham this time—they'll find him again." Shad took a slice of the dried buffalo from Toote.

She offered one to Jonah. He took one, then a second slice, glancing at the back of the lodge where Pipe Woman sat side-legged, the blankets pulled up beneath her chin. She was no longer looking at him the same way she had the day they met. Now, instead, there was an expression of horror on her face.

Jonah couldn't blame her. What he'd done . . . But, hell, he'd done it for her too.

Shad asked, "He say when they come north?"

"Half a year at the most, from what Laughing Jack told us. Says Usher figures to be slow at moving west—back to Deseret. With their prisoners. Gritta and Hattie."

"Usher won't give her away, Jonah. Remember that. Not until someone finds Fordham."

"They better not—or I'll kill Fordham myself."

He watched Jonah stand, finishing the last of his coffee. "Where you heading?"

"Don't see any use in burning daylight, Shad."

"Doesn't answer where—so a man knows how to find you."

"East from here. First I'll check around Sedgwick down on the South Platte. Wander on to McPherson, and Kearny. Don't hear any word there, I'll push on south a bit into Kansas. Someone—soldier or civilian—at one of the posts will hear of that bunch. If they're going back to Mormon country—there's one good way to get there."

"Then why the hell don't you stay here and wait for 'em to come marching by, Jonah?"

He shook his head. "Can't take the chance I'll miss 'em. Can't sit still—just waiting. I got to be looking."

"I understand, son."

Hook glanced at Pipe Woman a moment. Wishing there were something he could say to her, to make her see that he wasn't a violent man. But what else had he shown her? The look in her eyes last night when he was preparing to draw down on the man hurting her . . . the look in her eyes for that instant last night when she and Toote saw Jonah opening Jack's neck like a hog at slaughter—before Shad shooed them back into the lodge.

What do you say to such a beautiful young woman who you felt such an arousal for, such a heated yearning to feel flesh against flesh—but now saw in her eyes nothing but fear and loathing for you? He told himself maybe it was better this way—after all, she was Shad's daughter. And he had a wife out there . . . somewhere. Better in the long run that he just go.

"I'll be moving out now," he said quietly, pushing aside the door flap and stepping from the lodge into the cold.

Sweete and his family joined Hook in the gray light of early dawn.

"You need help—wire me here. The colonel will get word to me, for certain," Sweete said. He folded Hook into his arms.

Toote came into him next, murmuring some Cheyenne. Then she backed up, mist in her eyes, and said in English, "Thank . . . Pipe Woman . . . safe now."

He nodded, self-consciously, then turned to take up the halter on the pack horse. That's when she shuffled close, standing there so close he could smell her. Jonah turned, finding Pipe Woman at his shoulder, those wide eyes still filled with fear. But, perhaps now no longer any fear of the violence he knew was inside him—but fearful instead of what violence might do to him.

She put out her arms and came into him, her head buried against his bony chest.

"Thank you, Jonah Hook," she said, quietly against his wool coat.

He smelled her hair, drinking in its fragrance of smoke and hides and sage, deeply.

Then turned quickly, mounted his horse, and jammed heels into its flanks so that none of them could see the hot tears.

44

S PRING HAS A way of slipping in on the plains like no other season. Summer is always upon that land before you know it. Autumn arrives in the nonchalant way of a shy suitor. And winter usually blusters in with a fury, bravado, and sometimes sheer terror.

But spring most often of all sneaks up on a man with the seductive secrecy of a woman. Here he had been living through each winter day and night, surviving. Not really noticing that the sunlight grows longer by a few minutes each day. Perhaps not really noticing any change in the snowpack, realizing that what snow comes might be a little wetter, the winds a little stronger at times.

So it is with this beguiling seductive quality that spring arrives on the plains. Just like a woman will slip in on a man and tangle up his heart when he least realizes it. And when he finally opens his eyes one morning, she is there, she is everywhere, she is with him. And he is hooked. Madly, irretrievably in love.

Spring had come to the plains.

Here along the Missouri River, there were already signs that the great ice jams of the upriver were breaking. Sawyers and flotsam flowed past, tumbling in the muddy foam from up north, now headed east for a union with the waters of the Mississippi far downstream. An occasional buffalo carcass too, rocking slowly with the frothy, icy, mud brown Missouri. Water born of the high places. A land where Jonah Hook had only marched along the fringes. Not daring yet to penetrate. Perhaps never—he got his family back, and things settled down back in Missouri. Maybe go as far east as he ought—back to the Shenandoah, in the shadow of Big Cobbler Mountain. They'd be safe from harm there once more.

And put this all behind them.

But that was as much a dream as any Jonah experienced each time he closed his eyes.

Late March it was. After three months of backtracking from Fort Laramie, the hunt had brought him here to this country near the Missouri River, just inside Kansas. Upriver from the great bend and Kansas City. At Fort Leavenworth again, remembering that winter of sixty-five when first the Union army brought him west to fight Indians.

More a staging arena now than any fort Hook had seen out west. When first he got here days ago, it was as if he had stepped back into another world, one that had become unfamiliar in the years gone between. What struck him most about Leavenworth was that this grouping of neatly whitewashed buildings and close-cropped lawns and wide graveled walks, along with its band shell and central flagpole and drilling infantry had no business calling itself a western fort.

But perhaps that was it, he had thought. Maybe he was no longer in what could be termed the West. Perhaps this was the end of the East and the beginning of the frontier, that term others were using out here more and more now. Maybe the West started here at the Missouri.

Again Jonah Hook had prayed that here his journey would come to an end.

It wasn't that he didn't have reason to give voice to that prayer. He had damned good reason. The last three months had led him here—with word that he might find a bunch that sounded like the ones he was looking for. Men, the story had it, who'd come riding north out of the Territories on some of the best of horseflesh anyone had seen in a long time—tough, lean, and good configuration. And every man jack of them was well-armed, swaybacked almost under the firepower each sour-faced one of them carried.

They stayed off by their own and kept to themselves, he was told. Likely waiting for something, somebody. And they had to do with the sutlers when need be. Drinking whiskey among the watering holes and hovels near the fort. And dealing with the chippies and whores in their cribs back of those dingy, smoky places. But only in rotation, it was noted by a few who had cause to notice such things.

The entire group never ventured out of its camp as a whole. Always some staying behind while the others came in for leave. On schedule they rode into the settlement to take their recreation. On schedule they rejoined out front and remounted, riding back to their camp, where they bothered no man.

"They pay for what they need," a clerk at the mercantile had told Jonah of the band camped down by the river. "Never an argument on price or quality of what they buy. Good customers."

"There a tall one with 'em? Bald on top—long hair down to his shoulders?"

He had thought, then shook his head. "No. No man like that."

"How 'bout a fella that walks with a hobble, like this?" Jonah had inquired of the clerk days ago, hobbling across the floor as Riley Fordham had mimicked Boothog Wiser's peculiar clubfooted walk.

Again he shook his head. "No, sir. I'd remember something like that."

And with the news came a sinking feeling that the bunch camped out yonder were not the ones he wanted. Until he joined three of them in a card game one cold, blustery afternoon that slicked the mud puddles in the rutted street with ice scum and drove men indoors while their horses hunched around, rumps to the cruel wind, heads bowed at the rail.

"Gimme two," Jonah said to the dealer, a local. In fact, two other locals were sitting in on the game. Seven hands in all at the big, battered table beneath an oil lamp spreading yellow light and smoky shadow over them all.

A crack of lightning snapped his nerves taut as catgut, and seconds later came the slap of thunder stampeding in off the plains with nothing to slow it in the slightest. It made the low-roofed shanty of a gambling palace shake, rattling clapboard against quaking frame stud. Shaking the lamp above them, causing a few among them to shift in their chairs. The three he had been getting to know did not. Glued as they were, unnerved by the noise.

"That'un was close," said one of the locals.

Jonah laid his cards down when called. "Nothing more'n three of a kind." He knew he would be bested by the fleshy, jowly unspoken leader of the trio. But it was as he had planned.

Jowls grinned, creasing all the lines leading from his red-veined bulbous nose down to the five-day whiskers. His eyes gleamed at the other two. "We're making money, our time out, boys."

They both grumbled, as did the locals while Jowls raked his winnings from the center of the table.

"These two with you, are they?" Jonah asked, sensing he had to turn up the heat a bit.

It was time. He'd pried enough out of them to know the trio was from the ten or so camped down by the river. And the more they had talked during the three hours they had been trading cards and coins and scrip back and forth, Jonah had come to realize that the bunch had just spent time farther south, and east some too before that. Enough clues to pick up their talk among themselves about places he knew in southern Missouri, what with their talk of fighting Confederate sympathizers during the rebellion on the borderlands, and even referring at times to a prolonged stay down in the Territories. They were most proud of that—amused with the fact and not short of brag that they had eluded any man or posse or squad of soldiers sent to follow them.

"We was our own law down there," Jowls had claimed, with another big grin that brought smiles from the other two.

"How was them squaws?" ventured one of the locals, leaning in over the table to ask eagerly.

"We had one whenever we was needing to dip our cock in something warm!" exclaimed a man with a pinched rat face covered by a patchy set of whiskers.

"Your boss—he like poking them squaws like you fellas?" Jonah asked as he dealt a five-card hand around the green-blanket table.

"Me?" Jowls asked. "I liked it a whole bunch."

"No," Jonah replied. "I'm asking about your boss, mister. One running your outfit."

"Naw. He didn't stoop to poking squaws like us," Rat-face answered.

"That's right. Jubi—" and suddenly then the third man shut himself off, noticing the glares of the other two. He cleared his throat. "The colonel keeps hisself a woman what could answer all his needs of the flesh."

Like no struggle he had ever known, Jonah forced himself to sit there in the chair, slowly looking from face to face to face, measuring each one. Not for playing this hand, but for what he knew lay in store. He drew cards, folded, watching the rest play through the hand. Then he passed the deck on to Jowls. Jonah got lucky, and though his mind wasn't really there in the game, he ended up winning the hand. And the cards went on to the rat-faced gambler.

Time for Hook to force the play.

"You dealt two off the bottom . . . friend." Jonah's eyes leveled on the dealer, flicked once to Jowls to find the leader measuring Hook coolly.

Flicked next to the third man on the far side of the dealer, a flat-faced, nondescript man in whose eyes registered the first licks of fear. Flat-face laid down his cards and slid them toward the dealer.

"What makes you say that?" Jowls asked.

In his eyes, Jonah could see the fleshy one wasn't too sure how he should play it. Hook had only one hand on the table right then. The other somewhere in his lap.

"I saw it," Jonah replied, not taking his eyes off the dealer, or the flat-faced man. "Now, since I ain't lost no money on this hand, I'm not going to kill the dealer."

Jowls slowly eased back from the table with a loud scrape of his chair. "You better figure on holding a royal flush, mister—'cause you just bit off more than you can chew."

Bringing his pistol up from his lap into plain view, Jonah laid his cards down, then filled that right hand with a second pistol from his belt. "You can sit this hand out, you wanna, mister. My trouble's with this one dealing bad cards. But—since I get the idea you can talk these boys into trouble, or out of it—I'll probably blow your head off first if any of them two make a funny move on me."

Jonah watched Jowls flick a tip of his tongue out to lick his lips.

"Now, all three of you—here's the way we're going to play this hand," Hook said. "I'm going to give you three a chance to lay your hardware on the table, and slide it over to these fellas here. They look like honest folks—so we'll trust 'em with your guns."

"We do, what you fixing to do with our weapons?" Jowls asked.

"Hold 'em—while I beat the shit out of the dealer."

The rat-faced man flared. "You ain't got the balls—"

"I could shoot you in the balls right here and now under the table—and that'd end you ever having another squaw again, wouldn't it, mister?"

The dealer puckered with imagined pain. "You wanna fight me?" he asked with a nervous grin. "All right." Then he slowly pulled his pistol out and laid it on the table. It made a loud noise in the small, low-roofed room.

"Now the other one," Jonah prodded, anxious. "The both of you two, get shet of your weapons." He wagged his own pistols as the three stood and pulled coats aside, showing they now had empty holsters. "Gentlemen, watch these guns and these other two fellas for me while I teach this one bottom-dealing bastard how not to play cards with honest folk."

When he had waved Jowls and Flat-face back from the table, Jonah set his two pistols down in front of one of the locals, then strode past the fleshy man, heading for the rat-faced one who was moving off, volving his shoulders, bringing up his fists and flexing his ropy muscles.

With a crack, Jonah caught him unprepared with a quick jab. Rocking Rat-face backward. A second jab brought a spurt of blood as the man shook his head, bewildered. The room erupted into cheering and jeering. From the corner of his eye, he saw the flat-faced man balling his fists, uneasy, wanting in on the action.

That glance cost him.

Rat-face was on him with a crack to the side of the head that stunned Hook. It made his temple throb with bone against bone, and seeing stars. A big, powerful fist doubled him over, a fist on the back of his head brought Hook to his knees. As Rat-face stepped up, preparing to ram his knee under Jonah's chin, Hook moved aside and caught the leg, standing as he did it. The man spilled backward, cracking the back of his head on the edge of a far table.

Of a sudden the air was being choked out of him. Jonah felt an arm around his neck, fingers in his hair, reaching down for his eyes, a thumb clawing toward his mouth, gouging for all the man was worth. Shifting his weight, Jonah saw from the corner of one bloody eye that Jowls still stood his ground, yelling enthusiastically. It had to be the plain, pie-faced one. Jonah had not counted on this.

Now he jammed a heel into the man's boot. Feeling a lurch in his grip. A second time he jammed down, even harder with his heel. The arm came loose, just enough that Jonah spun beneath it, feeling some of his long hair come away in the man's grip. He drove one fist into the gut, the heel of his other hand came up beneath the man's chin, driving him backward.

Hook tasted the salty blood on his tongue, felt it dribbling from his nose. And the sting of torn flesh at the corner of his eye where the man's fingers had raked him good.

And then Jonah had his hands full again as Flat-face came at him, charging, head down, crushing Hook with both his arms as Jonah pummeled him on the back of the head, neck, shoulders. Arms locked him in a painful vise, choking off his breath. Hook couldn't get any air as the man shoved him against the wall, driving the last breath from him. Then, again he rammed Hook against the clapboard. A collision against the wall. Each time with a grunt from the Confederate.

"Drop the knife, Perkins!"

He heard someone yell. Not sure who. His eyes weren't clear—not for the blood and for the tears of pain.

"Leave me cut him, Hastings!"

Rat-face was there at Hook's side now. Knife out, he was badly bruised and bloody.

"He could have gut-shot you—but he didn't, Perkins," said Jowls, the man called Hastings. "Leave it at that." He was looking over the room like he knew good and well that none of them really could stand a chance of getting away from committing murder in this fashion.

"I'll finish him good," Flat-face said with a grunt, shoving Jonah against the wall a fourth time.

"Let 'im go, Colby."

Colby obeyed immediately, stepped back, and accepted his pistols from Hastings. Perkins was wiping himself off with the back of his hand, smearing the blood on the front of his greasy britches.

Then Hastings was in Hook's face. "You fight good, for being such a skinny fella."

"You need someone like me who can fight, don't you, Hastings?"

Jowls cocked his head slightly, his eyes getting real serious. "You want work, that it?"

"Easy work," Jonah replied. "Never cottoned to doing anything hard. Like my money come easy."

Hastings smiled. Then stepped back and appraised the Confederate a moment. "You just might do. But mind you, it ain't only my say."

"The major ain't gonna let him in," Perkins snapped sourly. "He's a Reb. You know how both of 'em feel 'bout Rebs."

"We'll see what the major says," Hastings replied. "My bosses both gotta want you in—or you can't stay."

"They out at your camp?"

He shook his head. "We'll be meeting up with one of 'em not for weeks from now. Planned on it being out to Fort Laramie."

"That's along the North Platte."

"You know it, mister?" Hastings asked with interest.

"I been out there. Fought Injuns a time or two. On the Sweetwater. Clear up to South Pass. I know that ground, and Fort Laramie too."

Hastings was grinning again as he came a step forward and slapped a hand on Hook's shoulder. "See there, boys? We got us a honest-to-goodness Injun fighter in our platoon now. Just what Boothog and Jubilee gonna want when we cross back over them damned mountains to Deseret."

45

"PERHAPS IT IS time we took a holiday from one another," Jubilee Usher told him as the big man slowly walked away across the canvas-sheeting floor of his massive tent.

Lemuel Wiser was relieved. Whenever he argued with Usher, Wiser was never sure how the argument would turn out. Except that he had long ago learned to make an idea sound like it was Usher's from the start. Convince the charismatic Saint that the idea was his to begin with, and then the man would defend it with a fiery passion.

"We have been moving across this country faster than we had planned, Colonel Usher," he said. "Hastings's group is likely already away from the Missouri and pushing west along the Platte toward our rendezvous."

Usher turned, grinning crookedly. "I certainly hope Hastings has the information we need for Brigham." For a moment he gazed into his glass of brandy, swirling it around. "All of Deseret will need that intelligence, Major Wiser."

"Hastings and his bunch are proven, Colonel. They won't let us down. You handpicked them yourself—the steadiest we have among the whole lot. They learned a lot about Kansas that last scout you had them on."

"Yes, I did pick them myself—most carefully." Usher took a drink. "I wanted the best to ride back north again with Hastings, because they would be the outriders plunging into enemy territory farther than any of the rest

354

of us. I had to know I could depend upon them to get the job done—clean and tidy. No messy mistakes. No deserters."

"No, not like Fordham."

Boothog watched the mention of the name twist Usher's features, making his eyes mere slits with a flinty center.

"No, Major. Not like Riley Fordham."

"But I do have four out looking for him already. I spread them out as you suggested. They'll cover everything north and west of here, sweeping the land clear before meeting up with us at Fort Laramie. I'm sure one of them will have Fordham's head waiting for you."

Usher smiled. "That was a novel approach to this ancient problem, don't you think, Major?"

"The burlap bags, Colonel?"

"Yes," Usher replied, sinking slowly into his canvas chair. "Giving each of those four I sent scrambling after our deserter a burlap bag."

"One of them will have the prize in his bag when we get to Laramie, Colonel."

Usher stared into his brandy. "The head of Riley Fordham."

"Yes, Colonel. And that man will win the prize."

Usher gazed up at Wiser now, the grin disappearing. He sounded almost sympathetic. "You so wanted the girl, didn't you, Major?"

Wiser had never been able to hide it. "She is every bit as beautiful as her mother, Colonel. Yes. The girl will bear a man many children, and make a Saint proud to have her for one of his wives when we return to the land of Zion."

He turned away, gazing wistfully at the roof of the tent. "The thought of that has such a peaceful picture to it. I tell myself very often now what it will mean—returning there to old friends and family. After all these years of waging war against the blaspheming Gentiles."

"Brigham Young will welcome you home with a parade, Colonel."

Usher threw back the last of the brandy and licked a droplet from his lower lip. "A job well done. Yes. The Prophet will reward us all for a job well done."

"Our job is not really over, Colonel."

He waved a hand in answering. "Of course, it isn't, Major. But I wish to be among my own people for a change. These . . . these Gentiles, nonbelievers—they taint our men, sully our faith at every turn. We need to return to our own kind—if only to renew our spirits as one would renew himself at a well he comes upon after crossing a vast desert in the land of Judah, the sands of Canaan, the wilderness of Sinai."

"A hero you will be, Colonel."

He turned to look at Wiser. "Where is it you've decided to lead your company of regulars?"

Boothog was taken aback by the sudden question that shifted the direction of the conversation. But then, Jubilee Usher was like that, adept at keeping men off balance, especially when he suspected those about him were polishing the apple. Usher was not the sort to allow his battalion of Danites to butter him up with false praise. Above all others, Usher knew who he was and needed no man to convince him he was just and righteous. He needed no one to tell him he would soon stand next in line to Brigham Young himself. Jubilee Usher was about God's work in a pagan land.

The rest were politicians, even Wiser had to admit that. Those members of the Council and the Quorum who surrounded Young were stodgy politicians, every last one of them trying to outmaneuver the rest. But Jubilee Usher—now here was a man who could command, every bit as powerful as Brigham Young himself. Perhaps that was why Young had dispatched Usher years ago, and gave him far-ranging orders and a free hand for his band of avenging angels.

Perhaps, Wiser thought more and more on it, perhaps Brigham Young in some way feared the power and charisma and charm of Jubilee Usher.

Come a day soon, it would be most interesting to see how Young would react to having the powerful man back at his side, seeing how years ago he had ordered Jubilee Usher to kill Jim Bridger with the words, "These mountains are not big enough for the two of us!"

Wiser brooded on that now, wondering if the valley of the Great Salt Lake where bloomed in glory the City of the Saints would now prove to be too small for Brigham Young and Jubilee Usher.

"I figure I'll point them north from here. As I understand from this map we copied from the post commander at Fort Harker, Fort Hays is not that far ahead of us along this river, called the Smoky Hill." Lemuel strode to the open tent flaps, taking a deep breath of the spring air. "I'll go due north—with your permission, Colonel. North until I strike the Platte not far from Fort Kearney in Nebraska."

"No longer a territory, Major," said Usher. "It became a state last year as I understand."

"Yessir."

"You'll march west from this fort . . ."

"Fort Kearney, sir. Yes. We can plan to rendezvous with the others in, say, the second week of July."

"That will give you enough time, Major?"

"It will."

"How about my battalion? Have you thought of a route I should take?"

Wiser took a hobbling step forward. "Perhaps it would be most prudent of you to march your wing on west, along the Smoky Hill. Past Fort Hays, Fort Wallace, and plunge into Colorado Territory, where you can strike north from there, to Fort Sedgwick."

"You've spoken of it—on the South Platte."

"Yes. Northwest of there within easy distance is Fort Laramie. Where we'll be waiting for you—should we arrive earlier than expected."

Usher smiled as he rose from his chair, pacing to the small camp table where waited the cut-crystal decanter. He poured himself another glass of brandy. Savored its aroma, then took a drink, swishing it around in his cheeks. Enjoying it fully.

"Yes, Major—that's where Hastings and I will expect to meet up with you . . . and the lucky man who carries the head of Riley Fordham."

Spring seeped out of the land and with it the rains of April, along with the cool days of May. And finally the passing of those first days of June.

July at last had come to bake the plains.

And with it the coming of Hastings's squad of twelve.

They had inched their way north along the Missouri until reaching the mouth of the Platte River. From there they struck out due west, following the great Platte River Road of the emigrants—those wayfarers of a quarter century moving west before them—bound for California, Oregon, and those Saints on their pilgrimage to the valley of the Great Salt Lake. This dozen trail-weary scouts too were bound for a home most had not seen for many years. A home some had never cast their eyes upon.

For now, they had pushed all the way to Fort Kearney, Nebraska. More properly, Hastings's platoon reined up not far from the fort itself, in a little settlement fondly called Dobe Town. Most among the dusty, saddle-galled long-riders found much to their liking in that squalid grouping of saloons, watering holes, whores' cribs, and even what was touted as an opera house—each structure really nothing more than a mud hut with some sort of storefront, clustered among the others along a rutted main street like some nightmare vision of sod walls and roofs that leaked on occupants when it rained, showered dust on occupants when the plains baked dry with the coming of July.

July was dry. And growing more than hot with each passing day.

"Some of us got all tangled up in what Jubilee told us, in that Bible voice of his—how he spoke his Bible words at us," explained Healy Stamps, one of Eloy Hastings's reconnaissance platoon, during the long days and nights of their march west from the Missouri River. "Few of us never was Mormons before Colonel Usher come along to save our souls and put our feet on the right road to immortal life."

"I s'pose I get a chance to meet the man, this Jubilee Usher—I'll learn about the hereafter myself," Jonah replied.

"You can't but be caught up in the righteous power of that great man," Stamps went on, lights glowing beneath his bushy eyebrows. "He is one truly anointed by God—a powerful and mighty elder in the one true church of Jesus Christ in the latter days."

"Sounds to me like Usher took you in when no one else would, didn't he?"

"Don't you know it," Stamps answered enthusiastically. "Back during the war, with nowhere for a loyal Union man to turn but what he didn't see Secesh on every side of him. I hope you don't take offense, Hook—you being a old Confederate soldier yourself."

"Man does what he damn well believes in, Stamps. I carry no grudges again' you, or most who fought in blue. I figure you always done what you thought was right, too."

"God Himself knows what is right for man. And God not only tells the Prophet Brigham Young, but those the Prophet chooses to ride at Brigham Young's right hand."

"Usher?"

"God speaks to the colonel all the time."

"Usher's battle plans?"

"Might say that. What to do, where to go."

"And most of all—just who to punish?"

He grinned widely. "In the name of God, I think you must feel the burning yourself!"

"Burning?"

"The burning in the bosom! Don't you feel it when you're doing God's work to stamp out evil on earth?"

"As one of Brigham Young's Angels?"

"As Angels of Jesus Christ in the latter days—our Lord and Savior! As the Prophet said it, and Colonel Usher reminds us—there are few called upon to do the dirtiest of work to prepare the way for the new Kingdom here on earth. Those who take up the sword in the name of Jesus Christ, to smite the evildoers, these will surely be anointed in Zion come the Judgment Day."

When Hastings's platoon arrived, they found more of their number already there to welcome them to the fleshpots of Dobe Town.

It was a joyous reunion, finding Major Boothog Wiser and his entire company awaiting news from the east. There was backslapping and pump-handle shaking of hands all around, sharing of jokes and stories of the trail and offers to buy a round of drinks for all. And apart from the rest stood the one Jonah took to be Wiser himself—down at the end of the bar, with a bottle all to his own and that custom-made boot at the end of his leg.

"Who's the new man, Captain Hastings?" Wiser called out from the far side of the noisy celebration.

Hook figured Wiser had caught him studying the major. He felt a nudge now and found Hastings at his elbow, prodding him down the bar, through the reveling crowd of horsemen just off the trail. To meet the major himself.

"This is a new man I picked up back at the Missouri."

"I see, Captain." He drank a little from his glass, eyes studying Hook over the rim. "Where you from?"

"Missouri."

"You sound Southern."

"I am. Born in Virginia."

"You fight for the Confederacy?"

"I did. General Sterling Price."

"I knew this Price," Wiser said. "Fought him myself. Perhaps we were on different sides of a battlefield at one time."

"Ain't likely. War ended early for me. I was captured."

"Prisoner, eh? What then? You see the light—and figure the grand republic was worth saving?"

Hook wagged his head. "Weren't that way, Major. The Union will take care of itself. I figured the Yankees and their grand republic can just leave me be and let me get on with my life."

Wiser grinned slightly and brought the glass from his lips. Then held out his hand. "Lemuel Wiser. I didn't catch your name."

"Jonah Hook, Major."

"Pleased to have you with us, Jonah. You care to stay with Captain Hastings's platoon of scouts—and if he wants to keep you with him—that's fine by me."

"By all means, I'd like him to stay with my outfit, with the major's permission," Hastings said. "Jonah's had experience fighting Indians."

"Indians?"

"Sioux and Cheyenne," Hastings replied to Wiser's question.

"Where was that, Jonah?"

"Out on the Emigrant Road. On the Sweetwater. North Platte. With General Connor's expedition to Powder River."

"My, my," Wiser said approvingly, glancing quickly at Hastings with a bright light in his eyes. "You just might do to ride back home with us, Jonah."

Hook felt the first wings of hope take flight. "Thank you, Major. I was hoping to meet the colonel himself soon too. Heard so much about you both."

"You've learned of Jubilee Usher?"

"Yes, Major. Is he with you?"

Wiser grinned, on his face a benevolent light. "The colonel will meet us at Fort Laramie, Jonah. He has taken a different route." He looked at Hastings. "And we will all go forth from here to effect that rendezvous with the colonel."

"How soon we pulling out, Major?"

Wiser looked back at Hook. "Captain, we have a few days to spare. And I plan on spending them here. The men with me have rarely had money of late with which to gamble. And when they have had the money—it seems most no longer have the heart to gamble with me."

"I take it you like to play cards, Major?" Hook asked.

"You a gambler, Jonah?" The light brightened behind his eyes.

"Let's say I get serious about a game of cards every now and then."

"Perfect! Simply perfect!" Wiser called out to the bartender to bring over two more glasses into which he poured drinks of the red whiskey. "Captain Hastings—first a toast to you for enlisting so splendid a recruit as Mr. Hook appears to be."

"I figured he'd do, Major."

"Indeed." Wiser studied this new recruit. "Any man who believes the U.S. government should damn well stay out of the affairs of its citizens— especially the religious affairs of a growing population—that man should do well upon our return to Deseret."

"This grand republic got no business telling any man how to run his life, Major."

"Splendid, Jonah! Just what we have been saying for years now. There is, you are aware, a separation of church and state in the Constitution drafted by our Founding Fathers?"

"I never knew that. No, Major."

"The Founding Fathers knew best—that it was God's plan that our government should keep its hands off the religious affairs of the people."

"I figure the Yankees and their Union ought to just keep hands off of most everything, Major Wiser."

Wiser laughed suddenly, a head-rearing, hearty laugh. He clamped a hand on Hook's bony shoulder. "To think we've found a kindred heart, Captain Hastings. In this land of the Gentile heathen, so far from Zion no less. And—a man who loves to gamble to boot!"

46

Early July, 1868

H E WAS THANKFUL the prairie nights cooled off the way they did. As short as that starlit respite was from the growing heat of summer come to sear the high plains.

Lemuel Wiser sat at the big table with Jonah Hook and the rest, fewer now than when they had started fourteen hours ago that very morning after a breakfast of eggs and potatoes and thick slices of ham with gravy served up by the former army mess cook in his smoky kitchen at the back of this saloon. Good biscuits on the side too, washed down with lots of coffee laced with sipping whiskey.

"Gets the old heart pumping for the game," Wiser had cracked as he tore open the first deck of cards for what had been a long, long day that saw players come and go. Very few of his men tried their luck. Soldiers mostly, in Dobe Town from Fort Kearney for a little recreation—some drinking, some gambling, and most surely some treasured but precious few moments behind those doors out back where the powdered chippies plied their trade.

Army troopers or Wiser's own soldiers—men always seemed to like the girls better than the gambling. Back there away from things, where a man was no longer self-conscious around his fellow soldiers, where a man could scream and holler and let it all out when the explosion came as he rode one of those fleshy or bony, coffee-colored or alabaster-skinned, whores.

From time to time men dropped in and out of the game, at times there were more than eight ringing the table with Wiser. At times down to no more than four. Yet the gambler in the soul of the new man kept him at the table. Jonah Hook won a little, lost a little, managing to stay just far enough ahead that he could afford to keep a bottle at his elbow through the last fourteen hours. He poured drinks for the other players and himself, and stayed far enough ahead that he was not driven to carding out like so many of the others who gave up and left, empty-handed.

Some of those losers stayed to watch. Others went out the door in silence. A few left noisily, grumbling their complaints as to the suspected lack of honesty in the good-looking stranger with the smooth tongue. It was not the first time Lemuel Wiser had heard such complaints, not the first time he had been accused of having an oily tongue or fast, slippery fingers.

Wiser enjoyed being a gambler in everything he did in life. There was enough boredom after all. And all a man had to do was open his eyes and look around him to see the desperate lives of little men to know that. Long ago, Wiser had promised himself he would not be one of them. He would make things happen, create his own world and along with it create a specific order to that world, mirroring most how he saw himself. So far, he had done well in that regard.

And with Jubilee Usher now returning to Deseret, it just might mean a promotion for Lemuel Wiser. If Brigham Young took Usher up the ladder, then Wiser would be the natural to step into the vacancy: to lead the Danites. To make of Young's Avenging Angels what only Lemuel Wiser could make of them. To fashion them in his own image.

What glory before God and the Saints!

Yet across the last two hours, with the whiskey growing stale and the cloud of old smoke hung thick about their shoulders, Wiser had steadily lost. Not much each hand. But enough that his winnings were dwindling. Some going here, some there to that soldier. But mostly his money had been dragged across the wide table until it now sat in front of Hastings' new man.

"I must say, Jonah—you've proved to be quite a good card player."

Hook smiled back, cracking that bony face of his with a disarming grin. "Just lucky, I s'pose, Major. Cards is a funny game like that."

"Man learns a lot about another man—watching him play cards."

Hook peered over his cards, tonguing aside a quid of moist tobacco he was chewing. "That so, Major? What you learned about me?"

"You're good, Jonah Hook. One of the best I've played. Not the best, mind you. Because I've never lost to any man before."

"Not even Colonel Usher?"

"I told you! Lost to no man." He said it a little harsher than he had wanted. But it did not matter. He had spoken.

Soon enough, Wiser told himself. Soon he would be stepping into Usher's role—*Colonel* Lemuel Wiser. A man to be reckoned with—by Saint and Gentile alike.

For the better part of the next two hours, the cards moved around the table. And the money moved between the last three of them left sitting at the table, in the center of the ring of onlookers who squinted down through the yellow, murky haze, a glow put to the tobacco smoke by the single oil lamp that hung just above their heads. Three remained. Wiser—sweating with more than the heat of this old summer night. An old soldier—who played his cards predictably as a barracks better, conservatively, and well. Jonah Hook—who now had all but a few of Wiser's dollars on his side of the table.

"There, Jonah," Wiser said, feeling a surge of confidence in the strength of his hand. A full house: kings and sevens. Boothog was certain, something in his gut telling him that his luck was about to take a turn for the better. A gambler who wins is a gambler who has to hang in there through a short run of bad luck and bad cards.

And Wiser knew he was truly a gambler.

"I'll raise," Hook replied, pushing more scrip to the center of the table.

Wiser watched the money come to the pot, then looked down at what he held in his hand. He studied what money he had left in front of him, next to his whiskey glass. It was as if Hook knew exactly how much it would take to wipe him out. And he suddenly hated the new man for it.

Wiser smiled, despising Hook. "Here you go, Jonah," he said with a silver lilt to his voice. "I'll match you—knowing that you don't stand a chance of beating me."

"That's all you got, Major?"

He held his hands out, guarding his cards. "You see it, Jonah. I'm just going to have to win back some of that money you won from me. And this is the hand to do it on."

Hook pursed his lips then took a swallow of whiskey from his glass. "I see. You figure you've got a hand good enough to beat me?"

"Let's call and see. What do you say, Jonah?"

He wagged a hand. "Not so fast, Major. If you think you've got a good hand—I want you to know I've got a better hand. And I'm willing to see just how much a gambler you are. But—you're out of money . . . so I guess you don't really want to play for high stakes."

Wiser leaned back in his seat, for a moment listening to the muttering of some of the spectators, soldiers and Danites both.

With a flair, he stood, pulling back the flaps of his rumpled coat to expose the two pistols. "You want my custom guns, don't you? Had your eye on them, I know. They are fine specimens—"

"I got guns, Major. Don't really need yours."

"Then . . ." And he looked over himself, wondering what he could offer. He was growing a bit edgy, from the hours in the chair, enough whiskey to put a sharpness to everything, and from this hired man's cocky attitude. "What is it you want me to wager?" His words no longer had that silver smoothness to them.

And that crooked smile Hook gave him made Wiser want to take the man's thin, sinewy neck in both his hands right now and squeeze until the smile was gone and the eyes bugged out, tongue lolling, gasping for air—

"You ain't got anything I really want. I s'pose the game's over—"

"More money? Take my marker! When we get to Laramie to rendezvous with the colonel—I'll honor my note." He quickly turned to one of the men. "Get me paper and a pencil. I'll write Mr. Hook my draft—"

"Don't want any more of your money, Major. Told you. 'Sides, what can a man do with just so much money?"

Boothog slammed a flat palm down on the table, exasperated with the Southerner. He was thumping the clubfoot on the floor noisily, drumming in rhythm with his warning. "You're trying to goad me, Jonah. And I won't stand for goading from any man."

Hook smiled back at the tongue-lashing, which vexed Wiser all the more.

"Few days back, you was telling me how much a gambler you was—how good you was too. Good at gambling in life too. I didn't figure you'd buckle under and go belly up like this, Major. Just 'cause a man whipped you at cards."

"You haven't whipped me at cards, Hook!" he roared, wiping beads of sweat from his brow, swiping the finger off on his vest gone damp in the sticky, still air of the saloon.

Hook peered carefully at the table. "I don't see you with any money left to call me. Appears I win this hand, and the whole game. It's over."

When the Confederate reached in with one long arm to rake back the pot, Wiser caught his wrist. "Hold it right there, Jonah," he said quietly through his teeth, desperately trying to maintain control of himself and the situation.

"What's that, Major?"

He started to choke on it. As much as he wanted to crack the man's skull—it just might have to come to that later. But for now, in front of all these people . . . in front of these men he would one day command from the top—Lemuel Wiser would have to be just what he claimed he was: a gambler.

"Yes. I do have something you might be interested in, Jonah," he said, releasing the Southerner's wrist.

Wiser leaned back, smoothing his vest lapels. "You been a long time without a woman?"

Hook stared at him without expression. "Long time, Major. Why?"

"I have a prize. I mean a really rich prize I can offer you." Wiser stared down at the money on Hook's side of the table, glanced at the old soldier who had folded and sat watching them both, and then back to the Confederate. "You say I'm not a gambler? Well, let's see if you are the gambler you claim to be. I'll wager what special treasure I have against everything you have—all that money sitting in front of you."

Hook dragged a hand through his long hair, then scratched a cheek as he gazed down on the pile of money. "This is a lot of money. But you got my interest up, I will admit. Just what you got that could be worth all this money? And what's this talk of me not having had a woman got to do with it?"

Wiser felt himself leap joyous inside. His tactic would work, he was sure of it.

"Palmer," he called out, wagging a finger to one of his men. Wiser whispered his orders in Sam Palmer's ear and watched the man go.

Seeing Hook's eyes follow Palmer's exit, Wiser said, "I'm having my wager brought here now to show you, Jonah. I think a man of your needs . . . you'll approve."

Minutes later there was a hush that came over the group, a scraping of boot soles as men moved back and a grin that crept across Wiser's lips.

"Here is my wager—against everything you've got. Winner takes all."

He watched Jonah turn and look at the girl.

She stood weaving between Palmer and Colby, one of Hastings' men, groggy and stupefied on laudanum. It was the safest thing to do, Usher had decided years ago. Keep the girl and her mother drugged so there was never any danger of them escaping. He had always wondered what the stuff would one day do to the girl's brain. But it did not matter now. Jubilee Usher wanted that deserter Riley Fordham so bad that the colonel had promised the girl as a reward to the man who brought back Fordham's head in a burlap sack.

The girl no longer mattered.

At last, Wiser looked at Hook, finding on the Southerner's face a strange, pinched look.

"You don't want the girl?"

Hook swallowed hard, trying to grin, not being able to. "This one—is she . . . is she still . . . a—"

"A virgin, Mr. Hook?" Wiser replied, then laughed easily. "Of course. That's the very reason she's worth all that money you've got in front of you."

Eloy Hastings edged from the spectators to bend at Wiser's ear. "Major, just how you gonna square this with Colonel Usher?" he asked. "I mean—he's got her promised to the man who brings in Fordham—"

"That's my concern, Captain," Wiser snapped.

He'd let the southerner win, if that's the way the cards ran against him this last hand. Wiser ran his hands over his five cards, lying face down on the table. Then tapped his fingers on them. And after Hook had gone off with the girl—he'd have the men kill the Confederate, just as he was about to sully his young, virginal prize. Wiser would have the girl back before Usher was any the wiser.

"Jonah?"

Hook gazed at Wiser, his eyes narrow, dark slits in his bony face.

"What's it to be?"

"Let's play this hand through, Wiser."

There was something to the tone in Hook's voice that struck Wiser as different from what he had heard up to this moment. Perhaps it was because Hook knew he might be beat—bested here at the last by a better man. A true gambler. Not just a man who played with money, especially other men's money. No, Wiser told himself, I'm a true gambler—making a wager on life itself.

"What do you have, Jonah?"

"A full house . . ."

Wiser felt his throat constrict, swearing he would not let any of the men see him sweat.

"Three tens . . ."

Seeing those cards, Wiser sighed in relief. That was the best Hook had. And Boothog looked down at his own three kings.

"And two aces."

Wiser's throat seized, a hot lump choking him. Very conscious of moving slowly now, to keep from lunging across the table, he leaned forward casually and studied the Confederate's cards. Then he sank back in his chair, standing finally, turning over his own cards.

"You have me beat," Boothog said. Then, with a wave of his hand he whispered, "You win the girl."

Jonah had brought Hattie here as quickly as he could, only briefly joining in the shrill laughter of the others as he dragged her out of that dingy, murky saloon into the clear, cool night air. Heading for the livery at the end of the dry, dusty street, where he told the others he would be bedding down his new-won prize.

That news had inspired more lewd cheering as the others gathered at the yellow-splashed doorway in those dark early-morning moments, bidding him luck, others saying he needed no luck now—all he needed was stamina. Then more crude jokes as the voices slowly faded behind him.

Hook glanced quickly over his shoulder. No one out on the street now. They had all gone back inside. He could hear them yelling and laughing back there, but only faintly.

He could make it out onto the prairie. Sure of it. Get two horses saddled. Get his daughter tied onto one so that she wouldn't fall when and if they had to make a race of it.

He prayed they would not be faced with that.

Yet he knew Wiser was not the sort to let Hattie stay with him. Never mind that it was Hattie . . . or any young woman for that matter. Boothog Wiser didn't seem like the kind of man who took easily to losing at all. Especially losing everything.

He had a pocket filled with Wiser's money. And he had the reward Jubilee Usher had promised to the man who found and killed Riley Fordham. There was no doubt in Jonah's mind that Wiser would be coming to get it all back.

With Boothog's money, Jonah could get someone to take care of Hattie for a few weeks. Maybe a few months. However long it would take to double back and ride west to Fort Laramie—where he would find Usher and . . . reclaim Gritta from her captor.

His stomach went sour.

Then he looked at Hattie as they pushed through the short door into the fragrant livery. Beyond, a half mile away or more on the flat prairie, he heard someone playing a mouth harp. Maybe a lonely soldier. Maybe one of Wiser's men in their camp by the river. Jonah could not be sure. He only had to find two horses now. Any two. Saddle them. And get lost going east.

Jonah set his daughter gently down among the aromatic hay in a vacant stall, listening to the snorts and pawing of hooves. He lit a single lamp and hung it on a nail, quickly looking over the stable, finding bit and saddle for two mounts. And hung from a nail some short lengths of rope that he would use to lash her atop her mount for their hard ride.

Better that they head south. He knew some of that country: the Republican, Solomon, Saline, and down to the Smoky Hill. Keep Hattie safe until he could finish with Usher and bring Hattie's mother home.

Get the girl safe and then he'd have to return to the Platte. It was here he would come to deal with Boothog Wiser.

After that—farther west. To the place called Laramie. Then he'd finally look in the eye of Jubilee Usher.

But first, he had to get Hattie atop this horse, tied on, and led out onto the trackless prairie, praying no man would follow them into the night as black as the heart of hell itself.

47

Wiser sent Hastings with a half dozen of his scouts around to the back.

Boothog himself would go in the front door of the livery stable. Backed up by four of his own men.

He knew they enjoyed this. Every last one of them. He had seen it burn in their eyes more than once. Whenever Wiser had been crossed and wronged and felt the burning need for taking revenge on one of the men. The rest—especially these most trusted by him—they all watched unflinchingly as Wiser had taken his pound of flesh each and every time.

He could remember seeing that love of it in their eyes. They had enjoyed watching the torture and the blood, the begging by the victim.

And Boothog Wiser knew they would take no small pleasure in what he, Wiser, now had in store for this simple homespun Southern sodbuster named Jonah Hook.

Wiser figured he had given Hastings enough time to get around by the run-down stable's double-wing back door, a stable that slightly listed to one side with age and the incessant prairie wind.

Silently moving to the small door, he tested the latch and hinges gently for noise. He wanted to be in the stable before Hook knew he had arrived. As Wiser was pushing in on the short door, a hollow shot echoed from within.

Wiser froze. A quick exchange of gunfire, intermingled with a pair of grunts. Then shouts swamping over everything from out back. Calling for him.

He glanced at his own men, then shoved his way into the stable, both hands filled with the fancy pistols.

It was dark in here—dimly lit at best. Four horses milled about, pawing, rearing at the noise. Some gun smoke hung in a murky haze at the far end of the stable, swaying with the rocking light of the disturbed lantern hung upon a long nail. Hay dust stirred, making it hard to see. Wiser could not make out what was happening.

"Major Wiser!"

It was Hastings' voice.

"Captain! What's going on? Where is he?"

"He's in here! Got two of my men! Get the sonofabitch!"

Wiser read the panic in Hastings's voice. Strange that a man as proven as the captain should express so much fear. Perhaps only the tension coming now at the end of a long scout. Then Wiser's belly convinced him of something different. Hastings would know, better than any, about the enemy they were up against.

"What's he got for weapons, Captain?"

"Those two pistols—all I saw him carrying."

"He's got something more," someone said from the darkness.

"What?"

"Dunno."

"Shuddup! Now get your boys to rush him," Wiser ordered, with his pistol waving two of his own to go down either side of the center aisle between the two rows of stables.

Boothog could read more than reluctance on their faces. He pointed the pistol at one of them. The man moved on into the murky darkness, carefully, his head pulled back in his shoulders like a gun-shy tortoise.

Wiser watched as a pair of Hastings's men argued with their captain at the far end of things.

"Get them moving! This can be over in a matter of seconds, Captain!"

Hastings shoved the two forward with his big, fleshy hands. They dived into the dim light shed from the solitary oil lamp. Something flickered across the corona of light—the shadow of a man. A bevy of shots rattled through the stable. Three of the gunmen fell. Two of them screaming before they passed out. The third crumpled silently.

The fourth lay wounded in the dust and hay, dragging himself back toward Wiser. A hand over a dirty blotch on his shirt.

"Bastard got us in our own cross fire!" hollered the wounded man.

"You think you're gonna die—that it?" Wiser shouted back at the man.

"I'm gut-shot, Major," he begged, crawling close to Wiser's legs. "It's a slow, mean way to go."

"Go to hell then!" Boothog cried, instantly aiming his pistol at the man's face below him and pulling the trigger.

The back of the gunman's head exploded in a spray of red that splattered the hay and dust with gore and crimson. Wiser stepped over the quivering body, waving the last two ahead with him.

"Hastings!"

"Major?"

"You and me gotta see to this—don't we now?"

"I suppose we do."

"You especially, Captain. You brought him in."

There was a moment of quiet reflection from the far end of the livery. "You're right. It's my doing. I'll . . . clean things up for you, Major."

"That's a good soldier."

A wild laugh split the shadows. "Ain't that just like you goddamned officers!" the drawl called out from the darkness.

"Ah, Mr. Hook!" Wiser replied. "How good of you to let us know that you plan to join the celebration."

"All you officers can do is send good soldiers to their death, ain't that so? And now you're gonna follow orders like the rest, Hastings? Or you gonna get out while you still can?"

"Go ahead, Captain," Wiser reminded stiffly. "Let's see you tidy this matter up."

"Sure—c'mon in here, Hastings. I'll put a couple of holes in you before any of the rest of your boys get close enough to finish me off. And what's it get you, Captain? A decent burial in a hero's grave back in Zion? Shit—you know damned well Wiser will leave you rot where you lay. Like he done with all the rest before you."

"Don't listen to him, Hastings! That's the devil's own hand servant in there! Let's finish this and get the girl."

"That's right, Hastings," the Southerner's voice called out. "The girl is all that Wiser wants. He don't care a good goddamn about you at all."

"Goddamn you, Hook!" Wiser spat.

"Say, Major—where's Hattie's mother?"

That stopped Wiser. And the major saw it had stopped Hastings in his tracks as well.

Hook called out again. "The woman's with Usher, ain't she?"

Wiser was slow making sense of it. How did the man know?

"I don't know what the devil you're talking about, Hook. Perhaps if you come out and give the girl up, we can sort—"

"The girl's name is Hattie. She has a name, Wiser."

Boothog smiled. He had it fitting together nicely. "And the woman? What was her name?"

"Gritta."

Wiser listened to the rumble of the two men left with him, and those still with Hastings. If they had been spooked by a man hiding in the dark before, they now were a little less than anxious to tackle someone who had tracked them across more than three years and hundreds of miles of wilderness.

"Three winters gone, Wiser. I been waiting a long time to put a name on the bastards come and stole my family. Now I got names. And I got you here with me. Whyn't you send the rest of these hired killers out of here, and you and me finish this—like the big man you're always bragging you are."

"You're a back-shooter, Hook. I saw it in your eyes when we first met. You'd never fight me fair."

"Shit—I'd never expect you to fight fair, you bastard. Your kind never does. You run and hide less'n the odds are in your favor."

"Live to fight another day has always been my credo."

"And let other men do your dying for you."

"I'm done talking with him, Hastings! Finish it!"

"Major—why don't we just burn the sonofabitch out. We can do it real easy—"

"I want the girl, Hastings!" he shrieked. Then, attempting to gain some self-control, he said, "The colonel wants the girl too. She's no good to us burned alive."

"None of us good to you killed, Major."

"You're not going in there to finish this off, Captain?"

Hastings hesitated a moment, finally wagging his head. "Never meant to fight a badger buried in a hole—"

Suddenly the captain was knocked backward a step, still standing, staring down at the tiny hole in his belly, a red blossom slowly spreading around it. He started swiping at the stain with one hand, wide-eyed—

—a second hole opened up in the center of his chest. Right where Wiser had aimed. Hastings looked up at the major with dull disbelief, trying to raise his own pistol to fire at Wiser.

Boothog fired a third shot, watching it connect low in the neck, spurting bright blood as Hastings stumbled backward against his men diving helter-skelter for cover. Near Wiser, the last two were scrambling out of the way. Boothog yelled for them to come to him. They did not.

He emptied one pistol at them taking cover in the dark, shadowy corners of the stable behind him. Then calmly holstered the weapon and shifted the other to his left hand, where he spun the cylinder, methodically checking the caps on each nipple.

Deciding he would have to finish off this goddamned Gentile himself.

He had heard the scrape of a boot out the back, too late to do anything about it.

But Jonah Hook didn't get back-shot. He had shoved Hattie back down in a dark stall, slapping the horses out into the dusty aisle between the rows of stalls for cover and confusion as he drew his first pistol. As he ducked back into the dark of a far stall, he dragged the Winchester from its scabbard beneath the stirrup fender.

So that was all he had, Hook thought as he made himself small. Two pistols and a seventeen-shot Model 1866. Maybe, if he was lucky and made each ball count, he could hold both sides of the stable at bay. Whittling them down one by one.

Then he heard some of them coming, whispering . . . footsteps from both directions. And he knew if they rushed him like that—it was all but over. He started to move to a crouched position, putting a hand out to steady himself, when he had found the flake of a hay bale. Big enough, he figured.

He waited, breathless and listening. Then flung the flake into the murky lamplight and shadows, across the aisle into the far row of stalls.

It had done the trick. The four gunmen spooked, firing into one another. And Jonah had himself made sure of two of them before he ducked back into the darkness once more.

From the sounds of things, the four were done and out of the way.

Then he thought on it hard and knew they still might rush him. And that would be the end—unless he put a little more fear into their hearts. More so some downright simple confusion to keep them off balance.

That's when he started talking to Hastings, recognizing his voice at the back of the livery. Hearing Wiser at the front of the stable. And glory of glories—it had worked.

Better than Jonah had hoped: the major shot Hastings. Gone right mad, Wiser had. Mad with frustration, even hate. He heard him shooting up there among the front stalls. Lead smacking wood, scattering hay dust. Gun smoke hanging like dirty gauze, suspended over the stable, made a greasy yellow by the single lamp.

Wiser was a madman. Shooting at his own men. None of the last shots came Jonah's way.

Then some quiet. Quickly sorting it out, Jonah figured Wiser was reloading. Or waiting with that second pistol—wanting Hook to grow impatient and show himself. How Jonah wanted to watch the bastard squirm. . . .

More than anything, Hook knew he had to swallow his own hate down now—keep thinking things through or he would not last. Not long enough to get Hattie out of there. And that fear of failing her stabbed something down deep inside him now.

"I'm with you, Major!" cried a voice from the back of the stable, near the big opened doors.

"Your glory will be made in Zion, boys!" Wiser called back. "Let's go in and get the Gentile!"

Hook stood, sensed where Wiser was, and pulled off two quick shots that barked but bit only stall uprights. Yet before he himself ducked back down, Jonah watched Wiser going for cover.

Overhead sang more than a half dozen bullets as Hastings's scout fired at the disappearing target. Jonah counted shots, with his left hand reaching for the security of the repeater.

More gunfire exploded at the back of the livery, although these did not echo like those before inside the stable. These shots were instead swallowed by the night. Outside. Beyond those big open doors leading onto the black prairie.

Jonah strained his eyes, shading them from the pale, murky lamplight—trying his best to get his night-eyes.

A man reeled backward into the barn from the doors. Then he made out three of the gunmen crouching, turning to fire into the night with quick orange muzzle blasts.

Then a second gunman sank back on his haunches, clutching the side of his chest. In a moment he lay down, rolled onto his belly, and did not move again.

The last two of Hastings's scouts yelled at one another and flung their voices to Wiser at the far side of the stables. Then the pair bolted to their feet and at a dead run plunged into the blackness of night, their pistols spitting yellow flames ahead of them.

There came a flurry of more gunfire outside the building. Not only pistols, but big guns as well. Booming amid the cracks of the smaller-bore pistols.

An agonizing silence followed . . . until Wiser called out.

"Men? The rest of you able, get back in here so we can finish what we've started!"

There came no answer.

Hook heard the shuffle of steps in Wiser's direction, the murmur of voices. Wiser was arguing with those two he had left in his command.

"Jonah?"

On guard, Hook snapped around, to the back of the stable.

"Jonah Hook! You in there, son?"

"Shad Sweete? That you?"

"By damn, it is—his own self!" Sweete roared.

He was flush with confusion, joy, relief, and then again fear. "Keep covered. This fella's got him some gunmen left, Shad."

A bullet whined overhead.

"How many, Jonah?"

"Don't know—"

"You're still mine, Hook. And the girl too!"

"Girl, Jonah?"

"My daughter, Shad."

"Hattie's there with you?" a new voice sang out.

Something familiar to it, but not like the hominess of Shad Sweete's colicky bellow.

"Who's asking?"

"It's Riley Fordham, Jonah."

"She's here with me, Riley," he called into the dark.

"Ah—Mr. Fordham!" Wiser cried. "What an unexpected pleasure. Not only will I get to watch Hook die—as slow and painfully as possible—but I will have the pleasure of killing you as well. Cutting off your head and presenting it to Colonel Usher when next I see him at Fort Laramie."

Wiser laughed, loud enough that Hook stood, without thinking, firing the last two shots in the one pistol, then aiming the second into the dark. One, two . . . then three shots—

A scream, then many footsteps pounded the hard earth, flinging the small door aside noisily. Until there was no more noise from the front of the stables.

Hook listened to the quiet for a long, long time.

"Go 'round front, Fordham," Jonah called out.

"Already sent him, Jonah," Sweete replied.

Jonah cautiously stepped to the corner of the stall, listening. All he heard between each of his own steps was the labored breathing of one of them. Then the creak of the hinges at the front door.

"The rest run off, Jonah," Fordham called out. "Likely they're on their way to their camp—get the rest. We gotta be making tracks, and now."

"Fordham's right, Jonah," Shad said.

"This ain't finished."

They joined him, finding Hook standing over Wiser, one boot on his gun hand.

Sweete knelt beside the man, putting his ear against his wet, dark-slicked chest. "He ain't got long, Jonah. You plugged him in the lights twice't. Who is he?"

"Damn." Hook used his boot toe to knock the man's pistol aside. "This one had Hattie."

"We gotta go," Fordham said anxiously. "Get her out—"

"G'won, then. I appreciate what you done, coming to help me. You can go now. Save your hide, Riley."

"Listen, dammit. I put my own neck on the line to come back to make sure Hattie was safe. No different from you, Jonah."

"She's safe."

"Where's she?"

"Back there. They got her pretty sleepy. She don't know nothing that's going on."

Fordham stepped away as Jonah knelt over Wiser. Shad shifted, turning his head first this way, then that, as he listened for sounds of the gunmen returning.

Hook stuffed the muzzle of his pistol up under Boothog's nose. "Before you go, you sonofabitch—why don't you die clean so you can meet your maker proper."

"You can go to hell, Gentile," Wiser gurgled. "Filthy vermin—"

"I figure I will go to hell, in the end. But right now—that's where I'm fixing to send you. I'll be a while getting there before I join you." With the muzzle and front sight, he lifted Wiser's upper lip, ramming the pistol in hard against the gums and upper teeth.

"He know where your wife is, Jonah?"

"He does—and I do too," Hook answered. "Now, Boothog—let's just come clean with your dying breath, you want to tell me where I can begin looking for my boys."

"I don't have any idea, sod—"

Jonah drew the hammer back with a loud click. "I thought I spoke good enough English for you to understand, Major. Maybe you just don't listen good unless it hurts real bad. That's it—ain't it? Your kind likes to hurt . . . enjoys it something special. All right then."

Hook pulled his pistol away from Wiser's mouth and jammed the muzzle against the man's thigh, pulling the trigger.

Wiser shrieked, almost biting through his lower lip as he squirmed on the floor of the barn. His pant leg smoked until enough blood seeped from the gaping bullet hole to snuff out the smoldering cloth.

"Tell me where I start to find my boys." He cocked the pistol and jammed the muzzle against the major's other thigh.

"Good glory, Jonah!"

"Die in hell, you dumb sodbuster!"

He fired. Wiser doubled up in pain, then Jonah brought the pistol butt down into his groin. And pointed it at the major's scrotum.

"Jonah!" cried Shad.

"I'll save your balls for later."

"Jonah—he ain't gonna talk—"

Shad was too late.

Hook flicked the muzzle just below the bottom rib on Wiser's left side and pulled the trigger. Wiser doubled up with a gurgling grunt, rolling onto that side as Jonah got out of his way.

"You're not gonna get a thing outta him, Jonah."

Hook kicked Wiser's head brutally to the side, then knelt again to hold the man's chin cupped in his left hand. "Is that right, Major? You figure I'll never get any word out of you?"

"J-just leave me die," Wiser gurgled. "The rest . . . they'll be coming for you now. Anywhere you go—"

"Let's ride, Jonah." Shad stood.

Behind them Fordham came up, the girl cradled across his arms. "She didn't get hit. It's a miracle, as much lead was—"

"Get her on a horse, Riley. Now!" Jonah snapped.

Fordham turned and was gone without a word.

Shad took off, then turned after a few steps. "You coming, Jonah? We ain't got a whole lotta time. Let that bastard die on his own. He'll take what he knows of your boys with him."

"Listen to that old man, Hook. He ain't stupid like you," Wiser spat blood up, coughing. "You'll never see the rest of your family again, you simple heathen."

Jonah gazed down at Wiser. Then turned aside, finding Sweete anxious. Maybe the old man was right. Leave Wiser to bleed like a stuck pig here in the dirt. Better to get in the saddle and ride—

"Jonah!"

As the old mountain man bellowed his name, Hook whirled back around. Finding Wiser pulling something from his boot—a double-bored, over-under derringer.

It spit flame, burning a tongue of pain along Jonah's neck as he brought his pistol up, firing at the instant Wiser's second barrel erupted.

Wiser's grunt exploded from his lungs as Hook put a hand to the damp ribbon of pain low on his neck. Jonah brought his hand away as Shad stepped up. Sweete peered down at the body. "This one's gone. You'll live—if we get you out of here now."

48

I N FIVE DAYS they had crossed the great, black-domed expanse of wilderness that "welcomed" any man suicidal enough to try that stretch of prairie south of the Platte River from Fort Kearney into the Smoky Hill country of Kansas.

Shad Sweete had driven them hard with what little darkness they had left that first night, leaving behind Dobe Town and its dusty huts and splatterings of yellow light as he steered them beneath the great dark map of the sky. Due south. Keeping the North Star over his right shoulder. Where he kept turning to look from time to time. Looking behind too, for he was sure they were following.

Yet as the sun tore itself in a bloody greeting from the bowels of the earth that first morning, the old trapper had still seen no sign of pursuit. Sweete led the others down into the cottonwood and willow and alder of the Little Blue River. For the next half hour they kept their horses plodding the middle of that stream, east for a ways until he found the mouth of a ravine that he thought would do.

It was there he told them to dismount, unsaddle, and picket the horses close by on the good grass just up the draw. When they were all back in the shade, he let the rest fall quickly asleep.

Shad woke Jonah Hook a few hours later as the sun climbed halfway to midsky. Without many words spoken between them, he showed the

Confederate where to stretch out in the tall grass of the riverbank and watch their backtrail over an immense expanse of country laid out before him.

"Don't you go back to sleep, Jonah."

Hook rubbed the grit from his eyes with both sets of knuckles. "I won't."

"Hattie counting on you to keep your nose in the wind and eyes on the skyline, son."

"I ain't let her down yet. Go grab you some sleep, old man. I'll be fine."

Sweete stirred later when he heard footsteps. Pulling his pistol, he rolled over and pointed the weapon at the mouth of the narrow ravine as Hook was creeping in. "Someone coming?" he asked in a harsh whisper, his blood pumping full in his ears as he sat up.

"No," Hook whispered back. "Just come to get Fordham. His turn to stand watch."

Shad had glanced at the sky, finding the sun halfway to the far horizon, on the other side of the ravine now. The Southerner had stood a good five hours or better.

Yet he felt sorrier still for Fordham as the Mormon was rousted from his sound slumber. Neither Shad nor the Danite deserter had slept in more than two days before their sudden appearance in Dobe Town, coming east from Laramie, hoping for some word of Jonah Hook or the small splinter group of Danites the Confederate was searching for. Instead of finding word among those huts clustered along the Platte River, Fordham had recognized two of Boothog Wiser's men still in the watering hole that dark morning, just about the time the shooting broke out somewhere down the long, rutted main street in that squalid little town.

By that time it had already been one hell of a ride for the two of them, tearing away from Laramie after a second of Jubilee Usher's bounty hunters showed up at the fort, following Fordham's trail that far. And before that second Danite died, he had spilled a little of the plans that Usher and Wiser were moving in separate battalions, north through Kansas—with orders to rendezvous at Laramie by midsummer, where they would celebrate the capture of Riley Fordham.

And for some reason that had again made the hairs stand at the back of Shad Sweete's neck. The two leaders dividing their command made the old mountain man feel the need for pushing east as fast and as long as their horses could carry them. A week of solid riding, brutal on his old body. Swapping lathered animals for fresh at road ranches along the way. Pushing faster, compelled by some need to hurry. Arriving in time.

Only by the power of his medicine. By the power of Shad's own spirit helper. Something Jonah Hook would likely never understand, he thought again now as he closed his burning eyes and tried for more fitful sleep that afternoon in the narrow ravine. He felt the ride more in his old bones than either of the younger men would ever realize.

Getting on in winters now—too many robe seasons behind him to go acting like some young bull who could ride all day and make love all night.

How he had longed for Toote to be curled under the shade of the willow with him as it grew hotter and the ants and beetles found his fragrant, sweaty body too much to their liking.

They saddled at sunset and rode that night until sunrise then hid and slept and kept watch until they rode again a third night beneath the swallowing prairie sky lit only by starshine and a late-summer moon that too quickly sailed overhead.

By the third day Hattie had begun to come around. It had taken time, day by day, hour by hour of the torture. But by the evening of that third day of hiding out the sun, as they were resaddling, refilling canteens at the little stream that Shad said they would follow south to the Solomon River, the girl had suddenly shaken her head, looked up and around at the sinking rose light in the sky, and found Riley Fordham tightening the cinch on his horse nearby.

Hattie started screaming, leapt to her feet, her throat filled with terror as she darted off—and ran right into Shad Sweete: the big man was a frightening stranger—surely part of Jubilee Usher's band of Danites.

It took a long time for Jonah to calm his daughter, cradling her in his arms as she collapsed there beside the little creek bordered with elm and alder and plum brush. Jonah had waved the other two men off while she sobbed, muttering incoherently as the laudanum released its grip on her. Rocking her against him, he murmured soothingly into her ear.

The sun had fully torn itself from the sky that evening before she tore herself from her father's embrace. She stared fully at last into his bearded face, touching him, kissing him, not really believing it was her own pappy. Then the terror caught in her throat as she remembered the two others who had been with her father. She turned, finding the pair seated close by.

"He's one of them," she whispered, pointing to Fordham.

"Riley Fordham, Hattie. He's took care of you before."

She said, "I never knew his name, but—I'll never forget his face."

"Riley—come on over here now," Hook said. "The other'n, Hattie—he's like a father to me now. Taught me, kept me alive a time or two. And they both saved our hides a few days back when I was busting you free of the ones had you prisoner."

"You remember me, Hattie?" Fordham asked as he came to kneel nearby. She nodded shyly, sliding behind her father. "Never knew your name." "I'm Riley."

Hattie glanced sheepishly at Jonah, then stuck out her hand to the man. Fordham took it and shook.

"You've got good manners, Hattie Hook."

"Her mama taught all the children good." Hook choked on the sour ball of pain the thought of the boys caused him.

"He . . . Riley protected me, Pappy," she explained in a whisper, holding her father all the tighter. "I never . . . without him—"

"Jonah, time we was going," Sweete suggested. "We only got so much dark these summer nights. Let's use every minute we got."

"I did not introduce myself," Hattie said. "Mr.—?"

"Shad Sweete," he replied with a big grin, bending at the waist gallantly there among the dried grass and rustling plum brush to accept her tiny hand. "Much pleased to meet you, Miss Hattie." Then he kissed the back of that filthy, alabaster, rope-burned hand.

"You see what he did? He kissed my hand, Pappy!" she exclaimed, suppressing a giggle.

Hook smiled at the old mountain man before Sweete turned to his horse. "That's right, Hattie. Shad Sweete's full of surprises."

The afternoon of the fifth day found them striking the Kansas Pacific tracks just east of Fort Harker. Riley Fordham suggested they ride east from there.

"First town ought'n to be Salina," Shad Sweete had told them.

"We'll find a rail stop there, won't we, Jonah?" Fordham asked.

"For certain we will," Hook replied. "You still want to do what you set your mind to do?"

"I do. I owe Hattie for running out on her—like I told you that first night as we rode south from Dobe Town. I'm gonna watch over her for you, Jonah. That's a promise. She'll be safe while you go fetch the rest of your family."

Hook had smiled, then glanced at Sweete, who nodded approvingly. "Looks like you got yourself a stepdaughter, Riley."

"More like my little sister."

By noon the sixth day they were riding into the outskirts of Salina,

Kansas—a town smelling of new-cut lumber and weathering sideboards, of cattle dung and horse apples and the sweat of honest men at labor on this midsummer's day. The commerce of the east probing west, ever west.

They stopped at a plain-fronted, two-story clapboard house set off the main street away from the whir of things, where hung a sign in a yard overgrown with too much ragweed and prairie bunchgrass. A rap on the door brought a fleshy woman wiping her flour-dusted hands on a dingy apron.

"Afternoon," Riley said, smiling and setting his tongue for charm. "My name's Fordham, and this here is Jonah Hook."

The woman nodded to each, her eyes coming back to the girl standing between them.

"And this is Hattie, Mr. Hook's daughter."

"Hello, ma'am," she greeted the woman softly.

"Hello yourself, young lady."

"Could we ask a favor of you?" Fordham inquired.

"Room-and-board prices posted on the sign by the door," she said, cutting him off.

"No, ma'am. We just want to know if Hattie could use some of your water, a clean towel, and a little of your lye soap to freshen up, a young lady and all . . . if you don't mind."

She was not long in eyeing the girl down, then up, once more, and determining the child was badly in need of a good scrubbing. "You come on in, young lady. We'll take you up to my room where we'll freshen you right up. You fellas, just make yourself comfortable on the porch here. I'll send my girl out with some lemonade for you."

The good part of an hour later, Hattie reappeared. While not washed, her dingy dress had been nonetheless dusted, and the many small tears repaired by the hand of a fine seamstress. The young woman stood before them, freshly scrubbed, cheeks rosy, eyes gleaming and bright, her hair washed, brushed, and newly braided, finished off with a scrap of ribbon.

"Her teeth were something awful, you ought to know, Mr. Hook," the woman said.

Riley grinned at Jonah when Hook sheepishly covered his own mouth with a hand.

"We thank you for seeing to her teeth too," Hook mumbled. "Lord, Hattie—it's been so many years. You've growed so. And look at you now!"

"What do we owe you?" Hook asked the landlady.

The woman looked at the girl, then Jonah and Riley, and finally the big man in greasy buckskins. She gave Hattie a gentle hug, then a playful slap on her rear.

"You go 'long now, Hattie. It was my pleasure, fellas. You all take care of that little lady now. She's something real special."

Hook brought his hand up to shake the woman's. "Real special. Thankee, ma'am."

They led their weary horses back onto the main, dusty street, not finding it hard to locate the rail station, where they counted their assets after inquiring the cost of a ticket east.

"Got enough to get her to Kansas City," Hook said.

"She needs to go farther than that," Fordham declared, staring at the scrip in his hand. "Clerk said it cost forty dollars to get to St. Louis."

"Only twenty's what he said," Hook replied. "But I don't have that much. It's for damn sure I ain't asking for your money, Riley."

"I'm paying. And I'm riding too—like I said from the start. Two tickets to St. Louis is forty dollars, and I've got enough for both." He patted his belly, beneath his shirt where he had belted a leather wallet. "I figure to have a lot left over from what I eased away from Jubilee Usher when I ran out on him."

"More'n enough to get you to St. Louis?"

"That, and enough to get Hattie enrolled in a good seminary."

"Seminary?"

"A girl's boarding school." Fordham looked down at the young woman. "If that's all right with you and your daddy."

She beamed, went to embrace her father. "May I, Pappy?"

"I only just got you back, Hattie." Clutching her to him, Hook finally smiled, crinkling the flesh on his homely, bony face. Moisture welled in the eyes that finally looked up at Fordham. "Whyn't you go on now, Riley—and buy them two tickets to St. Louis. This young lady's gonna need a proper escort she goes riding the rails east to boarding school."

As Jonah stood and drew up the cinch in the gray light of summer's dawn here outside Fort Laramie, he knee-popped the horse in the belly, causing the mare to blow. He yanked quickly and buckled—in, down, and in again. And remembered that sunny afternoon back nearly a month gone now. A July afternoon in a railroad town called Salina cropping up like a prairie weed beside the Smoky Hill and Kansas Pacific line.

With the whistle growing more and more faint, he and Shad Sweete had reined up atop the first row of low hills shouldered along the timbered river course, turning in their saddles to gaze back at those last few cars of the eastbound disappearing into the shimmering summer haze of that late afternoon.

"She's gonna be fine, Jonah," Sweete had told him.

"I know she is."

"Time we get to Laramie, chances are Riley's wire be waiting for you already."

"It's something I need to know. Where she is. Who she's with. For so long—"

"Any man can understand that. Especially Riley Fordham. He'll wire you where she is. The school matron's name."

Shad swiped at troubling, buzzing, green-backed flies tormenting the men and horses in the afternoon heat.

Still Jonah had sat, watching until the last smudges of billowing wood smoke was all that remained on the far horizon. "She wants me bring her mother home," he had said. . . .

Here at Fort Laramie now Sweete lumbered up beside the younger man as the cool breezes worked their way off the Medicine Bow Mountains to the west. Down the valley of the LaRamee River, through the smoked-hide lodges clustered in a small circle where the old mountain man and wife and daughter camped among the others in the shadow of the white soldiers' fort.

Hook tugged the diamond hitch on the pack animal before Sweete spoke.

"I want you know I was disappointed as you, Jonah—finding Usher's bunch already pushed through here before we got back."

"I'll find him," Jonah replied. "I know who. And I know where now. I'll get Gritta back home with Hattie. Like I promised the girl."

Shad motioned the women on over, Toote and Pipe Woman, when they emerged quietly from the lodge into the new light of day. "Any use me asking to go 'long with you, son?"

He turned to the old mountain man. "I s'pose there's still a lot for me to learn, Shad. But not this trip. The track is plain enough to read—and we both know they're headed back to that Salt Lake country. It's just a matter of time now."

"Man always needs someone watching out for his backside, Jonah."

He dropped the stirrup leather and strode over to the older man. "If ever I feel the need of that—I know one man I can trust to do it. You pulled my fat out of the fire a time or two."

"You're still a young hoss, too. Lots of time for us."

Toote hugged Jonah just as she had when he had pulled away on that trail east. But now, to everyone's surprise but her own, the young woman came forward into the arms Toote backed away from.

"Come back, Jonah Hook," Pipe Woman said quietly in her rough-edged English. She had clearly practiced for this leave-taking.

He gazed down into her pretty face, noticing the dark, cherry eyes misting over. He suddenly sensed the hurt of tearing away, like flesh from flesh.

"I got to find her." He looked at Shad for help. "Dead or alive. I got to—"

Sweete put his big hands on his daughter's shoulders and gently pulled her back from Hook. "We know. I'll make her understand why you're going, Jonah."

"You do, don't you?"

Sweete nodded. "Come gimme a hug, son. And tell me you'll be back. Tell Pipe Woman too. That you'll be back. One day."

He looked at her, snagged her arms again, and crunched her with all he had to give at that moment, feeling a little less hollow for human closeness. He brushed her cheek with his lips, knowing if he did anything more, he would be sorry for it. Like he was doing Gritta wrong because he would likely find himself staying when he had to be pushing on after Jubilee Usher and the Danites. There was a woman and two boys out there.

Releasing Pipe Woman, Jonah quickly hurried into the big man's arms and turned away before he betrayed himself.

"You know her heart is riding off with you, Jonah. Take care that you do come back to us."

Atop the young mare, yanking on the halter to the pack animal, then reining away, Jonah swallowed down the emptiness and hurt. He rode away, hard and fast. Not knowing for sure what else to do now with the hollow pain.

Knowing only that he could not stay while there was still blood and kin and half of him still out there among the deserts and mountains.

Still out there . . . somewhere.

Epilogue

Late Summer, 1908

T HE YOUNG NEWSPAPERMAN lay stretched on the freshly filled straw tick below the front window, where the night was beginning to cool at last.

In the back room, he heard the soft murmur of the old man's voice. A cooing really, to Nate Deidecker's ear anyway. That's how Jonah Hook half sang, half whispered his wife to sleep as night had eased down on this high land in the shadow of Cloud Peak.

Whereas of a time long ago gone the couple had lain together in the shadow of Big Cobbler Mountain in the Shenandoah—seasons before a long, long trail had brought Jonah and his wife here to the edge of the high plains, their backs against the Big Horns.

Deidecker's eyes burned beneath the poor light of the smoky oil lamp. Nate set his pencil upon the pad that lay beside the tick, reached over, and rolled the wick down, snuffing the lamp and plunging the room into momentary darkness—dark only for the time it took his eyes to grow adjusted to the moonlight rising over the vaulting land, starshine as bright as any ballroom back east in Chicago, Philadelphia, or New York.

He stuffed his hands behind his head as he rolled onto his back and drank deeply of the scents in the room. The freshly dusted tick, emptied of sour straw and refilled that afternoon by the old man.

He remembered Hook taking down the sickle from the porch wall and going to work only yards from the cabin as if he'd done the same every day of his life for a hundred years, slashing back and forth in a neat row across that small meadow where Nate's picketed buggy horse grazed contentedly. Fresh grass, growing summer cured beneath the high-country sun now late in the season, was what the old scout stuffed into the tick until it could hold no more. Then Hook buttoned it closed and dragged the mattress into the cabin's front room.

Here beneath the open window where the curtain was nudged into a gentle dance above him, casting teasing shadows over his outstretched body, the night was cooling.

Strange how quickly the night sounds came to him once the lamp was out and all was darkness once more in this world of consuming wilderness. Just outside that door, beyond this window only inches from his elbow— those crickets and locusts and tree frogs and the little toads down by the Big Piney. And from the distance, on that gentle, warm breeze came the first of the distant calls he was not sure at first he had actually heard.

A wolf.

Deidecker was sure that's what it was. Hook had explained the difference earlier that day. How the coyote yammered and yipped—a smaller cousin to the big, yellow-eyed, lanky-legged prowler of the high plains and mountains.

Out there now, that was a wolf.

Only then did he realize Hook was no longer singing to his wife. He too must be listening to that wolf, Nate thought.

Then the quiet, soothing rumble of the old man's voice drifted back to him once more. Renewed, as he cooed his wife to sleep. Like a man would rock his children.

And something struck him, a thought that his mind hung on the way a man might catch his coat on the head of a nail as he carelessly brushed past an old, weathered wall. In this way his thoughts brushing past in the summer night as he heard a different voice coming from the old man this night, in the black of that back room. A voice unlike the one the old scout had used to tell his story to the newspaperman—soft enough to put Nate Deidecker to sleep as well.

He savored that sound, like water running gently over its high-country streambed. Hook cooing to the silent, far-seeing woman who never spoke, never so much as looked at Deidecker but once all that day and into the long evening of listening to the old scout's stories. Rocking, forever rocking in her chair set down in the grooves worn into that old porch out front.

This wild, forbidden silence was their most private possession here in the darkness, with another summer night come stealing up the slope of these foothills. The light of a long day had hurriedly climbed over the Rockies.

As surely as Jonah Hook must have hurried west from Fort Laramie, over the Continental Divide, and marched to a rendezvous in that valley of the Great Salt Lake.

That part of the story would come tomorrow, Nate figured.

Enough for the newsman to digest in one day. Listening more than scribbling notes as Hook talked in that easy way of his so flavored by the things seen and heard, the things that had touched a heart gone old among these high and far places.

Nate had done enough of the writing though. But a lot of listening—to get the flavor of the old scout's speech. Deidecker had to capture it just so, if he was ever going to make something of it.

He had come here for a story. And beneath this window with the wilderness slowly creeping in on him from the darkness realized he had a book. Good Lord—did Nate Deidecker have a book!

He closed his eyes, thinking on the leather binding . . . the expensive deckle-edged paper . . . signing copies of this breathtaking biography for the likes of folks back east who would buy out of wonder and amazement and . . .

. . . hours later, as the newspaperman came slowly awake, sensing there was a reason he had, Nate listened to the night. Listened to the great, shrinking wilderness that would soon be no more. Then he realized that the moon had risen, journeyed, and was coming down in the western half of the night black sky. Its first gentle, silvery rays slipped through the window only inches over his bed on the cabin floor.

Deidecker turned on his side, away from the window, propping an elbow beneath his cheek, ready to close his eyes again and give himself back to sleep when that moonlight caught something and shined from it, like a gentle ribbon of quicksilver off a mirror.

Pushing the single blanket from his legs, Nate rose, padding barefoot across the roughened plank floor. Never taking his eyes off the object beckoning from the stone mantle above the small fireplace.

He took it down and carried it quietly back to the window, where he turned the dull brass frame in the light to rid it of reflection.

Staring down into the old, faded chromo, recognizing a background of crude Indian tepees . . . only then focusing on the foreground, where stood a stranger staring back at Deidecker.

A young man with the nose and eyes and mouth of Jonah Hook. Beside him, a beautiful Indian woman, held close beneath his arm, protectively: and standing before their parents, a pair of half-breed children. The little boy wore only breechclout and moccasins, the girl, a dress with fringe spilling down the little arms, nothing on her tiny bare feet.

Nate Deidecker had not been aware of this brass-framed chromo sitting so openly on the mantle for all to see, like a family portrait.

Then the hair on the back of his neck prickled as he lay back down on his straw tick, with both hands gently pressing the old, faded photograph to his breast there in the silver moonlight come down on him from the high places.

They were days now gone the way of the winds.

Nate remembered the words spoken by the old man earlier that day when reflecting on the man he once was, knowing he would never be again.

Days gone the way of the winds.